BLEEDING

DARKNESS

A STONECHILD AND ROULEAU MYSTERY

BLEEDING DARKNESS

BRENDA CHAPMAN

DUNDURN
TORONTO

Cover image: © Mark William Penny/shutterstock.com
Printer: Webcom

Library and Archives Canada Cataloguing in Publication

Chapman, Brenda, 1955-, author
    Bleeding darkness / Brenda Chapman.

(Stonechild and Rouleau mystery)
Issued in print and electronic formats.
ISBN 978-1-4597-4004-4 (softcover).--ISBN 978-1-4597-4005-1 (PDF).--
ISBN 978-1-4597-4006-8 (EPUB)

    I. Title. II. Series: Chapman, Brenda, 1955- . Stonechild and
Rouleau mystery.

PS8605.H36B64 2017   C813'.6   C2017-906240-9
                                             C2017-906241-7

1   2   3   4   5   22   21   20   19   18

We acknowledge the support of the **Canada Council for the Arts**, which last year invested $153 million to bring the arts to Canadians throughout the country, and the **Ontario Arts Council** for our publishing program. We also acknowledge the financial support of the **Government of Ontario**, through the **Ontario Book Publishing Tax Credit** and the **Ontario Media Development Corporation**, and the **Government of Canada**.

Nous remercions le **Conseil des arts du Canada** de son soutien. L'an dernier, le Conseil a investi 153 millions de dollars pour mettre de l'art dans la vie des Canadiennes et des Canadiens de tout le pays.

Care has been taken to trace the ownership of copyright material used in this book. The author and the publisher welcome any information enabling them to rectify any references or credits in subsequent editions.

— *J. Kirk Howard, President*

The publisher is not responsible for websites or their content unless they are owned by the publisher.

Printed and bound in Canada.   VISIT US AT

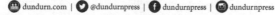

Dundurn
3 Church Street, Suite 500
Toronto, Ontario, Canada
M5E 1M2

For in that sleep of death what dreams may come.
—William Shakespeare, *Hamlet*

And the truth cannot be hid;
Somebody chose their pain,
What needn't have happened did.
—W.H. Auden, "A Walk After Dark"

For my girls, Lisa and Julia

CHAPTER ONE

When David McKenna opened his eyes, the morning light had weakened and filled the hospital room like clear, cold tea. He turned his head to see Evelyn still in place, her arm resting on the side of the bed and her head bowed. He wanted to tell her to go home but knew she wouldn't. She stirred as if sensing that he was awake, and a moment later, he felt her hand work its way into his. They hadn't been this intimate for years and her touch left him with mixed feelings. Mostly regretful ones.

"What time is it?" he asked. He licked his lips, chapped from his long sleep in the dry room.

She glanced at her watch. "Nearly four o'clock. Do you feel better? You slept a long while."

"Yes," he lied. "You should go home and get some rest too."

"I will. The kids are on their way."

"No need for that." He knew there was but wanted more time. More time to work in his garden, read books he'd always meant to, feel the wind off Lake Ontario on his face.

More time.

Evelyn must have buzzed for the nurse because she entered the room almost immediately and the pain that coursed through him was exchanged for the floaty oblivion he'd grown to crave. He'd never thought he'd end his days an addict, but terminal disease had a way of turning a lifetime of decisions on its head.

He dozed and half woke. Someone had straightened his pillows. Moistened his lips with crushed ice.

Evelyn's chair was empty and he wondered if she'd even been there. The dreams were real and reality a dream.

He drifted off again to the smell of juniper and rotting leaves. He was a boy running through his grandfather's field.

Jumping. Leaping. Free.

Sun cut through the hazy air, reflecting off the water flowing down the bank. He stopped and stared as a cloud crossed in front of the sun and darkened the marshes. The girl lay on her side as if sleeping, her long dark hair tumbling down her back, trailing into the mud. He stepped closer, needing to look even as the cold and horror filled him. He was no longer a boy, but a man with a man's grief.

He struggled to remain upright. Fought to keep from screaming.

"Wake up, Zoe. Wake up." He narrowly missed tripping on a tree root in his haste to reach her.

As he raised his face to the river, now transformed into boggy reeds, she pushed herself up onto her side and turned to look at him over the blood-streaked shoulder of her ruined sweater.

"You found me at last," she said. Her smile was filled with the sweetness that he remembered. Her eyes filled with tears. One escaped and dribbled down her cheek and came to rest on her chin. She sat up in a sudden motion and reached out both arms toward him. Blood dripped from her neck where it had been cut with a hunting knife. Her smile brought back the sunshine.

"I've been so scared of the dark, but now you're here to keep me company while we wait for the others."

He took her hand, so small and cold in his. "I'm sorry," he said. "For all of this. For not being able to stop it."

"I don't blame you," she said. She sat up straighter, a look of concentration on her face, her brow furrowed into crooked lines. She turned her face toward the reeds and tall grass with the woods a line of darkness behind and glanced back at him. A mist had stolen in and her face was fading into the fog. He could hear her voice high above the sound of rushing water. "Do you hear that, David? Do you hear them?" The panic in her voice was mirrored in her face. "The wolves are getting closer. We need to get out of here. We're nearly out of time."

CHAPTER TWO

"You have one fine set of knockers, you know that, right?"

Lauren propped herself up on the hotel pillows and knocked a cigarette out of the pack on the bedside table. She blew a perfect smoke ring while Salim's tongue worked its way from one breast to the other and licked its way down her stomach. Her hand found the top of his head and gently pulled until he stopped and looked up at her. His black eyes reminded her of a cat's, sly and otherworldly.

"What?" he asked.

She kept the regret she was feeling out of her voice. "I don't have time for round two. I'm leaving the city for a while."

"Where're you going?" His finger circled her belly button.

"My father's not well and I promised my mother I'd … God, don't stop whatever it is you're doing."

He grinned. "Did your schedule open up all of a sudden?"

"Yes. I mean no." She pushed herself off the pillows and lowered her face to kiss the top of his head.

She was going to have to be the one to show some self-restraint. She said with feigned conviction, "I have to go and you have to get back to the office, Salim."

He rolled onto his back and crossed his hands over his chest. The loud release of air through his nose expressed his frustration, but she ignored him. She stood and stretched her arms over her head, breasts and belly pushed forward, all the while knowing that he was looking at her body and liking the feeling. She dodged his hand as he reached over to pull her back on top of him.

"I can't get enough of you," he said, his voice low and thick with lust.

"Don't sound so surprised."

He plumped up the pillows she'd vacated and flopped against the headboard. "When you hired me, I had no idea this is what you had in mind, but I'm not complaining."

"No, I don't suppose you are." She crossed to the desk where she'd laid her clothes across the back of the chair. "I need to have the kitchen drawings completed before Monday morning."

"You're going to owe me one if I have to work on my day off. I have an idea how you can pay me."

"Whatever it takes." She smiled. "You've almost nailed the design but she's not happy with the position of the island and the flow into the dining area."

"I'll see what I can do. Will you be back early in the week?"

She hesitated on her way to stepping into her panties. "I have no idea how long I'll be away. Let me know when you've saved the drawings and I'll access them from my laptop. If worse comes to worst, you can take the meeting with the client and I'll call in."

"Hurry back."

"Believe me, I wouldn't even be going if I had a choice."

Three hours later, Lauren sat in the driver's seat of her Honda Civic, forearms resting on the steering wheel, staring at her parents' house on Grenville Crescent. The last time she'd been home had been the year before in the spring for her dad's birthday, having gone south for Christmas on an all-inclusive holiday with Salim to avoid the usual holiday depression. The trip home in April had been a quick overnight visit, and then back to the safety of her life in Toronto. Her parents had lived in this house since their wedding day forty years ago. A seventies split-level with a two-car garage on a treed lot — oak and maple now bare of leaves. Shingles on the roof were lifting in spots where snow hadn't accumulated. The white siding had turned a dull beige in the fading sunlight. A light snow had fallen the last hour of her drive from Toronto and coated the driveway and sidewalk. Her father would have cleared both by now if he'd been home.

She looked to the right of their property, at the Orlovs' house, and saw the same slow decay taking over the property. Boris and Antonia had been living there as far back as she could remember. They'd never had any kids and Lauren had resented them for it when she was younger. She'd longed for a girl next door to hang out with instead of her two brothers.

On the other side of her parents' house, the woods stood thick and dark, the deciduous tree limbs bare of foliage. A path cut through the trees, marking an opening to the Rideau Trail, almost four hundred kilometres of interconnected pathways through the back country between Ottawa and Kingston. She'd planned to bike the length of it once but never had. A boulevard of trees across from their house in the middle of the road blocked out the neighbours and made her feel as if they lived in the country.

She took another drag from the cigarette burned down to a stub between her gloved fingers. A car she didn't recognize was in her parents' driveway and she wondered which of her brothers had made it here ahead of her. Probably Adam. Tristan and Vivian would make an entrance as usual, or at least that's how the vivacious Vivian would arrange it.

She began to feel the chill through her thin wool coat, so she butted her cigarette out in the ashtray and opened the car door at the same time that her mother opened the front door of the house. Her mom stood backlit by the hall light. Clemmie was next to her, tail a waving flag as he looked up, waiting to see if they'd be going for a walk. She swiped a hand across her eyes and swore softly.

Damn it all to hell. I hate that I have to be here. I hate that this is happening.

Lauren hugged her mom, who hugged her back with one arm, her ear pressed to a cellphone. "Just talking to Ruth," she said. "I'll order pizza when we're done. Take your old room."

Lauren felt the familiar disappointment. Against all reason, she'd hoped for a warmer greeting this time with her dad so ill, but her mom put little pressure into the hug and turned away as she waved Lauren inside, already saying something into the phone. Lauren carried her suitcase upstairs and lay on the single bed for a moment, closing her eyes and breathing in the smells of her childhood. She knew that it was only the fabric softener, but it was the same fabric softener her mother had bought forever.

Welcome home, Lauren.

She found Adam in the den working on his laptop. He glanced up at her and back down at the keyboard. "Hey, kid."

"Hey," she answered and sat in the chair next to him. Clemmie flopped at her feet. She reached down to scratch behind his ears. She and Adam had never had a demonstrative relationship, but a hug wouldn't have killed him. "Mom's finishing up a phone call with Aunt Ruth and then she's going to order pizza."

"I'm starving so that's good news." He typed a few more words before shutting his laptop. He smiled at her. "I like your hair short and white. Very on trend. Hipster."

She touched the back of her neck, surprised at the compliment. "Thanks, I think. When are Tristan and Vivian expected to arrive?"

"Mom said tomorrow morning."

She studied her brother, whom she hadn't seen in over a year. He looked tired, his brown eyes that could snare a woman's interest with one glance bloodshot, and the way he slumped into the couch, dripping exhaustion. He'd lost weight since the last time they'd met up in Toronto on one of his stopovers. "Are you still on the western and northern routes?" she asked.

"I accepted a new itinerary at the end of the summer. I'm flying between Vancouver and Hong Kong now. Didn't Mona tell you?"

"No, but we haven't spoken in a while. That's a big change. Did you ask for it?"

"I was ready for something else."

"How does Mona feel about that?"

"Good, I guess. I'm home more now since half the stopovers are in Vancouver."

"I was hoping to see her this trip."

"It's hard for her to leave her class and Simon isn't good when his routine is disrupted, but she'll come for the funeral."

They were silent for a moment, thinking about their father's impending death without the idea of his passing seeming real. Lauren didn't want to contemplate the change this would bring to her family … at least, not before it happened. "What grade is Mona teaching this year?"

"Four, and Simon just entered grade three at the same school. He's got a full-time teacher's aide with him, which is helping."

Even though they hadn't seen each other in a long time, she knew her brother well enough to hear the frustration underlying his words. "I imagine it's been tough for you." She remembered how hard he'd taken having a son with special needs.

Mona had wanted to try for a second child but Adam had so far refused.

"Tougher for Mona," he said. "Your kitchen and bath design business appears to be doing well."

"Can't complain."

She started to talk about her latest kitchen project but before she'd finished her first sentence, Adam opened his laptop again and clicked on a couple of keys. He glanced up at her and back at the screen a few times, pretending an interest in her work that she knew he didn't have. She let her words trail off after a few moments and stood up. Clemmie was instantly on his feet, eager chocolate eyes fixed on her face. "Just heading out for a walk with Clem," she said.

"Right, see you later then." Adam glanced up and smiled one last time. She heard the keys tapping in earnest as she went in search of her coat and the dog's leash.

"Well, Clemmie," she said as she bent down to grab his collar, "At least you're always glad to see me."

Kala Stonechild pulled into the parking lot next to Joliette Institution for Women and took a moment to survey the red brick building behind a high metal fence capped with barbed wire. The trip had been a slow drive: three and a half hours from Kingston to Montreal, hampered the entire way by blowing snow, with the town of Joliette an additional hour and a quarter on Autoroute 40. Traffic had moved at a crawl the entire way.

She got out of her truck and stepped into a snowdrift. Snowflakes wet her face and gathered in the creases of her jacket. Cutting across the open space, the wind gusted and swirled wet flakes around her as she pushed her way to the entrance.

She was met by a guard, who radioed to somebody to come out and accompany her inside. In the meantime, she showed her ID and signed in before putting her phone and valuables into a tray and walking through the scanner. The place had the institutional smell of cleaning products and the lonely feel of hopelessness. Kala already felt depressed at the thought of the empty hours spent inside these walls by women who could not leave until they paid for their crimes, the majority of which had to do with drugs and prostitution.

The caseworker who shook her hand was a tall, stout woman with curly red hair and a kind, freckled face. "My name is Linda. Thank you for coming all this way. We were pleased when Rose asked to see you."

"How has she been doing?"

They started walking but stopped in front of a metal door. A second later, someone inside pressed a button and the door opened.

"A few months ago, she started going to the trailer where the Indigenous inmates gather for circle and therapy. This seems to be helping her get out of the depression. Today, they made bead bracelets and I hear that she participated."

Linda said this as if it was a big step forward but Kala felt sad at the thought of how small Rose's life had become. They waited for a second door to be unlocked from the inside. The caseworker looked sideways at her. "When I started working here, the inmates with mental issues were in the minority. Now, I'd say close to seventy percent have mental issues. We don't have nearly the resources to deal with the crisis."

"Has Rose been in solitary?"

"No. She lives in one of the residences with four other women. They cook for themselves and have some freedom to move around. Rose has been a model inmate but makes no effort to develop relationships." Linda paused for a moment. "She works every weekday in the prison shop sewing underwear for male inmates in other pens."

"It's good that she keeps busy."

Kala wasn't surprised that Rose had kept people at a distance. From what she remembered of Rose on the rez when they were younger, she'd been a tough teen with no liking for people. Linda led her down a green corridor that fed into a large room with a guard behind bulletproof glass at one end. He nodded at them and Linda raised a hand in greeting. Tables and chairs were bolted into the floor at discreet distances from each other. The room colour was a slightly brighter shade than the green corridor, but still depressingly institutional.

"Take a seat and a guard will bring Rose to you. I'm sure I don't have to tell you that the guard is listening in on your conversation through the mic under the middle of table. I don't expect any trouble, but you can signal the guard for assistance at any point. I'll return in twenty minutes to take you back to the front desk. Remember, no touching."

Kala took a seat facing the guard and thought about the last time she'd seen Rose. It had been over a year ago in the rundown apartment where she and her twelve-year-old daughter Dawn were living. Kala had spent months tracking them down but the reunion hadn't lasted long. A week later, Rose took Dawn and joined a new boyfriend to hold up a liquor store before fleeing into the west. The police picked them up in the prairies and Kala became Dawn's guardian because there was nobody else. Rose had refused to see her or Dawn before or after sentencing … until now.

She heard the door behind her open and waited as a guard escorted Rose to the seat across from her. Kala was surprised to see Rose dressed in regular clothes — a blue sweatshirt, jeans, and running shoes — having envisioned an orange jumpsuit as seen on television prison shows. Rose was skinnier than she remembered, her cheeks hollowed out and grey strands in her long black hair. She kept her eyes downcast, hands folded in her lap.

"How are you doing?" Kala asked. She wanted to reach across the table and hug her friend, but knew she could not.

Rose didn't say anything for a few moments. She kept her head lowered but finally said, "Three squares a day. Who can complain?" She raised her eyes to look at Kala and for an instant, Kala saw the cocky grin that used to come so easily. It didn't last long. "How's my kid?"

Anyone who didn't know her would think that she didn't care all that much, but Kala knew otherwise. "Dawn is good. Maybe I could bring her next time?"

"No!" Rose shook her head and lowered her voice. "No, not here. I don't want this place tainting her and I sure as hell don't want her seeing me locked up."

"I think it would help her if she saw you. She misses you."

"Has she said that?"

"Not in so many words, but she's struggling, Rose. She's keeping everything in. She sees a counsellor but hasn't opened up."

"She *is* my kid. Tough to the end."

"Well, sometimes tough is just hiding a whole whack of hurt."

"I never said it wasn't." This time, Rose lifted her eyes and stared into Kala's. "I need to ask you a favour."

"Name it."

"My ex, Dawn's *dad*," she spit out the word, "I heard that he got early parole but seems nobody thought to tell me. I need you to find out when he got released and track where he goes on the outside."

"If you told me his name, I've forgotten. What was he in for?"

"Bastard's name is Paul Dumont but the only one who still calls him Paulie is his mother. Everyone else calls him Fisher because it was all he ever wanted to do when he was a kid. Fish for pickerel or lake trout and he was good at it. Too bad he ever left the bush. Fisher got fifteen years for dealing drugs and B & Es in North Bay although I think the judge gave as long a sentence as he could because he assaulted a cop when they tried to arrest him. Last I heard he was in Millhaven."

"Okay. I'll look into it. Anything else?"

"Fisher's bad news, Kala. Not the murder-your-sister kind of bad news, but he can't hold a job and if there's trouble anywhere to be found, he's right smack in the middle of it. I need you to keep him away from Dawn."

Kala felt a coldness spreading through her. "Has he threatened to do something?"

Rose dropped her eyes and stared at her hands. She spoke without emotion, as if she'd long ago given up on anything turning out in her favour. "Fisher doesn't threaten. He sneaks up on you when you least expect him and robs you blind." She raised her eyes to Kala's. "The only thing I got worth stealing is Dawn. I need you to make sure he doesn't get his hands on her."

CHAPTER THREE

Tristan opened the door for Vivian and helped her manoeuvre a pile of snow that had drifted onto the driveway. "Watch your step," he said as he let go of her arm. "I'm not sure if your high-heeled boots were the best choice for this trip."

She laughed. "I've been wearing high-heeled boots since I turned thirteen, and that's not going to change. Bring it on, winter." She spread her arms wide and tilted her head to look at the sky before turning her face to smile at him. Her black hair curled over her shoulders and glistened with melting flakes.

He watched her step her way carefully up the snowy path to the front door of his parents' house before he hauled their suitcases out of the trunk. The snow had gotten heavier as they pulled into Kingston, a result of the lake effect. He was glad he didn't live here anymore and wasn't looking forward to the next few days. He'd promised Vivian they'd be back in Edmonton by the weekend, but really, the promise was for himself as much as her. She had no idea how much he hated this damn town and the memories. He'd always downplayed the worst of it.

Her footsteps were filling in with snow already as he tromped up the path. He entered the front hallway and dropped the suitcases. Vivian was sitting in the chair, taking her boots off with Clemmie jumping up and down, pawing her leg. Adam was bent over the dog, trying to pull him off, apologizing and telling the dog to get down at the same time. Vivian yanked off her boot and opened her arms to let Clemmie into her lap. "It's okay, Adam," she said as the dog licked her chin. "Seems I haven't lost my touch with animals." They both turned to look at Tristan.

"Hey," Adam said and closed the space between them to give Tristan a hug. "Good to see you, although not the best circumstances."

"No, but we knew this day would come. I'm just sorry Dad won't get to see his new grandchild."

"That's right," Adam said, letting go of him and turning to look at Vivian. "You're what, four months along?"

"Four months and two weeks, but who's counting? I'm getting a little bump." She rubbed her stomach through the fabric of her blue coat and smiled up at Adam.

Tristan felt the familiar nugget of happiness in his chest, still finding it hard to believe that he was going to be a father. He'd almost given up waiting for Vivian to be ready for a child, but she'd surprised him with the news in October. He'd been ecstatic since she told him that the ultrasound two days earlier confirmed that they were having a boy. Looking at his wife now, even more beautiful in pregnancy than before, he wanted to hold on to this moment.

He wanted to forget that he'd felt their marriage slipping away as late as the summer before and the jealousy that consumed his waking hours and disturbed his sleep. He asked, "Where's Mom and Lauren? She texted me that she arrived last night."

Adam nodded. "Lauren got here yesterday late afternoon. The two of them are at the hospital and with any luck they aren't fighting yet. I was on my way over when I heard you pull up."

Tristan said, "Viv wants to lie down for a bit, but I'll be right behind you after I get these suitcases upstairs. My old room, I'm guessing?"

"Yeah. Mom replaced your single bed with a double."

"Only a double?" Vivian frowned and set the dog on the floor before she stood up. She straightened the folds in her plaid skirt. "The way you flail around, Tristan, a king is barely large enough." She paused. "I thought Mona and Simon would be coming with you, Adam?"

"Mona called this morning and she's booked a flight to Toronto for later this afternoon even though I asked her not to bother yet. Simon will stay with her sister. She's renting a car and will be here around suppertime."

Tristan stopped with his foot on the first stair. "Is Dad that bad?"

Adam nodded. "He hasn't got much longer. Maybe a few days at the most. He keeps slipping in and out of consciousness."

"How's Mom taking it?"

"Stoically, of course. It's how we roll, remember?"

"There's not a McKenna born who shows fear or pain."

"Although we've been known to drink away our worries," said Adam. "Tristan, why don't I wait and we can go to the hospital together?"

"Yes, why don't we go in one car?" Vivian asked.

"I thought you wanted to lie down," Tristan said, pausing with a suitcase in each hand.

Vivian turned her luminous eyes on him. "If your father's that close to the end, I should make an effort to see him now. Give me a few secs to freshen my face and I'll be ready to go."

Tristan shrugged at Adam, letting him know that as far as women and decisions went, it was best not to question. Especially not when the woman was pregnant.

David opened his eyes and turned to see out the wide rectangular window on his right side. The snowflakes were falling thick and fast and he licked his lips, trying to imagine the taste and the soothing cold on his skin. Would he experience such sensation on the other side? He'd know soon enough.

"Your father's awake."

Evelyn's face came into focus. He shifted his gaze and Lauren's face leaned in next to his wife's. *Lauren*. He'd wanted to tell her something but his mind couldn't corral the thought. He tried to move his mouth.

"Get him some ice chips." Evelyn's voice. The tone she used with Lauren but not the boys. The books on raising kids had said not to show favourites, but Evelyn hadn't gotten the message. His extra attention to their daughter to try to balance the scales had only thrown gas on the fire. Just one more regret on a long list.

"How're you doing, Dad?" Lauren rubbed the ice chips on his lips and he tried to smile.

"Hanging ... in."

He felt her hand on his forehead for a moment and then Evelyn manoeuvred Lauren a few steps back out of his line of sight. "The boys are coming by soon. I'm still checking with the doctor to see if I can bring you home now that I have so much help."

He managed to say, "That would be good." *Good, but not likely.* He knew he was never leaving this bed except in a body bag. He was quite certain Evelyn knew it too. Her greatest strength had been twisting the truth to protect her version of the world. Not letting in any of the ugliness. Problem was that hiding from the truth had ruined them all.

At the bottom of it, he knew that he was to blame. Would he make the same choices today? Would he stay silent about what he'd done?

He closed his eyes and let himself float away.

Zoe tucked in his sheet before she stretched out on the bed next to him. Her matted dark-brown hair trailed over the side of the bed and her eyes, the colour of walnuts, were wide open, watching him. Blood dripped from the gaping wound in her neck, staining the white blanket underneath her a shocking crimson. Her delicate hand slipped inside his large, rough one.

"Am I dreaming or is this real?" he asked himself. This could not be real. He turned his face sideways and kissed the top of the girl's head, which was snuggled against his chest.

"No point coming back to haunt me for what I did after all this time," he said. "I did what I did for a reason. What would be the point of laying blame?"

He expected some sort of argument but got nothing from her. She lay still next to him, as deeply asleep as Lauren used to be when she was a baby and had drunk a bottle of warm milk. The girls had been inseparable friends from grade school on. Zoe petite and dark-haired, Lauren tall and slender with blond-streaked curls. How many times had he heard them giggling in Lauren's bedroom or watched them walking arm in arm down the road?

Lauren and Zoe. Zoe and Lauren.
I loved you both
As my own.
Two little peas in a pod.
Arms linked and faces shining
Until death did you part.

"I'm going to get some late lunch," Lauren said. She'd had enough of walking on eggshells with her mother and could do with a smoke and a vodka tonic. Make that three vodka tonics.

"Tristan will be here soon. Don't you want to wait until you've seen him?"

No mention of Vivian, as usual. "That's okay. I'll see them back at the house later today."

"Well, suit yourself." Her mother's face was wearing her tight, pinched look and Lauren waited for the other shoe. "You always do," Evelyn added, her eyes spoiling for a fight.

There was a time when Lauren would have engaged with her mother's rebuke, but she knew the battle would end up a draw and leave her feeling lousy. She picked up her purse from the floor and stretched herself to full height. "See you later," she said with fake gaiety. She beamed a smile even though the effort cost her.

She took the elevator and found her car covered in a layer of snow at the back of the municipal parking lot where the snow had drifted. After swiping off the thick coating on the windshield with her arm and waiting for the car defroster to blast out hot air enough so she could see, she worked her way over to Princess Street and continued south toward the waterfront. The snow had tapered off to a light sprinkle but the roads were slick with ice and she drove slowly. She took a left on Wellington and was lucky enough to find a parking spot near the Iron Duke.

She pushed open the door and took a stool at the bar in front of the long line of beer taps. She ordered a tall vodka with lots of tonic and ice, knowing she had to pace herself. The bartender set the drink on a coaster in front of her.

"You look familiar," he said.

"I used to come here a long time ago." She took a sip, deliberately keeping her eyes down, swirling the liquid in her glass as she set it back on the counter. She sensed he hadn't moved and tried to think him away.

"Lauren? Lauren McKenna?"

She slowly raised her eyes. Stout. Grey stubble and kinky hair. It took a few seconds for her to place his eyes. When she did, she grinned. "Hey, Clint. How've you been?"

"Well, you know. Trying to stay out of trouble. I started working here a couple of years ago. You were in Toronto last I heard."

"Still am. I'm home because my dad's not doing well. He's not expected to be with us much longer."

He frowned. "Sorry to hear that, Lauren. I always liked your old man."

"Yeah, me too."

He moved away to talk to a waitress and returned to fill glasses from the beer taps. "Is Adam flying in?"

"He's here and Tristan and his wife Vivian are en route."

"Tristan got married?"

She understood the surprise in his voice. Nobody could imagine her brother moving on after Zoe. To the rest of the world, her family's lives had been frozen in that one horrific moment in time. In her case, they weren't far wrong. "And they're expecting their first baby."

"Wow." The silence following his exclamation spoke volumes. "Is she from here?"

"Edmonton. It's where they're living now."

"Well … good for him. Couldn't have been easy."

Clint moved to the other end of the counter with some relief, Lauren imagined. She should have been used to the stilted conversations and awkward eye shifts as people searched for the right thing to say. Problem was, there was no right response when faced with a murderer's family member. To be fair, Tristan hadn't been charged with Zoe's murder, but that didn't stop anyone from believing he got off only from a lack of evidence. Hell, for a lot of years, she herself had half believed he'd done it.

CHAPTER FOUR

It was going on 9:30 when Lauren left the Duke and got into her car. She'd drunk the first three vodkas quickly and enjoyed the buzz while sipping on a fourth and fifth, chatting up the two men on the barstools next to her. The better-looking one had suggested she return with them to their hotel near the waterfront, and she'd considered it for all of half an hour. Before her cheeseburger arrived and the alcohol started to wear off. She'd lingered over two cups of coffee after they left and then been surprised to find how long she'd spent in the pub. She certainly hadn't set out to kill the entire afternoon and evening there.

She looked around the darkened street at the layer of pristine white snow glistening on the sidewalks and roadway like spun sugar in the light from the streetlamps. Errant flakes drifted through the air in their lazy tumbles to earth. She'd missed supper and her mother would be pissed off, no doubt, but the thought of facing her family en masse over a meal had been more than she could bear this evening. Adam had called while she was still with her mother to say that Mona was flying in early. She'd be there by now, forming a tight unit with Vivian to make Lauren feel the outsider. Even now, with night firmly in place, she found herself reluctant to go home.

She drove through the nearly empty streets toward the harbour and turned west on King Street, catching glimpses of the lake between buildings, the moon full with the stars pinpoints of light scattered in the blackness above. She drove the route on autopilot, skirting past Kingston General on her right where her father lay dying while driving parallel to the waterfront. At Portsmouth, she turned right and continued on past St. Lawrence College, crossing Bath Road and entering her own hood, the streets and trees as familiar to her as breathing even after all the years away. Instead of turning left and winding her way onto Grenville Crescent, the street where her parents lived, she kept going a few blocks more and turned right on Elmwood with another quick left onto Hillendale.

Zoe's house was halfway up on the right, a Victory white storey-and-a-half with red shutters and a sloped green roof. The siding looked greyer than she remembered and the shingles were blackened in places, much like on her parents' house, but not much else had changed. Lauren slowed and drove to the end of the block where she made a U-turn in front of the aging apartment building and doubled back, sidling up next to the curb across from the Delgado house and turning off the engine and headlights. She sat for a moment, staring straight ahead and stilling her breathing.

When she closed her eyes, she was fourteen years younger, walking up the sidewalk to the Delgado front door after school. Zoe was leading the way and swivelled her head to laugh at something Lauren said, her long black hair swishing across her back as she started up the steps. "Matt is helping Dad in the shop so we have the house to ourselves."

Their last afternoon together. Even though Zoe was dating Tristan, she kept her Fridays open for Lauren. Tristan didn't like it, but he had no choice. Zoe was Lauren's best friend long before she started up with him. That last Friday, they'd taken bottles of Coke and a bag of chips up to Zoe's bedroom and watched a taped episode of *Gilmore Girls* on Zoe's little TV before Zoe stretched out on her bed and Lauren leaned against the footboard hugging her knees to her chest.

"I don't know what you see in my brother," Lauren said. The words had become a joke between them. A phrase she used to start a conversation and one that Zoe thought she didn't mean. Zoe laughed as she always did. She couldn't have known that she and Tristan would break up by Sunday and that she and Lauren would miss the next Friday afternoon get-together for a reason Lauren couldn't recall now.

That's how Lauren remembered Zoe, always smiling and laughing. The one to light up a room. The one everyone circled around, wanting to get close to her warmth. She'd been drawn to her and so had Tristan. "We just need to get *you* a boyfriend," Zoe had said that Friday afternoon, her dark eyes glittering onyx. "Then we can double date."

If only.

Lauren had wanted to tell her about the past few months and her unexpected, exhilarating, breathless relationship with Zoe's brother Matt, but she didn't want to jinx it. Not yet. She'd known Matt forever as her best friend's big brother and he'd teased her like a little sister until that day they'd met by chance at the mall and he'd walked Lauren home. That was when he looked at her differently and she'd thought that her crush on him might turn into something more. She couldn't believe it when he'd found ways to see her alone. Later, she wished she'd told Zoe her secret even though her murder ended any chance she had with Matt. He acted as if he'd never kissed her or held her hand or told her he couldn't wait to see her the week before his sister's body was found in the woods less than a mile from Lauren's house. Not that she could blame him. At the funeral, he'd avoided her and looked away when he caught her staring, and she'd felt ashamed.

As she sat in her Civic in front of Zoe's house, she watched the front door opening and she ducked lower in the seat. A taller, more muscular Matt than she remembered stepped outside and stood for a moment in the porch light. He held the door for an older, greyer version of his father, Franco Delgado. They both wore red plaid jackets and carried mugs of coffee. They were talking easily to each other and she saw Franco smile as he looked across the top of the black Ford Escape at Matt before they both climbed in. Matt backed the car out of the laneway, glancing at her car to make sure he didn't hit it, but he didn't see her scrunched down in the front seat. She watched their red taillights disappear down the street and around the corner with a longing in her heart that made her want to chase after them. Not that she ever would.

Ten minutes later, she started the engine in her cold car and slowly followed their tire tracks down Hillendale on her way home. With any luck, everyone would be in bed and she could put off the big family reunion until the morning.

Lauren awoke earlier than she wanted to, but it was hard to sleep with doors banging and feet thumping up and down the stairs. Should she chance a smoke before getting up to face everyone? She seriously considered it for all of a minute but knew what would happen if her mother smelled smoke in the house. *Fuck, she was turning back into a timid teenager, scared to cross her mother and risk the fallout. Fuck, fuck, and double fuck.* She sighed heavily and swung her feet onto the floor.

Vivian and Mona were sitting with their heads together, looking at pictures on a cellphone and laughing over a photo when Lauren entered the dining room with a cup of coffee she'd poured in the kitchen. They both raised their heads and the moment of gaiety evaporated with the guilty look that passed between them. *Yeah*, Lauren thought. *Remember why we're all gathered. This is not the time for levity.*

"Hey Mona," she said and waved a hand at her. "Adam told us you were flying here earlier than you'd planned. Good of you to come."

"Of course I've come." Mona got up and came around the table to hug her. She smelled of vanilla and coconut and west coast sunshine. Mona, the glass-half-full gal who never forgot to call on Lauren's birthday and kept her updated on Facebook about Adam and Simon, putting a happy spin on the troubled world of their son.

Do you ever get pissed off, feel like hitting somebody? Lauren had once asked Mona's smiling picture, her blond hair freshly cut into its signature bob, her hand outstretched with a glass of white wine to toast the photographer. She'd had to squint to see Simon's moon-shaped scowling face in the background over Mona's right shoulder.

If I had a son like Simon, I'd struggle getting out of bed each day.

"You're looking *so* good," Mona said as she sat back down in her chair. "I love your hair. The cut suits you. Everything going well in Toronto?"

"Can't complain. How's life in Vancouver? Simon?"

"Oh, you know." Mona laughed. "Life is never dull. Adam's been away a lot but he has longer layovers now that he's started the Asian route. We have a new teacher's aide who works exclusively with Simon and he's doing wonderfully."

Vivian covered a yawn with her manicured red nails. Then she laughed. "This baby is making me tired."

Lauren doubted the yawn was from fatigue. Vivian always became bored if the talk wasn't about her.

Mona was kinder. "You'll need more naps for the first trimester especially, but soon you'll have your energy back."

"Oh, I hope so." Vivian reached for a bran muffin." I'm hoping my ravenous hunger drops off too or I'm going to be *huge*. Simply huge."

And ... ba da boom. The conversation has returned to you. Lauren let her gaze rest first on Vivian and then on Mona. Two polar opposites in looks and personality. Vivian, dark-haired and sloe-eyed with a petite, curvy body even in pregnancy, and Mona, blond and solid with farm girl fresh looks right down to the freckles on her face and arms. And yet, they got along fine. Lauren was the odd one out. "So what are your plans for today?" she asked.

"I'm going to take a long nap after I go for a walk this afternoon," Vivian said. "I'm not kidding when I say that I'm exhausted. I hardly slept at all. I'm at the spa this morning for a massage and facial. Tristan is on his own today."

"And Adam and I are going to see your father at the hospital this morning. Your mom's already there. After that, I don't know," said Mona. "Adam wants to meet up with someone from high school later. I plan to go shopping. What about you, Lauren?"

"I'll visit Dad this afternoon. I have some work to do before then."

"Oh yes, you're a businesswoman," said Vivian. "How I envy you." Her lips formed a rosebud pout, likely to remind them of her condition. Lauren knew that Vivian was not lacking attention from Tristan, who'd wanted a child for ages. Her lot in life was to be envied if anyone's was. Lauren was one hundred percent certain that Vivian was not envious of her at all.

"Once you have the kid, you'll have it made. Tristan will give you everything your heart desires." Lauren immediately regretted how churlish the words made her sound.

Vivian looked across the table at her. Her eyes were amused and her voice came across light but her message felt like a glimpse behind her carefully controlled facade. "I'm quite sure I have that now." She smiled. "You see, Lauren, unlike some people, I've always been lucky with men that way."

CHAPTER FIVE

The first thing Kala did when she got into the police station Tuesday morning was put in a call to Millhaven. She was still on hold when Paul Gundersund plunked himself down at his desk across from her. She covered the phone receiver and mouthed a good morning. He nodded back before standing up again. "Coffee?" he asked.

She nodded and watched him walk toward the machine near the window, stopping along the way to talk to Andrew Bennett. Gundersund had stopped coming by after work and on weekends to visit her and Dawn as he once had. She'd missed him at first but gradually she and Dawn had begun the long road toward getting closer. They took Taiku for meandering walks after supper and while they didn't speak much about the past, Dawn seemed to have forgiven her for the stint in foster care. At least, she never talked about it.

Gundersund set a full cup on her desk and Kala signalled a thank you. She had drunk half of it by the time a real person clicked online. "How can I help you?"

"This is Officer Kala Stonechild. I'm currently fostering Fisher Dumont's daughter and understand he got early parole. I'd like to speak to someone about his release."

"One moment."

She heard keys tapping. "Fisher Dumont made early parole."

"I realize that. Can you tell me why and where he's living now?"

"Is this part of an official inquiry?"

She could lie but wasn't prepared to risk getting into trouble. "No, not exactly."

"Dumont went before the Parole Board and they granted early parole with strict conditions. I'm not at liberty to tell you where he's living now without a written request and permission from above. As you know, privacy laws are strict."

"But what about his ex-wife and daughter? Don't they have a right to know where he's living? I have custody of his daughter, who is under eighteen."

"They'll have to fill in the form. It's online."

"You're kidding me."

"If you have a complaint —"

"I know. Fill in another form. This is the definition of insanity, you know that, right?"

"Have a good day, ma'am."

Kala was left listening to the dial tone. She was going to have to find another way to track down Fisher Dumont.

Dawn kept her head down and walked past the girls standing on the sidewalk. They were in her class, always sitting in a row at the front. Dawn preferred the back row near the exit. *Emily, Chelsea, and Vanessa.* She was surprised when one of them spoke to her.

"Hey Dawn. What did you get on the math test?"

She lifted her eyes. Which one had asked the question? She couldn't be sure, but thought it might be Emily, the leader of the pack. The blondest of the blondes. Before she could respond, Emily was walking beside her. The other two followed a few steps behind. "I passed," Dawn said at last. "Why?"

"I failed."

The two girls giggled from behind. One of them said, "Like Mr. Biggs said, Em has to find a tutor or she's going to fail her year too."

Emily's head bobbed up and down, strands of hair catching sunlight as she moved. "Mr. Biggs suggested you might be able to tutor me." She flipped her hair back over her shoulder and gently rolled her neck from side to side as she walked. "I can pay."

"No thanks." Dawn pulled her hood over her head and sped up her steps. She tried to put distance between herself and Emily without actually breaking into a run.

"Why not?" Emily's voice sounded incredulous as if she'd never considered the possibility of Dawn turning her down flat.

Dawn picked up her pace, Emily's red leather jacket stubbornly bobbing up and down in her peripheral vision. She felt anger well up from her gut. "I don't need your money."

"But I need your help." Emily's voice was pleading now, not the entitled tone she'd first used. She dropped it a few notches to something close to a whisper. "Please."

Dawn turned her face sideways and glared. Emily stared back at her without blinking or breaking stride. She flipped her lip glossed pout into a smile, which Dawn was all too aware was meant to win her over. "I'd be in your debt."

Dawn remembered all the times Emily had turned away and giggled with her girlfriends when she'd walked by. She remembered how small they'd made her feel. The snubs. It would feel good to make Emily feel an iota of that smallness. Dawn chewed her bottom lip before she stopped walking to face Emily. "I don't have much time to help you. It would have to be last spare of the day today."

Emily's voice bubbled out of her like it was filled with carbonated water. "That works for me. Thanks, you're the best."

I'm sure you really think that. Dawn started walking. "I'll be in the library. Bring your test."

They'd reached the front steps to the school and Emily fell back with her friends. Dawn climbed the stairs and entered the school without looking over her shoulder. She knew the three of them would be watching her and waiting until she was out of earshot to say something flip at her expense. She had no illusions about her own role in their drama. She and Emily would never become friends, and that was just fine with her.

She sat alone in the cafeteria after English and gym class, reading a book from the library and eating the ham sandwich and apple that Kala left for her in the fridge before hustling out the door to the office earlier than usual. She'd spent the day before on police business in Montreal and gotten home late.

Dawn had been living with Kala since November. She'd been placed with Kala a short time after her mother went to prison and had only been with her a few months before her court worker pulled her out and put her in a foster home. That hadn't worked out and now Kala was saddled with her again — that was how Dawn saw it. She felt like she was on probation, not sure who would decide she wasn't fitting in this time around. Dr. Lyman said she should start trusting her aunt, for that was how she thought of Kala, and it wasn't that she didn't want to ... but something inside her wouldn't relax. She was always watching and waiting for signs that her life was going to fall apart again. Her mother had told her that she had a gift. A sixth sense about the universe. Dawn knew it more as a bleak darkness that stole away her happiness.

French and biology classes filled her afternoon and Dawn forgot about meeting Emily until she slid into the seat next to Dawn in the library. "I almost didn't see you sitting here," Emily said. She dropped her bag onto the table and pulled out her math text-book followed by the recent test. A circled red 43 percent was written across the top. "I wasn't kidding about needing your help. Sorry I'm late."

Dawn glanced at her watch. Ten minutes left before the period was over and she had to catch her bus home. "I have time to go over the first problem."

An hour later, they were still going through the test. Dawn hadn't expected Emily to really try to understand anything and was surprised to find she was making an effort. Dawn could have left, but she liked the feeling of helping Emily make progress. Besides, she didn't have anything else going on at home. Emily finished jotting down the formula and worked through the answer before looking up at Dawn. "I think I get this part."

"Good, because I really have to go." Dawn started collecting her books and pens and putting them into her bag. She paused when Emily said, "I made you miss your bus. I'm sorry."

"I'll catch the next one."

Dawn didn't expect Emily to follow her out of the library and certainly not down the hallway to their row of lockers. Emily stood next to Dawn while she spun the numbers on her lock. "Do you want to go to Starbucks for a coffee before you go home? I'm meeting a few friends."

"I don't think so. I have to get home."

"Well, maybe next time."

Dawn kept her face forward and dug around in her locker. She heard Emily's footsteps going down the hallway and waited until she was busy at her own locker before heading toward the exit. The idea that Emily wanted her to join up with her friends was a nice dream, but Dawn knew better than to get her hopes up. Emily might not be as awful as she'd first thought, but the two of them would never be friends. Not once Emily found out that both her parents were in prison.

Dawn pushed open the front door to the school and stepped outside. The sun was nearly down and a cold stillness had settled over the empty street.

She pulled up her hood and walked down the stairs, careful not to slip on patches of black ice hidden by the fresh coating of snow that had fallen while she was inside working with Emily. The snow crunched underfoot like corn flakes as she trudged to the bus stop, hoping she made it home before Kala.

Fred Taylor buzzed through late afternoon as Paul Gundersund was putting on his jacket to attend a meeting with the police board. "You got time to take a call?" Taylor asked. "A woman wants to speak to somebody in charge."

Gundersund was acting staff sergeant while Rouleau replaced Captain Heath. Heath was now happily on a vacation in Europe with his mistress Laney Masterson and officially separated from his wife. "He chose my cousin and true love over marriage to a fortune," Vera, Heath's executive assistant, had said with a wry smile. "At least he's finally made a decision."

Gundersund looked out the window at the deepening twilight, violet shadows snaking their way across the winter day's satin-blue sky. He would have liked to have spent some of this glorious winter day outside, but his life was now endless paperwork and back-to-back meetings. How the hell could Rouleau stand this bureaucratic yoke around his neck day in and day out? He reined in his thoughts and said, "Sure, put them through."

A moment later, he heard a woman's voice. "Hello?"

"Officer Gundersund here. How can I help you?" He pulled over a notepad and picked up his pen, flicking the end against the desk while he waited.

"We're sure this is nothing." The woman hesitated. "She went out for a walk and it's getting dark. We were wondering if someone could put out the word so patrol officers are watching for her."

"I'm sorry, but who is this?"

"I told the person I was just speaking with. This is Evelyn McKenna. We're a bit worried, you see. It's not like her to not answer her phone."

"Is she of adult age, ma'am?"

"Yes, but she's from out of town. And the temperature is dropping."

Gundersund looked out into the main office and saw that everyone had gone for the day. He smiled as he realized this call would get him out of a meeting that would last well into the dinner hour. "Give me your address and I'll come by for a chat."

"We'd be so relieved."

"Sit tight, Ms. McKenna. I'll be there in less than half an hour." Gundersund hung up and grabbed his jacket from the hook on the door. He paused as the euphoria at getting out of the meeting fell away. He hadn't even asked the missing person's name. What was wrong with him? He rubbed a hand across his aching eyes and silently chided himself for being so lax. Then he walked out of the office and down the hall to the front desk where Taylor was speaking into the phone. Taylor put a hand over the receiver and said, "Going out on the call?"

"I am. Did you catch the name of the missing woman?"

"No, sorry. The woman on the line only said her name, which was Evelyn McKenna, and that she needed to speak to someone in charge. By the tone of her voice, I thought it best to punch her right through."

"You did the right thing." He could call Evelyn McKenna back or wait until he got to her place to pin down details. The second choice made him look less foolish. He took a step and turned back. "Did you see Stonechild leave by any chance?"

"Yeah, you just missed her."

Gundersund debated calling her to meet him at the address but decided it wasn't worth two of them being late for supper. Likely, whoever was missing had already made it home. He quickened his stride and was outdoors breathing cold air on a jog to his Mustang, slowing when he caught sight of someone hunched over on all fours near Stonechild's truck. It took him a second to realize it was Kala.

He cleared his throat and she looked up at him. "I dropped my lip-gloss container and it rolled away somewhere. I can't find it in this light." She straightened. "I guess it's not worth getting worked up about."

"Likely not."

"Playing hooky? I thought you had a meeting."

"A call came in about a woman on Grenville Crescent who went for a walk and didn't make it home yet. Apparently she's not from Kingston and the family's worried."

"Like some company?"

"I thought you'd want to get home."

"I have time for a stop."

"If you're sure. Might be good to have another set of eyes in case this turns into a search."

Kala pulled keys out of her pocket. "Give me a second to warm up the truck and I'll follow you over."

CHAPTER SIX

The house was an older split-level, set back from the street, lights shining from every window. A mirror-image house sat dark and silent close to the property line on the neighbouring lot, no fence separating one from the other, coniferous trees and bushes abundant on both properties. The trees stretched into a forest to the left of the McKenna property line. Gundersund parked in their driveway while Stonechild found a spot for her truck on the street. He walked back to meet her at the foot of the drive, quickly chilled by the wind. The sun was nearly down, twilight soon to be overtaken by the night. A half moon and stars would break up the darkness.

"Hopefully, this will be quick," said Gundersund. He thought about how long it had been since the two of them had been out in the field together. Stonechild and Bennett had been teamed up three weeks earlier when he'd taken over for Rouleau. He knew they'd started seeing each other outside of work and the thought kept him from falling back to sleep in the middle of the night.

"You never know with these calls. Could be a suicide."

"Hopefully not." He wasn't prepared to make the gruesome leap yet. Evelyn McKenna had said the missing woman went out for a walk — the woman from out of town. The likeliest scenario was that she ended up in a pub or restaurant out of the cold and lost track of time. He shivered and zipped up his jacket. It was looking like he'd have to pull out the parka. The warmer winter weather that had held through December was making a sharp plummet into the freezer.

Stonechild jumped up and down, stomping her feet. "Let's get inside before they find us frozen to death."

She strode ahead of him and the front door opened before her foot hit the bottom step. Two elderly women stood in the entranceway. The shorter one hovering in the background was wearing a black dress that stretched tight over a full bosom and fell past her knees, beige tights and sensible shoes, a red head scarf the only bit of colour. The one who had to be Evelyn, the more regal of the two with her grey hair tightly permed, held a black-and-white dog that appeared to be a spaniel and Boston terrier mix. The mutt was barking and squirming in her arms and looked ready to have a go at them.

"Clemmie!" she said in a voice so sharp Gundersund froze with one foot inside the doorway. She lowered the dog to the floor while keeping a firm hand on his collar and looking up at Stonechild. "Let him sniff you and he'll settle."

Clemmie took his time checking them out — lingering over Gundersund and growling low in his throat before Evelyn clipped out his name again — and then immediately lost interest in defending his castle, turning and walking away, his nails clicking on the hardwood. Gundersund's eyes tracked him down the hallway. *You're probably going to lie near a hot air vent where I would love to stretch out alongside, you lucky dog.*

After introductions, Evelyn led them into a living room to the right of the entrance partway down the hall. Gundersund smelled traces of pipe tobacco before furniture polish and cleaner overpowered the scent. The room was small, the furniture made from dark-stained oak of a long-distant age, the grey couch cushions frayed but clean, the carpet faded even in the lamplight pooling from two end tables. The couch faced a fireplace with a charred grate swept clean. Evelyn gave them the couch while she and the neighbour, introduced as Antonia Orlov, pulled wing chairs closer, one on either side of the room. The space was gloomy and claustrophobic and Gundersund felt himself pulling in air through an open mouth, trying to fight past an asthma attack and regain his equilibrium. Stonechild sat perfectly still next to him, her eyes taking in the room while her face remained its usual inscrutable mask.

Evelyn began speaking without prompting. Gundersund got the feeling she was used to taking control. "My daughter-in-law went for a walk in the early afternoon and nobody has heard from her since. The children are out searching for her."

"The children?" Stonechild asked.

"Well, my adult children. Adam and Mona are in one car and Lauren and Tristan in another. We're getting worried as you can imagine with Vivian pregnant and not from here. Her coat wasn't suitable but she refused something of mine."

As if this was a bigger crime than being lost. Gundersund leaned forward, arms on his knees. "Was Vivian experiencing any medical issues with her pregnancy?"

"Not that anybody told me. She certainly ate enough at mealtime and she insisted on wearing inappropriate high heeled boots even in her condition."

"How far along is she?"

"From what they told me, four months. Girls are so careless these days. I put no stock in her reliability about anything. Today is one more reason."

Gundersund felt as if questioning Evelyn was like trying to catch an eel with his bare hands. He was relieved when Stonechild took over.

"Let's start from the beginning, shall we? You said that Vivian is not from here. What is her full name and what is she doing in Kingston?

"Why Vivian McKenna, of course, since she's married to my son Tristan. None of this nonsense about keeping her maiden name. I insisted that if she was marrying my son, she had to take his name. They live in Edmonton but everyone is here because my husband is in the hospital."

Gundersund saw her chin quiver, the first sign of a chink in her prickly armour.

Stonechild's voice softened. "I'm sorry that your husband is ill. Can you tell me the other relationships for the names you gave earlier?"

Evelyn relaxed her shoulders. She appeared to focus on Stonechild for the first time. "Adam is my eldest. He's a pilot with Air Canada and his wife, Mona, is a teacher. They have a nine-year-old son, Simon, whom they left at home in Vancouver. Lauren is the second oldest, my daughter. She lives in Toronto and owns a kitchen design business."

"And what do Tristan and Vivian do for a living?"

"Tristan is a writer. He had a bestselling novel a few years ago and is working on a new book while also freelancing. Vivian works at the Bay in cosmetics." Evelyn's mouth drooped as if pulled taut at the ends by a string.

Her face was a series of tells that let them know exactly what she thought of the people in her life. Gundersund knew that Stonechild would be way ahead of him on this. She was as intuitive at reading people and situations as anyone he'd ever met. Except when it came to her own personal life.

The other woman had been sitting motionless across from Evelyn, half in shadow, and she shifted slightly so that he could see her. "You live in the house next door?" he asked.

Her eyes darted over to look at him. They were faded blue and startled above plump cheeks. "Yes, with husband," she said, but it was enough for him to hear a strong Slavic accent.

"Did you see Vivian today?"

She shook her head, the red scarf slipping lower on her forehead.

"What about your husband?"

"Boris is working all day in basement. He make birdhouses."

"That are works of art," said Evelyn. The two women smiled at each other.

"My Boris has gift."

Gundersund felt Stonechild's elbow against his arm as she stirred next to him. "It's early to file a missing-person report," she said, "but if you have a picture of Vivian, we could start our patrol officers looking for her and we'll check the hospitals in case she stopped in for any reason. If she isn't home by morning, we'll reassess the situation. If Vivian turns up or contacts you, please be sure to let us know right away."

"Of course." Evelyn rose and picked up a picture in a silver frame from the mantle. "This is their engagement photo from a few years ago. You can make copies and return it to me in the same condition."

Stonechild stood to accept the picture and Gundersund pushed himself off the hard cushion to stand beside her. He pulled a business card from his pocket and handed it to Evelyn. "Call me as soon as you hear from Vivian."

They left the McKenna house and crossed the street. Gundersund leaned against the side of her truck while they discussed next steps. Stonechild held the framed photo and studied it in the light from the streetlamp. "She's pretty: black hair, brown eyes, and Tristan looks vaguely familiar. I might have seen him on television or something to do with his book. He's got a pleasant enough face and quite piercing brown eyes behind his glasses."

"Let me have a look." Gundersund took the photo from her. "A good-looking couple. I can't say that I've ever seen either of them before. I'll keep this and go get things started back at headquarters while you get home to Dawn."

"Are you sure?"

"Yeah, no problem." He pushed himself off the side of the truck. They were standing so close that he could smell coffee and spearmint on her breath. He resisted the urge to cup his hand around the side of her face.

"You need to move and let me in the truck before my hands freeze up and I can't work the key." Her eyes held his and he felt something unspoken pass between them. Her smile was amused and regretful at the same time … or perhaps that was only his imagination.

He nodded and pulled away from her before crossing the street to his car. He had a few hours' work ahead of him and needed to get things moving. He'd handle the hospitals after he got word out to the officers on patrol. Hopefully Evelyn McKenna would call him with good news by the time he reached Division Street.

All the way to the station, he saw Stonechild's haunting black eyes — the eyes that filled his dreams and kept him from patching things up with his wife, Fiona. The eyes that he couldn't get out of his head. The only consolation was that she had no idea how much she filled his thoughts or the effect she had on him.

And now that she was involved with Bennett, he fully intended to keep it that way.

Kala found Dawn reading at the kitchen table when she arrived home just after eight, Taiku stretched out at her feet. She was bone weary but the sight of her niece and her welcoming smile lifted Kala's spirit. The smell of chicken roasting in the oven made her mouth water. "You're so good to come home to," she said, and then crouched down to rub Taiku's head.

"The chicken and potatoes will be ready in fifteen minutes," Dawn said, closing her book and standing up. "I thought you might not make it home in time."

"It *has* been a long day."

They ate at the kitchen table. Dawn said little in response to Kala's questions about her day. Dawn ate quickly and stood to clear the plates as soon as Kala set down her fork. Kala watched her scrape the plates and put the kettle on for tea. How much to tell her about the trip to Joliette?

While the tea steeped, Dawn washed their few dishes and left them in the rack to dry. She poured Kala a mug of tea and brought it to the table. "I'm going to skip our walk tonight," she said. "I have to study for a test."

"I'm going to skip the walk too. I'm exhausted. Sit for a minute."

Dawn glanced at her from under her long bangs and then lowered herself onto the seat next to her. She dropped her head. "Have I done something wrong?"

Will you be sending me back to foster care? Kala knew this was the question lurking in Dawn's mind every day, every moment. "Of course you haven't. I can't thank you enough for this meal and cleaning up. You've made this place a home."

Dawn raised her eyes to Kala's. "Have you decided to buy it?"

"I sign papers next week." *Dawn needs stability. Buying the property will start her believing you mean to keep her.* Dr. Lyman's words replayed in Kala's head. "Time you, me, and Taiku put down roots."

Dawn seemed to think about this before she said, "I've never lived in one place longer than a year. I wonder what it will feel like."

"We can take a holiday if we feel the need for a bit of freedom." Kala smiled at her. She took a cleansing breath. "I saw your mother today. That's why I went to Montreal." *No secrets.*

"Is she okay?"

"Yes, but sad to be away from you."

"Dr. Lyman said she made bad choices but that doesn't make her a bad person."

"Do you want to see her if I can arrange it?" She'd have to convince Rose but was sure she could if given time.

"I'll think about it. Do you need me to do anything else?"

Kala studied her bowed head and bit her bottom lip. Now might not be the time to spring her father's parole on her. Better to find out where he's living and what he's up to first. She might not have to tell Dawn anything at all if he'd moved away from the area. In all likelihood, he'd headed west to find work. She reached over and rubbed Dawn's shoulder. "No, we're good. Make sure you take a break from studying before bed. You'll sleep better."

"Okay."

Kala sat thinking and sipping tea long after she heard Dawn climb the stairs to her room. Dawn had been roaming the house in the wee hours of the morning for the past month, the only outward sign that she was struggling. Kala would fall asleep again only when she heard Dawn return to bed, Taiku padding behind her, trusted companion and the one source of comfort that Dawn would allow. If Dawn was considering visiting her mother, this was a big breakthrough. She'd refused to talk about Rose since Kala picked her up at the police station after a wild police chase in a stolen car across the prairies that saw Rose and her boyfriend Gil Valiquette serving long sentences in Joliette and Millhaven respectively.

Taiku stood from his spot at her feet and stretched. She rubbed his ears and said, "Such a life, my boy. So much pain in one so young." She pointed toward the hallway and raised her voice to a command. "Go find Dawn and keep her company. I'll be up in a bit. Go on now. Find Dawn."

Taiku followed the direction of her finger toward the entrance to the kitchen and moments later she heard him galloping up the stairs. Taiku had helped to heal her and he was doing the same for Dawn even if some days it felt like they had made little progress. Taiku was the tonic. She just had to learn to be as patient as her faithful dog.

David McKenna was dreaming that he was a boy again. His mother was in the kitchen mixing up something in a bowl. The radio was on and she was singing along to a Frank Sinatra song. He tried to listen to the words and recognized her favourite, "Moon River." She used to pick up his baby brother and rock him to this song while she walked around the apartment singing the words. *Oh, dream maker. You heartbreaker.* She was calling his name. No, it must be his father. *Wherever you're going.* He opened his eyes, expecting to see his father standing in front of him in his grey work shirt, a cigarette hanging from his bottom lip. *I'm going your way.* David squinted in the sudden shock of light.

"You're awake."

He turned his head. It took a few seconds for him to recognize his neighbour's grizzled face. He moved his lips to say, "Hey Boris," but wasn't sure the words came out. Boris was sitting in a chair as close to the bed as he could get. His head was at a level with David's own, less than a foot away. His breath smelled of stale garlic and cigarettes. Rye and coke.

"I would have come sooner but I've been busy in the basement building the houses. Trying a new model for chickadees. I have an order for ten and the store owner wants them by next week."

Boris was then quiet for a bit and David felt himself drifting off. His eyes jolted open again when

Boris said, "Do you ever think about her, that girl? That girl Zoe? She would have been in her early thirties by now." His voice was low. "I think about her sometimes ... and the other dead girls in Romania."

David blinked and moved his lips. Fear pulsed through him, an emotion dredged up from another time. He wanted to say, *We promised never to speak of these things. This is not the time to drag it up from the corner of hell where it belongs*, but his mouth wasn't working.

Boris scratched the white stubble on his cheeks. His breathing was laboured as if he'd been running. He wheezed softly as he spoke. "The police were by your house today. Not the same ones that came when the girl went missing. They're probably retired by now. Antonia happened to be there having tea with your wife, which could mean something or nothing." He cleared the phlegm from his throat. "Seems your daughter-in-law, the dark-haired one, went for a walk and didn't come home." He paused. "I hear she's pregnant."

He paused and David's mind felt as if it were free-falling through time and space. His heart was beating like a frightened bird in his chest, trying its damnest to get out. "Nooooo." He said it this time and was rewarded with a trickle of drool down his chin.

"What's that you're trying to say?" Boris asked. His face was inches from David's mouth and David felt the heat from him. Smelled his gamy sweat. Boris pulled back enough that David could breathe again.

"I'm looking after it. I just wanted to let you know in case this doesn't end well like the other time." He patted David's hand lying exposed on top of the bedspread. "I'll do what I can to make sure the past stays that way. You can rest easy knowing that. I just thought you should know before you heard the worst from somebody else."

CHAPTER SEVEN

Jacques Rouleau was in the office earlier than usual to meet with Gundersund and Stonechild after Gundersund texted at 6:00 a.m. to say that a pregnant woman named Vivian McKenna had not been heard from since the previous afternoon. He found the team already gathered in his office, which Gundersund was now occupying while he took over Heath's. Bennett was pouring a round of coffee when he arrived and he gratefully accepted a cup.

"I only now heard the name of the missing woman," said Woodhouse. "She's married to a guy who killed his girlfriend fifteen or so years ago. Tristan McKenna."

"He was never charged with her murder," said Gundersund, looking at his computer screen. "In fact, he denied killing her and there was no evidence that he did. They were high school kids. Zoe was in grade eleven and Tristan was in grade ten. What age would that put them at? Fifteen and sixteen?"

"I was a few years ahead of Tristan's older brother and at college when Zoe was killed. What was his name?" Woodhouse tapped his head. "Adam.

That's it — Adam McKenna. Anyhow, Tristan had been dating this girl Zoe Delgado and she'd broken up with him. She went missing soon after they split, maybe a week later, and her body was found a week after that in the marshland near the Rideau Trail. Her throat was cut open, but the knife was never found. Tristan McKenna might have gotten away with killing her, but everyone knew he did it." Woodhouse paused dramatically. "And now, his pregnant wife is missing."

"Well, why don't we just go arrest him right now and get it over with?" said Bennett. "Screw the part about collecting evidence."

"Sarcasm isn't helpful," said Woodhouse. "Even you have to admit that if another woman he's involved with is missing, this could lean toward the suspicious side of the street. Another woman with long dark hair, I might add."

Rouleau asked Gundersund. "How many hours has she been unaccounted for?"

"She left home around one thirty yesterday so that makes it eighteen hours since anybody heard from her. Her phone appears to be turned off. I've circulated her photo and description with the patrol officers. They haven't spotted her yet."

"I think it's time to get the team on this. Interview the husband and the rest of the family. You said in your text that they're here because the father is ill?"

"That's right. He's in Kingston General."

"It's early to put out a missing-person bulletin, but we need to have a clearer assessment before we sound the alarm, anyway. She might have had a fight with her husband and caught a bus out of here. You never know."

"Wouldn't be the first knocked-up woman to do something crazy. Their hormones get worse than at their time of the month." Woodhouse looked at Stonechild and she returned his stare without blinking.

"Sharp insight from the man whose girlfriend is a blow-up doll," said Bennett.

A round of laughter erupted as a purplish-red suffused upward from Woodhouse's shirt collar. He glared around the circle and let his angry stare rest on Bennett. "Talk shit now, Bennett, but remember you'll be returning to my charge in a few weeks. We'll see how funny you find things then."

Rouleau held up a hand. "Enough, children. The people who should be offended are all women and the men who respect them. Knock off the sexist comments, Woodhouse, and no need to sink to it, Bennett. Gundersund, keep me in the loop about this search and let me know if you need my assistance. God knows I wouldn't mind getting out of some of the meetings filling up my agenda." He wondered if he looked as tired as he felt, and the day was only getting started.

He returned to his office and stopped at Vera's desk on the way. "Any word from Heath?" he asked as he did every morning.

Vera's smiling red lips turned downward into a frown. "No, and nothing from Laney. She usually posts photos on Facebook but hasn't this trip."

"She could be thinking about Heath's divorce proceedings and not wanting to stoke fires with his wife."

"I think you're right." She picked up a file and held it out to him. "You should know that the *Whig* reporter Marci Stokes called again about twenty minutes ago. She said she heard that we're working on a missing-woman case."

Rouleau shook his head, partly in frustration but an equal part admiration. "That woman has tentacles everywhere. She'll already know that we have no comment."

He accepted the file and continued into Heath's corner office. The sun wasn't at full strength but it was early yet. Two days in a row of sun was a reprieve from the snow and gloomy cloud cover. He patted his stomach before sitting down. He felt the beginnings of a pot-belly from too much sitting. That settled it. He'd get out for a walk at lunchtime and start getting his life back together. He'd been allowing time and circumstances to have their way with him, but it was time to take control again. He owed at least this to Frances and all that she had sacrificed over the course of their marriage. Her memory deserved more from him than fermenting in grief and self-pity.

He picked up the file and pulled out a briefing note for an upcoming meeting. He sat lost in thought for a moment, staring at the photo of Frances he'd put on his desk after she died. It was his favourite of her, taken soon after they were married. She wore a flowered summer dress, with her hair loose around her face, her eyes dancing with happiness as he clicked her picture. That morning she'd told him she was pregnant and they'd gone on a picnic in the country to celebrate. *July.* It had been a hot month and the air conditioner was barely keeping up in their Lower Town apartment. He found a nicer two-bedroom apartment in Sandy Hill after she lost the baby five months later. As if a move would help her to forget the loss of their child.

He dragged his eyes away and looked out the window. Where was Vivian McKenna and what was keeping her from contacting her family? Gundersund had checked the hospitals and her family had been searching everywhere else she might have gone in the neighbourhood. Gundersund had sent out an unofficial call to patrol officers to keep an eye out for her. Her disappearance was worrisome and he would have liked to get more involved, but he couldn't spare the time until Heath came back ... *if* Heath came back. Vera was covering for her boss as best she could, but Rouleau feared Heath was having a mid-life crisis that could end with him chucking his job as well as his wife. He knew what he'd do now if given the choice between his job and the love of his life.

His eyes found Frances's face in the photo again. He picked up the frame. *I can't say that I blame Heath for finding his happiness. It's too bad I didn't come to my senses sooner too, eh love?*

Kala looked around the dining room at the assembled members of the McKenna family and tried to memorize their names and relationships from the quick round of introductions when she and Bennett had entered the room moments before. Only the mother, Evelyn, was absent from the family circle, having gone to the hospital to sit with her husband. Bennett had taken up a position near the hutch and had his notebook out. She directed her gaze at the missing woman's husband, Tristan. He looked as if he hadn't slept for days, judging by his bloodshot eyes and the dark bruising underneath. Now, he was standing with his back toward her in front of the window, looking out at the street. She raised her voice to catch his attention. "Can you tell me how your wife was feeling leading up to her disappearance, Tristan?"

He took a few seconds to turn and focus on her. "She was feeling good. Happy. We both want this baby so badly and we were making plans. She wouldn't simply have up and left, Officer. I'm going crazy with worry."

The darker-haired brother, Adam, who was standing at the end of the table holding a cup of coffee, said, "We're all incredibly concerned. Vivian isn't a flighty woman and she loves Tristan. She wouldn't run off like this because she knows how worried he'd be, not to mention the rest of us. We're already torn up about my father."

"You have to find her," Tristan said, his voice loud and anguished in the silence of the room.

"We will do everything we can to find your wife," said Kala, "but we need more information. Could each of you tell me about your last interaction with Vivian and where you were when she went missing?"

"The last time I saw her, she told me that she was getting a massage in the morning, coming home for lunch, and going for a short walk. She then planned to relax with a book and have a nap," said Tristan. "She'd been having trouble sleeping and had started resting in the afternoon. I slept in that morning and soon after I ate a quick breakfast I left to visit my father in the hospital. Mona came with me. That was the last time I saw my wife."

"I left after breakfast as well to go to the gym and meet up with a friend, who ended up cancelling last minute. I was already downtown so I grabbed some lunch from a coffee shop," said Adam. "Before I left the house, I passed Vivian on the stairwell when I went up to our room to get my gym bag and said good morning. She seemed in good spirits and said she was on her way to get some breakfast in the kitchen. That was it. No sign of distress or upset."

Kala looked from them to the two women sitting on the other side of the dining-room table. The sister with the short, peroxide-white hair looked up from typing on her cellphone. Her skin was ashen and her eyes bleary from lack of sleep.

"Vivian and Mona were having breakfast when I last saw her," she said. "We sat at this table and talked about how happy Vivian was to be having a baby. She and Tristan had been trying for some time. She talked about going to the spa before taking a walk and a nap in the afternoon, but I teleworked in my room all morning and left before lunch so I have no idea what she actually did."

"And where did you go when you finished working?" asked Kala.

"To the hospital and then shopping and a late lunch at the mall in the food court. I drove around for a while and got home around four after I got a text from Tristan asking if I'd seen Vivian. I called him right away and he sounded worried, so I came home to help track her down."

Kala looked at the sister-in-law. "And you, Mona?"

Mona had been listening to everyone intently and turned her head from Lauren to Kala. "Yes, I had breakfast with Vivian and Lauren came in as we were finishing up. I went to the hospital with Tristan and walked back here late morning. I was probably the last one to see Vivian. She was in the kitchen making tea when I got here. We said hello and then I went upstairs to call our son Simon in Edmonton before having a bath. I didn't hear Vivian leave for her walk. She seemed tired but fine otherwise."

"Was Evelyn home at all during the day?"

"She was at the hospital. I'm not sure if she came home for a break or not."

Adam walked around the table and stood behind his wife. He rubbed her shoulders as he said, "We've checked everywhere we can think of and driven the streets most of the night. What are you doing to find her?"

Kala tried to sound reassuring. "We've had officers watching for her since Evelyn called yesterday. We've checked the hospitals and clinics but she hasn't been brought in so this a hopeful sign. We'll be stepping up the search with a team on the way here to start a foot search of the neighbourhood. We could put out a public appeal if you give us permission. It's early but given the situation, it could prove helpful."

"I want you to do whatever it takes," said Tristan. "I want her home before another cold night sets in." He'd begun pacing and Lauren jumped up to intercept him. She put an arm around his shoulders. They were nearly the same height and standing so close to each other, Kala could see the strong family resemblance. Her touch seemed to calm him down.

"We all want that," said Adam, drawing Kala's attention back. "This is a difficult enough time for our family with Dad nearing the end. You can imagine how raw we are to begin with, never mind our worry over Vivian's whereabouts."

"We will do all we can to find her." Kala glanced at Tristan one last time before she motioned for Bennett to leave with her. It wasn't time yet to raise the matter of his dead high school girlfriend, even if she sensed an unspoken tension in the room. She'd noticed the looks that passed between the family members and the way they studied Tristan when they thought she was looking elsewhere. This family was teetering on the edge of a deep suspicion that could go one way or the other. So far everyone was playing their role to perfection, but the longer Vivian remained missing, the harder they would find it to keep up a united facade, to pretend to believe that Tristan was not involved in the unsolved murder of his ex-girlfriend or the disappearance of his pregnant wife.

Kala and Bennett stopped for takeout coffee and breakfast sandwiches on their way back to the station after Gundersund phoned to say that Woodhouse would be leading the neighbourhood search. She and Bennett sat in the Tim Hortons parking lot and watched traffic go by on Princess Street while they ate. She kept the engine running and the interior was toasty warm while the north wind pummelled the outside of the truck. The brilliant sunshine wouldn't make a dent into the frigid temperatures.

"I'm not sorry Woodhouse gets to be lead on the outdoor search," said Bennett, warming his hands on the coffee cup. "Geez Louise, but that's a cold day out there."

Kala nodded. "If Vivian McKenna spent the night outdoors, she could be in real trouble." She didn't want to say the word *dead* out loud. Not yet.

"From what they said, she doesn't appear to be a woman who'd just up and leave."

"No. I'd be more hopeful if she'd been less definite about the walk and nap."

Kala's cellphone buzzed and she took it out of her pocket to read a text message from Gundersund. "Sorry, Bennett, but you've been recruited to help with the search. I'll have to drop you off back at the McKennas before I go to the station. Rouleau wants a verbal update from me in advance of getting the media briefing set up, and this will give me a chance to read up on the case of the murdered high school girlfriend." She'd also use the time to follow up on the form she'd emailed to Millhaven tracking down Fisher Dumont. He was like a stone in her shoe. Not consuming her waking moments, but bothering her enough that she knew the only way to keep the problem from taking over was to find him and keep an eye on his whereabouts.

Bennett asked, "Do you really think Tristan McKenna is behind Zoe Delgado's murder and his wife's disappearance?"

"No idea yet, but I find it's always good to stay a step ahead." She crumpled up her sandwich wrapper and tossed it on the space between their seats, then put the truck into gear and turned her head sideways to smile at Bennett. "Time to get moving. I hope you put on your long johns this morning. You're sure going to need them."

"A day with Woodhouse searching the side streets, woods, and pathways. Perhaps I can bump him off in some secluded spot along the way."

Kala grinned. "I doubt very much he'll leave the warmth of his car except to issue orders, but it's always good to dream big."

CHAPTER EIGHT

Gundersund walked Kala back to her desk after her debrief with Rouleau in Heath's office. He seemed less remote than he had lately, prompting her to ask, "Have you heard from Fiona? When does she finish teaching the university term?"

"She decided to stay on for the winter semester so she won't be home until spring."

"Sounds like she's doing a great job, although must be tough to live away from home so long."

"She's managing."

There was the same grim set to his jaw that he got every time he talked about his wife. Kala had no idea the state of his marriage but she knew that Fiona was determined to make it work. She'd made that crystal clear the last time they were alone together and in the two emails she'd sent from Calgary before Christmas.

They walked as far as Kala's desk without speaking. She sat down and booted up her laptop. Gundersund stood watching her until she began to feel uncomfortable with the silence. He appeared to have something on his mind that he was having trouble broaching.

She asked, "Would you like to come by for supper tonight? Dawn would love to see you."

He hesitated and then said, "Let's play it by ear. This could turn into a busy day with the missing woman case."

"You're right. I wasn't thinking." She put her head down and waited for him to go into his office, but still he lingered. He was looking at her when she finally raised her eyes to his.

"You know that Fiona and I are separated," he said. He rubbed a hand across the scar on his cheek. "When I told you that our marriage was over a few months ago, I meant it. We'll be getting divorced when she comes back from her stint at the university."

"Sure." She could see that her one-word response wasn't what he was expecting and wasn't certain what emotion she saw on his face.

He put his hands into his pockets. "I'm not spreading the news yet, but wanted you to know." He turned without waiting for her to answer.

She watched him walk back into his office while she pondered their unspoken relationship. They both had reasons for keeping their interactions professional. Even if he was free of his marriage and they acted on their mutual attraction, once their affair ended — as she knew it would — working together would get awkward. She looked down at her computer and opened the Google search screen. No point even thinking about starting up with Gundersund. Fiona would never be out of his life anyway no matter what he believed now. Kala had the feeling that Fiona was biding her time out west and planning the best way to ensnare Gundersund once again. Their tempestuous relationship was common knowledge around the office and nobody seriously thought he stood a chance if Fiona wanted him back.

Kala searched out numerous reports in the *Whig* archives about the search for Zoe Delgado during the crucial first days when she went missing fourteen years earlier. After seven days of searching, her fully clothed body was found in the marshland a kilometre or so off the main Rideau Trail north of her neighbourhood. The paper had printed Zoe's high school photo and Kala studied it closely, trying to get a sense of the girl. She had a wide, happy smile, pert nose, and large brown eyes that reminded Kala of a baby doe. Her hair had been long, dark brown, and straight. She was small of frame, according to the paper: five foot three, 110 pounds. The paper had printed shots of the marshy location next to the woods and river where the police search had found her body and daily updates tracked the search for her killer, including pleas for anyone with information to come forward. Tristan McKenna's name was mentioned in every article as the ex-boyfriend and the main suspect. An arrest was expected but never came. The stories gradually petered out with the final headline six months later: *Who Killed Zoe Delgado?* A photographer had captured Tristan ducking from the camera, looking angry and guilty as hell. Several anonymous sources were quoted as saying they had no doubt he'd gotten away with murder. Zoe's father Franco Delgado said that justice had not been done in his daughter's case and they all knew who killed her. He stopped short of naming Tristan, but the implication was there in the articles.

Kala stopped reading and looked up as she heard someone enter the office. She smiled to see Tanya Morrison walking toward her carrying a stack of files.

"I've been recruited to give you a hand." Morrison returned her smile and set the files on Kala's desk and pulled over the visitor chair. "These are the files on the Zoe Delgado case that you requested from Records. Do you believe this cold case is linked to the missing woman?"

"I'm not sure yet." Kala rifled through the stack of papers until she found the picture of the woods and path where the police had found Zoe's body. "Does this location look familiar?" She waited while Morrison read the article. Morrison thumbed through the first pages of the police file until she found a description of the location with more photos of the area.

"I know approximately where this is although it might be harder to find the exact spot in the winter. These photos were taken early fall, by the state of the trees."

"How about we take a drive over there to have a look?"

Morrison checked her watch. "Sure, it's almost lunchtime and I could use some fresh air."

"Let me call Woodhouse to make sure we aren't stepping on his toes." Kala picked up her phone and then set it back down. "It's not like Zoe Delgado and the woman missing now are connected. At least not yet. I think we can safely visit the site without letting Woodhouse know."

"No need to poke the ugly grizzly with a stick."

Kala laughed. "Exactly. You haven't been working in Major Crimes long but you have Woodhouse pegged."

"Believe me, everyone in the Kingston Police Force knows about Officer Woodhouse. I think his picture is in the training manual under assholes to avoid."

Kala parked on Sherwood Drive where it dead-ended next to an entrance to the Rideau Trail. From here, it would be a twenty-minute walk to the McKenna house on Grenville Crescent but a less-than-five-minute drive. The sun was blazing in a cloudless sky although the air was cold and a brisk wind was blowing from the northwest. "It'll be protected in the woods and not this bitter," she said, pulling the hood of her parka over her head before tucking her hands inside her pockets. She was wearing gloves, but they were thin leather and not nearly warm enough for a day like today. Luckily, she'd put on her warmer boots before leaving the house.

"January is my least favourite month," said Morrison. "Spring always feels a long way off when it's minus twenty with a wind chill."

"I like the winter months when they stay cold. I can't get used to the freeze-thaw cycles in southern Ontario. Kingston winters are brutal that way. It's as if the weather can't make up its mind and commit."

"Sounds like my husband." She gave a sideways grin and Kala decided to let the flip comment go. She didn't know Morrison well enough to probe.

They turned left on the trail, passing a house and property at its entrance with thick woods closing off their sightline to other homes. The last layer of snow had been packed down by dog walkers and cross-country skiers, making walking easy and not unpleasant now that they were out of the wind. They were about ten minutes in when Morrison stopped and looked around. "We need to get off the trail and follow the blue route to the marshland. See the markers on the trees. Based on the written report and the photos, Zoe's body was found a kilometre or so into the brush at the end of this path."

"Are you quite sure that we're close to the right spot?"

"The police report was specific enough and I have a good sense of the area, having grown up not too far from here. I spent a lot of time in the woods as a kid. We might have to walk a bit, but I think we're close."

They set off farther into the woods. The snow was deeper, not as packed down, and their pace slowed. Kala inhaled the pine scent of the forest and listened to the swooshing of the wind through the boughs overhead. Periodically, sharp shafts of sunlight broke through the dark canopy of branches. The woods weren't so thick that they couldn't wind their way past trees and through bushes and undergrowth with relative ease, that is, except for wading through untrampled snow. It looked like nobody had been this way since the last snowfall and when they reached the tall grasses and reeds of the marshes Kala didn't see any signs of activity. They tromped south through the stalks, the trees and bushes on their left.

"Should be close now," Morrison said, her breath exhaling in smoky puffs of vapour that blew away in the wind. They'd been exposed to the wind's sharp bite since leaving the cover of the trees. They'd battled their way through the worst of it when Morrison pointed to a scrubby spot near a giant pine. "This looks like the location."

Kala walked alone to the place where Zoe Delgado had been found and knelt in the snow to study the terrain closely. The wind buffeted her more gently in her squatting position and the sun felt stronger near the earth. She bowed her head and said a silent prayer for Zoe's spirit before inspecting the ground and raising her head to take in the full expanse of the landscape. "How close are we to the McKenna house?"

"It's not far from here. Maybe ten minutes once we get back onto the Rideau Trail and then cut over to where it runs behind Grenville Crescent."

"Let's walk in that direction and then we can take the streets back to my truck."

"If you like."

They began making their way in single file down the narrow path with Morrison in the lead. It was easier going back since they could step in their own footprints, where they'd packed down the snow on their way in. Kala tried to imagine the woods that autumn fourteen years ago. Today, the branches were frosted with snow and the path was a narrow ribbon winding through the shelter of trees and bush. The smaller path branched into the wider Rideau Trail and the sunlight strengthened. They turned right and started south toward Grenville.

"The police found Zoe Delgado's body seven days after she went missing," said Kala. "Were you living in Kingston then?"

"Yes, I remember that time clearly because the city was on edge before and after she was found. At first, we thought a rapist was on the loose but then the news focused in on her ex-boyfriend as having killed her. After that, the story died away and the fear lessened. We went back to our regular routines."

"Was she killed where her body was found?"

"I believe that was the conclusion, but it rained solid for two of the days and it was hotter than normal for that time of year. Looking back on it now, I'd think much of the physical evidence would have been lost."

"Was she raped?"

"Initially, we thought so because the news reports said that some of her clothes were missing, and we were scared about a rapist, but I believe that was later refuted. The information should be in the files. Are you thinking of picking up the cold case?"

"While interesting, if Vivian McKenna turns up alive and well, I can't see that I'll be pursuing it."

They reached a curve in the trail and Morrison shouted over her shoulder, "We should be getting close to Grenville Crescent." She looked back at Kala and stopped walking, raising a hand to shield her eyes from the sun. She held up her other arm and pointed into the bushes. "I see something in that gap between the trees. That bit of blue. Do you see it there?"

Kala hurried toward her and squinted through the snow-laden branches. The blue was a sapphire shade and stood out starkly against the snow. "I'll check it out."

She waded through the thick snow and knelt next to the alder trees. The bit of blue was fabric and she carefully began brushing away snow. She knew that Vivian McKenna was supposed to be wearing a blue coat and pulled her phone out of her pocket and snapped several pictures before she looked back at Morrison.

From her position near the ground, she could see markings from a branch that had been used to smooth out the snow between her and the path and her heart quickened. She'd been on the lookout for Vivian McKenna the entire time they were in the woods, hoping she was wrong about the possibility of finding her body near Zoe's murder scene. "I'm going to dig a bit with my hands."

Morrison also had her phone out. "I've got that bad feeling again."

"Yeah, I know what you mean."

She'd accepted the worst before she cleared enough snow to see her. The woman was lying on her side, back toward the trail, hunched in on herself in a fetal position. Her long black hair was crusted with frost and snow that had blown around her body like a protective sheet. One arm lay extended in front of her, fingers rigid in a red leather glove. This was without a doubt Vivian McKenna … and her unborn child. Kala straightened and looked back at Morrison's anxious face, reddened by the wind and a startling contrast to the bloodless face lying on the ground in front of her.

Morrison's arm was raised, the hand holding her cellphone resting on her shoulder. "What have we got?"

"It's not good news," Kala said. "You can let Gundersund know that we've found Vivian McKenna. We're going to need Forensics and Woodhouse will have to be informed."

"Shit," said Morrison. "Shit." She shook her head and lowered the phone to call in.

Kala took a last look at the still form and said a silent prayer for her too before backing her way toward Morrison, being careful to use the same footprints that she'd made on the way in. They'd stay until the team arrived and wait for further instruction. Once back on the Rideau Trail, she pulled out her cellphone and texted Dawn to not keep supper waiting. Their lives were going to be put on the back burner for the foreseeable future.

CHAPTER NINE

"What kind of sandwich would you like today?" Vera asked as she slipped one arm into her coat. She stood in the doorway to Rouleau's office and he looked up from his laptop.

"No sandwich today, thanks. I'm going out for a break."

Vera looked skeptical. "You've never taken a lunchtime break before."

"I'm turning over a new leaf."

"Well, that's good. You've been working much too hard."

He put on his coat after she'd left and picked up a copy of the *Globe and Mail* on his way to his car. He'd find a quiet place to have lunch downtown and then walk along the waterfront. With a craving for haddock and chips, he found a parking spot near the Pilot House and entered to discover the tables full with only standing room left near the bar. He squeezed in beside two men discussing hockey in animated voices and ordered a pint of local beer, surveying the room as he drank. His gaze halted on reporter Marci Stokes, who raised her head from her laptop to return his stare from a corner table. Her face broke into a smile and she waved him over.

"Please join me for lunch," she said.

"I don't want to interrupt your work."

"No problem." She closed her laptop and took a sip from her glass, which he knew to be her usual gin and tonic. "I could use the company and you'll force me to actually take a break for once. I have a few hours to deadline and I'm on the edits now."

"Then how can I refuse?"

He sat and Marci motioned for the waitress to come over. They both ordered the fish and chips. Marci waited for the waitress to leave before she leaned across the table.

"That was a short press briefing this morning. I was expecting you'd take some questions, such as why was the missing woman's husband not there to ask for his wife's safe return?"

"I thought this wasn't going to be a working lunch?" He smiled but was already regretting his decision to sit with her.

She laughed. "I know. I'm incorrigible, aren't I?" She sat back in the chair. She ran a hand absent-mindedly through her hair, which had loosened from a clip at the back of her neck. The green sweater she was wearing had stretched and lost its shape over time but he would bet that she couldn't care less. "Okay, change of subject," she said. "What do you do for fun?"

"For fun?"

"On those long winter evenings when you're not at work? Do you have a secret life?"

"No, but now I'm wondering if you do." He thought of what to tell her and realized his world sounded boring no matter how he spun it. Simple honesty would have to do. "I spend most long winter evenings with my father, cooking supper and discussing the news over a glass of Scotch."

"That sounds lovely. I met your dad once and found him utterly charming."

"He is that. He's started working on a puzzle of a medieval city and recruits me to help slot pieces into place. Five thousand pieces of mainly grey and black is proving to be a challenge. He says it will help to keep Alzheimer's at bay. I'm starting to believe he's secretly offering this preventative measure for me rather than himself."

"Once a parent."

"Always a parent."

She toasted him with her glass. "No kids, Jacques?"

"No."

She tilted her head and rested her chin on the back of her hand as she studied him. "You would have made a good father. I was sorry to hear about the death of your ex-wife."

He nodded. Even now, he couldn't bear to talk about Frances. He asked instead, "And you? Any kids?"

"I raised my two younger sisters if that counts. My father died soon after Cicely was born and my mother became a hopeless drunk. She hid it enough to hold down a job but we never knew when or if she'd make it home. My dad was the love of her life and we were a poor substitute."

"I'm sorry." He could see more pain in her face than she was likely aware. He could imagine how these early experiences had shaped her into the reporter she'd become: dogged, closed off, and tough.

"No need. I've long since reconciled. Cicely and Wendy are both in long-term relationships and doing fine. I'm in good shape too." Her mouth raised in a self-mocking half smile.

They stopped talking when the food arrived. Marci ordered a second drink and Rouleau declined.

"So, will you be staying in Kingston much longer?" he asked after they'd both eaten a few bites.

"Good question. I've had another offer in New York, back at my old paper. I'm not sure returning would be a smart move. Plus, the *Whig* offered me the assistant editor job, which I turned down for now after some reflection. They've left the door open."

"Why did you turn it down?"

"Honestly? I like being a reporter and came to realize that I might be giving too much up after I took the editing gig for a few months. Be careful what you wish for, huh?"

"Is your ex still an editor at the *New York Times*?"

"He is. He's also the one asking me to go back with a raise and the job I've been after since I started. Top dog on the foreign desk."

"Sounds like he wants to get back with you."

"One would assume." She picked up her drink and sighed. "I'm not sure I can do it anymore." She took a long swallow and set the glass back down. "What would you do in my position?" Her eyes searched his face.

"I'm probably not the best one to ask."

"That's okay. I'm staying put anyhow. Kingston has grown on me."

"Well, that's good to hear."

"I'm surprised you would say that, considering how I'm often a thorn in the Kingston Police's backside."

"The role of keeping police and politicians honest can't be underestimated." He would have added that he respected her quick intelligence and enjoyed their conversations but his phone rang before he had the chance. He glanced at the number. "Sorry, I have to take this."

"Take your time."

He felt her eyes on him as he turned sideways and listened even though she continued eating. The call ended without him giving anything away. He knew he could leave without telling her about the tragic turn of events, but this seemed short-sighted given that she'd know soon enough and likely take back the neutral ground they'd forged over lunch. He raised a hand toward the waitress and signalled for the bill. "A woman's body has been found on the Rideau Trail and I'm heading there now if you want to follow. I expect the *Whig* will have a reporter there soon in any case."

Marci was already hitting speed dial on her cell. "Is it the missing woman?" she asked as she held the phone up to her ear.

"Too early to confirm."

She spoke in clipped sentences, holding the phone tucked between her ear and chin while standing to shrug into her coat at the same time. Rouleau was at the cash paying for their meals when she pulled her bill from his hand. "Thanks, but I'll pay for my own. Best not to owe. I'm to follow you out to the scene and a cameraman will meet me there." Her face was flushed and she looked almost radiant in her rush to get the story that would rock the city in a matter of hours, sooner if it was leaked on social media.

"I hope you have boots in your car," he said, looking down at her running shoes. Her fall trench coat wouldn't do either on this frigid afternoon.

"I can't get used to your northern weather, but I have clothing reinforcements in my back seat for these last-minute occasions." She patted his arm as he stepped aside so that she could use the machine to pay. "Thanks for this, Rouleau. Believe me, I won't soon forget."

The day reminded Lauren of that time fourteen long years ago when they'd been waiting for news of Zoe. The same frantic feeling in her stomach. The same sickening sense of foreboding that hovered in the house like a dark sorrow, waiting to swoop down and fill every crack and crevice. She'd been relieved when mid-morning Evelyn had announced that she was going to the hospital. Ever eager to please, Saint Mona had gone along to keep her company on death watch. She was the daughter Evelyn no doubt wished she'd had.

Lauren stared across the room at Adam, once again typing on his laptop. He looked exhausted, dark stubble on his cheeks, posture slouched back on the couch with his feet on the coffee table and knees bent, resting the computer on his legs. Tristan was on the phone to his publicist in the kitchen, explaining why he was going to miss an author event they'd booked for him at the end of the week in Calgary. His voice was wheedling, then fake jolly, asking the publicist to line him up anything she could later in the month. For the first time, Lauren wondered how badly her brother needed the money from these speaking engagements. His only truly successful book had been five years ago and she knew that sales had dropped significantly the year before. A reprint had been put on hold.

With the police now looking for Vivian, they'd stopped making their desperate drives down city streets with stops at every bar, restaurant, and store. Each time, Adam would circle the block while she and Tristan entered the businesses and approached the staff. Tristan would talk to the owner or clerk while she checked washrooms and change rooms on the remote chance that Vivian was passed out somewhere. Absurd, but she'd played along to keep Tristan from falling apart. Mona had come for the first run but begged off on the second. Lauren would have liked to do the same.

She heard Tristan end his call and a moment later, he plopped down on the couch next to Adam.

"How'd that go?" Adam asked, fingers resting on the keyboard.

"I might have lost the best interview of the year but I'll get over it." He looked across the room at Lauren. "This is killing me."

She knew he wasn't talking about his writing career. "I know it's hard, but we'll get through it." *Like last time.* "I'm taking Clemmie for a walk around the neighbourhood. Would you like to come?"

"Yeah, why not."

"I'm going to stay and man the fort," said Adam. "Trist, I'll call your cell if there's any news."

They bundled into parkas and winter boots and set out with Clemmie tugging on his lead. Lauren liked the bracing cold and felt the sluggishness from one too many Scotches the night before begin to lift. At least it wasn't snowing but only because it was too damn cold to snow. She took a flask from her jacket pocket and handed it to Tristan. "Have a drink. It'll take the chill off."

"Thanks." He took a long pull and handed the flask back to her. She did the same and closed her eyes as the golden bite hit the back of her mouth and the burn travelled down her throat. Tristan pulled a joint out of his pocket and shielded it from the wind with his gloved hand as the flame from his lighter bobbed in the wind. He took a drag before offering it to her but she waved him off. "One addiction at a time."

They started walking east on Philips Street without conscious thought. Philips crossed Portsmouth and they kept going until they reached the intersection at Hillendale. It would be natural to veer left toward the Delgados' as they had so many times before Zoe died. Lauren glanced at Tristan but he didn't appear to notice how far they'd walked. She took another swig from the flask.

"Were you and Vivian getting along?"

"Yeah, more or less. We'd had a bit of trouble last year when I thought she was going to leave me but she's happy about the baby. We both are."

"She's not an easy woman to live with."

"No. She can be a right bitch sometimes, but I can't imagine my life without her. She keeps me going and pulls me out of my depressions. I know she can seem self-centred, but she has a great sense of humour and honestly doesn't take herself as seriously as it appears. I will admit though that she has this pathological need to be front and centre." He turned his face toward her and grinned. "I half think she's disappeared for attention. We've all been preoccupied with Dad and she isn't a woman who can stand being out of the spotlight for long."

"I hope that's what's going on." Lauren bit her bottom lip while she pondered how to broach the subject of Zoe. Had enough time gone by for him to open up about what had happened to her? Did she even want to know?"

Lauren turned south, away from the Delgado house, and for the first time Tristan appeared to realize where they were. He looked back toward the Delgado side of the street. Lauren looked too, disappointed not to see any sign of Matt, not that she'd expected to. He and his dad would be at work.

"The Delgados still hate me." Tristan hunched into his jacket and sucked on the spliff.

"Maybe not. They have no reason to … right?" This was as close as she could come to asking him if he'd killed Zoe. She'd never asked, not when Zoe's body had been found, nor in the fourteen years since.

He stopped walking and squinted down at her, exhaling the weed in a slow stream of smoke. "Et tu, Brute?" he said softly.

Lauren stared back until she couldn't take it any longer. She raised her middle finger and started walking. "Fuck off, Tristan. You know I'm on your side."

He kept a few steps behind her. "Forget it, Laur. I know we're tight. It's just ... what if something bad happened to Viv? How am I going to explain it?"

"Are you asking me to cover for you?"

"We could cover for each other. Say we were together that afternoon."

Lauren knew he was just scared of reliving the Zoe witch hunt when he was in the police's sights. She was too. She tried to make her voice sound confident. "You're jumping the gun. Vivian is probably sitting pretty somewhere, laughing at the lot of us and biding her time before she makes a grand entrance and asks what all the fuss is about."

"Yeah, maybe."

"For sure maybe."

They turned right on Elmwood, heading in the direction of home.

"Fuck, it's cold," he said.

At Portsmouth, a police car sped by and they stopped walking to watch it turn left onto Phillips. Tristan threw away the second roach he'd pulled from his pocket and tucked away his lighter. Lauren had a flash of the future and knew that they'd look back at this moment as the crossroads between waiting and knowing.

"Christ, I don't know if I'm ready for this," Tristan said.

"It could be good news." Lauren put an arm around his shoulder and hugged him hard.

Afterwards, she'd remember the defeated look on his face and the certainty in his eyes that the police were bringing the worst possible news. She'd wonder later, when sleep eluded her, why she couldn't shake the feeling that he'd known Vivian would turn up dead.

CHAPTER TEN

An unmarked police car was in the driveway. The aboriginal cop and a new, older one were standing with Adam in the front hall when Lauren and Tristan entered the house ten minutes later. Lauren recognized Officer Stonechild from her previous visit. The older, bald cop introduced himself as Staff Sergeant Rouleau. His eyes were the unusual colour of green sea glass and she looked away quickly so that he wouldn't read anything into her stare. She kicked off her boots and crossed the hallway to stand in front of Adam, whose face was looking as white as freshly fallen snow. She felt her own heart start to speed up in fear. "What is it?" she asked, but she already knew what these two police officers on their doorstep meant.

Tristan was rooted in place near the door and her question propelled him to move past the cops to join her and Adam. All three turned to face the two police officers who were standing close together wearing grim, watchful expressions.

The cop named Rouleau spoke. "We've found a woman's body on the Rideau Trail not far from here.

I regret to say that we believe it is the family member whom you reported missing, Vivian McKenna. We'll need someone to come with us to make a conclusive identification. I'm very sorry to bring you this news."

"Vivian?" Tristan screeched the single pain-laden word and stood swaying as if he'd topple over. Lauren gripped him from one side and Adam grabbed him from the other. "She was pregnant. My wife was pregnant. We were having a baby." His voice cracked. "We were having a baby."

"How did she die?" Adam's voice was harsh. "Did she fall in the woods and couldn't make it back?"

"We're investigating her cause of death now. This will take time, but we'll keep you informed as soon as we have information." Staff Sergeant Rouleau's voice was not unkind and Lauren sensed him to be a compassionate man even through the whirl of emotions that were filling her like poisonous gas.

"If we'd gone up the Rideau Trail the day she went missing, could we have saved her?" Lauren asked, and then wished she hadn't. The shock of this news was making her lose her filter.

"No," said Rouleau, his eyes now squarely on her. "You could not have saved her."

"Thank God for that," said Adam. By the tone of his voice and the expression on his face, Lauren could tell that he was angry she'd asked the question. *Insensitive bitch.* She could see what he was thinking because the same words crossed her mind as soon as the words were out of her mouth.

She felt somewhat vindicated when Tristan said, "I'm glad you asked because it would have eaten me up not knowing if she was waiting for us to help her, all alone in the cold and dark."

"Tubular Bells" blared from somebody's pocket, the ringtone replacing one awkward moment with another.

"Mine," said Adam, pulling his phone from his shirt pocket. He glanced down and back up at Rouleau. "It's my wife. Should I answer?"

"Of course."

"We should tell them in person," said Tristan, his voice close to panic. "I don't want Mother to find out second-hand."

Adam nodded at him as he said into the phone, "What is it, Mona?"

He listened for a bit. "Okay, I'll let the others know. Someone will be over as soon as possible. I know we should all … I'll try to get them organized." He tucked his phone away. "Dad's slipped into a coma. Doctor thinks this is it."

The two police officers looked at each other and it seemed to Lauren that they read each other's thoughts. Officer Stonechild said, "We only need one of you to identify the body."

"I'll do it," said Tristan. "I need to see her."

"Then I'll go with you." Lauren thought that their father wouldn't know if she was there or not. She'd rather visit the morgue than spend a stifling, guilt-laden afternoon with her mother. She was tiring of the lot of them, if she was honest.

"That leaves me to pick up the reins at the hospital," said Adam. He added under his breath. "As usual."

Lauren looked to see if he was kidding, but no, he seriously was acting the put-upon eldest child. She supposed they had their roles from childhood with little chance of them changing the few times they got together. Adam was the high achiever, the serious, dependable one who always stepped up to the plate and shouldered what others could not. He needed these attributes to be a star pilot and to be Simon's father. She was the middle child, the rebellious only daughter who wasn't expected to amount to much. Her father's favourite and her mother's cross to bear. She'd been closest to her baby brother Tristan — younger by a year, but her responsibility when their mother was doing her volunteer work at the church. Tristan was forgiven everything and given whatever he wanted. Toys, sports memberships, cellphone, new clothes, extra dessert. They'd been close, but she'd learned not to cross him or he'd run tattling to their mother and she'd end up on the losing end. She'd forgiven him every slight and betrayal and was still doing it. The three of them continued dancing the dance.

"We'll come as soon as we can," she said to placate him. The effort of saying it made her weary. She wondered how long she'd have to do this family time before she could slip out to the bar and forget about them and death for a few hours. God, maybe she really was a bitch, or at least she was one when she came here. In Toronto, she had friends and lovers. She got along with people and quietly went about her business. She didn't let anyone walk all over her. Only in Kingston, in the bosom of her family, was she reduced to the person she wouldn't want to sit next to on a bus. Only here could she imagine killing one of them without suffering a moment of regret. Vivian would have been her second choice, however. Next in line behind Evelyn.

God, I could use a drink.

She drove Tristan to police headquarters in her car. They went into a cold room where they were storing Vivian, now a lumpy form on a gurney, concealed from them under a white sheet. Lauren had a grip on Tristan's arm more for her own comfort than his. He identified Vivian matter-of-factly, no sign of his earlier grief on display. Lauren turned her head to look at him, unsure what this new behaviour could mean. He was staring straight down at Vivian, his features sad but controlled. Lauren shifted her eyes downward as well. She hadn't liked Vivian much, but the sight of her waxen face and the gold heart earrings still in her ear lobes made her want to weep. The idea that Vivian had put these gold studs in her ears the morning of her death without a clue of what lay ahead was heartbreaking. She thought it strange how the mind could take a death and accept it until one detail such as a pair of earrings could break the façade of control. The technician had only pulled the sheet back to below Vivian's chin and she wondered if this was the standard way to identify someone or if he was concealing some injury.

"I'd like some time alone with my wife and baby." Tristan's words were loud and defiant in the quiet room.

All eyes turned to look at him.

Officer Stonechild stood on his other side. Her voice was low and calm. "I'll take Lauren with me, but Clarence needs to stay. He'll give you space to have a quiet moment with Vivian. Take all the time you need." She nodded at the coroner and he nodded back. She touched Tristan lightly on the arm before escorting Lauren into the hall.

"Would you like to go for coffee in the cafeteria or sit in the hall to wait?" Officer Stonechild asked.

"I don't want to be too far away in case Tristan needs me."

"Let's take seats over here then."

They sat without speaking for the first few minutes, although Lauren felt herself relaxing in the still presence of the officer. The tightness in her chest eased and the tears cleared from her eyes. Officer Stonechild's arm rested warm and comforting against her own.

"How close were you to Vivian?"

"Not very. I live in Toronto and they met and married in Edmonton. I visited them a few times on business trips and last summer I spent a week with them on vacation in Hawaii. Mona and Adam were there as well."

"Can you give me your impressions of her?"

"Impressions?"

"It helps me to have a feel for the person. For instance, was she outgoing or introverted?"

"Vivian was an extrovert, no question. She loved parties and social events." Lauren again felt the full force of her brother's loss. She swallowed hard. "This baby was going to be a complete change of life for her, for them."

"She was looking forward to the baby?"

"Seemed to be. Tristan was over the moon."

"A pregnancy can be hard on a marriage."

The officer's mildly uttered statement hung in the air like a warning signal but Lauren couldn't stop herself from saying, "I have no doubt a real live child would be hard on Vivian since she always had to be the centre of attention, but the pregnancy was giving her that. Let's say that she was not averse to milking the pregnant card. To be honest, I was surprised that she let herself even get pregnant, but Tristan badly wanted a child."

"So, their marriage was solid?"

"From all that I saw, yes."

"I realize this sounds like gossiping and I apologize." Officer Stonechild gave an apologetic smile. "Again, I'm only trying to get a sense of Vivian's state of mind."

"Of course."

"You appear close with your brothers. Are you?"

Lauren considered the question and where her answer could lead. This cop was too easy to talk to and she had to be on her guard. Past experience with the police had taught her this if nothing else. "We're a close family," she said. *Let them prove otherwise.* "Vivian's death is going to take a long time for all of us to get over." Her eyes welled with tears again and she didn't stop one from sliding down her cheek. She supposed this sorrow came from shock. She wasn't used to crying in public.

"I'm sorry again to ask questions at this difficult time."

The door to the viewing room opened and Tristan walked toward them. Lauren could tell that he'd been crying but he'd composed himself before leaving Vivian. He raked a hand through his hair as he strode with seeming purpose down the corridor. "Should we go to the hospital to see Dad, then?" he asked when he reached her. "I need to tell Mother what's happened before she finds out another way." He looked at Officer Stonechild and seemed to challenge her with his tone. "That is if *you* don't need anything more from me."

Lauren knew he was putting on false bravado. If he didn't, the feelings inside him would shatter his rigid facial features into a million snivelling pieces right before their eyes. She'd been witness to it before. The officer studied him but hid what she was thinking about his insolence, for that's how Lauren saw it. She was impressed when Officer Stonechild spoke in the same sympathetic voice as before.

"Yes, we're done for now. We'll be in touch soon with more information. Here's my card if you have questions. You can call me directly at this number."

"Thanks," said Tristan, slapping the card against the top of his hand. "We'll see ourselves out."

Lauren sensed the officer watching them make their way to the end of the long green hallway, but when they reached the elevator, she looked back and there was nobody there.

CHAPTER ELEVEN

Their mother was in full queen mode when Lauren and Tristan entered their father's room: seated next to his head, holding court while nurses went silently and efficiently about their business. Mona was in a chair at the foot of the bed and Adam had gone for coffee. The blind was drawn and the curtain half pulled around the bed so that the light had a yellowish cast. Lauren thought she could smell decay when she bent over her father and kissed his cheek. His face was so porcelain pale as to appear bloodless and his papery skin tasted salty on her lips. She pressed her leg against her mother to lean in since Evelyn refused to move from her place of honour even though it made proximity to their father awkward. Lauren thought unkindly that this was her mother's intention.

"What is the news on Vivian? Adam told us there's been a development but we should wait for you to arrive with the latest update," Evelyn said to Tristan, who was stationed at the end of the bed, watching Lauren and waiting his turn to draw close to their father.

Tristan looked decidedly uncomfortable but spoke clearly enough. "Vivian is dead, Mother. They found her body a few hours ago off the Rideau Trail not far from our house. Lauren and I just came from police headquarters where we went and identified her."

"No!" Evelyn pushed herself out of the chair. Horror filled her face and she raised a trembling hand to cover her mouth. She moaned, "How can this be?" Realization of what was to follow seemed to quickly supersede any feeling of grief. She glared around the room. "I will not have this a second time. How will we bear being scrutinized like common convicts with your father dying? They'll make your life — our lives — a living hell."

Tristan straightened his shoulders, ignoring the tear that leaked from the corner of his eye and slid onto his cheek. "I didn't do it and I have no fear of an investigation just like I had no fear when Zoe died."

"Good God, you don't think the police will link the two deaths and pin them on you? I know that I would if I were looking for a prosecution."

"She might have died of natural causes," Lauren said, secretly moved by her brother's attempt to keep himself together enough to stare down Evelyn. "We don't know anything yet about how she died."

Evelyn's shoulders dropped but the hard line of her mouth remained. "I hope you're right." She lowered herself back into the chair, looking older and washed out. "She was carrying my grandchild."

Her last words were nearly drowned out by Mona's wailing, which had been growing in intensity once the impact of Tristan's words sunk in. Lauren wanted to walk over and slap her senseless but was prevented when Adam pushed the door open and walked up to the bed. His eyes went around the space and landed on Mona. He set the tray of coffee onto the bed and crouched down to put an arm around his wife. She rested her head on his shoulder and he rubbed his hand in circles on her back. Lauren felt herself relax as Mona's caterwauling gradually subsided. "Tristan told you," he said.

"Vivian really is dead!" Mona cried. She tilted back her head and looked up at Adam. "How will we bear this?"

"We'll find a way. Poor Vivian."

Adam's voice was as anguished as Lauren had ever heard and tears welled up again. She had to get a grip or she'd be wailing right along with Mona.

Adam straightened, releasing Mona from his arms, and asked, "Are you okay, Tris?"

"I'm in shock. I can't believe I'll never see Vivian again. It's like I've fallen into a nightmare all over again."

"Of course you're in shock. I'm sorry." Adam looked at each of them in turn and dropped his voice. "With Dad not able to take charge this time, I'll remind everyone that we have to stick together. We know that Tristan is innocent, but the husband is always the first one whom the police suspect. This combined with Zoe's unsolved murder and Tristan is in real danger. We might not get another chance to talk privately before the police are swarming around, so let's back him up and get them to look for the real killer."

"Thanks, brother," said Tristan, and Adam crossed the short space and grabbed him in a hug.

"The police in this town are idiots," said Evelyn. "They harass good upstanding families and ruin reputations. I will do everything I can to make sure they don't get away with it this time."

"I support you fully, Tristan," said Mona, drying her eyes with her sweater. "I know you couldn't have done this."

We're circling the wagons, thought Lauren. *The McKennas might be dysfunctional in private, but by God, we put on a good show of solidarity when it counts.* A shiver travelled up her spine and for a second she was overcome by the feeling of impending disaster. Something evil had been unleashed and they were not going to escape this time. She looked at her father and listened to the rasp of his breath, fainter now than when she had entered the room. She'd grieved when she'd first heard that he had cancer and had been heartbroken the last several months when his health declined. Now that his final days or hours were here, she was numb, unable to grieve anymore. His death would be a release from his suffering and for this she was grateful.

"What about you, Lauren? Are we agreed on this?"

She lifted her head and looked at Adam. He'd released Tristan and they stood side by side with Adam's hand resting on his brother's shoulder. Adam's dark eyes demanded that she answer him. They were all watching her, waiting for her to proclaim her undying support to the family unit. She heard a noise and looked toward Evelyn, who'd opened her mouth to say something but shut it again like a big blowfish sucking in air. Lauren's eyes swung back. Saint Mona's china blues were round, glistening spheres of suffering. Tristan looked as if he was having trouble holding his head up and Lauren directed her response to him. "I'll do whatever it takes to keep you from being wrongly convicted," she said. "You know that I've always been on your side."

Tristan nodded. His eyes would not meet her own and the black premonition exploded inside her again, unleashing a fear that made her want to run back to her safe condo in Toronto and the anonymous life she'd carved out for herself. A life without drama or people judging her as the sister of the teenage killer who'd gotten away with it. A place where her nightmares had stopped and she'd made peace with her dead best friend.

This isn't going to end well, she thought. *This isn't going to end well at all.*

They gathered in the meeting area. Gundersund was pinning the last photo of the crime scene to the wall when Kala took a seat between Andrew Bennett and Tanya Morrison. Woodhouse was in the corner, legs stretched out and chin on his chest with his eyes shut.

"Is Rouleau coming?" asked Kala. She expected Heath to return from vacation sooner than later and Rouleau would be returning to the head up Major Crimes. He needed to get involved in the case right off the mark.

Gundersund turned. "No. He's stuck in meetings, but I'll fill him in later. I want to divvy up the workload now."

Kala nodded and glanced over at Woodhouse. Could he look any more disinterested? Was he even awake? Gundersund appeared unfazed by Woodhouse's apathy. He asked if the coffee was ready and invited them all to fill their mugs before he started the briefing. They took him up on the offer and even Woodhouse stirred himself to get a cup. Once resettled, Gundersund began by going through the facts that they had so far, followed up with new information from the coroner and Forensics.

"As we knew from looking at the body, she was strangled and Dr. Shumaker reports that her own scarf was used to strangle her from behind."

"Do you think she wandered up the path and someone took advantage? Could have been a stranger," said Bennett.

"Or a family member. The husband comes to mind," said Woodhouse. "From all accounts, he got away with one murder already when he was in high school."

"All options are on the table," said Gundersund, "including Zoe Delgado's unsolved murder and links with this one. Rouleau wants Stonechild to look into the Delgado cold case while Woodhouse leads the investigation into Vivian's death. The two of you will be speaking with the family again and interviewing neighbours. Fortunately, we already have the initial interviews taken by Stonechild and Bennett when Vivian was reported missing, but alibis will need checking and stories going over again. Morrison will be helping both teams with research or whatever is required and Bennett will assist Woodhouse. We've been lent a couple of beat cops to help Woodhouse with door to door. I'll be coordinating from head-quarters until Captain Heath gets back from holiday and Rouleau returns to head the investigation."

Kala didn't mind being charged with the cold case because she knew it might tie in to the McKenna murder. The obvious links to Tristan McKenna would need to be scrutinized. She wondered, however, why Woodhouse was being handed such a key role in the investigation. She supposed it came down to Rouleau's assignment and a lack of resources. She'd heard chatter that Rouleau had been trying to place Woodhouse with another division. She hadn't asked Gundersund or Rouleau, not wanting to get drawn into giving an opinion about Woodhouse. She would find it hard to be kind and so preferred to say nothing.

"I'll want Morrison and Bennett on door to door," said Woodhouse. "I'll re-interview the family, starting with the suspicious husband." He grinned.

"The father is dying in Kingston General," said Gundersund. "Try to be sensitive, Woodhouse, as much as you can."

"Sensitive is my middle name."

"Only if you hyphenate it with prick," said Bennett under his breath.

Kala looked around but she was the only one who'd heard him. She put a hand over her mouth and smiled. "See you later?" she asked, looking up at Bennett as he stood to leave.

"Yeah. I'll check in."

She and Bennett had been going to the gym together a few times a week and grabbing a quick bite on the odd Friday after their workout before she went home to Dawn. Kala didn't consider them dates and hadn't wanted anything more. Still, she found herself wondering what it would be like to start up with him. She hadn't been physical with anybody for a long time and Bennett was attractive, amusing, and obviously interested. She could do a lot worse. She looked toward Gundersund at the front of the room. He was talking with Morrison but watching her as he spoke.

She stayed until the others had filed out and approached Gundersund, who was gathering papers from where he'd left them on a table. He didn't notice her right away and she waited for him to raise his head. He jumped when he saw her standing so close to him but recovered and gave her a quick smile before his face turned serious. "Do you have a question for me, Stonechild?"

"Sorry to startle you. I was wondering if I should begin by interviewing Zoe Delgado's father and brother. This might be a stretch, but they could be harbouring some hatred for Tristan if they believed he killed Zoe. I checked and they still live in the neighbourhood."

"Sounds like a good place to start."

"I might be crossing into the new case."

"A chance we'll have to take." He grinned and she knew he wasn't concerned about her treading on Woodhouse's turf.

"Any idea when Captain Heath is coming back?" She didn't care really but wanted to keep talking to him for a few moments more. She'd missed their easy friendship more than she would ever admit. He'd had a way with Dawn and she'd come to rely on his help in the past.

"No word yet. Vera is trying to track him down in Tuscany."

And now, the real reason for waylaying him. "Do you happen to have any inside track with Corrections?"

"I've got a few contacts. Why?"

"A guy named Fisher Dumont got early parole from Millhaven a few months ago. I'm attempting to find out where he's living since he was released."

"Is he connected to any of our cases?"

"Not directly."

"I'll see what I can find out."

"I'd appreciate it, thanks."

She swallowed the twinge of guilt she felt at her subterfuge. If she'd told Gundersund that it was personal, he might not be willing to break rules and she'd be back to wading through the red tape, and she hated red tape more than anything.

CHAPTER TWELVE

Kala returned to her desk and read the entire police file on the Zoe Delgado murder. It was hot in the office and she took off her wool sweater and draped it over the back of her chair. She rolled up the sleeves of her black turtleneck but still felt the sweat soaking through under her armpits. The rest of the team was gone and she could focus without interruption, getting up once to brew a pot of tea. At quarter to one, she bundled up again and got into her truck to grab some lunch on her way to the Delgado garage on Centennial Drive off Gardiners Road. The cold snap was continuing another day under a cloudless blue sky. The sun was strong, but not strong enough to get the temperature above twenty below zero. Closer to twenty-five below with the wind chill. She didn't envy the officers doing door to door or searching the trail for forensics evidence.

She drove west and cut north past motels, gas stations, and an A&W with the wind lifting gusts of snow against the windshield. Even wearing sunglasses, the sun was dazzling and she squinted as she looked at the twin lines of snowbanks on both sides of the road. The Delgados' shop sat on a flat, barren stretch of land across the road from the Exit 611 truck stop and next to Neilson Dairy. A sign at the entrance to the property said DELGADO AUTO with a finger pointing in the direction of the building. The snow had piled against the west side of the one-storey garage and covered the cars waiting for service in the lot. The low building had a flat roof and was made of concrete block painted dark grey with two bays for working on vehicles attached to the office. One scraggly clump of cedars was trying to stay alive next to roll-off bins tucked in along the east wall.

She parked near the cedars and fought to stay upright as she battled the wind to the front door. The office walls were lined in pine and the aroma from a half-full pot of coffee on a filing cabinet hit her as soon as she walked through the door. That and the oil smell. Nobody was behind the counter but a bell had tinkled her arrival when she opened the door so she positioned herself near the counter in full view of whoever was inside the bays. The office was cramped but clean. Her eyes fixed on a calendar of fifties pinup girls — a red-haired woman in a yellow bustier and silk stockings graced January — hanging next to a Mickey Mouse clock. Mickey's white gloves were indicating quarter to three. A minute or so later, a grey-haired man in navy coveralls walked through the connecting door wiping his hands on a greasy rag.

"Can I help you?"

"Mr. Delgado?"

"That's right. I'm the owner. That your truck outside?"

"It is, but that's not why I'm here." She pulled out her ID. "I'm Officer Stonechild with Kingston Major Crimes and I'd like to ask you and your son Matt a couple of questions if you can spare some time."

His welcoming grin changed to a frown. "What's this about, then?"

"You haven't heard the local news today?"

"Never got around to turning on the radio. Had a late night in the shop yesterday and back early this morning. We've been working flat out all week, trying to catch up."

"We're looking into the recent murder of a woman whose family was investigated as part of your daughter Zoe's murder." She'd tried to word her reason for bringing up Zoe's killing as generally as she could, but her explanation sounded convoluted even to her own ears. Mr. Delgado was looking at her with a puzzled expression so she tried again. She asked, "Had you heard that the police have been searching for Vivian McKenna for the past two days? She went out for a walk and never returned."

"Tristan's wife?"

"Yes."

"Can't say that we knew."

"Unfortunately, her body was located yesterday afternoon on the Rideau Trail not far from where Zoe was found fourteen years ago."

"Christ." His face drained of colour. He ran the oil rag across his forehead leaving a smear of black grease. "I need to sit down."

They took the two chairs near the plate-glass window after she pulled one of them out to turn and face him. He rested his hands on his knees and bent forward. His face was turned from her in profile. He was looking out the window, appearing to compose himself. The wind rattled the glass and puffs of snow blew across their sightline. The noise of an air gun punctured the silence at regular intervals. Kala waited.

"Was it Tristan this time too?" His voice was harsh. A silent struggle was going on behind his eyes but anger was winning out over his pain.

"There's no evidence that he was involved with either death. I've spent the morning going through Zoe's case."

"Then you'll know he got away with killing my daughter."

"We have no evidence that he did."

"I know that the police had nothing conclusive, but for the life of me, I know of nobody else who would have killed her."

"I've found that it's unwise to convict someone without proof, although I completely understand the need to bring Zoe's killer to justice and your reasons for believing the killer was Tristan. I am going back through the case to see if the investigation missed anything, but we need to keep an open mind. We can't decide the killer and then only look for evidence to convict them. That would not be justice."

Franco rubbed a hand across his eyes. "Her death killed my wife too. Not right away. It took some time, like a slow-moving disease, but she never recovered. Fit that into your system of justice."

"I'm very sorry. You've been through some terrible tragedy."

He looked at her. "Vivian McKenna. How did she die?"

"Dad? What's going on?"

They both looked toward the door to the bays. A good-looking man in his midthirties stood with one hand holding the door open. Kala judged him to be six feet tall and in good shape, likely into working out. His black hair was cut short and he had the same black eyes as his father.

Franco stood up. "Matt, this is Officer Stonechild. Officer, my son Matt. Looks like Tristan McKenna's wife Vivian turned up dead on the Rideau Trail, not far from where they found Zoe." He looked back at Kala. "The officer wants to find out if her murder is linked to your sister's."

Matt remained standing in place, his eyes going from his dad to Kala and back again. His jaw tightened. "Tristan?"

"As the officer here told me, we can't rush into judgment. She's going to go through Zoe's case again. Maybe the truth will come out after all."

Kala stood as well. "What has your contact been with the McKenna family since Zoe died?"

The two men exchanged glances and Kala felt the mood in the room change. Their eyes became guarded.

"Let's say we've kept ourselves informed about the McKenna family," said Franco.

Matt stayed silent but nodded agreement.

Kala asked, "Did you know the McKenna kids were back in town?"

"We knew," said Franco. "David McKenna is on his deathbed and I heard they'd come back for his last few days. I liked David and I'm sorry that he's dying, but I can't forgive him for sheltering his son."

"How are you staying informed?"

"Their next-door neighbour Boris Orlov brings in his car for service twice a year and brings me up to speed. I used to see David walking his dog on occasion. He made a point of stopping and asking how we were doing but we didn't get beyond that. Last week, Matt met Boris in Tim Hortons and he mentioned about David being sick."

"What kind of dog do you have?"

"A mutt. Part poodle and part something else. You?"

"Black lab."

"Can always tell dog people." He gave a smile that she took as meaning nothing personal about his anger.

"Have either of you met Vivian?"

Again, a look passed between them. Matt answered. "I saw her and Tristan a few times last summer when they were home. Once at the dog park and once at the grocery store. That's it. We didn't talk though."

Franco added, "I saw the two of them pass by in his mother's car. Can't say I spoke to Tristan since the police wrapped up their investigation into Zoe's murder. Wait, that's not true. He came by one day a month or so after the police stopped their investigation to give his condolences but I didn't want to hear them. Maybe we should have warned Vivian about what she was in for."

"Dad," Matt said with an edge of warning in his voice.

"Yeah, I know, son. I can't keep going there."

"I hate to ask you to relive any of this, but what can you tell me about the day Zoe went missing?" Kala asked.

Franco said, "I was at work all day but left early when I got a call from my wife that Zoe hadn't made it home from school. Matt and I drove all over the neighbourhood looking for her while my wife stayed home and made phone calls. We got the police involved the next morning. I'm sure it's all in the police file."

"It is, but I wanted to hear it from you. Matt?"

"I was at school. I saw Zoe at her locker after last period and she said that she was going home. I had basketball practice or I would have gone with her. I never saw her again."

"She didn't mention being worried about Tristan and their breakup?"

"She said that he was taking it hard and she felt bad, especially since she was still friends with Lauren and kept running into him."

"That would make it tough."

Matt nodded. "I wouldn't say that she was overly concerned for her safety, though. None of us was. We'd known the McKennas forever. Dad, Mr. McKenna, and Boris Orlov used to go fishing together. I hung out with Adam and had even taken Lauren on some dates. All of our friendships died that day along with my sister."

Franco stared at Matt and said, "I didn't know you dated Lauren, son."

"It was nothing. Teenage stuff." Matt's voice was dismissive but his cheeks reddened.

"Just surprised I didn't know."

"It wasn't a big deal, Dad."

Kala left the garage without learning anything more and cleaned a coating of snow off her truck before climbing in. While the heater warmed up, she took out her phone and called Dawn. She'd be done class for the day and on her way home. Dawn's phone went to voicemail and Kala left a message saying that she was still at work and would be late getting home.

She threw her phone onto the seat and paused before putting the truck into gear. Snow had already filled in the back windshield as she pulled away. Should she call again to find out why Dawn didn't answer or was she being paranoid knowing that Dawn's father was out of prison? The likelihood that he was even looking for a daughter he'd never known seemed a remote possibility, and Kala decided not to worry about it for now. She'd finish up her work quickly and be home by seven, an early enough night for the first days of a murder investigation. Maybe not being the lead investigator would prove a godsend this time around. She'd spend more time with Dawn and continue developing the trusting relationship that Dr. Lyman kept telling her was the key to mental health.

CHAPTER THIRTEEN

Dawn's phone was in her knapsack and she didn't hear it ringing until it was too late to answer. She fished it out and listened to Kala's message, feeling relieved to hear that she was working late so there was a chance to beat her home again tonight. Otherwise, she'd have to explain why she was coming home so late herself. Every time Dawn thought about sharing how she was feeling or what she was doing with Kala, she felt a knot in her chest that kept her from talking. Reaching out meant risk; sharing led to loss. Better to keep quiet and not open herself up to pity or pain.

"Anyone important?" Emily asked. She'd stopped working on the math equation and was stretching her arms over her head. Her long blond hair shone in the light as she moved. She was wearing large silver hoop earrings and a tight jade-coloured sweater. She smelled like pink bubbles or something sugary and sweet. Dawn knew that every guy in the library was keeping an eye on Emily, hoping she'd turn her head and notice him.

"My aunt letting me know she'll be late getting home."

"You live with your aunt?"

"I do."

"Well, that's great she's going to be late. You can come with me for a coffee. I'll buy since you agreed to meet me again today. I think I'm actually getting this problem so you deserve something to eat too." Emily's smile lit up but Dawn wasn't fooled. Emily was using her to pass her course and wanted to humble her somehow, to restore the balance of power.

"That's okay. I should be getting home to let the dog out."

"That's too bad."

They packed up their books and again Dawn was surprised when Emily walked with her down the hall to her locker. She lingered while Dawn opened the lock. Dawn hesitated before pulling on the door. "Are you meeting your friends?" she asked, hoping Emily would take the hint and leave.

"Not today. Can't your dog last another half hour without you?"

Dawn turned her head sideways to study her. Something sounded off in Emily's voice. An uncertainty that made Dawn curious. "I guess I could spare half an hour if we go somewhere nearby."

Emily's face lit up. "I could drive you home after. I have my car."

Of course you have your own car. "I don't want to put you out."

"Not like I haven't put you out enough. I'll go grab my coat and meet you back here."

They were at the front entrance when Emily said, "We may as well take my car to the coffee shop. It'll save time."

They decided on Coffeeco on Princess. The coffee was fair trade, organic, and tasted divine, or so Emily said to convince Dawn to drive that far out of the neighbourhood. Emily chattered the entire way about different kids in their class and cheerleading. She was captain of the squad and spent a lot of hours practising. Dawn listened and inserted the odd word when needed but overall she was happy to let Emily carry the conversation.

A mixture of dark roast coffee and tea smells greeted them upon entering the small shop and they each ordered a cappuccino and carrot muffin. They were the only two customers and chose a table next to the window.

Emily shrugged out of her coat and looked around. "I love this cozy place. Where do you usually go for coffee?"

"Home."

"Really? You don't have a place you hang out?"

"No."

She didn't have any friends to sit around drinking coffee with, but she wouldn't tell Emily. Already, she was wondering what Emily was after. To make fun of her later with her friends? Dawn took a bite of muffin.

"Did you get tickets to the Shawn Mendes concert next week at the K-Rock Centre?"

Dawn was beginning to feel as if Emily was working to prove how uncool she was, not that it was that difficult. "No, I'm not going to the concert," she said. After a few seconds of silence, she asked, "Are you going?"

"Yes! Chelsea's dad knows somebody and got us tickets near the stage and backstage passes. We're going to meet him after the show."

"That's great."

"Isn't it?"

Dawn drank her coffee and ate the muffin quickly. She looked over at Emily. She'd barely eaten anything and her cup was still full. Dawn hadn't taken off her coat and was starting to sweat. She knew she sounded ungracious but this whole outing had her on edge. "I have to go soon."

Emily jumped a little and picked up her coffee. "Of course. Sorry. I'll take this to go and can drive wherever you want."

"Just to a bus stop would be fine if it's on your way."

Emily reached across to grab her muffin and Dawn stared at her arm where the cuff of her sweater had bunched halfway up. A series of cuts, some fading and others new and angry red, stretched up the inside of Emily's forearm. She raised her eyes to Emily's face and Emily glanced down. She yanked her sleeve to cover the welts and tucked the muffin into her purse while standing and picking up the coffee.

"Ready to go?" she said, her eyes challenging Dawn to say anything about what she'd seen.

Dawn hesitated but stood too and silently followed Emily outside. The snow had started falling and darkness was settling in when they were inside the coffee shop, and they stepped outside to find slightly warmer temperatures but a damp wind. Dawn listened to Emily chatter about the new clothing store she'd found online and agreed that she should forward Dawn the link. Emily was speaking at accelerated speed as if she was trying to keep Dawn from talking.

They cleared the snow off the car before starting back toward the school. Emily was a careful driver, stopping at all intersections for longer than necessary while her head swivelled back and forth, scanning both directions. The heater was blasting hot air and Dawn felt sweaty in her down-filled parka.

"Thanks for coming with me," Emily said as she pulled over to the curb near Dawn's bus stop. "I didn't want to go home."

"Why not?"

"My mother likes to sleep in the afternoon."

Dawn paused, one hand on the door. "Is she sick?"

Emily laughed. "No. She plays tennis in the morning at an indoor club in the winter and takes a break before making supper."

Dawn didn't know how to respond. She had no history with a mother who had time to play a game all morning and sleep all afternoon. Where did one even put that? "I'll see you tomorrow," she said and stepped out into the cold and darkness.

Luck was with her for once. The bus's headlights were coming toward her through the slanting snow and she wouldn't have to wait alone wondering when the next one was coming and trying to keep warm. She'd be home in time to take Taiku for a walk and get supper started before Kala arrived and still have time to replay this strange outing with Emily to try to figure out what her sudden interest could mean … and why Emily was cutting herself when she seemed to have everything good in the world going for her.

"Knock, knock," said Gundersund, hand raised but not striking Rouleau's office door. "Got a few minutes?"

Rouleau looked up from his computer and waved him in. "I'm almost done here. Give me a sec."

"Sure." Gundersund took the visitor chair and stretched his legs, trying to work out a cramp in his calf muscle. The room was in darkness with the exception of the desk lamp and the glowing screen. Rouleau's face looked ghostly in the white light. He finished typing and shut down the computer. He pushed back his chair and folded his hands on his chest.

"What's up?"

"I did what you asked and put Woodhouse in charge of the McKenna case including interviews and door to door. Tell me why we're doing this again?"

Rouleau reached inside his desk drawer and pulled out a bottle of single malt. "Pour you a shot of Heath's special stock?"

"Sure, why not?"

Rouleau stood and retrieved a couple of plastic cups from the filing cabinet. He didn't address Gundersund's question until they'd both had a healthy sip. "HR is worried and this seemed the only way to head off trouble with Woodhouse and the union. He's threatening to lodge a complaint. Says he's being discriminated against and being held back while new officers waltz in and move up without earning it."

"He's talking about Stonechild."

"Among others."

Gundersund took another drink and thought about the possible repercussions. "There's nothing to what he's saying."

Rouleau spoke after a pause. "I'd like to think not, but in the name of fairness, I'm trying to see this from his point of view. Giving him lead on the field-work will go a long way to diffusing the situation."

"What if he screws it up?"

"I have every confidence that you won't let that happen."

"I hope that's not misplaced." Gundersund couldn't get a read on Rouleau's mood. Was he really backing up Woodhouse on this nonsense? "He's not the most sensitive cop. We could have lawsuits on our hands when this is over."

"A chance we'll have to take." Rouleau looked at his watch. "Sorry to cut this short but I promised Dad I'd bring home supper."

"Yeah, I should push off too." Gundersund swallowed the last of the Scotch and stood up. He was unsettled with how this conversation had gone but he couldn't put his finger on why. "See you tomorrow?" he said as he walked toward the door.

"Bright and early."

Rouleau turned off the lamp after Gundersund was gone and sat in the dark, thinking. He was walking a tightrope but couldn't say much to Gundersund. Even the bit he'd told him tonight might have been too much. Woodhouse had done more than threaten to file a complaint. He'd started formal proceedings and aimed allegations at Rouleau and Stonechild, accusing Rouleau of hiring her without going through the proper competition and promoting her beyond her experience above other more experienced officers, such as himself. Woodhouse had a signed statement from his now-retired partner, Ed Chalmers, praising his work and supporting his allegations. He'd also managed to get letters of support from three other long-time cops. Human Resources had advised Rouleau to give Woodhouse a bigger role in the next investigation to try to get him to withdraw his complaint and he'd agreed to give it a shot. He'd be meeting with the HR and the union reps late in the morning to discuss the complaint.

Rouleau stood and walked across the room to get his jacket from the coat rack. His father was working on a research paper and would have forgotten to eat lunch. He'd stop at the butcher and pick up a couple of steaks. They'd go nicely with the New Zealand Pinot Noir he'd bought on the weekend.

He stopped by the main office down the hall on his way out. The only one still working was Kala Stonechild, hunched over her keyboard and oblivious to him watching her from the doorway. He'd been avoiding being alone with her since he'd learned of Woodhouse's complaint, partly to keep from any compromising situations and partly to keep her from guessing what was going on. He had no way of knowing how she'd react, but suspected she'd disappear as easily as she'd arrived in Kingston if it meant making his life easier. It wasn't in her nature to fight for herself; he believed that her childhood in foster homes had taught her that escaping from bad situations was the least painful route.

He saw Kala raise a hand and run it absentmindedly across her forehead and stepped back into the hallway out of her line of vision. He wanted to tell her to pack it in for the night and head home to Dawn, but he stopped himself. She'd be like a bulldog on this case until it was solved, and he hoped against hope that she'd be the one to succeed. Even better if Woodhouse came out incompetent and disproved the glowing assessment Chalmers had given and knocked down his own inflated view of himself. The morning meeting would give him a good indication of how seriously the board members took Woodhouse's complaint.

He'd decide what to do from there.

CHAPTER FOURTEEN

At exactly 4:22 a.m., David McKenna sighed his last shuddering breath and passed on to the next world. Evelyn was alone in the room, sleeping beside him in the leather hospital chair. Adam, Tristan, Lauren, and Mona had taken advantage of her falling asleep to go in search of a vending machine. They returned with cups of coffee to find a nurse standing next to the bed with their father's wrist in her hand. She looked at them. "He's passed," she said and rounded the bed to bend over Evelyn. She gently shook her shoulder. "Mr. McKenna has slipped away, dear. I've buzzed for the doctor on call and he'll be here any minute. It's comforting to know that he's been released from his pain."

Evelyn stood, eyes bleary with sleep. She looked down on her husband. "The Lord bless his soul," she said, making the sign of the cross. "It was time his suffering ended. He's gone to a better place."

Lauren later remembered the room full of medical staff, but only briefly, and then the interlude of stillness in the room as they waited for the attendants to arrive with a gurney to take her father's body away.

Evelyn had gone into the hallway to speak with the doctor and Tristan was in a chair near the window with his eyes closed, snoring softly. Mona and Adam were off finding a pharmacy to buy migraine medication for Mona, who'd felt one coming on. Lauren moved closer to the head of the bed where Evelyn had stubbornly sat throughout the vigil and reached out a hand to touch her father's forehead. His face was free of pain and his mouth had relaxed into what could pass for a smile.

"You look so peaceful, Dad. I'm glad you aren't going to have to be here to face the fallout with Tristan." She checked that her brother was still sleeping and then looked toward the door to make certain she was alone. Satisfied, she lowered herself into Evelyn's vacated chair. She wasn't sure if her dad's spirit was still hovering in the room, as recounted by those who had near-death experiences, but she felt something or someone's presence and wanted to believe. "I'm going to miss you, Dad, but I've been missing you for a while. She rested her cheek on his arm and closed her eyes, trying to feel him with her. "I wish I'd had a chance to tell you how much I love you, but I'm banking on the fact you knew. I'm sorry I haven't made you prouder but I'm going to try. I won't let you down." Tears seeped from under her eyelids and down her cheeks. She whispered, "I'm so tired, Dad. I wish you were here."

She heard the door push open and footsteps on the floor. "What are you doing? Lauren, sit up!"

She opened her eyes to see her mother's furious face bearing down on her. This is how it feels to stand outside your own body, she thought, a curious spectator watching her mother fly toward her like a raging bull.

"Don't touch him. I can't bear for you to touch him." Evelyn's face was bright red and her eyes shot daggers.

Lauren pulled back and her mother's open palm landed on her shoulder instead of her face.

"Stop it, Mother!" said Tristan and Lauren saw him striding across the floor to grab onto Evelyn's arm. "You're distraught. You don't know what you're saying."

"I don't want her near him."

"It doesn't matter. I'm leaving," said Lauren, pushing her way past them both. "I don't need this shit."

She grabbed her coat and purse from the chair and shoved the door open, colliding with an overweight bald man as she stumbled into the hall. "Are you okay, ma'am?" he asked, steadying her with both hands as she shoved and manoeuvred her way past him and the man standing behind him.

"I will be," she said.

The cops have come for Tristan, she thought, but she kept running down the hall toward the elevators, slowing to a walk when she reached the door to the stairwell. She swiped at her eyes with the back of her hand to clear the tears and blurriness and climbed down the three flights to the street. Exiting onto the sidewalk, she breathed in great gulps of frosty air and calmed herself enough to form a plan. She'd return to the house and throw her things in the car and be in Toronto before lunchtime. Tristan could fend for himself and the rest of them could go to hell for all she cared. This would be the last time she set foot in this town.

Over. This is over.

Lauren had put her suitcase into the trunk of the car when she heard someone calling her name. She slammed the trunk shut. Boris Orlov was standing on the front steps to his house in his housecoat and slippers, waving a rolled-up newspaper.

What now? she thought but she walked toward him on the snowy path that Boris had cleared between their two properties.

"Are you leaving?" he asked. "Is there news of your father?"

"I'm sorry to tell you, Boris, but Dad died this morning. I'm going back to Toronto."

He squinted. "God gave, God took back. Your father lived a good life. Come in and have a cup of tea before you go. Antonia will need to be told."

"I really have to get going."

"I just made a pot. You have time to sit for a moment." His words became an order. "Come in. I'm getting cold standing here."

"Just for a minute, then."

Lauren climbed the steps and followed him into the house. She removed her boots and went after him down the hallway into the kitchen.

The Orlov home had the same heavy smell that she remembered from childhood: beets and cabbage with an underlay of furniture polish. She remembered

Antonia working all the mornings of her childhood scrubbing and cleaning with afternoons spent in the kitchen making borscht, cabbage rolls, perogies, bread, corned beef — food that forever tied her to her homeland. For as long as Lauren knew her, Antonia had been a stout, buxom woman with a silent, hang-dog face who wore black skirts past her knees, nude knee-highs, and flowered aprons that only came off when dinner was served. Lauren now wondered if her strong Romanian accent was the reason she kept to a silent presence seemingly content to be in the background. She had no idea what Antonia thought or dreamed about. What made her happy.

She took a seat at the kitchen table and Boris poured tea into chipped mugs, the roses faded from bright red to pink in the dishwasher.

"Antonia!" he called. "Lauren is here." He added sugar to his tea and pushed the bowl toward her. "She hasn't been feeling well."

"I hope it's nothing serious."

Boris shrugged. "God's will." His eyes bore into hers. "Tell me, did your father say anything before he died?"

"No … he slipped into a coma and didn't wake up again." She turned her head to listen. "Is Antonia okay? I don't hear her upstairs."

"She's fine. She's fine. Your mother. How did she take your father's passing?"

"Not well."

"*Ach*, then. Nobody does." He slurped his tea, rough hands large around the cup. Your father was a good man. He always put his family first."

Lauren paused. "Maybe he shouldn't have. Not always, I mean." The tea was stronger than she liked. She reached for the sugar bowl.

"When you live through a Communist state like I have, you will understand that all you really have is your family. You can trust nobody else. Your father knew this truth."

Lauren had overheard snippets of the Orlovs' history although she'd never given their previous lives much thought. "You grew up in Romania," she said, thinking back to a conversation with her father. He'd explained to her why they had accents and ate different food when she'd asked. She was in grade two and her new best friend had come to play. She'd made fun of Antonia's clothes and the way she spoke to them when she offered them cookies. Lauren had made fun of Antonia too and her father had overheard.

"We came to Canada after the revolution. After they executed Nicolae Ceaușescu."

"Dad told me that he was a brutal dictator, but I don't know much more about that time. What was it like living there?" She was embarrassed that she'd given the Orlovs so little thought. They'd just been the neighbours, older people of no interest. Part of the furniture of her life.

He looked past her, his eyes distant, reliving something long ago. "What I have seen would give you nightmares. Antonia is my reminder of what evil people are capable of. Nobody is immune."

"What happened to Antonia?"

He refocused on Lauren. "It was a long time ago. You take for granted all that you have in this country."

He motioned toward the door. "It is time for you to be going. I will tell Antonia that you came by with your news. She will be sad that David is gone."

Lauren was startled by the rough change in his expression and she stood, bumping her knee on the table. "I hope she's feeling better soon. Thank you for the tea."

Boris nodded, but didn't make a move to get up. He resembled a bear, his broad shoulders hunched over the table. "We will visit your mother later. Let her know that."

Snow was falling when Lauren stepped outside. It coated her car and would need to be cleaned off before she began the drive home to Toronto. She pulled up the hood of her jacket and started back across the lawn. Before she reached the driveway, a car drove up and parked on the street. Adam jumped out of the driver's side and waved at her.

What the hell now? she thought and kept trudging through the snow toward her car. Adam couldn't stop her from leaving. She should have hit the road when they were all at the hospital.

He trudged his way through the snow to her. "The police have taken Tristan in for questioning. Hauled him out of Dad's hospital room." He glanced across the yard. "What were you doing at the Orlovs'?"

"Letting them know about Dad. They haven't charged him?"

"Not yet."

"What do you mean not yet?"

"You have to know he could have done it, Lauren."

"What about that musketeer speech in the hospital? One for all and all for one?"

"That still applies, but we have to be realistic."

She stared at him. She remembered all the times he'd gone his own way and left her and Tristan to fend for themselves. Nothing had changed. Nothing ever changed. She walked past him and opened the trunk of her car. She kicked the rear fender. *Shit, shit, shit*. She reached in and took out her suitcase and slammed the trunk shut.

"Were you leaving?" he asked, his voice incredulous.

"I was, but can't very well now, can I?"

"Fuck you, Lauren. Our father just died and Tristan lost his wife and baby and you were running away like you always do. Thinking only of yourself."

She turned and Adam was standing motionless glaring at her. Hair glistening with snow as the sun came out from behind a cloud. Looking so bloody perfect in the glow from the heavens.

"When have you ever been there for me?" she yelled. "When did you ever put our family first? Because I'm not so sure I'm the one who let everyone down. You ran away to Vancouver and left Tristan and me with her." She jabbed a finger toward their house. "So don't talk to me about being selfish or tell me what I should or shouldn't be doing. You can go fuck yourself."

He held up both hands in mock surrender. "Okay. Okay. You're right. I'm a big hairy ass and I'm sorry. But we have to —"

"I know. Stick together." She hoisted her suitcase and started back toward the front door. "I'm staying but only because of Tristan. Once they let him go, I'm out of here. Back to Toronto and my life that has nothing to do with this dead-end town and my seriously deranged family."

She stomped up the sidewalk and slammed her way into the house. She heard Adam's car rev away from the curb as she was kicking off her second boot.

"Just great," she said to her face in the hall mirror. "Why didn't you leave when you had the chance?"

She carried her suitcase back upstairs, lay on the bed, and stared at the ceiling. She needed to figure out the best way to help Tristan when all she really wanted to do was go back to the bar and have a drink. She sat up and swung her feet onto the floor. Some of her best ideas came over a shot of hard liquor. Why should solving this problem be any different?

CHAPTER FIFTEEN

"Did you know we brought in Tristan McKenna?" asked Bennett on his way to his desk. "Woodhouse is letting him cool his heels in interview room one before we have a go at him. Woodhouse thinks he can get McKenna to confess."

Kala looked up from her computer. "Did Rouleau okay that? I heard David McKenna died early this morning."

"I have no idea but I'd be surprised if he did."

"Well, whatever. I made a pot of fresh coffee ten minutes ago."

"Thanks, I could use a cup. The dampness has gone right through me."

Woodhouse strutted into the office and Kala went back to reading. She looked up again to find him standing next to her desk.

"What's going on with the Zoe Delgado file?" he asked.

"I interviewed her dad and brother but they didn't tell me anything that wasn't in the files."

"So you essentially have squat that I can use?"

"If you want to put it that way."

"Well, keep on it, Stonechild, and let me know if you come up with anything. I want to connect the two murders with some solid evidence. They're obviously linked by the killer."

She didn't bother to respond. What would be the point? Woodhouse's dark presence drifted away and she went back to reading. She observed Gundersund come out of his office and motion for Woodhouse to join him. He didn't include her so she continued making notes. Woodhouse exited the office five minutes later looking as if he'd eaten a lemon.

"Let's go, Bennett," he said on his way past Bennett's desk. "Naptime is over."

"See you later," Bennett said to Kala. "Are you going to watch us interview McKenna through the two-way?"

"I don't think so."

"Get the lead out, lover boy," said Woodhouse. "Fraternize on your own time."

"Don't rise to his bait," Kala cautioned quietly. "He'll only get worse."

"You don't need to tell me."

She waited a few minutes after they left before knocking on Gundersund's door. "Got a minute?"

"I do. Take a seat. Still feels weird being in this office instead of the main one."

"The perks of power." She smiled and sat across the desk from him. "Tanya Morrison seems to be settling into your old chair."

"I might have to arm-wrestle her for it."

The chair creaked as he leaned back and put his hands behind his head. His hair was getting long and wild-looking and he seemed like someone who should be sailing a large boat on the Atlantic or climbing Kilimanjaro rather than stuck behind a desk. "So lay it on me and I hope this has nothing to do with Woodhouse."

"No. I was wondering if you had a chance to follow up on the whereabouts of Fisher Dumont?"

"I have a call in. Is this urgent?"

"Important but not urgent."

"I'll follow up this morning."

"Thanks."

He was openly searching her face but kept to himself whatever he was thinking. "What are you up to today?" he asked.

"I've been rereading the Zoe Delgado file and interviewed her family yesterday. I'd like to have spoken with David McKenna, but that's obviously out of the question now. I was going to drive over to their house to speak with other McKenna family members, but I think I should give them a day to grieve his death."

"Woodhouse didn't show the same restraint. He picked up Tristan at his dead father's bedside."

"I know. I might have waited until after lunch to bring him in."

"But you have the milk of human kindness running through your veins." He grimaced and ran a hand across the scar on his cheek. "Anyhow, enough about Woodhouse. My eye's already twitching."

"I might make a run over there anyway to speak with the neighbours. The Orlovs. They lived next door when Zoe went missing and were never seriously considered suspects since they gave each other an alibi. They might have insight into the McKenna family back then."

"Apparently, they've given each other alibis for Vivian McKenna's murder too."

Kala heard a question in his voice. "Do you think there's something there?"

"No idea. What's their story, anyway?"

"They emigrated from Romania in 1990 and moved to the house they're living in now. Up until their retirement, Boris worked for the provincial government as a clerk and Antonia cleaned office buildings in the evenings."

"No kids of their own?"

"No."

"Okay. It's a good idea to have a chat with them. I'm expecting the autopsy report on Vivian McKenna to be sent over soon. Maybe it will reveal something linking the two murders."

"They were both young women having relationships with Tristan McKenna and both killed on the Rideau Trail near his childhood home. On the other hand, Zoe's throat was slit and Vivian was strangled — a glaring difference."

Gundersund agreed. "It's unusual for a serial killer not to use the same method. However, the same killer could have seen an opportunity and improvised. Might be a stranger."

"So the killer happened to meet Zoe Delgado fourteen years ago in the woods and killed her on a whim. Then fourteen years pass by without another killing until a chance meeting with Vivian alone on the same Rideau Trail. The murderous urge takes over him again and he strangles her? Sounds far-fetched."

"But possible."

"The unexplainable coincidence is their relationships with Tristan."

"Bringing us back to him or someone in his circle."

Kala thought for a moment. "Another possibility is that Tristan killed Zoe and one of the Delgados killed Vivian out of revenge, banking on Tristan being found guilty of both."

"You interviewed Zoe's father and brother. Did they say anything that makes you suspicious of them?"

"Not really. I'm only brainstorming theories at this point. I'm not married to any of them."

"Good enough." He stretched his arms over his head and looked at his computer screen.

Kala took the hint and stood up. "Well, I'll leave you to it. Let me know when you hear from your contact about Fisher Dumont."

"I'll follow up if they don't call me back by lunchtime."

She returned to her desk unsettled by the feeling of going around in circles. She sat staring at her dark computer screen.

Tanya Morrison was working at Gundersund's desk. She looked over. "You appear deep in thought, Officer Stonechild. Planning your next move?"

"Feel like coming with me to interview the McKenna neighbours? We could grab some lunch afterwards." Kala surprised herself by the offer. She usually preferred being alone.

Morrison threw down her pen. "I'm in."

The sky was leaden grey and snow had started sometime earlier after a brief respite in the morning. Kala's truck was covered in a heavy, wet layer and they both cleaned it off before leaving the parking lot and heading south on Division. Kala found herself relaxing in Morrison's easygoing company. Her friendly freckled face and wide smile didn't appear to be concealing a hidden agenda. Morrison was reading her cellphone while Kala drove. She lifted her head and looked at Kala. "You said the Orlovs emigrated from Romania in 1990. That was the year after the dictator and his wife were executed by firing squad at Christmastime."

"Communist regime I'm guessing."

"Yup. Names of Elena and Nicolae Ceauşescu. He was a nasty piece of work."

"Oh yeah. How exactly?"

Morrison looked at her. "Some of this is familiar from history class. You never learned about it in school?"

"Nope. I wasn't all that keen on high school. I might have missed a few classes here and there."

Morrison's mouth lifted in a half grin. "You would have been too young at that time but I was a teenager during his dictatorship so I remember bits and pieces. It's entirely likely that the Orlovs emigrated because of the nastiness going on in their country. I don't recall anything in their file, though."

"It wouldn't have been considered relevant to Zoe's murder, I guess."

"No, I suppose not. It would have even less relevance to Vivian McKenna's death."

The truck in front of them was making a sudden left turn without signalling, coming to a sudden stop and pulling partway into the oncoming lane. Kala braked and her rear tires fishtailed on the icy road. She tapped the horn as she managed to swerve around the car, narrowly missing its back bumper.

"Idiot," said Morrison. "Some people shouldn't be on the road."

"Gets the heart pounding."

They arrived at the McKenna house without further incident. Kala got out of the truck at the same time as Lauren McKenna stepped out her front door.

"She looks ragged," said Morrison.

"I'd love to talk to her but expect she's on her way to join her mother."

"Don't look now but she's seen us and is coming our way."

As Lauren got closer, Kala could see her red, puffy eyes and pale skin. She looked gutted. Kala touched her on the arm. "I'm sorry about your dad. This has been a tough week for you and your family."

"We've had better." A quick smile. "My brother Tristan. Have you arrested him?"

"Not as far as I know. He's only being questioned."

"This is insane. He and Vivian were getting along and he was so happy about the baby and becoming a father."

"We're only working to get at the truth."

Lauren looked at Morrison and back at Kala. "My father told me a confidence last summer that I think I should share now that he's gone."

"Is it relevant to the case?"

"Yeah, I think so."

"Would you like to come into the station to make a statement?"

Lauren looked back at the house and down the street. A car drove slowly past the driveway but didn't stop. "What I'd like is to sit somewhere warm away from here with a cup of coffee and tell you off the record first. Is that possible?"

Kala considered the request. Lauren looked on the verge of falling apart and they might not get this chance again. She said, "All things are possible. Tell us where you want to go."

"Do you know the Tim Hortons on Princess?"

"Sure," said Morrison.

"I'll meet you there. It should be quiet this time of day."

Back in the truck. Morrison looked over at the Orlov house. "Guess they'll still be here later," she said.

"If this doesn't take too long, we can come back afterward. If not, there's always tomorrow."

Kala turned the heater on high, switched on the windshield wipers, and pulled slowly away from the curb. She squirted washer fluid on the glass at regular intervals as she tried to clear enough ice from the windshield to see the road ahead. Each swipe of the wipers left smears of ice crystals in frosted patterns, making visibility difficult. Luckily, traffic had slowed to a crawl. Morrison kept an eagle eye on the road from the passenger seat, straining to see past the ice and scanning the street and walkways for pedestrians. "Bloody horrible weather," she said.

They passed a car facing the wrong way, spun out in the ditch. The driver was waving his arms talking to a tow-truck operator parked on the shoulder of the road. By the time Kala pulled safely into the coffee shop's parking lot, Mother Nature had blanketed the earlier layer of fresh snow on the roads and trees with a topcoat of hail that continued to pour down from the swollen clouds in icy sheets.

Lauren considered skipping the rendezvous with the two female cops and heading straight to the bar, but thought better of it in the end. She reminded herself that the only reason she was sticking around was to help Tristan and this was an opportunity to change the story. At least she'd chosen a coffee shop on her route to the Iron Duke.

The two cops were already seated with cups of coffee when she arrived. They'd paid for hers and the kid behind the counter handed her a full mug upon entry. She took the vacant seat next to the older woman in uniform, across from the intense-looking aboriginal one. They waited until she had her coat off.

"You had something to tell us," Officer Stonechild said.

Wasting no time. Lauren took a deep breath. "Dad told me that he thought Tristan might have killed Zoe Delgado at first but he knew later that he didn't. He told me that he knew for sure that Tristan didn't kill her." She could see skepticism in Stonechild's eyes, but the officer kept it out of her voice.

"Did your father say that he knew who killed Zoe?"

"Well, that's what I understood. Why else would he say that he knew for a fact the killer wasn't Tristan?"

"Did he say how he knew or whom he suspected?"

"Not specifically, but he said that because of what he'd done, he couldn't come forward. He had no proof and he'd be blamed. His exact words were that it would do nobody any good if he came forward."

The two officers looked at each other. They seemed to be silently coming to an agreement on whether or not her story was credible. Lauren kept her eyes steady on the aboriginal cop and willed her to believe. Their eyes met.

"The thing is," Officer Stonechild began, "this doesn't change anything. You've only given us what amounts to hearsay and sadly we can't confirm anything with your dad now."

"I was afraid of that but I was hoping you wouldn't just focus on Tristan for these murders; that this would have you looking at others who could have killed Zoe, and now Vivian."

Stonechild appeared to be thinking. She drank half of her cup of coffee before setting it down and resting her arms on the table. "Do you have any idea what your father did that would have him blamed for Zoe's murder?"

It was Lauren's turn to hesitate. She'd hoped that she wouldn't have to give up this detail but knew she'd opened the can of worms and couldn't go back. As it stood, her mother and Adam would never forgive her. Once she broke family loyalty, she'd be more of a pariah than she was already. She sipped her coffee and looked toward the door. She could leave now with her father's secret and they'd never find out.

"We won't tell anybody if it's not relevant." Officer Stonechild's gaze was direct. Her unwavering black eyes invited trust.

Lauren swallowed all the reasons she should remain silent. "All right." She breathed in and released. "Dad found Zoe dead behind our house next to the garage in the early evening, before anyone knew she was missing. He said that he was in shock but knew he had to protect Tristan because his first thought was that my brother had killed her. He told me that he was running on adrenaline and acted without thinking anything through. He told me that it was only later that he came to know that Tristan was innocent. When he found her, Dad hid Zoe's body in the woods behind our house and moved her farther down the Rideau Trail when it got dark. He washed away the blood and said the rain started in the night and helped even more. Also, the police never had a good look in our backyard because of where she was found on the trail."

"Why would he have done that?"

"I told you. He thought Tristan had killed her and was trying to protect him. It was later that Dad found out Tristan hadn't done it and by then it was too late to admit what he'd done. He told me that he always felt terrible about moving her, especially when everyone was searching for her. She was like a daughter to him."

"He could have come forward when he knew Tristan was innocent, if he really believed that. Did he say anything about finding a knife?"

"No."

Stonechild shifted in her seat but continued staring at her. "You only have your father's word that any of this happened as he told you."

"I know my father and he would never have hurt Zoe. Never. She wasn't raped, I know that. The police told us and we were all relieved that she hadn't had to spend her last minutes dealing with that horror."

Morrison said, "She was found fully clothed."

Lauren nodded. "That's what we were told. Dad must have been in torment, keeping silent. He was still wracked with guilt when he told me. I was home for his last birthday and he confessed this to me. He'd found out a few months earlier that he had cancer." Lauren didn't like how the two cops were staring at her. "I was the only one Dad told and he swore me to secrecy. Was I wrong to tell you?"

"You're never wrong to tell the truth no matter how much time has passed. Lauren, I need to ask. Was your father's mind sharp when you saw him last?"

"What do you mean?"

"Could he have imagined what he told you? Could his mind have played tricks on him as he neared the end of his life? He might have been taking drugs for the cancer."

"I never saw signs of dementia if that's what you're asking."

Officer Stonechild sat still for a moment before she stood up. She looked down at Lauren. "I know this wasn't easy but you've done the right thing. Do you have anything more to tell us?"

"No."

"We'll be in touch soon once we sort out what this

could mean. If I could ask one thing of you, Lauren: Please don't share this information with anyone else."

"Believe me, Officer, that's the last thing I'll be doing."

"And if you remember any more details from what your father told you, even ones that seem inconsequential, please get in touch with us."

"Of course."

Lauren watched their truck skid out of the parking lot through the frost-streaked window and finished drinking her lukewarm coffee. Had she done the right thing? She had no way of knowing. They might doubt what she told them, but she knew she'd given them something new to chew on. Information they couldn't ignore.

They might skip the part about her dad saying he found out Tristan hadn't killed Zoe and use the fact she'd been moved from their backyard as more proof that he had. If she'd told them that her father had found the knife and thrown it in the river, she knew for sure they would have blamed him or maybe even gone after her father. He'd believed the killer had got the knife from his unlocked workshop. He knew how it would look to the police.

No, she'd been right to keep silent about the knife.

She checked her watch. Two thirty already. By the time she got to the bar, it would be close to three and a respectable hour to have that drink. A reward for sacrificing her sanity to spend another day in this town. And if one drink stretched into four or five or six, a night of oblivion wouldn't hurt anybody.

God knows she'd earned a night off.

CHAPTER SIXTEEN

Rouleau's late-morning meeting with Sally Rackham from Human Resources and the union rep Larry Thibault took place in Heath's office at a round table in front of frosty windows with a view of steadily falling snow. Rouleau positioned himself to face the window and he watched the storm battering against the glass while he waited for Sally to start the meeting. Woodhouse was not present but Thibault would represent him in this opening jockeying for position.

Sally, pregnant with her third child, was sipping a carton of milk and eating a bran muffin while shuffling through papers she'd pulled out of a manila file folder. Larry tapped the table with a pen as if the staccato jabs would hurry her along. She wasn't to be rushed.

"Ah, here it is. The Woodhouse grievance, which I'll summarize, although you both should have received a copy. Jacques, he complains that you did not hold a competition for the acting position now held by Officer Paul Gundersund. He also claims that you've given preferential treatment to Officer Kala

Stonechild, whom he says is on loan to the force and has been routinely given the lead investigator role on homicide cases spanning the last sixteen months. He accuses her of taking credit for his work and gives the Della Munroe case as an example." She rubbed the underside of her belly as she talked.

Rouleau was half expecting her to ask him how he wanted to plead. He cleared his throat. "Paul Gundersund and Kala Stonechild are both productive, capable team players. Whatever tasks they've taken on are merit-based. I might add that Paul Gundersund's recent acting position while I am acting for Captain Heath was expected to be for a short duration. Woodhouse's claims against Stonechild are baseless."

"Officer Zach Woodhouse has been on the force longer than either of them. He's gotten an excellent review from his previous partner, Officer Ed Chalmers, who had a thirty-five-year exemplary career with the Kingston force, as well as from three other distinguished members of the force." Thibault sat back in his chair after he spoke and crossed his arms across his chest. He looked every inch an ex-cop gone to seed: the buttons on his white shirt stretched to popping over an out-of-shape belly, paunches of fatty skin saggy under his eyes. He'd slicked back his black hair with gel that glistened in the fluorescent lighting. Vera had prepped Rouleau by telling him that Thibault had been an average cop who took the union job early on in his career. He was a lot of bluster but had the union's power behind him. She'd warned that he was quite capable of making Rouleau's life difficult if he chose.

"They were partners, yes, but I would say that Officer Chalmers eased out of his position some time before his actual retirement date."

"Are you saying that he wasn't performing up to his capacity?" Sally asked.

Rouleau paused. "His performance reports will show a lack of initiative, particularly in the latter stage of his career. I would also say that up until this point, Officer Woodhouse has not demonstrated leadership skills or above-average policing ability. However, he is taking a lead role in our latest homicide investigation. This will give him experience as well as the opportunity to demonstrate his overall competence."

Sally smiled. "Very good. I'm also now clear to share with you both that Captain Heath is taking a year's sabbatical and we will be running an acting competition for his position. You will be encouraged to apply, Sergeant Rouleau."

"I was hoping Captain Heath would be back soon." Rouleau kept his face impassive but inside he was in turmoil. *An entire year.*

"We'll insist on a second competition for whomever is replacing Sergeant Rouleau if he should take Heath's spot for the year," said Thibault.

"Of course," said Sally. "Everyone will have an equal opportunity."

"Well then, I'll speak with Officer Woodhouse and ask him if he wishes to withdraw this complaint."

"Good. Any questions or concerns, Sergeant?" asked Sally.

"No."

"Well then, I think we've come to a good resolution."

Rouleau tracked down Gundersund in his old office as soon as he left the meeting.

"You look down and out," said Gundersund. "Take a load off and tell me your troubles."

"It's been a long day already." Rouleau stretched out in the visitor chair across the desk from Gundersund.

"Feels like you should be on this side of the desk." Gundersund eyed him with concern. "So, what's going on?"

"Heath is taking a year away. I've been asked to apply for his position for the duration."

Gundersund's face relaxed. "Is that all? Seems to me you're doing a great job. You were born to lead."

"I'm not convinced I want the burden for a year, even acting."

"I'd be glad to have you back here. Paperwork is not my thing. However, this could be a golden opportunity for you to make an impact on the force. We'd be lucky to have you at the top."

"There'll be a competition and, if I get it, a competition for my substantive job."

Gunderson shrugged. "We'll cross that bridge."

"I could see Heath never coming back and being stuck with his job. Not sure that would suit me. My father's going to need more of my time as his health fails, not less."

"You can reassess and turn it down if he decides not to come back after a year. Your career is heading into the final stretch. I suppose you have to decide where and how you want to spend it."

"Yeah, lots to mull over." What would it do to the team if Woodhouse managed to wrangle the acting job to replace him while he was replacing Heath? The thought of Woodhouse leading Major Crimes was inconceivable. Rouleau shifted positions in the chair. "So, how's it going with the McKenna murder? Any progress?"

"If two hours of Woodhouse questioning Tristan McKenna is progress, then there's that. I watched from behind the two-way. Woodhouse is surprisingly adept at interviewing suspects once they're confined to a twelve-by-twelve room. He got McKenna to admit that he and his wife had had periods of rockiness in their marriage, mainly about money. He said all that was behind them, though, and he denied killing her or even wanting her dead."

"Where's Tristan McKenna now?"

"Some lunch was brought in for him. Woodhouse plans to question him again this afternoon after he stews a bit. Vera is off getting sandwiches for the team, but the snowfall is likely slowing her down. You're welcome to share mine when she makes it back."

"No, but thanks. I've got a working lunch and then back-to-back meetings. Let me know how the afternoon session goes with McKenna."

"I'm going to sit in with Woodhouse. I'll fill you in at the Merchant if you'd like to meet up at the end of the day."

Rouleau glanced at the snow still falling thick and fast outside the window. "I won't be free until six. Let's see what the storm is like then and decide when the day's work is done."

CHAPTER SEVENTEEN

Kala decided against returning to the McKenna neighbourhood after they left Lauren at the coffee shop. Driving was getting treacherous and there was no sign of the storm abating. She also needed to report on Lauren's startling revelation about her father saying he relocated Zoe's body and to consider its implications.

"What do you make of what she told us? Wouldn't Forensics have noticed that the body had been moved?" asked Morrison as she blew on her fingers to warm them up. She'd taken her glove off to write notes on a pad before the truck's heater kicked in.

"There was nothing in the report. It was a rainy autumn and she was in the woods a full week before she was found. It rained the night she went missing, which would have washed away the blood in the McKenna backyard if anyone had looked for her there, which they didn't. A lot of physical evidence was destroyed by the elements."

"I'd say that if the dad, David, found her body in the McKenna backyard, it's even more likely that Tristan did it."

"Or someone who wanted Zoe's death to be pinned on him."

"Here's a thought." Morrison tapped her forehead. "Lauren killed Zoe and Vivian and is now trying to get her brother blamed by pretending to believe in his innocence. After all, what she told us is more damaging than helpful for Tristan's case."

"And what was her motive?"

"Some twisted form of jealousy? They seem overly close for siblings."

"I don't know," said Kala. To her, Lauren seemed a long shot to be the killer. Zoe had been Lauren's best friend in high school and she'd had little contact with Vivian over the years. Motive appeared thin for both murders. "I see Tristan as the killer over Lauren, but we have no certainties yet."

"Except for two women who were both involved with the same man being brutally murdered fourteen years apart."

Gundersund called the team together after they arrived at the station. Woodhouse had finished with Tristan McKenna and sent him on his way — for now. "We shook him up," said Woodhouse to Gundersund at the front of the room. "Just a question of time."

"Don't you want to wipe that smug look off his face?" said Morrison out of the side of her mouth to Kala.

"Tell me about it," said Bennett as he took the chair directly behind them.

Officer Bedouin entered and took a seat next to Bennett. "They've called in the reinforcements to crack this one," he said. "I'm here to save the day."

"Hey Bedouin," said Morrison, turning and smiling at him. "Long time no see."

"Thought you were rid of me, eh, Morrison?"

"Like a bad penny."

"If you're implying that I'm discontinued and worthless …"

"Which I would *never* do."

"Right."

"You two," said Bennett. "Like an old married couple."

"We're having a conscious uncoupling," said Bedouin. "Getting along for the sake of our children, which would be you lot."

"Let's get this party started," said Gundersund, drawing their attention to the front of the room. "Updates. Woodhouse, would you like to start by filling us in on the Tristan McKenna interview?"

"Right," said Woodhouse standing next to him. "Tristan McKenna has no alibi for the time frame of his wife's murder. He admitted to having marital problems last year, but insisted they were resolved and mainly to do with money. He kept repeating that they were both excited about the baby and had been trying for some time. He volunteered that there had been no physical violence during their marriage. However, as we all know, in the instances of pregnant wives being murdered, the husband is found to be guilty in the vast majority of cases."

"You let him go?" asked Bedouin.

"I did, but I plan to bring him in again for another grilling tomorrow. Let out some line, reel him back in. A little more line, a little more reeling. How did your interviews go on the Zoe Delgado case, Stonechild?"

The look he gave her felt like a challenge and she knew he expected her to have nothing.

"Morrison and I had a conversation with Lauren McKenna. She told us that her father confessed to her that he found Zoe's body in their backyard the evening she disappeared and moved her to the Rideau Trail where she was found a week later. He told Lauren that he thought he was protecting Tristan only to discover later that his son hadn't killed her. He never came forward to the police investigators at the time for reasons we don't know. Lauren also told us that her dad said he had not found the knife used to kill her."

Silence. Everyone except Morrison looked surprised, working out what this could mean.

"Are you sure she's not making this up to divert us from her brother?" Woodhouse asked. "Mighty convenient that she comes forward with this information now."

"It's more likely her father was confused. After all, he was sick, but we can't be sure he wasn't confessing to what actually happened." Kala needed to share her own reservations about the information.

"What does Forensics have to say, Stonechild?" asked Gundersund.

"I'm going to talk with them when we finish here."

"Fourteen years is a long time to backtrack."

"I'm hoping someone is still there who worked the Delgado murder scene."

"Good. We'll keep this under wraps for now until we know if her bombshell has any merit and what it means if it does. Rouleau and I will be holding a news conference tomorrow morning with the objective of allying fears about the serial killer rumours being spread on the Internet. We've been getting calls from worried citizens. I've borrowed a few officers to work the phone line, including Bedouin. Thanks for helping out."

"Happy to be of service."

"Vivian's autopsy report should be ready tomorrow and will hopefully shed some light. Anything else, Woodhouse?"

"I'm coordinating the door-to-door search with officers and it's ongoing. I'll be interviewing the McKenna family members one by one now that the old man has died and they can't use the death watch excuse for not being available."

"Your empathy astounds once again," said Morrison.

Woodhouse grinned and saluted her.

"And with that, off to your stations," said Gundersund. "Keep an eye on the storm and leave early if you have to get home. Can I have a word, Stonechild?"

"Sure."

She remained seated while the others filed out. Morrison gave her a sympathetic smile.

Gundersund took the seat next to her. "I heard from my contact in Corrections."

"And?"

"Fisher Dumont is living in a halfway house in Toronto. He checks in every week with his parole officer. So far, no problems." He handed her a piece of paper. "This is his parole officer's contact info."

"Is Fisher working?"

"He's washing dishes in a restaurant on Yonge."

"Thank your friend for looking into this for me."

"No problem." Gundersund ran a hand across the scar on his cheek. "Are you up for a drink at the Merchant on your way home? Rouleau is stopping by after his last meeting."

"Sorry, not tonight. The weather is dicey and I want to be home with Dawn."

"Another time."

"Sure, another time."

Darkness had fallen and the temperature had dropped by the time Kala turned onto Old Front Road. The wet hail had changed into steadily falling snow that slanted against the windshield and covered the icy roads a foot deep in places. Wet, heavy snow bowed the spruce and pine branches until they almost touched the ground.

The plows had not cleared this end of the city, but her truck made it through the drifts without difficulty. Gundersund's car wasn't in his driveway, but she hadn't expected it to be. She neared her driveway in time to see the plume of snow from the neighbour's snow blower clear out the last of her laneway, the throb of the motor loud in the otherwise silent evening. She rolled down her window and waved as he crossed the road in front of her on his way home. He waved back — a retired university professor named Frank who wouldn't take money for his kindness.

Taiku was waiting for her when she opened the truck door. She found Dawn at the side of the house shovelling the walkway and went inside for her warmer boots and parka to help finish the front steps. The snow kept falling, and they finally gave up, leaving the shovels near the back door for a second round when the snow stopped.

"Omelettes okay?" Kala was at the fridge pulling out cheese, a red pepper, mushrooms, milk, and eggs.

"I'll help chop."

Kala took sideways glances at Dawn as they worked at the counter. Dawn seemed to have settled back in to living with her, but Kala wasn't fooled. Silences that had once been easy now seemed filled with worry and distrust. Dawn had started off introverted and aloof when she lived with Kala the summer before but had made good progress until she'd been sent to live with the foster family. Now she was watchful and waiting again ... waiting, Kala knew, for a sign that she would have to go to a new home. Dawn had become even more closed off than the first time, although her grades were back up and she wasn't skipping school. Whatever peer group she said that she'd been hanging around with when she lived in the foster home appeared to have drifted away.

"Any trouble getting home today?"

Dawn started to shake her head but stopped and said, "I caught a later bus."

"Were you kept after school for some reason?"

"No."

And that's all you're going to tell me. "I'm ready to start cooking the onions if you want to get some toast going."

"Okay."

Food ready, they ate sitting across from each other at the kitchen table. Kala took a bite and asked, "Have you given any thought to visiting your mom?"

"No."

"You could write a letter to her if you want to break the ice that way."

"I'll think about it." Dawn pushed her plate away and rested her elbows on the table. "What do you know about my ancestry?"

"Your ancestry?"

"Yeah. My mother and father. Where do we belong?"

Kala's heart jumped. Had Dawn heard from her father? "Any particular reason you're asking?"

"I've been wondering. I haven't had any education about my ancestors or our heritage. I look like you, but are we from the same band?" She bit her bottom lip before saying, "If you don't want to tell me, it's not important."

"No, heritage is important." Kala struggled to recall details. She'd been raised mainly by white foster families from the age of three but had faded memories of life on Birdtail Reserve for a short time when she was a child. "We're descended from the Dakota. Your mother and my mother were Dakota but your dad is Métis and my dad was Ojibway, which would have been rival tribes way back. Within the Dakota side, we're Yankton. The Dakota first lived in Wisconsin and Minnesota and then South Dakota. We have ties to Birdtail Reserve in Manitoba, one of three Dakota reserves in Canada."

"Were they warriors?"

"More farmers, I think. I don't know all the details."

"Why don't you know?"

"I never gave it much thought."

I was separated from my family, my roots, my home. I was ashamed.

They are part of me but not me.

"Did you know your parents?"

Kala shook her head. "I don't remember much. They lived off reserve in Winnipeg and I was very young when I was taken from them."

"I'm going to find out more about our ancestors. Is that okay?"

"I'd like to know what you find out."

"I've got a math test tomorrow but I might have time to start searching before bed." Dawn stood and picked up her plate and glass.

"I'll tidy up. You scoot."

"Are you sure, Aunt Kala?"

"I am." She looked out the window. "Look at that snow still coming down. Maybe we can do some shovelling before bed if it lets up. Otherwise, we'll need to dig our way out first thing in the morning."

"Call me when you're ready."

Kala stood staring out the window over the kitchen sink for a long time after Dawn had gone upstairs, thinking about the young girl she'd once been and her lonely memories of living on Birdtail Rez. Her reflection seemed ghostly in the glass, the snow softly falling against the backdrop of darkness.

She and Dawn were not that different. They were joined by a history of loss. Would knowing more about their ancestors help them move forward? All her life in the white world, she'd sensed that her heritage and darker skin made her inferior. The idea of embracing what she'd tried to deny was foreign to her. Foreign and frightening, but maybe just that bit hopeful too.

CHAPTER EIGHTEEN

"Can I go downstairs?" asked Antonia, her face scrunched into a pout. The sound of her whiny voice grated on Boris's ears and he reminded himself to breathe deeply and be patient.

He'd looked out the window in his bedroom that faced the front yard and Grenville Crescent before walking down the hall to check on her. Eight a.m. and all was quiet. No sign of activity at the McKenna house and no unmarked police cars parked on the street.

"I'll make you some tea," he said. They spoke in their native Romanian as they always did when they were alone. He'd learned English in school as a boy but she had spoken only Romanian until they came to Canada. She was never comfortable with the new language. "We'll sit in the kitchen."

"Thank you, Boris."

She held up her arms and he helped her from the bed, swinging her legs onto the floor and slipping her swollen feet into her bedroom slippers. Then he retrieved her housecoat from its hook on the door and held it up, guiding each of her arms into a sleeve.

"I'll give you the medicine when you're back in bed."

"I don't like it."

He ignored her and held on to her around the waist as he walked her down the stairs and into the kitchen. She blinked at the harshness of the overhead lighting.

She reminds me of a little sparrow startled by its own shadow, he thought as he set about making the tea.

"Here you go, my dear," he said and set a cup of black tea in front of her along with the sugar bowl.

She eagerly scooped sugar into her cup while he buttered toast and brought it to her on a china plate.

"I didn't do it," she whispered.

Her eyes were button-bright and devious. He took away the sugar bowl and she let the spoon drop to the table. "Too much sugar isn't good for you," he said.

"I need to go to the grocery store."

"I've done the shopping this week," he lied. "Eat your toast and I'll help you into the bath afterward."

She took a bite of toast and then another. She looked around the room and back at him. "I need to scrub the floor. It's getting out of hand."

"I'm going to wash the floors while you nap. I'll clean the walls and dust the furniture."

"I should do this, Boris. You need to let me ..." her voice drifted away and she let the toast fall back onto the plate.

He moved his chair next to her and took her left hand in his two large ones. He rubbed her fingers and massaged her palm. The sight of her sitting like this, so diminished and defenceless, made him sad.

Fatigue was making him maudlin. How long since he'd last slept more than an hour here or there?

"Will we go outside soon?" she asked. "I'm tired of my room. I need fresh air or I will die."

"Shush. Spring will be here soon and we'll sit in the park and feed the birds."

"You promise? You promise me, Boris?"

"Yes. We'll feel the wind off the lake and dip our toes in the fountain. But for now, finish your tea and I'll help you to bed. You need your rest."

"And you will scrub the floors and make borscht for our supper?"

"Of course."

They managed the stairs and, while the bathtub filled, he brushed her hair and tied it up with pins on the top of her head. He helped her out of her night-dress, careful to avert his eyes, and into the tub. She was tiring from the pill he'd given her and lethargic when he finished washing her back. He lifted her from the water and dried her with a towel before slipping a clean nightgown over her head.

When the police officer arrived at the door at quarter to nine, Antonia was fast asleep and Boris was sitting at the kitchen table reading the paper and drinking the last of the pot of tea.

Our secrets are safe for another day, he thought. *Antonia won't be putting us into danger for the time being.*

It was the aboriginal cop and she was alone. She stomped snow from her feet before taking off her boots on the mat by the front door. Her hair was tied back in a braid and her face was lean, cheekbones high and pronounced. Her friendly good looks didn't fool him. He could see the sharp intelligence in her large black eyes.

"Sorry I haven't had a chance to shovel the walk yet," he said before he invited her to sit at the kitchen table with a courteous smile. "Tea?" he asked. "I can make a fresh pot, no problem."

"Tea would be lovely."

He felt her eyes following him around the kitchen as he boiled the kettle, refilled the pot, and took down a mug from the cupboard. She accepted milk but not sugar. Finally, he sat across from her, unable to avoid her questions any longer.

"Where is your wife, Antonia?"

"She's been ill with the flu. She's in bed now sleeping after a terrible night. I was up with her and am tired too but I need to keep the house going. I promised her some homemade soup later. I'm hoping that I don't get sick too."

"I was hoping to speak with her but I don't want to disturb her now if she's unwell."

"Perhaps another day?"

The officer sipped her tea and her all-seeing eyes watched him over the rim of the cup. "You moved to this house from Romania?"

"Yes, in 1990. A long time ago." He laughed and cleared his throat immediately afterward. "We lived in Bucharest."

"I've been reading about that period in your country's history. It was a difficult time."

"It was a horrendous time under Conducător Ceauşescu. The people were starving while he and his evil genie wife Elena and their children lived the high life. Antonia's village was torn down and she was moved into a housing slum in Bucharest. It was a long time ago, but could have been yesterday."

"That is tragic. How did you both cope?"

Her empathy seemed genuine, which surprised him. "We did what we had to do." She was skating too close to past torments that he needed to forget. "What did you want to speak to me about today?" he asked.

Her eyes let him know that she wasn't fooled by his clumsy attempt to change the subject, but she didn't press.

"What do you remember about Zoe Delgado?" she asked.

"The girl used to visit next door. She was best friends with Lauren McKenna when they were in high school and then the girlfriend of Lauren's brother Tristan. I would see them coming and going. Sometimes a group of them played horseshoes in the backyard or sat on the steps talking. In the summers, there were barbecues on the deck."

"Did you speak much to Zoe?"

"Not that I recall. I would say hello to all of them when we were outside at the same time. Antonia and I know the McKenna parents more than their children. Antonia is not comfortable around many people. David told me about his children so I heard most stories about them second-hand."

"The day that Zoe went missing and that entire week before she was found, what do you remember?"

"Fourteen years is a long time but I recall that it was autumn. Cool with a lot of rain. More rain than normal for that time of year. The day she went missing, I was working at my job downtown until four o'clock. Antonia was out shopping that afternoon and I picked her up and drove her home from the mall. She reported to the police that she did not see the girl because she wasn't home. I helped with the search through the neighbourhood the second evening. It was raining hard but several people came out to help. I remember that the girl's father and brother were frantic as the week went on. We were all shocked when they found her body hidden off the Rideau Trail less than two kilometres from her home."

"Did David McKenna tell you that he found her body in the backyard the evening she went missing and moved her to the Trail?"

Boris could feel his cheeks grow hot and flushed and knew they'd betrayed him. "Who told you this?"

"David confessed to his daughter before he died."

Boris imagined his blood pressure was reaching danger level. *Stay calm*, he told himself. *She doesn't have the entire story or she wouldn't be here alone on this fishing trip.*

"I knew, but only much later. David felt a lot of guilt and shared what he had done with me." He raised the palms of both hands to the ceiling. "This information changed nothing. The girl was still dead and the police —" he shrugged "— still did not have the killer."

"This evidence might have been the piece the investigators needed to put everything together."

"I don't see how. They couldn't even figure out that she had been moved. I doubt their level of competence would have been aided by this knowledge."

"You can't believe that."

"But I do."

"This would point to the killer not being a stranger."

"Perhaps. Perhaps not."

"David also told Lauren that he knew who had killed Zoe. Did he tell you?"

"No and I doubt that he knew. I'm sure he would have said something to me."

Their staring match ended when he looked down and picked up his mug.

"Did you see Vivian McKenna at any time during this trip home?"

He drank. Took his time. "Might have. We were never introduced."

"She went for a walk on Friday afternoon. Did you see her then?"

"No. I was in my basement all afternoon working on birdhouses. Antonia would tell you if she was awake. I drove her to the grocery store that morning but neither of us went outside Friday after lunch."

"You're certain?"

"Yes."

"Can you tell me about the McKenna family and how they got along with each other?"

"It's not my habit to gossip about the neighbours but I will say that David and Evelyn had a good marriage and their children were a source of pride. David told me many times that he wished the children and their families lived closer."

"The McKenna family must have been under extreme stress when Zoe Delgado was murdered."

She made the observation as mildly as if she were commenting on the weather. Boris wasn't fooled. She was still fishing. "The entire neighbourhood was upset and stressed by what happened," he said.

She looked at him a moment longer before draining the last of her tea. She stood and he did as well. "Here's my card." She leaned it against the rooster salt and pepper shakers. "Call me anytime if you remember something you haven't shared. I'll check back in a day or two to see if Antonia is well enough for a visit. I appreciate your help."

After she was gone, Boris was left with an uneasy feeling in his gut mixed with a big helping of relief that she hadn't insisted on going upstairs to see Antonia. He wondered if he would have stopped her and was glad that he didn't have to make that decision. There was a time he would have snapped her neck without a second thought. He'd lost the taste for it though. Now, all he wanted was to build birdhouses and be left in peace.

CHAPTER NINETEEN

Lauren rolled over and squinted at the clock. *Nearly 9:30.* The shot of Scotch when she got home from the Iron Duke at 1:00 a.m. had finally put her over the edge and she'd slept even though she'd been certain she wouldn't. She groaned softly and rubbed her forehead. Definitely a three-Advil morning.

She went downstairs to get some pain tablets and found Adam in the kitchen working on his laptop. She took the pill bottle out of the cupboard where her mother kept all her medication and swallowed some with water before pouring herself a cup of coffee and joining him at the table.

"Where are the rest of our happy clan?"

He glanced up from his typing. "You're looking rough."

"I have reason, don't you think?" The throbbing behind her eyes had spread to the back of her head.

"Alcohol is never the answer."

"*Au contraire.* Booze is my religion. Answers all my prayers and helps me find nirvana."

He looked back down. "They're still sleeping. I

was waiting for you to help me shovel the driveway."
He shut his laptop and stood.

"What, *now?*" She looked out the window. She could use some exercise and maybe fresh air would help with the headache. "It's stopped snowing at least. Let me finish this cup and I'll join you."

"Drink up."

The cold made her dizzy when she stepped outside. She took in big gulps of air that hurt her chest but she managed to remain upright.

"Christ, you look like hell," said Adam handing her a shovel. "Why don't you start with the walkways and I'll tackle the drive."

"Yeah, perfect."

The snow was wet and heavy and covered an icy surface that she chipped at without success. Adam yelled at her to leave it and he'd get out the salt after they removed the snow. She saluted him and continued lifting smaller shovelfuls that didn't strain her back. Halfway down the walk, she spotted the Orlovs' side door open, followed by Boris stepping outside in his navy duffle coat and black toque. He waded through the snow like a hulking black bear to his back shed and returned with a shovel and started clearing out the walk from his back door. The next time Lauren looked up, he'd rounded the house and started on the front steps.

She leaned on her shovel and watched him while she caught her breath. Adam came over and said, "I'm getting a mug of coffee. Want one?"

"Sure, if you're buying."

"I'll be right back." He looked over at the Orlovs'. "I wonder why Antonia hasn't been over yet to console our mother. She's usually shadowing Evelyn around the house at some point in the day like a lost dog."

"She'll probably be over later."

"I guess."

The next few moments passed in slow motion. Adam was walking on the path she'd cleared when Lauren turned her head and glanced over at the Orlov house. Boris was swinging his shovel and snow from the top step was arcing onto the bushes one second and the next the shovel was flying up in the air while Boris was waving his arms like a whirligig as he tried to regain his balance. Lauren's breath caught and she took a step forward as his feet shot straight up in the air and his body flew through space and smacked the bottom step before rolling a few feet onto the snowy walkway. She screamed for Adam and fought her way through the piles of snow to kneel next to him. Low moans signalled that he was still alive and breathing and Lauren fought to get her own heart rate under control. Adam was beside her before she could find out if anything was broken. He had his cellphone out and was speaking to an emergency operator. He hung up and knelt beside her.

"Best not to move him," he said. "The ambulance is on its way."

"I'm … fine. No ambulance," said Boris but his face was red and his breathing laboured.

"We need to make sure you're okay." Adam looked at Lauren. "He's breathing and talking so no need to start CPR."

"No shit Sherlock."

"Why don't you go inside and get a blanket?"

The rush of adrenaline that had propelled her across the yard was subsiding, now replaced with annoyance at her brother. Ever the one to take control, he was treating her like his lackey.

"Yeah, why don't I just do that?"

By the time she found a blanket folded on the couch inside the Orlov living room and returned outside, the ambulance was pulling onto the street without its siren on. She stood to one side while they checked Boris over and watched as they loaded him onto the stretcher. He appeared to have hurt his left side and was grunting in pain when not telling the paramedics that he didn't want to go to the hospital.

"I'll take my car and meet you, Boris," Adam assured him. "Once they check you over, I'll bring you straight home."

"Do you really think they're going to let him go home?" asked Lauren as Adam strode past her toward the house. She hurried to keep up, mindful of the slippery bare patches.

"Probably not, but why tell him that now? My guess is that he had a heart attack."

"Or he slipped."

"Or that. Let Mona and Mom know where I've gone. I'll send you a text when I know what's going on."

"Don't worry. I'll still be out here shovelling when you get home."

Lauren finished clearing the walkways and started on the driveway. Adam had removed some of the snow left by the city snowplow at the end of the drive and she started on the remainder. It was heavy slogging and she stopped every few scoops to stretch her back. The exercise had her sweating and her hair felt damp under her wool cap. Her head had mercifully stopped pounding.

She looked over at the Orlov house. It sat in shady darkness, the line of pine and oak trees blocking the direct sun. The house was still. Waiting.

Shouldn't you be up by now, Antonia? Why didn't you come outside to see what happened to Boris?

Lauren pushed her shovel into the snow pile and started walking toward the Orlovs'. Her own house was quiet, but they had reason to sleep in after the last few exhausting days and nights. She'd still be sleeping herself if not for the headache. Someone needed to alert Antonia to what was going on with Boris. She should have thought of it earlier.

She went around to the side door and tried to peer through the lace curtain on the window. No sign of Antonia, so she knocked, lightly at first, followed by harder raps on the glass. She waited a few seconds and rang the doorbell. No sounds from within. She tried the handle and the door opened. She stepped across the threshold.

"Antonia? Antonia, it's Lauren McKenna from next door! Are you okay?"

The furnace turned on and the clock on the stove sounded loud in the empty kitchen. Dishes were piled on the counter and in the sink, which surprised her. The smell of cleaning products was not as strong as it usually was the few times Lauren had been in the house. How often had her mother ridiculed Antonia for her cleanliness obsession when she wasn't over visiting them?

Lauren's head snapped around. She'd heard a thump on the ceiling over the kitchen, like a shoe falling on the floor above. There was no leaving now. She'd never forgive herself if Antonia was in distress and she didn't check into it. The entire situation was strange enough as it was.

She took off her boots and padded down the hall to the bottom of the stairs. Hunter-green carpeting, well worn but clean, covered the dark oak stairs and the landing. Lauren had never gone upstairs and felt odd as she set foot on the first step.

"Antonia!" she called, craning her neck to look upwards. "It's Lauren McKenna. I'm coming up to see if you're all right."

Still no answer.

Lauren reached the landing and looked inside the bedrooms as she walked down the hallway. The first two on her right were small with flowered wallpaper and beds covered in crocheted afghans and embroidered pillows. The bathroom was on the left. Pink tile and seventies fixtures. The door to the last room was slightly ajar and she knocked lightly before pushing it open.

Her eyes took a few moments to adjust to the light coming through red curtains in an otherwise darkened room. When they did, she saw a double bed with a crocheted blanket covering Antonia's still form, her head turned sideways on the pillow. Lauren crossed the floor, leaving the door open, and reached with her fingertips to feel Antonia's cheek.

It was warm to her touch and Lauren let her breath out slowly. She hadn't realized how much dread had travelled with her up the stairs to this back bedroom. She shook Antonia's shoulder and called her name until the elderly woman's eyes opened.

"Antonia. It's Lauren McKenna. Are you feeling okay?"

"Lauren?" Her face creased in puzzlement. "Why you here?"

"Can I prop up your pillows so that you can sit up?"

"Ya."

Lauren helped her into a sitting position, angling two pillows behind Antonia's head as it rested against the headboard. Lauren looked up. A sorrowful Jesus hanging on the cross looked down at them. He was next to a black velvet painting of the Virgin Mary. Lauren drew her attention back to the woman in the bed.

"Boris was shovelling snow and fell on the steps out front about an hour ago. He's gone to the hospital with Adam to be checked over. I'm sure he's fine but he might have sprained his arm or leg. He should be home soon."

Antonia blinked and her mouth opened but she didn't say anything.

Lauren waited a moment and added to fill the awkward silence, "I should have come right over to tell you. I'm sorry."

"Boris is fine?"

"Yes, at least, he will be once the doctor has a look at him." She peered around the room. "Can I get you some water?"

"Ya."

An empty glass sat on the bedside table and Lauren filled it from the tap in the bathroom. Antonia drank greedily, like a thirsty child, and seemed to rally a bit afterwards.

"I've been sick," she said, wiping her mouth.

"I'm sorry to hear that. Are you feeling better now?"

"Little bit."

Lauren had spotted photos in frames on the ancient oak dresser and pointed to one. "Is that your family in Romania?" She walked over and picked up the photo. Black and white. A mother and father and two kids. The girl was pretty. About twelve years old with dark hair and eyes. The boy was slightly older and taller, his face sharp like a fox. The picture was faded with age.

"Boris, me, with our parents."

Lauren stood holding the photo and looked back at the bed. "But I thought Boris is your husband?"

"Brother. Boris is ... Boris my brother."

Lauren picked up the second photo of a different couple with two children, also a boy and a girl, although they looked to be one and three years old. She held it up at eye level. The woman was an older version of the twelve-year-old girl in the other photo. Stunning dark eyes with long black hair over one shoulder. Could this beautiful woman really be a younger version of the old woman lying in front of her? "Is this you, Antonia?" She moved closer to the bed and handed the photo to her.

Antonia smiled. "My husband Cezar and our babies Gabriela and Iuliu."

"I don't understand."

"Taken." Her smile trembled. Tears were streaming silently down Antonia's cheeks. "All gone. Many years ago."

"In Romania?"

Antonia lifted the photo to her lips and kissed it. "Tired. I want to sleep now. You go." She closed her eyes but clutched the picture frame against her chest.

"I'm sorry for making you cry."

"Go."

"I'll come back to check on you if Boris is kept at the hospital. I'll let Mom know you're here alone."

Lauren stopped at the door and looked back. *Was the woman hallucinating or had she and Boris let everyone believe they were married all these years?* The photos seemed proof that she was telling the truth. How horrible if she'd lost her family, but how and who would have taken them?

Had her parents known the truth?

So many questions arising from two old photographs. She'd leave Antonia for now, but would have to let her mother know to check on her if Boris was much longer. They were friends, after all.

Lauren left the Orlov home and trudged through the snow to shovel out the last of the driveway. The uneasy feeling in her gut could be leftover nausea from her night in the bar or it could come from the newfound knowledge she'd gained into the secret past lives of her neighbours. If she'd grown up thinking of the Orlovs as an old, boring married couple and they were anything but, who else had she misjudged? More importantly, what should she do with these startling revelations about their relationship? Should she ask Boris to explain what was going on or would he think she was meddling? He'd never been the most approachable man. He'd kind of scared her as a kid, to be honest.

She finished shovelling the driveway and still had no answers. Adam texted her as she was carrying the shovels back to the shed.

On our way home. Boris sprained his wrist and bruised his side but okay otherwise. At pharmacy now getting Tylenol. Get the coffee on.

She shoved her phone into her pocket. *Yeah, I'll just trot right into the house and get that coffee going because I have nothing better to do than wait on you.*

She looked across the yard toward the Orlovs' property. At least the problem of taking care of Antonia was solved for the time being if Boris was coming home. She'd tuck away what she'd learned about them until she'd had time to digest it.

CHAPTER TWENTY

In the end, Woodhouse decided to wait a day or two before bringing Tristan McKenna in again for questioning. He'd never admit it to anyone, but he'd used up all his ammo for getting a confession. He needed time to reload.

He looked across at Stonechild. She'd come into the office late in the morning and been on the phone ever since. He was beginning to think her calls didn't concern police work. He opened the file he'd started on her in his personal drive and made a note to that effect. Date and time she sauntered in and length of time on personal business.

"I can see you now, Woodhouse."

Woodhouse lifted a hand. "Be there in a minute." No way he was going to let Gundersund think he was at his beck and call. He shuffled through some papers on his desk and heaved himself to his feet a good five minutes later.

"You wanted to see me?" Gundersund asked, glancing up from his computer.

"Is Rouleau making another request to the public for people with information to come forward later today?" Woodhouse stood with his hands on his hips, feet shoulder width apart.

"Last I heard. Why?"

"I'd like to put Stonechild on the phones. Morrison said she and Bedouin were swamped with callers earlier this week and they'll need another set of hands once we put out another public bulletin."

"Stonechild is working the Zoe Delgado cold case."

"Exactly. It's cold and a few days working the phones won't slow down her progress, which, I point out, has been zero after a week, oh yeah, with the exception of that dubious confession by a man now dead and unable to defend himself about moving her body."

"A week isn't exactly a long time when you consider the case is fourteen years old."

"My point. It's not pressing." He didn't like Gundersund's cold stare but gave as good as he got. Gundersund was the first to look away. He sighed and rocked back in his chair.

"You might be missing the bigger picture, Woodhouse, if you don't consider that Zoe's and Vivian's murders could be connected."

"*Au contraire.* I'm quite sure that the same murderer did them both in and I'll even go out on a limb and state the obvious: Tristan McKenna was nailing both dead girls and he's the most likely killer. We don't need to spend resources on the Delgado murder because once we get him for his wife's and lock him away for the rest of his life, we'll have justice for both."

"Interesting approach."

"Yeah. It's called efficient police work."

"Stonechild stays on the Delgado case. I can get another officer to help with the phones."

"Your call. The buck stops with you."

"Yeah, my call. Anything else?"

"I'm going to interview the McKenna family one by one. They've had a day to deal with the father's death, although that shouldn't come into play in a murder investigation, in my view."

"Go for it."

"You surprise me. I thought you'd want me to put on the kid gloves for a week."

"No, you're right. We need to move this case forward. A pregnant woman has been murdered and she deserves our best effort. I also don't like the idea of an unpredictable killer out there."

"Great." Woodhouse started backing out of the room. "I'll drive over to the house and get started."

"Are you taking Bennett?"

"I've got him on the door to door. I can handle this on my own."

"I could come with you if you need another set of ears."

"Nah, I'm good."

Woodhouse stopped for a burger and a beer at Harper's on Princess before reaching the McKenna house at 1:30. The dead man's wife opened the door. He searched his memory and came up with her name.

Evelyn. He flashed his ID and asked to speak with her inside unless she'd prefer to go with him to the police station.

"I'd prefer to answer your questions right here," she said.

He tilted his head in what would pass as agreement and stepped inside. A mangy-looking mutt skidded around the corner and growled at him deep in its throat from a few yards away.

"Clemmie!" Her voice was sharp, but she made no move to intercept.

"Lock that dog in another room or I'll have to do something about it."

That got her moving. He watched her drag the dog by its collar into the den and shut the door. Its barking kept up for another ten minutes but was muffled by the thick walls.

"That's not like Clemmie," she said leading Woodhouse into the living room. "He normally likes people."

"That's okay. I'm not a dog person." He took the couch and undid his jacket. She kept the house hot. "Is anyone else home?"

"No. My sons and daughter-in-law, Mona, have gone to the funeral home to make final arrangements for my husband's cremation. I have no idea where my daughter, Lauren, has gotten to. Likely, you'll find her in a bar somewhere."

"Sorry for your loss." He checked his watch. "Bit early for the pub."

"Not for her it isn't. You're not here about my husband, David, and my children, though."

"No. I'm lead investigator looking into Vivian's murder. I'd like to ask you some follow-up questions if you're up to it."

And even if you're not, just because I'm the police and I can.

She was a severe-looking woman with short grey hair that she hadn't bothered to dye when she'd had it permed into curls. She was tall, which he liked in a woman, but pear-shaped, which he did not.

Bottom-heavy with no tits. Beats me why anyone would marry someone who looks like you.

Her eyes flicked over him and a sour look made her appear even older. "Ask away."

He took out a tape recorder and set it on the coffee table. "Do you mind? This is more reliable than taking notes." He hit record without waiting for her response. "When and where did Vivian meet your son and what can you tell me about their relationship?"

"They met in Edmonton about five years ago when Tristan was there on a book tour. It was about the time his book was climbing into bestseller territory and he was appearing on all the talk shows. She thought he was a celebrity and he didn't do anything to make her think otherwise. He should have told her that one book does not a millionaire make, especially in Canada. They got married within six months of meeting each other and Tristan moved to Edmonton."

"And how was that working out?"

"Good, although they went through a bad patch last year. I'm sure she was disappointed when she found out he wasn't making money hand over fist. He's working on another book but he's more a plodder than a genius."

"Not a high assessment of your son's talents."

"I'm only telling you this, Officer, so you understand that Tristan doesn't have the cunning or smarts to pull off one murder, let alone two."

"Although he did write a bestseller. What was it about anyway?"

"It was science fiction. My son read an article about drones before there actually were drones available to anyone who wants one, and he used the premise to write a futuristic story. He had a terrific editor who should have gotten co-author status but didn't."

"Are you telling me that your son's success was a fluke?"

"There's a reason he only had the one bestseller."

Woodhouse was used to non-supportive parents — hell, his could have taught a master class — but this woman was running laps around them. "How about your other kids? How are they doing?"

"Adam is an Air Canada pilot who flies the larger planes overseas. He married Mona, a teacher and a compliant little thing. A ray of sunshine if you like that sort. They have a handicapped son. Autistic, but on the higher end of the scale, although he has a violent streak. I guess Mona's sunny ways help to keep her and Adam from pulling out their hair. They live in Vancouver. As for my middle child, Lauren, I believe we already established that she's a disappointment."

"Lauren lives in Toronto?"

"Yes, and has a bathroom and kitchen design business. She's keeping her head above water."

Woodhouse checked that the tape recorder was working. Nobody was going to believe this conversation if it wasn't. Talk about a negative piece of work. "How would you describe your son's relationship with Vivian this trip? She was pregnant so that must have changed things."

That brought a smile. "Tristan couldn't do enough for her. The baby was all he talked about."

"Who do you think killed her, Mrs. McKenna?"

"Why, I have no idea. It must have been a stranger."

Woodhouse took a few seconds to go over what she'd told him so far. "You seem to be saying that Vivian was a gold digger. Is this your opinion of her?"

"Perhaps initially, but I came to see that she was good for Tristan. They built a life together and were starting a family. He was happy."

"Did they come to visit you in Kingston often?"

"No. They hadn't been back since last summer and they came because we'd only found out that David had cancer. I saw no sign of animosity between the two of them although Vivian spent a lot of her time in the spa. She was one for getting beauty treatments. She worked at the Bay in cosmetics."

Are you for real, lady? The sour look on your face could curdle milk.

"Did you see Vivian and Tristan the day she disappeared?"

"No. I'd gone to the hospital before anyone else got up. She was missing when I got home late in the afternoon and I phoned you people."

"When was the last time you saw her?"

"The evening before. We had supper together here at the house and all Vivian talked about was the baby."

"Who else had supper with you?"

"Tristan and Adam. Mona arrived as we were having dessert. She flew into Toronto and drove from the airport that afternoon."

"Did Vivian have plans for the next day?"

"She kept saying she was tired and would have a spa treatment in the morning and rest in the afternoon. I can't recall if she said anything else."

"Well, I guess that about does it. We're going through her cellphone and the agenda she kept in her purse. Do you know if she kept a diary or anything like that?"

"I'd be surprised if she did. I never heard that she read books or spent much time thinking about anything besides fashion, makeup, and spa treatments."

"But you said that she met Tristan at a book signing?"

"I thought that odd too until I found out she was there with her co-worker, who was the science fiction reader."

Woodhouse stood and Evelyn did as well. He walked to the front door with her right behind him as if she wanted to make certain he left. He stooped to pull on his boots. "One more question," he said, looking up at her. "Was Tristan ever violent?"

He didn't expect her laughter.

"Goodness, no. Tristan could get angry like any of us, but he's the biggest coward I know when it comes to physical altercations. His sister Lauren fought his battles for him."

"Lauren?"

"I can see that I've surprised you, Officer. Women can be tougher than men when we need to be. Surely you know that."

"I'm beginning to."

He opened the door and a rush of cold filled the hallway. The sunshine sparkled off the snow, making him squint. He looked toward the neighbours' house. They'd been questioned but hadn't seen Vivian this visit if they were to be believed.

"How well do you know your neighbours?" he asked as he put on his sunglasses.

"We see them around. Antonia usually comes over for tea at some point in the day. They don't have any other friends that I know of."

"Odd people, are they?"

"If keeping to themselves is odd, then I suppose so. David and Boris liked building things out of wood and became friends over time. Antonia is quiet and shy but she liked coming over to have tea, as I said. Her imperfect English embarrasses her. We've been neighbours a long time and gotten used to each other's ways."

"I wonder if they're home."

"Boris sprained his arm this morning shovelling snow and is likely resting. I haven't seen Antonia for a few days. She's been sick off and on so I imagine she's laying low. Boris told me she was sleeping a lot this week, getting her strength back."

"I'll catch them when I return later to talk to the rest of your family."

"Calling ahead will ensure they're here."

"No idea which pub Lauren might be in?"

"I don't keep tabs on her."

"Well, thanks for your time."

She shut the door and he heard it lock behind him. He'd thought about asking her if David had said anything about moving Zoe's body fourteen years ago but decided against it. Let Stonechild follow up since she was working on that end of the case. Probably not important anyway at this point, if it was even true.

He was opening his car door when the mutt appeared in the living-room window, jumping up and down and barking like it was possessed.

God save us from yappy little dogs and old women with nothing good to say about anyone, he thought as he gave it the finger before climbing into the front seat.

Boris got off the couch and watched the latest cop drive away. He'd been home a few hours and napped for most of them. He'd shaken off Adam McKenna's offer of assistance and made the short walk from the car on his own steam and glared at the front steps on his way past. *Damn fool place to fall.*

The house was silent and he smelt the layer of musty dust that had settled in since the McKenna woman's murder — *or was it only his imagination?*

Christ, he ached. His arm was throbbing like an infected tooth times a hundred and his side was stiffening up but nothing broken, thank the great god above. The painkiller they'd shot into his arm was starting to wear off.

He hobbled toward the stairs like a much older man, clutching the banister with his one good hand

and leaning heavily against the wall to catch his breath. Was this what it was going to be like in the years ahead? He hoped he died in his sleep before that happened.

He'd left Antonia alone for just over four hours. The sleeping drug he'd given her wouldn't have knocked her out for this length of time but he couldn't hear her moving around on the floor above. Maybe there was enough in her system to keep her groggy and out of it. He reached the landing with his senses on high alert. Why did he have the feeling that someone else had been in the house? He put it down to anxiety for having left her alone so long.

He stepped into her bedroom. The curtains were still drawn, keeping out most of the afternoon sunlight and casting the room in a red glow. Antonia looked small under the covers, propped up on the pillows and holding something against her chest with her eyes closed. He moved closer.

"Antonia?" he said. He repeated her name a second time and her eyes opened. "What are you holding? Did you get out of bed?" He spoke in Romanian and she responded in the same language of their homeland.

"What have you done to yourself, Boris?"

"I fell shovelling snow. My wrist is sprained, but it is nothing serious. Was somebody in the house?"

"Nobody. I wanted to hold my family. I went to the bathroom and got the photo off the dresser when I came back to bed. That is all."

He searched her face for evidence of a lie but she was half in shadow and he couldn't be certain. Still …

"Are you hungry? I could heat up the borscht from yesterday."

"Yes. Can I come downstairs and eat in the kitchen?"

He thought about it but shook his head. "You must rest. I will bring it to you on a tray."

"But your arm."

"I can manage."

He left before she could protest further. He still had no idea what he was going to do with her. It would be so easy to put her to sleep forever and put them both out of their misery. The thought was becoming more attractive with every passing hour, but for now, for this moment, he would heat up enough soup for both of them before going into the basement to put the finishing touches on his birdhouses.

CHAPTER TWENTY-ONE

Kala waited around the station until five for Fisher Dumont's parole officer, Dennis Wilburn, to return her call. She'd used the police line to make her inquiry seem official, knowing that Kingston Police would come up on the caller ID. Wilburn let her know that Fisher was still in Toronto and nothing had changed since she last phoned. He'd shown up at work on time all week. While she'd been waiting for the return call, Woodhouse had come and gone with Bennett in tow. Morrison and Bedouin were still working the phone lines with another officer, and Gundersund was meeting with Rouleau. This seemed like a good time to pack up and go home.

She phoned Dawn while she waited for the truck to warm up and the window to defrost. "Hey. Checking to see if you want me to pick up anything for supper. I'm on my way from the station." She could hear people talking in the background. "Where are you?"

"On the bus. I'm almost home. I took some pork chops out of the freezer this morning."

"Glad one of us was thinking ahead. I'll see you in about twenty minutes."

She threw the phone onto the seat and put the truck into gear. That was odd. Dawn hadn't mentioned going anywhere after school. It was likely nothing to worry about, especially since she knew Dumont was living in Toronto and answering to his parole officer. Her instincts told her to tell Dawn about her father so that she knew the dangers, but she'd promised Rose that she wouldn't. She sincerely hoped this decision wouldn't come back to haunt them all.

She arrived home as Dawn was returning from a quick run up the road with Taiku. Dawn smiled when she saw her and Kala started to relax. She wasn't used to having the happiness of someone else impact her own and still found herself on edge whenever they both returned home at the end of the day. They went inside and warmed up with a pot of tea while Dawn made a salad and Kala fried the pork chops. She cut thick slices of brown bread instead of boiling potatoes, which would have taken an hour. They were both too hungry to wait.

"How's school going?" she asked when they were well into the meal.

"Fine."

"You stayed late today?"

"I'm helping another girl with math after school."

"What's her name?"

"Emily Morgan."

"Is she nice?"

"I guess." Dawn took a drink of milk. "We're not friends if that's what you're wondering."

Kala took a bite of salad to stop herself from probing. Dawn hadn't made any friends at Frontenac High School since she'd started grade ten in the fall. She'd returned to spending evenings in her room doing homework and appeared to have no interest in outside activities. Dr. Lyman had said to try to get her involved in something that got her socializing, but so far, she'd resisted all attempts. Tutoring another student was a start at least.

"Do you know where the name Sioux comes from?" Dawn asked. Her eyes shone with interest as she waited for Kala to answer.

"Can't say that I do."

"It was the name that the French gave to the Dakota and comes from an Assiniboine word that means snake or enemy."

"That explains why our people don't like being called Sioux."

"I found a book in the library. The Dakota fled out of the States in 1863 because the American army was slaughtering entire villages. Men, women, and children. Just because they were Dakota and trying to get back some of the lands that the Americans took from them. Canada was so weak militarily in the West that they let the Dakota stay even though the Americans tried to get permission to chase them across the border to kill them. They tried to live peacefully but the other Indian bands and the Métis weren't happy to have them move in. The Ojibwa attacked a few of their settlements before finally leaving them alone."

"Didn't I tell you that we didn't always get along? How many Dakota were in Canada back then?"

"Not many. Between one and two thousand and they were divided into three bands within the Dakota. They were good farmers and trappers but also worked for white settlers and the army. They had to be smart and resourceful to survive. I have more reading to do."

"I'll wait to hear what you find out."

"If I get my homework done, I'll read another chapter tonight."

"We could take Taiku for a walk before bed if you like."

"Not tonight. I have too much to do."

Long after Dawn had gone upstairs and Kala had cleaned up the kitchen and made a pot of beef stew for the next night, she called for Taiku to go outside with her. He had lots of energy and they walked down Old Front Road in the direction of Gundersund's house.

It was a beautiful evening: moonlight shining on the coniferous boughs laden with snow. The air was fresh and invigorating; stars punching through the black sky overhead. *I should have made Dawn come with me*, Kala thought. Taiku bounded ahead, disappearing into the woods every so often and returning with a face glistening with snow.

She didn't set out to walk as far as Gundersund's house but Taiku was far ahead of her and halfway up his driveway before she could call him back. Two dogs ran back toward her. Taiku had found Minnie, and walking behind them was Gundersund. He stopped a few feet away from her.

She bent and petted both dogs before they raced away into the darkness.

"Lovely night for a walk," he said. "Mind if we join you?"

"Looks like Minnie and Taiku have already decided you should. I was about to head back but Taiku got ahead of me."

"I'll join you for a bit, then."

They walked in companionable silence. At the big bend in the road, Gundersund asked, "Are you making any headway with the Zoe Delgado file?"

"The killer wasn't a stranger."

"Based on …?"

"Her being murdered in the McKenna backyard."

"I agree. Who do you think did it?"

"It could have been any of them. They're covering for each other and have been from the get-go. Tristan is the most likely killer but the father who just died or his mother or siblings might have had a reason that we haven't uncovered yet."

"Anyone else?"

"The neighbours? Zoe's father or brother? A boy she was involved with whom we haven't identified? The list hasn't been whittled down much."

"If we assume the same person killed Vivian McKenna, it sure looks like the link is Tristan. Most often husbands are the ones who murder their pregnant partners."

"Yes. However, we have no evidence that it was the same killer besides the fact that it seems obvious that it was." She wanted to ask what he thought of Woodhouse's approach but knew it wasn't her place to question Rouleau's decision to put him in charge of the field investigation. Instead she said, "I like

Tanya Morrison. She'll make a solid member of the team if she transfers permanently."

"I think so too."

They were nearing her driveway and she could hear the dogs nearby jumping through the snowbanks. "Thanks for walking me home." She stopped and touched his arm. "You should come by again and see Dawn. She misses you."

He looked toward the house. "Is she settling into school?"

"I don't know. Her grades are back up but she hasn't made any friends. I'm thinking of taking her on a long holiday this summer to give her a change of scene."

"I'll come by soon. Once this case is done with."

"For supper?"

"Yeah." He looked down at her. He was standing close enough that she could see the intense expression in his eyes. "I'll miss you if you're gone for the summer. I've gotten used to you being down the road."

"We'll be back."

"My worry is that you won't. Have you signed a contract with the Kingston force?"

"I'm transferred here temporarily but plan to stay a while."

She didn't tell him that she'd put in an offer to buy the house that she and Dawn were living in. Marjory, the owner and her friend from Birdtail rez had been postponing putting the property on the open market for a year until Kala made up her mind. She'd had trouble committing to land ownership and staying in Kingston because the open road had an equal if not stronger pull. It came down to what was best for Dawn in the end. She needed roots to feel safe.

He took off his glove and touched her cheek with warm fingertips. His thumb brushed her eyelid. "You have frost on your eyelashes," he said. "Time to go in before you freeze completely."

She stood very still, feeling him run his fingers across her face and push back a strand of her hair. He had the tender look in his eyes that he seldom let her see. They started moving closer when the dogs bounded up and ran a circle around them, barking and tumbling against their legs. Gundersund dropped his hand and took a step back. He grinned at her and called for Minnie to heel. She bent and caught hold of Taiku's collar, not wanting Gundersund to see how flustered she was by his touch.

"Maybe they know something we don't," he said.

"Like jealous children."

"I'll see you tomorrow. Sleep well." He turned and walked away from her the way they'd come.

She listened to him whistling until she could no longer make out his retreating presence in the thickening shadows. She had an urge to call to him but bit back her words. *He's not free to be with you yet.* The thought kept her in place but it was not enough to prevent a seed of hope from planting itself in her being. They were not done this dance of souls, she was sure of it. *The time is not right but someday our stars will align.*

She began whistling the same tune as Gundersund as she followed Taiku up the driveway toward the lights of home.

CHAPTER TWENTY-TWO

Lauren sat at the bar nursing her sixth vodka and soda, this latest one bought for her by the man in the business suit three stools away. He was older than she liked but appeared fit when he removed his jacket. They'd already made eye contact and exchanged a mock toast from across the bar when her drink arrived. She felt her resistance slipping despite knowing better.

You swore off one-night stands, she reminded herself. *Remember how gutted and sick you feel after they leave.*

The emptiness that had become part of her waking hours was falling away with every drink. She no longer cared that she was the odd one out in her family. The daughter her mother never wanted. The one expected to be a fuck-up. Mindless sex would fill the void for an hour or two.

I'm getting too old for this shit.

She turned away from him and when she looked back, a heavily made-up redhead with a low-cut shirt had a hand on his arm, talking into his ear.

Decision made.

Lauren lifted her glass and looked to her left. She'd felt as if she was being watched for a while but thought it was the man in the suit. Another pair of eyes met hers and she squared back around to face the bartender.

What, do I have a sign that says hot and ready on my forehead?

"Clint have the night off?" she asked.

He came closer, wiping the counter in circular motions with a white cloth. "He's in tomorrow. Four o'clock. Anything you want me to pass along?"

"No, that's okay."

"The regulars are arriving." He waved the rag toward the door as a crowd of men surged in with a blast of cold air. "They play pickup hockey every Friday night through the winter and then hit the Duke. Need anything else before I get busy?"

"I'm fine, thanks."

The noise level went up several notches, drowning out Garth Brooks singing about friends in low places over the loudspeakers. Lauren took her time finishing her drink, not wanting another, but not wanting to leave the anonymous warmth of the bar. She sensed without looking the man standing next to her.

"I'm not interested," she said.

"Good to know."

The voice was familiar. She turned her head.

"You're looking good, Lauren. Been a long time."

Her heart jumped but she kept her voice level if slightly slurred. "I'm surprised you're talking to me, Matt Delgado."

"I've had time to think about things. Zoe wouldn't have wanted me to freeze you out."

She looked into the drink on the counter that she was gripping with both hands. "But that's exactly what you did."

"Mind if I sit for a minute?"

"It's a free country."

He got onto the stool next to her and set down his beer. "Sorry to hear about your dad."

She kept facing straight ahead, working not to catch his eye in the mirror over the bar. "Thanks. My sister-in-law was murdered this week so we're not exactly having the best of times."

"I heard that. Horrible. How're you coping?"

She lifted her glass. "Not well, obviously, but this is helping."

"I'm sorry. You deserve better."

"A better family, you mean? Or a better life? I wouldn't mind one without people dying all around me."

"As I recall, you've always had to shoulder a lot. How's your mother?"

"Evelyn is … Evelyn is only sliding deeper into nastiness. But enough about my fun clan. What have you been up to since our last date fourteen years ago?"

"Nothing special. Got married. Lasted five years before we got divorced. She kept the house and the dog, which bothered me for a long time." He took a drink of beer. "I loved that dog."

"Did I know her? Your wife, I mean. Not the dog."

"Candice Jorgenson. She was in your class."

"Ah yes. Candice with the bouncy brown hair and cheerleader body."

"She was that. Still is, but left me to live with another woman."

"My turn to say I'm sorry."

"Thanks." He signalled the bartender. "Would you like another?"

"I have to drive home eventually so a soda and lime would be great."

He placed the order and then went to say good-bye to his fellow hockey players, who were getting up to leave. He came back after a trip to the wash-room and brushed her arm as he sat down.

"I heard you moved to Toronto after high school."

"I'm still there. I own a kitchen and bath design business that employs four. Doing okay, I guess."

"That's great."

"You're working with your dad?"

"I wanted to go to university but he needed me. Then I had that cheerleader wife to support."

Lauren let him work his way slowly to the elephant in the room. Matt asked after a pause, "Are you still defending Tristan even though all the evidence points to him? His wife's murder a few days ago shows a pattern." His voice trembled with anger and pain that she understood and could not fault him for. She wondered if this was the real reason he'd approached her.

"I've always looked out for him and always will. I don't believe he murdered Zoe or Vivian if that means anything to you."

"He hides behind you."

She turned and looked Matt square in the eyes. "I loved Zoe and wouldn't protect her killer."

"Even Tristan?"

"Even him if I knew for sure he'd killed her."

They stared at each other as if trying to see what the years had done to their cores, the intimate part of each other that they'd known and liked. She felt the years drop away and returned his searching gaze with an openness she'd long ago stopped giving. He seemed to see the girl who'd tagged along behind him with his little sister because he smiled the wide teasing grin he'd kept for her.

He said softly, "You were the best kisser I ever met, Lauren McKenna. I dreamed for years after you'd gone about those evenings when we walked over to Grosvenor Park and necked under the trees."

A pulse fluttered in her throat like a trapped butterfly. She laughed. "Those memories kept me warm on many a lonely Toronto night."

"Good to know I was there in spirit."

"I never stopped missing Zoe," she said after taking a mouthful and setting her drink down. She twirled the glass in the beads of moisture on the bar's wooden surface. "Because the police never charged anybody, I could never shut off what happened to her, wondering if I could have saved her. If I'd walked her home from school that day instead of staying late, would she be alive? Was I to blame in some cosmic trick of fate? Stupid, I know."

"You're not saying anything I haven't thought a million times. I can't forgive myself for not being there for her when she needed me. Why did you stay late at school?"

She turned and looked at him then. "I was waiting for you, but you must have already left."

"For me?"

"You said to meet in the library the night before. I guess you forgot."

"I must have."

They finished their drinks quickly, not talking any further about that day, and he helped her on with her coat. He didn't have to say anything because she knew that he would see her safely home. She handed him her car keys before they left the pub. He took her by the arm and helped her negotiate the icy sidewalk and settled her into the front passenger seat before getting into the driver's side.

Lauren huddled into her coat and Matt glanced over at her. "Your heater takes a while to get going."

"The cold air is helping me to sober up."

She was starting to find this entire encounter surreal. The two years after Zoe died, she'd had fantasies about Matt and her getting back together. The hope that he'd stop blaming her for Zoe's murder — or stop blaming her family — had faded away to nothing by the time she finished high school. The question was, why now? Why was he being nice to her out of the blue as if the fourteen years of silence would be easily forgotten? By the time Matt pulled in front of her house, she'd made up her mind. She turned to look at him with one hand on the door handle.

"Look, it's been nice catching up, but we really live in different worlds now. I haven't led the most exemplary life since Zoe was killed and I'm still struggling, if truth be told. I've had way too many men, too much alcohol and drugs, and too much self-loathing to pretend I'm the same innocent girl you once knew. I'm trying to get my shit together and some days are better than others. All I want to do now is make it back to my condo in Toronto, grieve for my father and Vivian, and lose myself in work." She paused and gave a self-mocking grin. "Thanks for driving me home and sorry you have to walk a couple of blocks." She shoved the door open, feeling the cold air rush into the car.

"Wait."

She hesitated and turned her head to look at him.

"How about a coffee before you go back to Toronto?"

"Why?" She held up a hand. "Doesn't matter why. I don't think that would be a good idea, Matt."

"My turn to ask why."

"Because I can't see the point."

He got out of the car and met her as she walked behind it to cross the street. He dropped the keys into her outstretched hand. "I'm sorry about everything that's happened."

"Me too."

"Shake?"

"Sure, why not?" She reached out her gloved hand and he grasped it and pulled her to him. Before she knew what was happening, his mouth was on hers in a kiss that felt nostalgic and sweet. She found herself responding but only for a moment. She stepped back.

"What was that, Delgado?" she asked.

"I don't know." He started walking away from her. "I'll call you later and maybe you'll change your mind about that cup of coffee," he called over his shoulder. "Sleep tight."

She was still smiling when she let herself into the darkened hallway and tiptoed up to her room. Yet underneath the flicker of happiness was a nagging uneasiness that grew as she got ready for bed. Where had Matt Delgado been after school that day Zoe went missing and why was he being so friendly now? She wanted to trust in the boy she'd thought she'd known, but was she a fool to even go there? Before she drifted off to sleep, she decided that she should go for coffee with him if only to find out what he was up to. If the idea of seeing him again made her heart pump a little faster, so be it. She'd had the feeling often enough with enough men to know that it wouldn't last.

CHAPTER TWENTY-THREE

Marci Stokes woke up long before the sun Saturday morning and couldn't get back to sleep. At 6:00 a.m. she threw back the covers and shuffled into the kitchen to brew a pot of coffee, which she drank while reading the news online in the small living room at the front of her limestone house. She'd finally moved out of the hotel to rent this half double on Earl Street near the downtown, slightly draughty but comfortable. She slept in the bedroom above the living room. The place had come furnished, the main reason she'd taken it — that and the black shutters, which she'd found charming against the grey stone.

At seven, she opened the front door to check for the newspaper and the stray cat she'd been feeding for the past week appeared on the steps, meowing and looking at her with forlorn green eyes. She thought it shivered in the cold but this could have been a flight of fancy. *Do cats even shiver?* "I like your survival instinct," she said. "I'll get you some milk but you can't come inside."

She turned and felt the brush of his fur as it scooted past her into the hallway. "Damn it, cat," she said. She found it huddled next to the radiator in the kitchen at the back of the house. She squatted a few feet away. "I don't need a pet. If I did, it wouldn't be a mangy cat like you." She reached out a hand and touched its fur for the first time. Its purr was loud in the silent room. She straightened. "First some milk and then a bath if you plan to stay inside for a bit."

She left the cat with a full belly and a wet fur coat sleeping next to the radiator with a warning that it would be back outside as soon as she returned home, and set off to her office at the *Whig* on Cataraqui Street. It was a short drive, staying on Wellington and cutting across Princess, past Molly Brant Point, and right toward the river on Cataraqui. She entered the three-storey red-brick building and climbed the stairs to her desk on the second floor. She didn't need to be here today, but she had little else to occupy her time except for laundry and grocery shopping. She'd much rather spend the morning staying on top of the Vivian McKenna murder.

She'd settled in nicely with another cup of coffee and the McKenna file open on her computer when Rick stopped by her desk with his parka on. He was a Chinese man who wore silk pastel cravats and a brown felt fedora and covered the entertainment beat. She counted him as one of her few friends on staff. "How's it going?" he asked

"Quiet. Looks like you've got something on. Where're you headed?"

"Covering the opening of a new ballet at the Grand Theatre. Did Scottie come talk to you about the anonymous tip that came in concerning your police beat?"

"No, but I just got in. What's it about?"

"The acting chief Rouleau has an internal complaint lodged against him for creative hiring. Might become a human rights issue, according to the source."

She stared at Rick, taking a second to find the words to respond. "Not sure we can put much stock in an anonymous bit of slander. How did it arrive?"

"Email, but an untraceable IP address."

"What does that tell you?" She tried to make the muscles in her face relax, realizing that he was giving her a curious look.

"We've gotten good tips before from anonymous sources," he said.

"You're right but more often than not someone's got an axe to grind and trying to stir up trouble."

"Well, see what Scottie wants to do about it."

"I will. Thanks for the heads up."

"No problem."

After he'd gone, she walked the length of the building to Scottie's office. He motioned her in when he looked up and saw her in the doorway. "I was about to come see you," he said leaning back in his chair. "Although I wasn't sure you'd be at work today."

Scottie had promoted her to assistant editor and she knew he hadn't agreed with her decision to step back into the reporter job. He'd said at the time, "This is a struggling industry Marci, and you should take the promotion and bank the money. You might need it sooner than you think."

She hadn't argued but wasn't ready to give up investigative reporting and the writing that she loved. If the paper died, something digital would have to replace it and good reporting would be needed more than ever to counter all the misinformation spewed out by wannabe journalists and spin doctors, not to mention the fake news stories circulating on social media. She asked, "What's this about an anonymous tip and Sergeant Rouleau?"

Scottie bent forward and picked up a paper that he handed to her. He was a small, bullish man, late forties and single, and she was still trying to figure him out. He reminded her of a chameleon that changed with whatever leaf it landed on. She didn't know how much support he'd give if she got into a dicey situation. He said while she read the printout of the email, "I want you to check if there's anything to it."

She attempted to appear neutral and not let on that her sympathies were with Rouleau until she knew the validity of the allegations. "I'll take a run over to the station and see what I can uncover. I want to find out if they have anything new on the McKenna murder anyhow."

"Good enough."

All the way to the station she pondered how to approach Rouleau and what she would do if the anonymous tip was true. She didn't like to think that he would compromise himself this way because she'd grown to like him. However, she was a reporter first and would remain objective.

As luck would have it, Rouleau was not at police headquarters and wasn't expected in that day. Most of the Major Crimes team was busy and Marci made no headway trying to get the desk sergeant to ring upstairs for anyone, telling her to return Monday when more staff were around. Not for the first time, Marci found the differences between the ways of New York City and Kingston frustrating and fascinating. Did these people think the news took two days off?

She left the building and started toward the parking lot, scrolling through her phone for Woodhouse's number. He wasn't her first choice for getting the information, but he'd have to do. She needed to bring Scottie something and Woodhouse usually delivered even if she left their encounters feeling the need for a scalding shower.

Kala rose early and Dawn was still sound asleep with Taiku at the foot of her bed when she got into her truck at 6:00 a.m. Bennett's car was already in the gym parking lot when she arrived and she went straight to the change room before going to the indoor track to run laps. She caught up with Bennett in the weight room half an hour later. She thought he seemed preoccupied but left off conversation until they finished their workouts, showered and changed, and met up again in the lobby.

"Felt good to get in some exercise," she said by way of an opening. They started walking toward the entrance. "You look as if you have something on your mind. Everything okay?"

He held the door for her. "Not sure. I think Woodhouse is up to something."

"What makes you say that?"

"He's been on the phone a lot and not about the case. I overheard him telling someone that he's prepared to push things as far as they need to go."

"He could have been referring to anything."

"I don't know. He's got that self-righteous thing going on and he made a few comments about Rouleau."

"Well I know that Woodhouse is no fan of mine but I'm surprised if he's found fault with Rouleau. I'll try to find out what's going on."

"I'll see what I can find out too from Woodhouse, but he plays his cards close to his chest." They reached their vehicles. Bennett asked, "Are you going into HQ or would you like to grab some breakfast?"

She checked her watch. "It's getting late and I want to get over to the McKennas to speak with whichever one of them I can corner. I'd also like to talk to Antonia Orlov. She's been sick but should be up for a visit now."

Bennett's eyes seemed worried. "Are you keeping Woodhouse up to date on your interviews? He told Gundersund that you've been interfering in his investigation by running an unnecessary parallel one of your own."

"Oh? What did Gundersund say?"

"He backed you up. Said you and Woodhouse were each focusing on one of the murders and he was working from the premise that the investigations complemented each other. He told Woodhouse that he'd been assigned the higher-profile one. I think Gundersund said that to keep his ego buttered up."

"Woodhouse must feel that he has some leverage if he's complaining to Gundersund. Rouleau isn't in the office today but I'll track him down. You're right. Something is going on."

She sat in her truck staring at the sky and thinking about what to do until the heater began blowing warm air. Every part of her balked at the idea of answering to Woodhouse, but she needed to find out if her investigation was harming Gundersund or Rouleau. She'd never paid attention to the politics inherent in any police force, not interested in climbing the ladder. Yet she knew Woodhouse had allies and he could do damage to the unit.

She pulled out of the lot and turned south on Division toward the harbour. If she was lucky, she'd catch Rouleau before he left his father's condo and get him to share what was going on. At the very least, she could warn him that trouble was afoot.

Delgado Garage was open on Saturdays. Even before Kala arrived at the gym for her workout that morning, Matt and Franco had already gotten the coffee going and repaired the brakes on a Chevy Malibu and given a grease and oil to a Lincoln Continental. At quarter past seven, they took a coffee break in the cramped office.

"You made the coffee extra strong this morning," said Franco, grimacing and lowering his mug, "and I noticed you got in late last night. Hungover, son?"

"Nah, but I didn't sleep all that well." Matt avoided meeting his father's eyes. He could tell that Franco was

fishing for information, but trying to appear uncon-
cerned by the casual tone of his next question.

"Anything to do with what's been going on?"

He could lie, but if his father found out, he'd
read more into it than would be good for either of
them. "I talked to Lauren McKenna last night at
the Duke. She was sitting alone at the bar when my
hockey team went in for a pint."

His dad nodded his head and rubbed a hand
across his chin as he did whenever he was mulling
something over. "Doesn't hurt to get close to them
to find out what's going on. What's that expression?
Hold your friends close and your enemies closer?
Did she let anything slip about Zoe or this latest
murder of her sister-in-law?"

"No, Dad."

"Well, you can always try again to get close to
her. From what I hear, she likes a drink and that
usually leads to loose lips."

"I'll see what I can do."

His father picked up on the sarcasm. "Don't be
flip, son. Giving them the cold shoulder for going
on fifteen years hasn't helped get Tristan put away
for Zoe's murder. We have to change tactics."

"I couldn't agree more." Matt pictured Lauren's
face when he'd leaned in to kiss her. "I'll see about
corralling Lauren for coffee later."

"As long as it's an Irish coffee. If she's anything
like her old man, she won't be able to stop at one
drink and you'll have a chance to wrangle the truth
out of her. I always believed Lauren McKenna knew
what happened to your sister. You only have to

re-establish the connection you had with her back in high school and get her confessing what she knows."

"That won't be easy."

The phone rang and his father reached for the receiver. "I have faith in you, boy. Zoe and I are counting on you."

Matt took his coffee into the shop away from his father's probing eyes. He had his own reasons for wanting to get closer to Lauren McKenna that he'd kept from his father for fourteen years. Franco would never believe the truth and now was not the time to shake up his world.

CHAPTER TWENTY-FOUR

Lauren joined her brothers and Mona in the dining room after pouring herself a cup of coffee. For the first morning in a long while, her head didn't need painkillers to stop from pounding. She'd slept like a baby: deep, dreamless sleep that had eluded her for years. *So this is what it feels like*, she thought.

"We're taking a drive to Brighton for lunch," said Mona. Today, she wore a soft mauve turtleneck and long silver earrings in the shape of doves. "Would you like to come with us?"

"Are we able to leave town?" asked Lauren.

"We're not prisoners," said Adam. "Tristan phoned in and the police aren't interviewing him today. He can be back in an hour or so if things change. They're keeping Vivian's body for another few days at least." He reached a hand over to grasp his brother's shoulder and Tristan nodded with his head down.

"We need a break," said Mona. "Why don't you come?"

"I think I'll pass." Lauren looked across the table at Tristan and almost relented. She'd seen the light on under his bedroom door and smelled the ganja when she'd walked by on her way to bed and knew he wasn't doing well. His face was starkly pale, emphasized by the contrasting dark circles under his eyes. A plate of congealing eggs and toast lay untouched in front of him.

"I heard you come in late," he said, voice slightly accusing.

"I needed some space."

Adam was staring at her with a look on his face that let her know he thought her behaviour was substandard and a let-down for the family. She stared back but didn't say anything. He wouldn't understand how close she was to cracking. He'd never backed down from anything. "Will you be home for dinner tonight, then?" he asked.

"I'll try."

"We need to support each other," said Mona, her words an echo of Adam's and Lauren knew that they'd been discussing her while she was out of the room. She was saved from searching for a retort when Evelyn's footsteps sounded in the hall. They all looked toward the doorway. Lauren had successfully avoided her mother since the scene in the hospital. She steeled herself for what was about to happen.

"All together then," Evelyn said. Her voice lacked its usual volume and her movements were slow. Tired.

Mona leapt up from her chair. "Sit here, Evelyn, and let me get you some tea and toast."

"I don't want to be a bother."

Since when? Lauren thought as she met Tristan's eyes. For a moment, she could tell that he shared the same thought and she looked down at the table before anyone noticed.

"Of course you're not a bother." Mona's voice swelled with forced gaiety and Lauren admired and hated her chirpy outlook in equal measure.

"Well, I could use a cup of tea." Evelyn ignored Mona's offered seat and settled herself at the head of the table. She looked at Tristan and Adam, but not Lauren. "Are you getting any sleep at all, Tristan?" she asked, her voice as soft as it ever got.

"Some." He paused and seemed to realize that more was expected. "How are you feeling today, Mother?"

"The grief comes and goes but I'm comforted that your father is not in pain any longer."

"I haven't seen Antonia around," said Mona, reappearing from the kitchen with a mug of tea that she set down in front of Evelyn. "Is she well?"

Lauren leaned forward to listen.

"I suppose I must get over to see her." Evelyn sighed and picked up the mug with both hands. "She has these sick spells once and a while. She's had them since I've known her. Her constitution is poor but the doctor hasn't found a root cause."

"How terrible," said Mona.

"Was she married to Boris before she came to Canada?" asked Lauren. Everyone looked at her with surprised expressions on their faces. Lauren shrugged: "I realize how little we actually knew about the Orlovs growing up and I'm curious."

"Yes," said Evelyn, her voice tightening. "They came from Romania after the revolution as a newly married couple." Her eyes flicked across Lauren and back to Tristan.

"How fascinating," said Mona. "What did they do in Romania?"

"Do?"

"For work."

Evelyn drank from her mug and set it down. "Boris had a job as a clerk in the government. Antonia cleaned office buildings at night and looked after their home during the day. That was the normal life for women back then although I'm sure you young people today find it hard to believe. We cooked and cleaned and did laundry and that was enough for us."

"Goodness, I sometimes wish we could go back to those days!" Mona laughed. "With all I have to do juggling work and Simon, well, it's not easy with Adam away so much. Did something happen to them in the revolution that made them leave ... Romania, was it?" Mona was edging back toward the kitchen for the toast.

"All these questions." Evelyn's voice was cross. "I suppose there was something that went on. The Orlovs didn't speak of it and I never asked. Boris might have confided in David."

"We're going to Brighton for a drive and lunch," said Adam. "All of us except Lauren. Would you like to come with us?"

"I could do with a change of scenery, so yes, thanks for asking. Why aren't you coming, Lauren?"

"I have a conference call with my office in an hour."

"Well, I hope you'll be staying home tonight for once and out of the bar." Evelyn stood as Mona set down a plate of toast and the jar of strawberry preserves from the fridge. "I've changed my mind about the toast since we'll be having lunch soon. I'll go put on some clothes for the outing."

Lauren took a grim satisfaction watching the looks on her brothers' faces when Evelyn swept from the room. Even sunny Mona looked dumbstruck as she looked down at the uneaten toast and full cup of tea.

Lauren knew her brothers hadn't expected their mother to accept the offer of an outing but now they were stuck with her. *So much for being the dutiful sons.* "Well, if Mom doesn't want it …" She reached for the toast and jam and pulled it across the table. "No point letting good food go to waste."

Lauren had only just wrapped up her conference call with Salim and two others in her Toronto office when she heard the family leaving downstairs. She glanced over at the bedside table. *Eleven thirty.* She walked to the window overlooking the driveway and watched the car pull away. Adam was at the wheel with Evelyn in the front passenger seat and Mona and Tristan in the back. For as long as she could remember, Evelyn never sat in the back.

The sky was overcast and a wind had come up that rattled the glass and buffeted the house. No snow falling yet, although the wind lifted sheets of it from the ground and off the rooftops, giving the illusion of snow drifting down. The top tree branches were swaying back and forth in the wind, clumps of snow encrusted on their feathery boughs. The day had a gloomy, grey cast to match her mood.

She went toward the stairs and stopped halfway down to look out the window in the direction of the Orlov house. She remembered her conversation with Antonia in her bedroom and felt the hum of disquiet start up again as she thought about the old woman lying in the semi-dark. Lauren had thought at first glance that Antonia was drugged but believed now that she'd only been groggy from sleep and flu. Yet, had she been disoriented enough to call Boris her brother in the first photo? Lauren had to admit that, on closer inspection, he had resembled Boris the man: same big ears and icy stare. In the second picture, Antonia had definitely been the woman posing with another man and two children. How could they be her family? Her mother had sounded certain about Antonia and Boris being married at the breakfast table and she *should* know the truth. Lauren hadn't detected any sign of obfuscation in her voice. Was Antonia simply crazy in the head or muddled from being feverish and ill?

She reached the bottom of the steps and entered the dining room, crossing to the side window that looked out over the Orlov property. A half circle of light spread in a yellow glow across the snow outside the basement window, but the rest of the lights in the house were off. Antonia should be in the kitchen by now preparing lunch for Boris as she did every day, according to Evelyn. Lauren smiled when she remembered her dad teasing their mom about neglecting him whenever he made their lunch those times she was off to the hairdressers or a PTA meeting. He'd wink at Lauren and they'd be co-conspirators buttering bread and stuffing as much as they could between the slices to eat in the living room in front of the television. "Don't tell Mum I let you eat in here or we'll never hear the end of it," he'd say.

God, I miss you, Dad.

As she stood lost in thought, the Orlovs' basement light snapped off and a few moments later, the light by the back entrance came on. The door opened and Boris stepped outside, pulling on his black toque with his one good hand as he carefully negotiated his way down the walkway toward the street.

Her father and Boris had been friends when she was growing up. Better friends than her mother and Antonia even though Antonia spent an hour or two every day at their house. Boris and her dad liked to build things and go fishing. Franco Delgado had a boat and the three of them would spend part of every decent weekend in the summer puttering around a lake or river north of Kingston. Sometimes, they'd sit in the Delgado backyard drinking whisky in the evenings, playing horseshoes, smoking cigars, telling jokes. All that ended with Zoe's death. Oh sure, her dad and Boris still spent time together, but sadness replaced Franco as their third companion. Sometimes, she sensed guilt hanging over the two men for a reason that she couldn't pinpoint.

She craned her neck as far as she could before walking into the living room and standing in front of the window. She kept close to the heavy gold curtains, uneasy about Boris finding out that she was watching him. He stood, an old man hunched into his parka, looking down the street and checking his watch two times before a cab drew alongside. The driver got out and helped Boris into the front seat. They sped past her and turned left onto Sherwood. Boris was looking straight ahead and the cab driver was speaking into his headset.

Lauren watched the taillights disappear and stood still, thinking this might be her only opportunity. Boris would likely be gone half an hour at least. She took one last look down the street and went in search of her boots and coat.

She decided to approach the Orlov house from the road rather than crossing the lawn where her fresh footprints would stand out in the snow. Uneasiness was making her cautious but she didn't want Boris to know she'd been by when he was away. She remembered the intensity of his stare whenever he would look at her even when she was a teenager. He was a man who missed nothing. She walked up the side of their driveway, keeping to the shovelled section. The path to the back door was trickier, but she tiptoed in the boot prints left by Boris on his way to the taxi. She hoped the drifting snow would fill them in before his return.

She rang the bell and knocked several times, trying to peer past the lace curtains into the house. She wasn't surprised when her pounding went unanswered and after a suitable wait, reached down to turn the doorknob.

Locked. Damn it.

She struck the door again with her fist before giving up. Antonia was likely upstairs in bed asleep. Wasn't this getting odd? She'd been in bed since the day after Vivian went missing. Surely, if she was that ill, Boris would have taken her to the hospital. She'd always seemed like the one soft spot in his prickly personality.

Lauren trod carefully in his footprints back to the driveway and was happy to see the blowing snow fill in the crevices behind her. By the time she reached her mother's front door, she'd put away the seeds of worry by promising herself that she'd visit Antonia when Boris returned home from wherever he'd gone. Hopefully, Antonia would be lucid this time and clear up the mystery of her family, including her relationship with Boris.

CHAPTER TWENTY-FIVE

Kala spent the day researching the Ceauşescu years, perhaps sparked by Dawn's discussion the night before about a book she was reading on the Dakota. "Did you know that the Dakota were advanced in agricultural practices when they fled up north into Canada from the U.S.?" Dawn had asked. "The Dakota also were instrumental in defending the Canadian border against the invading armies in the War of 1812."

"Did not know that," said Kala, "although I'm not surprised."

"Why is that, Aunt Kala?"

"Because we're a resourceful people."

Dawn had dropped her head back to continue reading but not before Kala saw the ghost of a smile that looked a lot like pride. Their conversation had gotten her thinking.

She needed to learn more about the people in Zoe's life, starting with the neighbours and the Delgado family. The Orlovs and Franco Delgado were both first-generation immigrants. Franco and his wife would have come to Canada from Italy in search of a better life, but they hadn't been running away from war. The Orlovs were another story. They were fleeing a tyrannical, harsh regime. Their similar yet distinct experiences contributed to who they were, how the Delgados raised their children, how the Orlovs interacted with their neighbours. She needed to dig deeper to understand the relationships amongst the three families.

She was unsettled by the knowledge that David McKenna had moved Zoe's body from his backyard onto the Rideau Trail, the information now supported by Boris Orlov. The murder site ruled out the killer being a stranger in her mind. According to Franco Delgado, the three men had been fishing buddies up until Zoe's murder. He continued to believe that Tristan had killed his daughter because she'd broken up with him. Zoe had been best friends with Lauren, pulling the Delgado and McKenna families even closer. If for the purpose of this exercise, she went with the premise that Tristan was not the killer, who else had motive and access? Who would have followed Zoe into the McKenna backyard with a knife?

Kala clicked through some sites and landed on one that gave the history of the Ceaușescu Communist dictatorship in Romania from 1967 until his Christmas Day trial and execution in 1989. His wife Elena was tried and executed alongside him.

Savage. Brutal. Paranoid. Repressive.

The words used to describe Nicolae Ceaușescu's control over the country. Said to be more Stalin than Stalin. She clicked on the video of Nicolae and Elena in front of the tribunal on the day of their deaths and watched with increasing apprehension as the events unfolded.

Locked forever in time, Elena stares severely into the camera, her gray hair pulled back in a severe bun, small but defiant-looking in her winter coat with a dark fur collar. Next to her, Ceaușescu looks drawn and tired in his black overcoat and tie, the last clothes he will ever put on.

Kala leaned closer to the screen.

An army officer in navy uniform and thick glasses reads out the charges in Romanian. The room is bursting with men in uniform, all standing while Nicolae and Elena sit on white chairs at a table. Ceaușescu gets to his feet, argues, sits again, argues, and is silent. The army brass leaves moments later and Elena and Nicolae stand up. She picks up her purse and an envelope from the table, straightens her scarf, adjusts her coat. He stands next to her, hat in hand. Officers in sepia uniforms move in and tie Elena and Nicolae's wrists while Elena yells in anger. Nicolae's voice joins hers as they struggle to stop what is about to happen. The camera work is blocked by the backs of the officers as they hustle the Ceaușescu couple outside. Moments later the sound of automatic gunfire, and then the camera passes over their lifeless bodies in the courtyard. Just over six minutes from sentencing to execution.

Brutal.

"What's that you're watching?" asked Woodhouse from behind her right shoulder.

She jumped and tried not to let him know that he'd startled her. She minimized the picture on the screen. "Nothing important."

"Looks like you're wasting time on the job."

"I wouldn't say that. I'm doing research." She hated feeling the need to explain herself to him.

"What kind of research?"

She rolled back her chair and turned so that she was facing him. "I'm checking into the neighbours. The Orlovs." She paused. "Do you want me for something?"

"Someone has to go to Edmonton to talk to Tristan and Vivian McKenna's neighbours, friends, and co-workers. I'm going to tell Gundersund that I'm sending you."

She thought it over while they locked eyes. His were daring her to contradict him. To put up a stink. She smiled. "Makes sense, although I haven't actually been working on your team."

"The reason we can spare you for a few days."

"You make it sound like I've been sitting around doing nothing." He made a face as if to say *if the shoe fits* that she ignored.

He asked, "Have you got anything for me that links the Delgado murder to Vivian McKenna's?"

"No."

"Well …" he let his voice trail off. "Be ready to leave in the morning. Vera's booking your flight and hotel. Sunday should be a good day to hold interviews since most of the people you need to talk to won't be working."

"As long as Gundersund clears it."

"He will."

After Woodhouse went into Gundersund's office, she tried to get her mind around two days away. She didn't feel right about leaving Dawn alone and would have to think of something. She got up and walked to the coffee machine to centre herself following Woodhouse's interruption. Rouleau entered the office as she was pouring a cup and he crossed the room to join her. She poured a second cup and handed him one.

"Haven't seen you around much, stranger," she said, sipping from her mug. "We miss you. I came by your condo last night to talk to you about something but you were out."

His eyes surveyed the room as they walked back to her desk. "I miss you too, and this office. How's it going?"

"It's going. I thought I should broaden our background checks on those close to Zoe the summer she died and was doing research on why the Orlovs came to Canada in 1990. Apparently, in Romania during the Ceauşescu era, the secret police were keeping tabs on just about everybody. They kept files that indicated eavesdropping and surveillance of most of their citizens. They were called the Secretariat."

"You're wondering if files were kept on the Orlovs."

"It's possible, don't you think? I don't know how we'd ever find out, though."

Rouleau rubbed his chin. "I worked overseas on a task force for a couple of years after Frances left me. I made friends with a cop who works in Bucharest and we've kept in touch. I could give him a call."

The intangible tingling that came when she knew she was on to something travelled up her spine. She had to keep herself from being too hopeful. "It's a long shot," she said.

"Sometimes the long shots are what pay off." He studied her and said, "I'll make this a priority."

"You never spoke about working overseas."

"I was part of a tribunal looking into war crimes. Heartbreaking work that took my mind off my own broken heart." He gave her a wry smile.

"I admire you for taking that on."

"The experience was eye-opening. The Orlovs could have suffered a past that they'd like to forget. The Romanian regime under Ceaușescu was increasingly repressive as it went along. Many people who spoke out disappeared into prisons where they were tortured and quietly killed."

"I'd like to have some knowledge of what they went through before I approach them again."

Rouleau nodded. "Then I'll see what I can find out." He took a few steps away from her and stopped. "Did you come by the condo for any reason in particular?"

Woodhouse was on his way back to his desk and Bennett had entered the office. Kala shook her head. She couldn't chance Woodhouse overhearing. "Nothing worth discussing now. I'll catch up with you later."

The rest of Kala's day was spent lining up interviews in Edmonton with the help of Tanya Morrison and Bennett.

"I don't know why they're sending you alone," said Bennett after Vera stopped by to discuss Kala's itinerary.

"I don't mind." Kala preferred working alone and was eager to carry out the assignment now that the wheels were in motion. "We've got all the legwork done today and it's only a matter of following the plan."

She was putting on her coat to go home when a call was punched through to her desk phone. She sat down and picked up the receiver. "Officer Stonechild. Can I help you?" Empty air. "Hello?" She listened to the silence a few moments more before starting to lower the receiver.

"Kala? It's Rose." Her cousin's voice sounded urgent and worried.

Kala again raised the receiver to her ear. "Rose? Is everything okay?"

Rose had never called her from prison before. She could have been right next to Kala, whispering in her ear. "He came to see me. Yesterday."

"Who came to see you?"

"Fisher. He said he wants to meet Dawn. Can you believe it? For the first fourteen years of her life, he never gave a fuck and *now* he wants to be a father? 'I've changed,' he said. Like he could." Rose's breathing was heavy as if she'd been running a race and a keening wail filled Kala's ear.

"Hold on. Hold on, Rose. Does Fisher know that Dawn is living with me?"

"I didn't tell him but he knows she's in Kingston."

"How could he know?"

"I might have told somebody who knows him. I should have kept my mouth shut. When will I learn not to trust anybody?"

"Oh."

"Can you take her away? Where he can't find her?"

"I don't think —"

"I did it once. I got her away from him."

"I thought you said that he was never in the picture after Dawn was born."

Silence.

"Rose?"

"I might have wished he wasn't. I ran away with her when she was two."

"He could have rights, Rose. You might not be able to keep her from him."

"Even if he was crazy drunk and doing drugs half the time? Even if he gambled away all our money?"

"I'm guessing you don't have sole custody?"

"No."

"Is Dawn's last name Dumont? I always thought she had your last name: Cook."

"I changed her name to mine after we left him."

Kala breathed deeply while she thought about what to do. She couldn't run away. Dawn couldn't take anymore turmoil. They had a life here. She said, "I'll keep her safe, no matter what."

"I need you to promise me."

"I promise."

"No, you need to swear on all you hold sacred that you will keep her away from him."

"I swear on all I hold sacred that I will keep her safe."

But I can't promise to keep her away from her dad if he's determined to find her.

Kala heard background noises on the phone and somebody talking. Rose covered the receiver and said something before saying to Kala, "Time's up. Gotta go."

"Take care, Rose. Don't worry about Dawn."

"Yeah. You take care too. Make sure you look after my girl."

CHAPTER TWENTY-SIX

Vera had booked Kala on the 6:45 a.m. direct WestJet flight to Edmonton Sunday morning. The flight arrived on schedule at 10:20 and Kala awoke disoriented and groggy as the wheels hit the runway. She hauled her overnight bag off the plane and caught a cab to police headquarters at 103A Avenue situated west of the North Saskatchewan River and northeast of the downtown. The sand-coloured building took up an entire city block, a grouping of interlocking rectangular concrete boxes with blackened windows breaking up the monotone monotony. Kala was greeted by a young female officer in a navy uniform named Julie Gaudette, who escorted her to a meeting room on the first floor. Gaudette asked if Kala would like coffee and said that a woman who worked with Vivian was waiting inside the room. Officer Gaudette would meet up with Kala afterward and they could go over the interview list and the search warrant.

Vivian's supervisor and co-worker from the Bay, Beth Engels, was a smartly dressed woman in her early forties with lips painted a luscious red that reminded Kala of candy apples. The scent of sweet lavender settled around her like an invisible cloak as Kala sat down beside her. Beth opened by saying without prompting, "Vivian worked for me the last four years. I can't believe she's dead."

"I know that this has been a terrible shock. What can you tell me about her state of mind last time you saw her?"

"She was excited about the baby for sure."

"I hear a but."

"Welllll … I don't like to gossip," Beth leaned forward and her silk blouse slipped lower over her cleavage, "but I was surprised when Viv announced she was pregnant and even more surprised that she wanted the kid."

"Why's that?"

"Because she was ready to leave her husband the year before."

"Did she tell you that?"

"She did." Beth bit her bottom lip. "She was having an affair."

"Who with?"

"She never told me the name. Very secretive about it, I think because Tristan was such a jealous guy. She was apprehensive about the scene he was going to make when she left him for good."

"Did she say if Tristan suspected or knew about the affair?"

"She said that he didn't have a clue and it was better for everyone that he didn't."

"Do you know if Tristan was ever violent with her?"

"No, Viv never said that he was, and there were no signs, you know, like bruises or black eyes. She knew how to handle herself. Self-confidence in spades, that one. I think she was more concerned with him not letting go of her even if he found out that she was running around on him. She told me more than once that he was more obsessed than in love with her. I think it went both ways, quite honestly, at least in the beginning for Vivian until the money got tight."

"Did you meet Tristan?"

"Only a few times when he picked her up after work. Couldn't say that I know him except from the things Vivian told me about him."

"Which would be …?"

"Well, like I already said about him being the jealous sort and underperforming when it came to his career. They had a chunk of money from his bestseller some years back but he hadn't done much since and they were living frugally. Vivian complained about having to cut back on more than one occasion. She seemed, I don't know, disappointed in him? She said he spent a lot of time slothing around the house. I could see why she looked elsewhere."

After spending the rest of the afternoon working with Gaudette, Kala caught a cab to the Holiday Inn where Vera had booked her a room for the night. Resting her head against the back seat, she thought about soaking in the hotel tub followed by room service. First, though, she'd call in the tidbit about Vivian's affair to Gundersund and see how Dawn was doing. He'd promised to pick up some food and bring his dog Minnie over to keep Dawn company.

It would have been nice to be there with them but at least she could get a good night's sleep knowing Dawn was in good hands.

Sunday evening, Gundersund finished his phone conversation with Kala and looked across the kitchen table at Dawn. "How was the steak?"

"Great. I'm glad we decided to cook instead of eating takeout. The corn on the cob was good for the middle of winter."

"They're growing every vegetable under the sun somewhere in the world three hundred and sixty-five days a year. Our world is getting smaller."

"And tastier."

He laughed. "How about we clean up and then take the dogs down by the water? It's a clear night and we'll have a good view of the constellations."

"I need to study."

"Studying can wait. A walk will clear your head."

"Well, okay."

He hadn't spent any time with Dawn since she'd returned from the foster home the summer before and hadn't been sure if she'd accept him back into her life. But the easy camaraderie he'd felt with her had resumed where it left off, for which he was grateful.

They stuck to the path of packed snow that Kala, Dawn, and Taiku had made from their repeated trips to the back of the property. The dome of indigo-black sky spread before them when they stood on the flattened bit of land above the drop to the water, stars twinkling like sequins, the quarter moon casting a shimmery white light across the black water. The shoreline was sparkling white, ice and snow mounded in sugary heaps over the rocks. Gundersund lifted his face to the cold wind off the lake, a welcome feeling after a day spent working in the stale office air. The dogs and Dawn stayed close to him and he felt as if they were the only ones left in the world, cocooned from time and troubles in the enveloping darkness.

"Aunt Kala said that you don't come over anymore because you're trying to get your marriage squared around. Is that true?"

"Not exactly."

They'd started walking back to the house and she was ahead of him with the dogs racing in front of them both. "Then why haven't you come over? Are you mad at us?"

"Never. I'm not sure why I haven't been over, to be honest, although work has kept me busy. I also thought your aunt needed space. She's been seeing another officer from work."

"You mean Andrew Bennett? They go to the gym after work but that's not exactly a relationship."

He was quiet for a moment, reading between the lines. "Perhaps I should start stopping by again."

"Perhaps you should."

They reached the back steps. "How's it going at school?" he asked.

"Good. I'm helping one of the girls in my class with math at the end of the day before I catch the bus home. She passed her latest test."

"No more skipping?"

"No."

"You do me proud, kid."

Long after she'd gone upstairs to study with Taiku following her like a bodyguard, Gundersund stretched out on the couch with Minnie at his feet. The room had a comfortable feel. Indigenous art on the walls, a stone fireplace, Hudson's Bay blanket folded on the footstool. The smell of wood smoke and jasmine incense soothed him, and before he had time to think about what Kala had told him over the phone about the affair Vivian apparently had been having while Tristan was away, or to worry about Woodhouse, his eyes had closed and he drifted into sleep. He didn't stir until morning. He awoke before sunrise, surprised to find a blanket covering him and Minnie upstairs sleeping with Dawn and Taiku.

Marci Stokes was waiting by the window in the Delta hotel lounge, an empty gin-and tonic glass and a full one standing side by side in front of her. She was staring out the window at the harbour, chin resting on one hand, her laptop uncharacteristically closed on the seat next to her. Woodhouse slid into the seat across from her and set his beer on the table. He looked her over.

"Ah, you didn't need to get your hair done just for me," he said.

"You flatter yourself. I get a haircut once a year whether I need to or not."

Christ, was that a smile on her morose face? "You wanted to see me?"

"I did. I'm looking into a possible internal complaint about Staff Sergeant Rouleau. Might even be a human rights complaint. Do you know anything about that?"

For a second he didn't have to feign surprise. Then he remembered that Ed Chalmers had said he was going to leak the story to the press. His instincts had told him not to go that route but Ed had disagreed. Now, he was going to have to play along. "How did you find out?"

Nice and innocent. Slightly outraged.

She kept her eyes riveted onto his face. "You weren't the source?"

"No. I don't air my grievances in the media. You should know that." He pretended to be thinking. "What if I told you that I'm the one who made the complaint, but I don't want my name out there? This isn't about making myself famous."

She shook her head as if to say she'd known he was behind this all along. Her voice was flat. "What is the complaint against Rouleau exactly?"

"It's not frivolous. He's been giving acting positions without fair competitions and assigning the case lead to his favorites without regard to seniority or merit."

"Which would be you, presumably."

"Yes, among others. You can speak with Human Resources."

"Okay. Anything else?"

"No, but I've been made lead field investigator on the Vivian McKenna murder, which in my mind is an irrefutable admission of guilt on the part of management. I'm thinking of withdrawing my complaint since they appear to have acknowledged the error of their ways and are open to making changes. I've also heard that competitions will be running to replace Captain Heath for a year and to replace his replacement."

"Which you feel responsible for initiating with your complaint?"

"One could say. Aren't you going to take notes?"

"I will after you leave. I have a memory like a steel trap." She poked a finger at the slice of lemon floating in her drink. "Anything new on the McKenna investigation, since you brought it up?"

"No comment." He threw back the last of his beer and stood. "Been nice chatting with you again, Ms. Stokes, but I really have to run. Thanks for the beer. I put it on your tab since you dragged me out here on my Sunday."

"I'd expect nothing less."

He savoured the flash of dislike in her eyes before she turned her head to look out the window. She was a smart old cow and he enjoyed matching wits with her. She might figure out one day that he held all the good cards, but until then, he'd use her on his path to the job he deserved in the Kingston force.

CHAPTER TWENTY-SEVEN

Lauren had honestly meant to confront Boris about the state Antonia was in, but her family returned home before Boris did, one thing led to another, and before she knew it, the day had disappeared. Invigorated after her trip to Brighton, Evelyn had a cleaning bee in her bonnet and insisted that everyone pitch in with a general tidy-up, including washing all the bedding and scrubbing the floors. Tristan and Adam weren't included in the divvying up of chores — another "Evelyn Rule of Life" that decreed men should not do women's work, so by everyone, she meant Mona and Lauren. Adam and Tristan bought Senators tickets online for the afternoon hockey game and left for Ottawa purportedly to "keep out of the way." While Lauren thought she could happily tell them both where to stuff themselves, she was relieved to see Tristan occupied and out of his bedroom.

At 5:30, Lauren squeezed out the mop one last time and climbed the stairs down to the basement to rinse the bucket and put away the cleaning supplies. Her back ached but she'd found the work mindless and oddly rejuvenating. Shovelling snow and now scrubbing floors and cleaning toilets were so far outside her current life as to be novel activities. She had cleaners for her condo and business, and a service took care of the condo grounds. She couldn't recall the last time that she'd cooked a meal.

Mona called to her as she started back upstairs. "I've made tea."

"I could use a cup." Lauren reached the landing and entered the kitchen. "Something smells good." She looked around the room. "Where's Evelyn?"

"She put a roast in the oven and went to lie down. Supper should be ready at eight and hopefully the men will be back."

Mona poured two mugs of tea and they took the easy chairs in the den. Lauren hadn't been alone with her sister-in-law since Vivian disappeared and felt an awkwardness between them. It got even more awkward when Mona set down her tea, stood up and hugged her. Lauren smelled sweat and talcum powder and was thankful when Mona released her and returned to her seat.

"Even though it's been over a week, I keep expecting Vivian to come through the door. How are you holding up, Lauren?" Mona had the earnest, caring look on her face that set Lauren's teeth on edge. The sweetness made her want to lash out … or cry.

"I've been through this before, remember? Violent death gets easier with practice." She picked up her phone from where she'd set it on the coffee table.

"Still."

"Yeah, none of this is easy." She looked at the crease lines on Mona's forehead and the suffering around her eyes and softened. "Don't mind me. Perhaps I'm having a harder time than I can admit even to myself. How're you doing?"

"Not great. I can't believe any of this. Adam is having nightmares and keeping us both up. I'll be glad when we can go home to Simon and get into our routine again. That'll be the only way to get some perspective on this horridness and put it behind us."

Lauren knew that Mona's words were wishful thinking. They would never completely recover from this blow no matter how often they talked about their feelings or found solace in work. The dead would be with them forever: haunting, bleeding, taking away the joy. They'd go through the motions, but the ghosts would not let them return to that carefree life they'd taken for granted. Broken. They were all broken for good. The knowledge made her kinder.

"Time heals," she said. "You're right."

She picked up her phone and clicked to open the screen. Three text messages waiting. Two from Salim with attachments and one from ... Matt Delgado. Her finger hovered over the phone and opened the one from Matt.

Hey, want to grab a drink or cup of coffee around seven?

She texted back: How did you get my number?

Called & your sister-in-law Mona gave it to me. Said since I was a family friend. Seemed nice.

Lauren raised her eyes and looked at Mona. So clueless and not worth getting upset with. She began typing and started over three times. She wanted to see him but didn't want to see him. The idea of him hopping in and out of her life gave her a stomach ache.

I'm going to walk Clemmie later. Could meet me outside our house.

Time?

After supper. Closer to nine thirty. Will text before I leave.

K. Later.

"Work?" Mona asked.

"No. It's that person you gave my number to when they called earlier."

"Sorry, I meant to tell you. He said that you went to high school together and that he wanted to get in touch. I hope that it was okay giving him your number. He sounded so nice."

"He said the same about you. No, it's okay." Lauren stood and stretched. "I'm going to have a shower before dinner."

"And I'll get the potatoes peeled and a salad made so we're set to eat when the guys get home."

Lauren climbed the stairs to her room. *I will not feel guilty for leaving Mona with the rest of the work*, she thought. *It's her choice to be the martyr. Not mine.*

Clemmie needed to be coaxed from his sleep after supper to be taken outside into the cold winter night. Lauren had second thoughts herself but once they'd tromped down the driveway and onto the snowy road, her mood lifted and she was happy to be striding through the darkness with stars shining above her like a tray of sparkling diamonds on a cloth of plush black velvet. Small boulevards of trees and bushes cut the streets in two and added to the feeling of being in the country. The air had the damp, soon-to-snow smell that she associated with Kingston and her childhood. She half expected that Matt wouldn't show up because she wasn't allowing herself to expect anything. When he appeared at the end of Grenville Crescent where it turned into Phillips Street, she relaxed and kept walking toward him.

"I thought you'd bring your dog," she said by way of greeting.

"Jupiter's getting up there and not much for long walks anymore." He hadn't shaven and she could see a smudge of grease under his chin that he'd missed. His eyes were tired and she wondered why he'd insisted on seeing her after a day working in the garage. The thought crossed her mind that she shouldn't be out here alone in the dark with him with two murders unsolved, but she dismissed it as quickly. She knew Matt and he would never hurt her. At least the Matt she used to know wouldn't. She glanced over at him, trying to read his mood.

"Hard day at the office?"

"Up at four so I start to run out of steam around now. I'll get a second wind."

"Is the garage ever closed?"

"Mondays. I have tomorrow off. We hired a new guy a few weeks ago and have an ad out for another mechanic so I'm aiming to get two-day weekends. Dad's getting up there along with Jupiter and will soon only work the books and front desk."

"I gather you're going to inherit the business one day."

"One day."

"Clemmie's getting up there too and his paws look to be cold. We shouldn't go too far tonight."

They made a right onto Portsmouth and another right on Elmwood. Traffic was light and Lauren imagined most people were spending the night in, getting ready for Monday and the start of another work week.

"Does your dad know that we've met up again?"

"He does."

"And he's okay with it?"

Matt took a few seconds to answer. "He wants me to find out what you and your family have kept back about Zoe's murder."

"Is that why you've asked me out? Playing at being a spy?" She stopped walking and Clemmie turned back on the lead and sat at her feet. She bent down to rub his head so that Matt wouldn't see how much his answer mattered to her.

"No. I realized when I saw you the other night that I'd missed you."

She took a deep breath and straightened to face him. "We won't work, Delgado, you must know that. You live here and I'm in Toronto. You can't leave your dad and I sure as hell am not giving up my business or my life. I also know that we don't stand a chance as long as Zoe's killer is running free. You suspect my brother and that will always be the wedge between us. So telling me that you missed me is empty words."

"You never struck me as a quitter, McKenna." He grinned at her until she smiled back. She swatted him on the shoulder.

"I get why I like you but have no idea why you like me." She turned and tugged on Clemmie's lead to get him walking. "I'm a jaded, bitter woman with a dicey past. Broken relationships, loose morals, and a self-centred existence."

"A woman of intrigue."

She looked sideways at him. "That's one interpretation, although probably not the sanest."

"Maybe I've lived my life too sanely and carefully. I've done time with a cheerleader and prefer your honesty ... to be honest."

They reached Grenville Road and turned toward home. The street was deserted with houses few and far between on their left and woods on the right.

"This street always creeps me out a bit at night," she said.

"You need to be careful."

His warning floated eerily in the darkness and she shivered inside her wool coat, aware of how easy it would be for her to be dragged into the seclusion of the trees. When it came down to it, she didn't know Matt anymore and he hadn't made any attempt to reach out to her in the past fourteen years.

"Has there been any progress with Vivian's investigation?" he asked.

She wondered if he intended to sound offhand. Was he digging for himself or his father, or was his question normal curiosity? Paranoia and self-preservation had been with her for so long that she couldn't tell honest interaction from nefarious. She said, "Not that I'm aware. The police haven't told us we can go home yet, though."

"I guess nothing new about Zoe yet, either."

"I'm sure the police would have told you."

"You'd think."

They reached Grenville Crescent and passed the brush and path leading into the Rideau Trail. The trees formed a thick black barricade, separating the road from the marshes, which extended in a thick swath above the river. Lauren was chilled through and exhausted from her day cleaning and the emotional roller coaster she'd been riding since she'd arrived at her parents'. Even now she wanted to spend time with Matt but she knew that she shouldn't.

"Thanks for the walk," he said. "I still owe you that coffee sometime."

Her heart rose and fell with his words. She knew then that she'd been hoping for more even as he must have realized that she'd been right about the futility of starting up again.

"I won't hold you to it," she said.

This time he didn't lean in to kiss her before he walked away and she didn't stand to watch him go. She'd let Clemmie off his lead and could see him waiting for her on the front steps. She started toward him. As she trudged up the driveway, she looked across the snowy yard to the Orlovs'. Their house was in complete darkness.

I need to get over there to check in on Antonia. She thought about how little interest or concern Evelyn had for her neighbours, but couldn't shake the feeling that something wasn't right. *Tomorrow,* she promised herself, *tomorrow I'll get to the bottom of the Orlov puzzle.*

CHAPTER TWENTY-EIGHT

Dawn had brought her lunch from home Monday morning as she always did: tuna sandwich, apple, and carton of milk. She hadn't liked to ask Kala for lunch money even though it was considered cooler to buy food in the caf, which she stood in now, scanning the room before making her way to the nerd table. The noise level was high and she felt invisible as she started across the floor. She'd come to like sitting with the other misfits who now said hello before leaving her alone. She made the mistake of glancing to her right and spotted Emily a few tables down, waving for Dawn to join her. For a second, Dawn thought about pretending she hadn't seen her, but then remembered that they were supposed to meet in the library after school. She hoped Emily was calling her over to cancel. She walked between two tables to reach the end where Emily was sitting while several pairs of eyes watched her progress.

Emily pointed to the only empty seat, which was directly across from her, next to Vanessa. "Why don't you sit with us?"

Chelsea yanked on Emily's arm. She whispered loud enough for Dawn to hear, "Are you crazy? Brett's on his way over."

Vanessa looked at Dawn. "Sorry, but I saved this seat for someone."

The entire table had gone quiet, as well as the tables on either side, and Dawn was glad that she didn't have to fake not caring. She looked over their heads and said, "Thanks, Emily, but I've got a seat over there." She kept her head high as she walked away, telling herself to ignore the tittering laughter going on behind her.

"Wait up!" Emily's voice cut through the ridicule of her friends and across the room.

Dawn looked back and saw Emily picking up her tray. She kept walking and didn't stop until she reached the nerd table. The regulars sitting at the table were looking away, probably glad that they weren't the ones in the spotlight of shame this time. Dawn sat and tucked her head, trying to disappear inside her jean jacket. She didn't raise her head when Emily slid in next to her. She didn't look up when she said, "I don't need your pity."

Emily's hand was on her arm. Her voice was low. "This isn't pity. I want to sit with you."

The three grade nine boys at the end of the table, who looked as if they could be characters on the show *The Big Bang Theory*, were glancing over and Emily waved at them. She picked up her carton of milk. "You're smart to bring your lunch. I'm getting sick of this cafeteria food. Did you get a good mark on your English essay?"

Dawn could tell that the exaggerated lightness in Emily's voice was false bravado and was surprised to realize that Emily was nervous. Dawn turned her head toward her and, after a few beats, said, "I guess. You?"

Emily smiled. "B-plus, which is a minor miracle. I usually get a C."

"Mind if I join you?" Brett McDonald was standing at the end of the table holding a tray. Dawn knew who he was but had never spoken to him. He was on the swim team and his parents were both doctors.

Emily waved him to the other side of the table across from her. "Brett, you know my friend Dawn?"

"Hey, Dawn."

"Hi."

The three boys had finished their meal but weren't going anywhere. Martha, a Chinese girl who always ate alone, started walking down the length of the table and stopped when she saw Brett.

"Hey, Martha," he said. "This seat's free." He pulled out the chair next to him.

Dawn could tell by the expression on Martha's face that she was surprised he knew her name. People like Martha didn't expect people like Brett to know their name.

Dawn found it easy to listen to Brett and Emily talk, respond when asked a question, and laugh at Brett's jokes. This would likely be the only time they ever interacted, so Dawn decided to relax and enjoy his company. When he got up to leave, he said, "Bye, Martha. See you around, Dawn, Em."

Emily arranged the dishes on her tray as she also prepared to leave. "See you in the library later. I can't stay long today, though."

"I need to get home too, so we can skip it today if you want to."

"No, I need your help with a couple of math problems, so if you can spare twenty minutes, I'll owe you one."

Dawn finished up her afternoon with biology and English and waited in the library for ten minutes before Emily rushed in with her winter coat on. "I can't stay after all," she said, out of breath. "My brother's flying home from university and we're on our way to Toronto to pick him up."

"I didn't know you had a brother." As soon as she said the words, she thought, *Why did I say that? None of my business.*

"Shawn is studying environmental science at UBC. He's five years older than me. I feel bad for making you wait. Did you miss your bus?"

"I'll get the next one."

"I won't be at school tomorrow morning, but wanted to know if you'd come with me to the Shawn Mendes concert Saturday night? My way of repaying you for getting me through math this semester. I wouldn't have passed without you."

"You don't need to do that."

"But I want to. I already have the tickets."

Dawn started to say no thanks, but Emily was walking toward the door. "It's at the K-Rock

Centre and we can meet up outside," she called over her shoulder. She didn't wait for an answer and disappeared as quickly as she'd arrived.

Dawn left the school with shadows casting long fingers across the road. A few students straggled out of the front doors with her, but nobody else was walking alone. She was partway down the steps when she looked across the street. A man dressed in dark clothes stood under the lamppost and he appeared to be watching the school. She pulled up the hood of her parka and took another look from under the fur-lined rim. His hair was black and long and tied in two braids; his skin was brown and lined and he was skinny to the point of looking unwell. She reached the sidewalk but he'd already left the spot where he'd been standing and was walking away, head down with his hands in his pockets.

She didn't linger to see if he'd turn around but stayed on the same side of the street and walked as quickly as she could in the other direction toward the bus stop. She couldn't figure out why the man had looked familiar and pondered where she might have seen him before. She also wondered why a man who looked to be down and out would be standing in the cold watching students leave the school.

Especially an Indigenous man.

"Detective Woodhouse wants all of us available today," said Evelyn, hanging up the phone. "Apparently, he wants to go through *everyone's* statement again to confirm where we were when Vivian went missing."

Tristan groaned and Adam pounded the kitchen table with his fist. "When are they going to let us go home? Surely they can't keep us in Kingston much longer. I have a plane to fly." Adam paused, then put a hand on Tristan's shoulder. "Sorry, brother. That sounded more insensitive than I meant it to."

Mona looked up from her knitting. "Perhaps we'll be free to leave after the detective goes through everything one more time. I'm going to insist that I need to get home to Simon. Evelyn, did you decide whether to have the memorial service for David now or wait until the summer?"

"The summer. Once this is behind us."

Lauren was holding Clemmie in her lap, rubbing his head and talking softly into his ear. She looked up. "I know the police told you to stay but they never told me that I couldn't leave."

"I suppose because you only live a few hours away," said Mona.

"That could be. Anyhow, I'll be in my room working, so call if the cops want to talk to me again."

She climbed the steps with Clemmie at her heels and they both jumped onto the bed. The dog found a comfortable spot on the pillow and immediately went to sleep while Lauren pulled open her laptop and began working on a bathroom design. A moment later, Tristan knocked on the door and entered without waiting for her to answer. He flopped down at the foot of the bed and leaned his head against the wall.

"I can't take much more of this."

"I know."

"Two weeks since Viv and our baby died and then Dad … I still feel like I'm in a fog. Like the world has caved in and I'm trying to climb out from under the rubble but it keeps falling back and knocking me over."

"It's going to take time. You have to let yourself grieve."

"Just like you are." His tone was accusatory, but she didn't react. Tristan was little more than a boy child and attacking her was his way of working off his own weakness. The strategy had worked when they were kids in the schoolyard. He'd pick on her when they were with his friends so they wouldn't notice his fear or lack of backbone. She liked to think he did this because he knew that she could handle herself, and she always had. She'd protected him however she could, even if it meant taking the blows. Looking at him now, she could tell that he was close to breaking.

"Will you stay in Edmonton?" she asked to deflect him.

"Christ, I haven't given it any thought. There's nothing for me there anymore." He banged his head lightly against the wall: one time, two times.

"You could move to Toronto and live near me."

"That's all you'd need." He smiled at her. "Me crying next door and you propping me up."

"I'd like to have you close by."

"Thanks, Laur, for everything. I mean it. We've always been a unit against the world and I don't know if I'd function so well without knowing you had my back."

Just what are you telling me?

She tamped down the feeling that she'd sold her soul and said, "Anytime." She propped herself up on the pillow next to Clemmie.

"You and Mom still on the outs?" he asked.

"We're civil. I think for once she might feel some shame for what she said to me in the hospital. God knows, it's a new emotion for her. Say, do you know much about the Orlovs? I have to say Boris has started to give me pause."

"What do you mean?"

"Why hasn't he gotten medical help for Antonia if she's been sick for two weeks? How come she never leaves her room?"

"They've always been reclusive. They show up over here whenever it suits them and keep to themselves otherwise."

"Do you think they're married?"

"What, to each other? Of course."

"What if I told you that Antonia said Boris was her brother?"

"When did she say that?"

"I went into her bedroom to find out if she was okay when Adam took Boris to the hospital after he fell. She even had a photo of what looked like her and Boris as kids with their mother and father."

Tristan laughed. "She had to be on drugs and hallucinating. They couldn't carry off a lie like that all these years."

"Tristan, I'd like to get her alone again and make sure she's okay. Would you keep Boris busy in the basement after supper while I sneak upstairs to see her?"

"Are you crazy?"

"More like worried. The other thing …"

"Yeah?"

"Somebody killed Zoe and Vivian and they had to know our family, don't you think? What if Boris …" She couldn't make herself put the thought into words.

"Killed them? Are you kidding me? That's plain nuts." He stared across the bed at her and their eyes held. His went from incredulous to skeptical. "Dad would have known. He and Boris spent a lot of years fishing and building things together. No way Boris could have killed Zoe and gotten away with it. Mom might tolerate Antonia, but Dad and Boris were real buds."

"So, after supper you'll help me to confirm that I'm imagining all this?"

He tilted his head from side to side and gave her an amused grin. "Sure, why not, but only because it'll be entertaining when you discover how flawed your detective skills are. We should make a bet. Five bucks says that the old couple next door is as exciting and mysterious as Mom's pot roast."

"You're on."

He pushed himself up from the bed. "I'll leave you to it then, and get ready to face the copper. What do you think of them?"

"The police?"

"Yeah."

"I think the one in charge, Woodhouse, has an agenda and I don't like him much. I trust the woman, though."

"Stonechild."

"She seems patient and clever. I'd be surprised if much gets past her."

Tristan nodded and ran a hand across his chin. "She's the one we have to look out for. Woodhouse is easily handled, but if she takes it into her head that I'm guilty, you'll be visiting me in the pen for the rest of my life."

"Then we won't let her find you guilty, will we?"

Officers Woodhouse and Bennett interviewed them individually in the dining room. Lauren was the last to be called at 4:30 and she could tell that Woodhouse was frustrated with his lack of progress with the others. She said nothing to improve his mood. She felt sorry for Officer Bennett, who acted as a mute sidekick, sitting off to the side, taking notes. As Woodhouse wrapped up his questions, she glanced over at Bennett and could have sworn he shot Woodhouse a disrespectful glare before lowering his head. Perhaps because of her own subservient role in the McKenna family, she was more sensitive to those in the same position in other relationships. The sense that Woodhouse bullied his partner emboldened her.

"Have you any evidence as to who killed Vivian," she asked, "or are you making our lives a living hell because you've got nobody else to harass?"

From the corner of her eye she caught Officer Bennett raising his head as she held Woodhouse's stare. She imagined that prodding a bull with a stick would elicit much the same look on its face. "If we were harassing your family," he said, "we'd have you all down at the station today instead of giving you the courtesy of being interviewed in the comfort of your home."

"I understood that you couldn't force us to be interviewed at the station if we refused. We could also ask to have a lawyer present."

Woodhouse took his time answering and then spoke as if he was explaining the way the world worked to a foolish child. "You're not under suspicion, so a lawyer isn't needed. If you're worried about something you haven't revealed to me, you should spill it now because it will come back to bite you. As I've said before, it might be premature, not to mention costly, to bring in a lawyer now, but hiring one is your right." He studied her with a phony perplexed look on his face. "I generally find that the innocent don't want a lawyer present when they're simply answering questions about where they were at the time of the murder. I thought you'd be pleased that we're being so thorough seeing as how it was your sister-in-law who was murdered."

"I don't understand why we keep going over the same ground." She could feel her stubborn streak rising up. She lifted her chin. "You continue asking where we were that day and we keep telling you. Nothing has changed and you're wasting time that could be put into finding the killer. When will you be releasing Vivian's body so we can give her a proper burial?"

"The autopsy report is expected tomorrow and we should release the body by the afternoon. I've told Tristan that he can make arrangements."

"So we can return to our lives in other cities now?"

"Yes, but you might need to return if called upon. When will you be going to Toronto?"

"I'll leave when Tristan takes Vivian's body to Edmonton. I plan to accompany him." She added the last sentence without thinking but realized as soon as she said the words that this was the right thing to do. She could afford a few more days away from the office if she kept teleworking and would be able to make sure Tristan got through his return home.

Woodhouse eyed her with interest. "You seem exceptionally close to your brother. I understand that you vouched for his whereabouts when Zoe Delgado was murdered."

His observations were made mildly without a question attached and Lauren bit back a retort. No good could come of matching wits with this cop who held the power to make the investigation into whatever he wanted. He didn't need evidence to leak innuendos to the press, or to continue pressuring them into a confession, or to trip them up The police had thrown everything they could at Tristan when Zoe was murdered and nothing would stop them from doing it again. She met his stare and neither spoke. The seconds ticked by.

Officer Bennett cleared his throat and ended the impasse. They both looked across the room at him. "Should I warm up the car if you're done asking questions?" he asked, shutting his notebook.

Officer Woodhouse's eyes shot bullets and Lauren braced herself for an outburst. She was surprised when he said in a jocular voice, "Yeah, because I guess we won't be finding out anything new from this one. Miss McKenna thinks we should be back on the road tracking down the *real* killer." He touched a finger to his head and saluted her. "While you're at it, Bennett, call Gundersund and tell him that we're on our way in. I'll be out in a few minutes once you've got the car toasty warm."

CHAPTER TWENTY-NINE

Gundersund tucked his cellphone into a pocket, ran a tired hand through his messy blond curls, and said to Rouleau, "That was Bennett. He and Woodhouse are done at the McKenna house and on their way in."

"Make any headway?"

"Bennett says no."

"Two weeks and we're not much further ahead than when Vivian McKenna's body was found. Murder is bad enough but to kill a pregnant woman ..." Rouleau couldn't finish. Frances's miscarriage and inability to conceive again had defined the tragedy of their marriage. "How's Woodhouse doing as lead investigator out in the field?"

"I want to be fair but he keeps re-covering old ground, setting his sights on Tristan McKenna."

"He could be right this time. Tristan wouldn't be the first husband to kill his way out of a marriage."

"I know and we have the second murder of Tristan McKenna's high school girlfriend to compound the suggestion of his guilt."

"I was surprised that Woodhouse sent Stonechild to interview people in Edmonton. I would have thought he'd want to go himself."

Gundersund lifted his mouth in a half smile. "He wants to delegate and save his skills for getting the truth out of Tristan McKenna. He calls it turning the screw slow and steady."

Rouleau's desk phone's red light flashed and he picked up. Just as well he didn't have time to comment. "Yes, Vera?"

He listened for a moment and said, "Put her through." He raised a finger to let Gundersund know the call wouldn't take long.

"Yes, Marci, how can I help you? How about six thirty? Okay, see you there." He hung up and said to Gundersund. "Marci Stokes has something to tell me and wants to meet for a drink at the Merchant. Feel like coming along?"

"No, I'm keeping an eye on Dawn while Kala's away and should get over there. I got a text from Kala and her flight gets into Toronto tomorrow late morning so she'll be home around lunchtime. That's another long night alone for Dawn so I'll go check in on her."

"How're they doing?"

"Well, I think it's promising that Stonechild didn't zip off to Edmonton and leave Dawn to her own devices for two days. I was over making supper last night."

"My dad wants to take all of you out for a meal one night soon. He's fond of Kala and Dawn and thinks he should get more involved. He intends to propose something to Dawn over a plate of Chinese food."

Gundersund stretched out his right leg and kneaded the muscle in his thigh. "I get the sense Dawn is struggling even with Kala's attempts to make her feel wanted, so your dad's involvement might be what she needs."

"Dad has a steadying hand and a gentleness that troubled souls respond to. He would have made a good social worker or minister. Sore leg?"

"Yeah. I fell asleep on Stonechild's couch and woke up this morning twisted out of shape."

"I'm sure Stonechild will be grateful that you stayed over."

"Dawn was happy to see me still there in the morning, anyway." Gundersund hesitated. "Any decision on running for top cop?"

"I have a meeting with HR in a few minutes. I intend to turn the acting position down." Rouleau saw the relief in Gundersund's eyes before he hid the emotion with a poker face.

"I'm happy for the team, but are you sure you should turn down the opportunity?"

"I've not interested in furthering my career. I'm content in Major Crimes with you lot."

Gundersund grinned. "Then I'd say it's our lucky day."

Sally Rackham entered his office munching an apple and rubbing her belly, which looked even larger than Rouleau remembered from the week before. She spread her feet and lowered herself into the visitors' chair with a grunt. "You caught me on my last week before I go on leave," she said. "This baby can't come out soon enough."

"Doesn't look like you have long to wait."

Her laughter filled the room. "My husband's been convinced since the fifth month that I couldn't get any bigger." She spoke down to her stomach. "Guess we're showing him."

"You said you had an update on Woodhouse."

"I do. He called today and withdrew his complaint."

"Well that's something. Any idea why?"

"If I had to guess? I'd say he's gotten wind of Captain Heath's leave of absence and is thinking about becoming your replacement if you continue acting for Heath."

"About that. I've decided not to apply for Heath's position so let's hope Woodhouse doesn't decide to backtrack when he finds out."

Her mouth formed a circle of distress. "Oh no. May I ask why not?"

"I prefer heading up Major Crimes."

She was silent but her forehead crinkled into a series of worried lines. "The thing is," she said after appearing to give his words careful thought, "the board wants *you*. I'm quite certain they aren't going to be pleased that you're turning the acting job down."

Rouleau looked out the window. Darkness had fallen around 4:30 but he could make out a frosted pattern on the glass that had snaked its way up from the sill. He knew she was being tactful. He wasn't going to get off easily if he went against the board's wishes.

He pulled his gaze away from the icy window and back at her. She held the half-eaten apple in midair and the anxiety on her face made him hesitate, but not for long. He said, "Let the board members know I'm not interested and they'll have to go with someone else. It's not like I'm the only qualified cop."

She looked far from convinced, but took a bite out of the apple before saying, "I'll tell them. Then I'll totter off on my maternity leave extremely happy that I don't have to deal with the fallout."

"They'll simply have to accept my decision and move on."

"I wouldn't bet on it, but we can dream. You know that you're doing an excellent job acting for Captain Heath now, don't you? The rank and file are as contented as I've ever seen them under your watch."

"Are you working to get me to change my mind?"

"Maybe." She smiled.

He returned her smile. "My mind's made up, but nice try."

After she left, Rouleau checked the outer office. Vera had gone home for the day and he remembered her saying something about hosting a book club and needing to pick up wine, crackers, cheese, and pâté. He'd forgotten what it felt like to have a circle of friends outside of work. He could take a lesson. It was time to expand his lunchtime walks into an activity that would widen his interests. He admitted to himself that he was getting restless. Dissatisfied with his life.

His desk phone rang as he was putting on his coat. He almost ignored it but old habits died hard and he picked up, tucking the receiver against his shoulder as he slipped one arm into the sleeve. He experienced a jolt of pleasure when he realized his old friend Petran Albescu was on the line.

"Petran, thanks for getting back to me so soon. I was going to follow up on my request in a few days."

"No need. I cannot talk, my friend, except I wanted to tell you that I'm taking the overnight flight and will be in Montreal tomorrow afternoon. I'd like to meet up."

"Tomorrow afternoon?"

"Yes, I arrive at three thirty at the Pierre Elliott Trudeau Airport. I'll hire a car and drive to Kingston." His accent gave a rolling quality to his words not unpleasant to the ear. Rouleau recalled that Petran spoke five languages fluently.

"Or I could drive to Montreal and we could meet there."

"That would be too much to ask."

"No trouble at all. I'll give you my cellphone number and you can text me when your plane lands. I'll meet you out front of the airport. Have you booked a hotel already?"

"You are indeed the friend I remembered. Don't worry about my accommodations. They've been looked after."

Rouleau detected a smile in his voice. "Can you tell me anything about your visit?" he asked.

"Not over the phone. You understand."

"I'll wait until I see you in person. I'll likely bring a member of my team if that's okay."

"Good. Until tomorrow. It's been a long time, Jacques."

"Too long. We have a lot of catching up to do."

"That we do."

Rouleau sat deep in thought after he hung up. Petran would not be flying to Canada unless he had something important to share. Something he wasn't comfortable saying over the phone because guarding against eavesdropping was a way of life in Romania or any country that had been under Communist rule. He'd take Stonechild with him to Montreal because this was her lead. He was intrigued but would set aside the implications of the call until they spoke with Petran in person.

Marci Stokes was waiting for him in the entranceway to the bar when he arrived at the Merchant a half hour later. Since it was a Monday night, they had their choice of tables and took one in the corner near the front window. Rouleau studied her as they sat down. She was wearing her usual black coat but looked different.

"You've cut your hair," he said as they pulled out their chairs. "It suits you."

"The grey has also been eradicated, although you're too much the gentleman to comment on that."

She appeared flustered under his gaze and he dropped his eyes to look at his beer. It wasn't just the hair that made her look different. The colour in her cheeks and the lightness in her step were new. She seemed happy. "Has something good happened in your life?" he asked.

"Ridiculously, it appears I've adopted a stray cat. Not sure how good that is in the scheme of life, but I feel like I'm settled for the first time in a long time. Perhaps the arrival of the cat was a good omen. He keeps showing up even though I did everything possible to shoo him away."

"I can see you owning a cat."

"Can you? I never could. My life has been all about not being tied down. My *New York Times* editor knew that at the heart of our relationship, I didn't need him. Not really. I'm afraid lust followed by familiarity is a decidedly different animal than love."

"I loved my wife Frances even after we separated. I realized after she left me that I hadn't done enough to nurture her spirit while we were married." Rouleau surprised himself with this admission and took a drink of beer to stave off further confessions.

Marci tilted her head and studied him. "You're a decent man, Sergeant Rouleau. You give me hope."

"Hope?"

"That there are more men out there like you and I won't end my days jaded and alone."

He returned her smile. "You had something to tell me?"

"I shouldn't be sharing this but I'm tired of all the underhanded tactics to get news reported, and I use the word *news* loosely of late, at least on the Internet." She leaned closer across the table. "We got an anonymous tip at the station that a complaint has been lodged against you for improper hiring and favouritism. I've had confirmation and am tasked with writing this up for tomorrow's paper."

"The complaint has been dropped."

"You know this for a fact?"

"I had a meeting with HR before I came here."

She pushed back against her chair. "Well, thank the good lord above for that. You've made my day and conscience a lot easier. Hold on a moment." She pulled out her cellphone and typed furiously with her thumbs. "A message to my editor. That ought to put the article to bed," she said. "Why don't you drink up and we can go over to my place and I'll cook us some omelettes and introduce you to the cat. You can help me give it a name."

He thought about her offer. His father was out for the evening and he wasn't looking forward to his own dreary company. "Did you bring your car?"

"I did but you can follow me over." She turned to look out the window. "The snow is holding off. You'll be able to park on the street."

He picked up his glass. "Then what are we waiting for?"

Rouleau entered Marci's limestone half double and was pleased to see that the interior was as warmly decorated and down to earth as the woman he'd come to know. She likely didn't consider herself either of these qualities, but he'd seen beneath her tenacious, tough exterior. He liked that she didn't fuss with her appearance or put much thought into how others saw her. In his mind, this made her more attractive, not less.

She took his coat and invited him to sit on a stool at the island with a pint of craft beer while she whipped up eggs and chopped onions, peppers, and mushrooms. "I used to be a good cook when I put my mind to it," she said. "Now I eat out or come up with something simple."

The cat had shot out of the house when they'd arrived but returned to sit on the window ledge outside the kitchen and was now indoors, licking its paws at Rouleau's feet. Grey and undernourished, it had watchful green eyes that studied Rouleau fixedly as it began to wash its face. It jumped as if dodging a kick when Rouleau shifted positions on the chair.

"Is the cat male or female?" he asked.

"I assumed male but can't say I looked that closely."

"We can eat here if you like." She set a plate of eggs and toast in front of him and began work on the second omelette. When it finished cooking, she poured them each a glass of red wine and sat on the stool next to him. They clinked glasses and ate without talking. She was comfortable in silence, as Frances had been.

"You haven't asked about the McKenna case," he said when he'd had the last bite and set down his fork.

"I'm taking a break for the evening." She sipped her wine. "But I wouldn't be averse to you chatting about it if you feel the need." Her eyes sparkled above the wineglass.

"Nothing new to report, sadly."

She set down her glass and pushed her plate away, resting her elbow on the counter and cupping her chin in her hand. "It's looking like the husband, isn't it? I've reported on a few husbands who killed their pregnant wives. The American Scott Peterson for one. Remember he was at a vigil for his missing wife Laci and called his unwitting girlfriend to say he was in Paris? Her family and the couple's friends said he would never have murdered his wife, and they fervently believed in his innocence until the girlfriend came forward to expose his lies. Now, he's on death row."

"The motives were rising debt and a desire to be single as I recall."

"He was a callous piece of work. Have you found any girlfriends circling around Vivian's husband?"

"None that we've located, but Kala Stonechild is in Edmonton now carrying out interviews."

"Good. If anyone can suss out the tangled relationships, it will be her. I truly am sorry about that article that we printed on her time living on the street. I wrote it but had asked that it not be issued until I had her okay. She didn't deserve to be broadsided like that."

"No, she didn't. I've often wondered why you even thought to dig into her life before she became a cop."

Marci blinked and stood in one quick motion, picking up their plates as she talked. "A routine search. I was interested in learning more about your team." She put the plates into the sink and picked up the kettle. She asked without turning completely around to face him, "Cup of tea to end the meal?"

He checked his watch. "Not tonight, I'm afraid. I need to get going because I have a few calls to make before it gets too late. Rain check?"

"Of course." The smile had returned to her face along with an easing of the tension in her shoulders.

Rouleau knew somebody had fed her the story and he had a strong suspicion who, but he wouldn't press. She'd be conflicted but wasn't in a position to tell him because of her code to protect the anonymity of sources, and he wasn't in a position at the moment to accuse Woodhouse without proof.

At the front door, he took a last look around the cozy living room: the plaid easy chair with an empty mug resting on a folded newspaper on the table next to it, the worn purple velvet couch, the soft yellow glow from a standing lamp with an antique glass shade. Marci held his coat while he put on his boots. He straightened and took it from her and their hands touched.

"Thank you for your company and an enjoyable meal," he said. "We never did get around to naming the cat or figuring out its gender."

"Another time." She was standing close and her tawny eyes were watching him. Her scent was light and pleasing: coconut and rose petals. He bent down and kissed her on the cheek and then her mouth was on his, her arms wrapped around his shoulders. When they broke apart some time later, she took a step back and looked up at him. "Dammit, Rouleau. If we're not careful, this could turn into a thing."

He pushed back a stray lock of her hair that had fallen into her eyes. He'd always been attracted to her intelligence and quick wit but hadn't imagined this feeling would become physical. Looking at her now, he realized that there'd been something more between them all along.

"I'm game to see what kind of thing this turns into if you are," he said, smiling, and she nodded.

"I think we should."

He opened the door, letting in a blast of cold air. He was reluctant to leave but knew this was not the time to take things further. "Sleep well, Marci. I'll be in touch soon."

She stooped to pick up the cat circling around her legs. "What's his or her name and I will be waiting for your call."

Chapter Thirty

Lauren rose before everyone else Tuesday morning — unusual, she knew — but the health of Antonia Orlov was playing on her mind and kept waking her up from an already restless sleep. After her interview with Officer Woodhouse the afternoon before, she'd gone in search of Tristan to go with her to the Orlovs' as they'd planned. He'd agreed to distract Boris while she snuck upstairs to check on Antonia. Unfortunately, Tristan had been in no condition to talk coherently to the dog, let alone Boris. He'd coped with the latest round of police questioning by smoking joints all afternoon and listening to music on his iPhone. Lauren had then herself coped by taking a cab to the Duke and getting hammered on vodka cocktails, some of which had been bought for her by a bearded man with the words *love* and *hate* tattooed on the knuckles of his hands. She'd stopped short of leaving with him but not because of any moral high ground. She'd been in the ladies' room throwing up when he'd gotten tired of waiting and gone home without her.

She tossed back two Advil with a glass of water and put on a pot of coffee, climbing back upstairs for a shower while it brewed. She pulled on faded jeans and selected a red sweater to distract from the redness in her eyes, then returned to the kitchen for her first cup of coffee. The rich smell of java turned her stomach but she closed her eyes and breathed in and out deeply until she got her queasiness under control.

What the hell am I doing? she thought. *Is this as good as it's ever going to get?*

She took her coffee into the dining room, where she stood at the window looking out toward the Orlov house. A light was on in the kitchen and a flicker of hope eased her aching head. Perhaps Antonia was up making breakfast and back on her cleaning schedule. Lauren imagined that she'd be over to drink tea and trail after Evelyn this afternoon.

The sky was lead grey with the wind bending tree boughs and skimming snow into swaths of filigree that danced across the white lawn. While she stood sipping from her cup, trying to keep the coffee from coming back up, snowflakes started falling from the bloated clouds, a sprinkle at first, quickly turning into a tempest driving hard against the window pane.

She returned to the kitchen and turned on the radio. Evelyn had it dialed to the CBC and Gord Downie was belting out "New Orleans Is Sinking" in his powerful voice that never failed to make her feel like dancing, protesting, loving somebody. She sang along with his words telling her that she had to do what she felt was real.

She slumped against the counter. *But how do I know what's real?*

The pounding drum and squealing guitar brought another round of nausea and she turned down the volume. On a better morning, she'd be cranking it up. She rubbed her fingers back and forth across her forehead. The song ended and the announcer began reading the news at the top of the hour. She waited until he started on the weather report and spun the volume back up.

Expect snow to end by eleven with a second system moving in late this afternoon, bringing strong winds and freezing rain turning to snow overnight all along Lake Ontario. There'll be ten centimetres of new snow on the ground when you wake up tomorrow so get your shopping done early today and hunker down. For those flying out of Toronto this evening or tomorrow morning, check that your flight hasn't been cancelled before setting out to the airport.

"That's just great," grumbled Lauren out loud to the empty room. "Even if Tristan is ready to leave, we're stuck here another day."

She sat back down at the table with a full cup of coffee and took small sips while slumping in the chair with her eyes closed. She heard Clemmie's nails clicking down the hallway toward the kitchen and then her mother's footsteps. She straightened and tried to appear less ill than she felt as Evelyn stopped in the doorway and stared at her.

"My goodness, Lauren. You look as if you're one step away from skid row."

"Thanks, Mother. You always know what to say to make me feel better about myself."

"You're not a child, Lauren, although you often act like one. All I want is for you to pull yourself together and —"

"Find a husband, give you some grandkids, and settle down to a life of servitude as you have. Not happening, Mother." She stretched her fingers to the ceiling and yawned, feigning indifference while inside, her stomach was churning, and not only from the hangover.

"Is this coffee fresh?" Her mother held up the pot.

"Half an hour old."

"I'll make another pot." She dumped what was left into the sink and reached for the coffee filters.

"The snow should taper off by lunch but there's a larger storm moving in later this afternoon," said Lauren, deciding it wouldn't kill her to be civil. "I expect we'll all make plans to leave tomorrow. Will you be coming to Edmonton for Vivian's burial?"

"I already told Tristan that I'm not up for the trip." Evelyn sat down at the end of the table to wait for the coffee to brew. "I'll go in a month or so once everything's settled here." She paused. "Thank you for going with him."

"Of course."

Her mother's face had aged since her dad's death and for the first time, Lauren wondered how she was going to cope with him gone. He'd been the one to pay the bills and handle the upkeep of the house and yard. He'd been the one to call Lauren on Sunday mornings, always carefully timed for the hour when Evelyn was grocery shopping. "She'll be sorry to have missed you," he'd say at the end of every conversation.

Her mother was looking at her, head tilted to one side. "Did you hear what I said?"

"No, sorry. I was daydreaming."

"I'm going to sell the house and move west to be closer to your brothers. Mona raised the idea and says there's some nice townhouses nearby. Adam told me that he'll be happier knowing I'm in the neighbourhood to help with Simon while he's away."

Lauren's first thought was *with Dad barely cold in the ground*, but she bit back the words. Of course, Evelyn would sell this place as fast as she could. She wouldn't care if she saw her husband in the tulips and daffodils that he planted every fall or in the roof he'd replaced the year before or the new tile in the kitchen that he'd laid with such care. Her mother had never felt the poetry of another's existence. "You'll be able to see more of Tristan too, help them all through this tough time," she said and could see that her response satisfied her mother. Lauren wouldn't put up a fuss or say she was moving too fast, and her mother could relocate closer to the sons she'd always adored.

"Well then," Evelyn stood as the coffee finished dripping into the carafe. "Would you like some French toast and bacon? I'll be making enough for everyone."

"I'll set the table."

As she was taking the plates down from the cupboard, Lauren looked across at her mother and said, "It's odd that Antonia hasn't been over to visit."

"She comes and goes as she pleases." Evelyn tied an apron around her waist. She looked out the kitchen window. "Although I'd have thought she'd be over to see how I'm doing by now. Maybe she thinks I'm looked after with the house full."

"We could walk over and check on her after breakfast."

"I don't like to go out in this snow and ice with my bad knee. You could go offer to shovel their drive when this storm passes, through. Boris will be struggling with one arm."

"I'll do that and I'll drag Tristan along to help."

CHAPTER THIRTY-ONE

Officer Gaudette picked Kala up at 6:30 Tuesday morning and they beat the worst of the morning traffic, cutting east across the downtown to Cloverdale, a small Edmonton neighbourhood situated immediately south of the North Saskatchewan River. The McKennas owned a two-bedroom condo in Waterside Estates, a stone and stucco low-rise surrounded by trees and adjacent to Muttart Conservatory, a spectacular array of glass pyramids housing botanical gardens that Gaudette said Stonechild should visit if time allowed as she pulled into visitor parking. She hoped today would be more productive than Monday. The stream of interviews hadn't elicited any new information to further the case.

"I'm catching a flight as soon as we finish here and at the retirement home," said Kala. "Maybe next time. How much do you figure these condos go for?"

"Three to four hundred thousand. Nice family area near the river. My partner and I looked at a place here last year but ended up in Century Park in the south end."

The super was waiting for them and let them into the McKennas' third-floor corner apartment after checking the warrant. "You'll find the woman across the hall in 303 is home and I told her you might want to talk to her."

"Thanks." Gaudette entered the apartment ahead of Kala and walked over to look out the balcony window. She turned and said, "Forensics just arrived. They'll go through the electronics and will help with the search."

Kala nodded. "May as well get started. I'll have a look in their bedroom."

"We'll begin in the second bedroom, which I see they've made into a den-slash-office."

Kala started with the bedside tables and worked her way methodically through the two chests of drawers and the closets. Vivian had large collections of makeup, costume jewellery, and shoes. Her clothing was good quality and expensive from what Kala could tell. She must have had a store discount although her wardrobe would still have cost a pretty penny. Tristan's clothes were on the worn, comfortable side: jeans and sweaters with several shirts, mainly white, and leather jackets.

She found a datebook for the past year tucked away on the top shelf of Vivian's closet. *Jackpot*, she thought, but set it aside while she finished her search of the room.

Gaudette met her in the living room a half hour later. "We're taking the home computer and a laptop we found on the kitchen table. No home phone and their cellphones are with them, I'm guessing. He keeps a datebook but must have tossed last year's. Not much in this one yet."

"Maybe he kept an electronic calendar."

"We'll look for one."

Kala waved the datebook. "I found this in Vivian's closet and it's for last year. I'd like to make a copy to take back with me."

"There's a photocopier in his office. We can print it off now."

Kala left Gaudette and the team to finish searching the rest of the apartment and crossed the hall to speak with the tenant in 303. Wendy Ferris was a retired grade two teacher who used a cane to lead Kala into her living room.

"Devastating news about Vivian. I'm still reeling. Just push Snowball off the chair and sit yourself down."

Snowball wasn't keen on moving, so Kala picked the cat up and set it on her lap. "How well do you know the McKennas?"

"Well, Tristan works from home and liked to come by for tea in the afternoons around three. We talked politics and books and I have to say that I looked forward to our chats."

"Did he ever speak about Vivian or his marriage?"

"Not often. He appeared unhappy last year and said that he and Vivian were working a few things out. He joked that she'd thought she married a wealthy author only to find out he was mortal. He was struggling to find a publisher for his second book and talked about self-publishing. He'd started on a third manuscript, which he said was a departure."

She looked uncomfortable and Kala prompted her to continue. "Anything you say could help us to find out why Vivian died."

"I'm not one for gossip and I certainly don't want to say anything to hurt Tristan because he has been awfully good to me. Do you know he replaced the taps in my bathroom last month? The super was away for Christmas." She stopped what she was about to say and smiled. "But perhaps you don't want to hear me ramble on."

"Tell me what you remember and I'll ignore whatever is not germane to the case."

"Very well then. Tristan was away on trips off and on last year, travelling around the province for workshops and book signings. He even made a long publicity jaunt across the southern U.S. He was depressed about his royalties from the first book dwindling away and was trying to get his career back on track."

"I understand."

"Vivian had a gentleman caller sometimes when Tristan was gone. Not every time, but the reason I started watching was because of how quiet they were coming in and out, as if they didn't want to be noticed." Wendy looked down at her hands folded in her lap.

"Did you know who he was or can you give me a description?"

"No. I never saw him except for his back when he went into her condo a couple of times. He was taller than Vivian and always went in ahead of her. Wore a dark coat, I think navy. She'd stand in the hall and shut the door after them."

"How do you know that he was a regular visitor if you only saw his back a few times?"

"I'd hear their voices through the door."

Kala paused before saying, "You'd leave your apartment and listen at their door, is that what you're saying?"

"It sounds so snoopy hearing you say it out loud, but yes, I'd cross the hall on my way to the garbage chute and listen at their door. I was worried for Tristan, you see. I knew how upset he'd be. I needed to be sure I wasn't imagining the worst of Vivian without giving her the benefit of the doubt."

"Perhaps they were simply friends."

"I'd like to have believed that."

"Why don't you?"

"I heard him leave very early one morning. I'm sure they thought I was asleep but I'm something of an insomniac."

"But you didn't see him?"

"No, by the time I got to my peephole, he was at the other end of the hall and Vivian was shutting the door. She was wearing a filmy red nightgown, I can tell you that."

"Do you know the dates that he visited?"

"That's asking a lot. I didn't write them down or try to keep track but I can tell you that the visits stopped last summer — or was it later in the spring?" She tapped her forehead. "Retirement makes all the days slide into each other. Sorry, I'm so obtuse."

"Did you tell Tristan what was going on?"

"No, dear. After thinking it over for a long while, I decided that telling him would do more harm than good. What happens between him and his wife is not my business. I only came to this conclusion after a lot of soul searching. Then Tristan seemed so much happier what with the news of the baby and I believed that their troubles were under the bridge." Her eyes widened. "Do you think Tristan found out on his own?"

"Not that we've uncovered."

"That's a relief. He's the kind of man needs protecting. Sensitive, with no protective shell. Maybe that's what makes him such a good writer."

"Did he ever speak about the death of his high school girlfriend?"

"Goodness, no." Wendy clutched at the shirt fabric over her heart. "How did she die?"

"She was stabbed in the yard behind his house. The killer was never charged."

"Why that's tragic. No wonder Tristan was so fragile. I'm honestly shocked."

Kala studied the woman in front of her. She saw no guile on her face, nor any sign that she was acting to protect the man she thought of as her friend. "The question of Tristan's guilt in these two deaths does not seem to have crossed your mind," she said, keeping the skepticism out of her voice.

"Tristan? A killer?" Wendy pursed her lips as she frowned and thought over the idea. "Of course, we're all capable of murder, and we can never fully know a person, but if Tristan killed either of those poor girls, I'd say that I've completely misjudged him. The Tristan whom I came to know would more likely be the victim than the killer."

Gaudette drove Kala to one last stop before taking her to the airport for a direct morning flight to Toronto. It was still early morning in the East and with the two-hour time change, she'd be home by lunchtime. Rosedale Manor was an assisted-living facility across the street from Edmonton General Hospital. Vivian's mother, Bea Peterson, was in her wheelchair, awaiting Kala in the downstairs living room near the gas fireplace. The room was bright and warmer than Kala liked, especially as fatigue was setting in. She'd be better off interviewing Bea outside in the fresh air but knew that would never happen.

"Thank you for seeing me." Kala sat on the leather couch across from her. "I'm so sorry for your loss."

Bea's head wobbled on her long neck and one eye twitched behind thick lenses. "I never thought Vivian would go before me. When will she be coming home so we can bury her?"

"I think soon but I'm not the one to decide. I can tell you that the length of time we keep the body is not unusual in cases such as Vivian's."

"I'd like to have gone to Kingston but my doctor forbade the travel. Vivian's father died ten months ago or I know wild horses wouldn't have kept him away." Her hands trembled and she laced her fingers and folded them in her lap. "Did she suffer?"

"No. She died quickly and likely didn't know what was happening." Kala spoke with certainty even though she had no true way of knowing. What good would it have done now to distress this woman further?

"Thank God for that."

"Can you tell me anything that could help us to find Vivian's killer?"

"Such as?"

"How she and Tristan were getting along, other relationships she was involved in, her state of mind this past while, or whatever you can remember her telling you about her life."

"Vivian was happy about the baby, which I have to say came as something of a surprise."

"How so?"

"Vivie never wanted kids. Liked being free and unfettered."

"Did she feel the same way about her marriage?"

Bea smiled. "She always was a hard one to pin down. Her dad spoiled her something rotten, you see, and made her into his princess. Bothered me now and then but they were two of a kind, really. My role was to be their cheerleader, which I accepted and grew okay with over time because I never liked the limelight. They were a pair of peacocks, if you know what I mean."

"I think I do." Kala reached over and rested a hand on Bea's hands. They felt bony and frail and were shaking uncontrollably under her touch. "I hate to have to ask you this, but was your daughter having an affair last year?"

Bea's right leg began jumping involuntarily but she met Kala's eyes without acknowledging her body's betrayal. "If she was, she never told me.

However, it wouldn't surprise me. She was a lot like her daddy, as I already said."

"What did you think about Tristan and how he treated Vivian? Were they good together?"

"Tristan?" Her smile returned. "Such a thoughtful man. He calls me every day from Kingston, you know. He would have made such a good father." Tears welled in her eyes. "Vivian didn't know what a decent man she had and gave him a bit of a hard time before she got pregnant. She thought he was a failure because he wasn't bringing in much money, but he had a new book idea that he told me would put him back on the bestseller list. His agent was excited too. Vivian would have settled down once everything fell into place."

"Were Tristan and Vivian fighting?"

"Well now, if they were, it was behind them. Vivian had a sharp tongue and never hesitated to tell Tristan that he had to get his act together, but he never let on that it bothered him. At least not in front of me. As for arguments behind closed doors, I never pried."

"And you're certain you didn't know if Vivian was having an affair?"

Bea pursed her lips and rubbed a hand jerkily across her eyes. "I can't say anything for sure about what Vivian was up to after she left home. I only knew what she wanted me to know. The closest she might have come to telling me her plans was on our last visit when she said that she was waiting for the right time. It was like she was thinking out loud, but when I asked her what she meant by that, she clammed up.

Then she laughed like she did when she was working to wrap me around her little finger and said, 'But you'll never judge me, right, Mommy?' and she laid her head on my arm like she did when she was little and I patted her hair. That's one of my last memories of her. It's how I'm going to remember her."

Kala met Officer Gaudette in front of the nursing home and they compared notes as she sped across town to the airport, letting Kala out in the drop-off zone. Before Kala stepped out of the car, Gaudette promised to send everything they gleaned from the computers, including a search for the name of the man with whom Vivian had allegedly been having an affair the year before.

"You've been a great help," said Kala, shaking Gaudette's hand. "I'll be waiting to see what else you uncover."

"I should have something to you by the end of the week. If McKenna killed his wife, we'll do all we can to get the prosecution."

Kala had to run down the corridor before the door to the WestJet plane closed and only just made it. She sank into her seat, legs aching, out of breath, but happy to be going home. The flight would give her lots of time to read through Vivian's Day-timer and search for signs of the mystery man. She'd also type up a report with what little she'd learned so far. All in all, the trip had given some new insight into Vivian and her marriage that Kala was eager to share with Gundersund and the team.

CHAPTER THIRTY-TWO

Lauren thought that she and Tristan made a fine pair when they finally went outside at 2:00 to shovel the snow, which had stopped falling an hour before. She was still feeling the effects of the hangover and Tristan had the vacant, dishevelled look of a man barely hanging on. He'd slept through breakfast and had only gotten out of bed when Evelyn banged on his door.

Adam's car was nearest to the road and he went out before them to clear it off and warm up the interior. Mona, with Evelyn on her arm, tromped through the snow ten minutes later and the three of them drove off for groceries and a liquor store run.

Your bad knee didn't stop you from an outing to the shops, Lauren thought.

"Don't expect us back until late in the afternoon," Adam said as he helped Evelyn into the front passenger seat. "We'll stop somewhere for lunch first."

Tristan leaned on his shovel and watched them go. "The terrible trio departs while the dastardly duo is left to clear out the laneway. You've heard that Mother is moving to Vancouver to be close to them?"

"She told me this morning. Saint Mona's doing, if I had to bet."

"Adam's not as enthused."

"I imagine you'll be getting many visits, too."

"I might need to move east." He pulled a half-smoked joint out of his jacket pocket and turned out of the wind to light up.

"A little hair of the dog?" he asked Lauren, offering her the joint after he'd taken a long toke.

"No, thanks. Keeping a clear head." She hadn't even smoked a cigarette in a week, but didn't want to jinx herself by admitting she was trying to quit.

"Suit yourself."

Between them, they cleared the driveway and the walkway in under an hour because the snow was light and easily removed. The snowplow hadn't been by so the end of the laneway wasn't filled in yet, making their lives easier. The plow operators were probably waiting to do the crescents and side streets until after the second storm dropped its load later in the day and overnight.

Lauren had begun to feel better. Surprisingly, the bracing air and exertion were becoming her hangover tonic. The cloud cover was blocking out the sun and the dull light was keeping the throbbing behind her eyes at an acceptable level. She called Tristan over to her at the end of the drive. "Are you okay to start on the Orlovs' driveway now?"

"I thought you wanted to get into their house?"

"I do, but if we shovel their driveway Boris might let you in to look at his birdhouses."

"Leaving you free to sneak upstairs and root around."

"The best plans are simple ones."

"Can't argue."

They worked alongside each other, heaving snow onto the already substantial banks lining the Orlovs' driveway. Partway up the drive, Lauren lifted her head and spotted Boris in the living-room window, watching them work, but he didn't return her wave before he disappeared deeper into the room. By the time she and Tristan reached the house, they were both sweating under their toques and down jackets, Lauren's having been borrowed from Evelyn's closet.

"I vote we go home and forget about the Orlovs," Tristan said. "I could do with a shower."

"You promised you'd help me with this."

"With what, exactly? If by some bizarre twist in the universe, Boris Orlov killed Zoe and now Vivian, which stretches incredibility to the breaking point, and oh yeah, his wife is really his sister and they've been KGB spies living next door for thirty years with a ham radio in the attic transmitting the goings-on of the neighbours to Mother Russia, then what are we waiting for? You and I are fully equipped to bring the two pinko spies in from the cold and turn them in to law enforcement."

"I know you think I'm being paranoid, but I'm worried. Something isn't right."

"Good Christ Almighty, Lauren." He scowled at her and dropped his shovel before stomping his way over to the Orlovs' side door and pounding on it with his fist. "Hello, anybody home?" he yelled.

She had no choice but to follow and hope that he didn't say something stupid. Nobody answered his knocks and Tristan half-turned to look back at her with a grin on his face. "Maybe they're up in the attic plotting the downfall of the West." Before he could take a step toward her, the door swung open and Boris was filling the entrance staring at them. He hadn't shaved and grey stubble marked his cheeks and chin. His eyes were steady, unblinking like a snake.

The bravado drooped out of Tristan's shoulders. "Hey Boris," he said. "How's it going, man?"

"Good."

Lauren stepped forward and nudged Tristan aside. "We got the last layer of snow off your drive and we'll be back to clear it again after the next storm ends. We were wondering how Antonia's doing. Does she need to go to the grocery store or anything?"

"No. We have lots of food."

"Is she up and about yet? Mother's been asking when she's coming over to visit."

"She's in the kitchen drinking tea. Would you like to say hello?"

Lauren blinked. "Why yes, we would."

She felt Tristan poke her in the side through her jacket but ignored him and followed Boris into the house. Tristan came too and they took off their boots and entered the kitchen where Antonia was sitting at the table with a pot of tea and a half-full cup in front of her. She was wearing a salmon-pink housecoat with black slippers on her swollen feet and her hair was hidden under a silk scarf tied at the nape of her neck. She nodded and smiled at them, her eyes darting between them and Boris like a little mouse on high alert.

"So good to see you up," said Lauren, moving closer to the table. "How're you feeling, Antonia?"

"Goot. I'm goot." Antonia stretched her neck to see past Lauren to Boris, who was leaning against the counter.

Lauren made another effort to draw her out. "Mother wonders when you'll be over for tea."

"Storm coming," said Antonia. "Will be bad one."

Lauren turned and looked at Tristan. He was standing in the doorway with his toque in his hands looking uncomfortable. He caught her eyes and coughed. "I'd love to see your birdhouses, Boris."

Boris scratched his head. "They're not put together yet. I have to go out later to get supplies at the hardware store. Come back another time."

"Sure. I could do that."

Lauren made a face at Tristan but he didn't take the hint and push the issue. Neither Boris nor Antonia made any move to ask them to sit down or to have tea and she felt her opportunity to speak alone with Antonia slip away.

Tristan shoved his toque onto his head. "I'll tell Evelyn that you'll be over after the storm," he said. "Coming, sis?"

Boris followed them to the door. "Antonia's had the flu but is getting back on her feet. Let your mother know we'll come by to help her out when you've all gone home."

Lauren and Tristan didn't speak again until they'd crossed the yard and were back in their own driveway.

"She doesn't seem in distress," offered Tristan, using his I-told-you-so voice.

"I'm not so sure. Boris wouldn't leave us alone with her, did you notice?"

"I didn't take it that way."

"I haven't got an explanation yet for the photo of her with two children and another man, or the photo of her with another kid who looks a lot like Boris, whom she said was her brother."

"She was hallucinating. You told me yourself that she appeared drugged."

"I'd still like to get her alone." Lauren walked ahead of him up the steps. "I just have to work out how."

Boris watched David's kids walk across the snowy lawn to their driveway where they stopped to talk. The girl, Lauren, who never seemed comfortable inside her own skin, had a sour expression on her face and glanced toward his house a couple of times as she said something to her brother. Boris stepped closer to the window, trying to read her lips but without success. He watched as the brother crossed back to the driveway and picked up the shovels from where they'd left them on the ground. He walked past his sister and leaned the shovels against the garage before following her inside the front door. Boris waited until he was certain the McKenna kids weren't coming outside again before he returned to the kitchen.

"Would you like something to eat?" he asked Antonia in English.

"Ya, thank you, Boris."

"I'll make some scrambled eggs and toast. Then you can go back to bed for an afternoon nap while I go out for a while. I have to get something for supper and buy more paint."

"For the birdhouses."

"I'm almost done but didn't want to show them to anybody yet."

After they finished lunch, he helped her up from the chair and half-carried her up the stairs to her room, his good arm around her waist. She was lighter than he remembered, the two weeks in bed taking their toll. The first week, she'd refused to eat for six straight days, turning her head away from him when he entered her room even though he'd told her over and over that this was for her own good. The steady diet of drugs hadn't helped her appetite and he'd been lessening the dosage the last couple of days. She seemed docile and sweet but he suspected that she was waiting to see his next move before making her own.

She swallowed the pills that he handed her without resisting this time. She'd sleep while he was gone but not as deeply or as long as the last few weeks. He knew the police would be returning soon to question her and he couldn't afford to keep her under much longer. He'd have to keep a watchful eye and hope she towed the party line. He smiled grimly at the reference to his Communist homeland and other times best forgotten.

His wrist was throbbing this morning, along with his aching ribs and leg, but he'd ignore the pain. He'd get a rest in after he returned from the store before Antonia woke up toward suppertime. She needed a bath and he'd have to manage getting her into the tub with one arm.

His sixth sense told him that Antonia was keeping something from him. Finding her holding on to the photo from the dresser had been odd. He knew that he should have gotten rid of the pictures long ago but she'd begged him not to and he couldn't deny her at the time. The pictures had faded into the room and he'd forgotten they were even there. He'd thought she had as well.

Her eyes were closed and she was snoring softly when he left her room and went into his own for a heavier sweater. If he hadn't promised the birdhouses for the weekend, he'd have stayed home, but with the storm coming this might be his last opportunity for a while to get the red paint for the trim. It took him several tries to put on the sweater and his outdoor clothes and boots. The clouds were lower in the sky and had turned from light grey to gunmetal when he finally stepped outside. A sharp wind was blowing in from the east and the first flakes of snow were caught in its slanting force. He turned to face the wind and closed his eyes, enjoying the damp coolness rocking his body and making him stagger backward half a step. *This is what it feels like to be alive*, he thought.

The two McKenna kids had done an adequate job clearing out his driveway and he supposed he owed them his thanks. He could have taken a cab again to the store, but decided to take his car, which he kept in the unheated garage at the head of the drive. He eased the old Buick out of the garage and stopped, letting the engine warm up enough to melt the layer of frost on the inside of the windshield. He'd worried that the car battery might have died and was thankful the engine turned over without much coaxing. He backed slowly down the driveway and onto the road using his one hand on the wheel. Sweat beaded on his forehead from the exertion but he wasn't done yet. He'd have to carefully navigate the icy streets and hope to God that he didn't get stuck anywhere. With luck, he'd be back home within three quarters of an hour.

As he pulled onto Grenville Crescent, he kept his eyes scanning the road for black ice and so didn't see Lauren McKenna standing in her living-room window, watching his slow progress down the street. If he'd seen her look from his car across the yard to his house, he might have had second thoughts about his shopping trip into town.

CHAPTER THIRTY-THREE

Kala retrieved her truck from long-term parking at the Toronto airport late that morning and took Highway 401 home to Kingston. The snow had tapered off by the time she pulled onto Old Front Road soon after lunchtime. The snowplow hadn't made it this far yet but her truck had little difficulty cutting through the drifting snow. She craned her neck to look up Gundersund's driveway but his car was gone and she remembered that he was at headquarters. Dawn was at school and only Taiku greeted her at the door. She let him out for a run around the yard before she took the stairs two at a time, stripping off her clothes as she went. A quick shower and a fresh change of clothes in her overnight bag and she was ready when Rouleau pulled into the driveway half an hour later. She waved to him from the window and wrote a note for Dawn before she locked up the house and joined Rouleau in his idling car.

"Sorry to drag you out of town again so soon," he said while backing out of the driveway.

"I don't mind." *Except for not seeing Dawn.* Gundersund had said he'd keep track of her one more evening if they didn't make it back so she could relax and concentrate on the case. "How do you know this Romanian cop. Petran …?"

"Petran Albescu. We worked together on a war crimes case in Serbia about twelve years ago and stayed friends."

"But he's from Romania?"

"Yes. We were part of an international working group headed up by Department of Justice lawyers from each country."

"He's the one you called about the Orlovs?"

Rouleau nodded. "I have no idea what he wants to tell us but he didn't feel comfortable doing it over the phone. A lifetime of being watched and eavesdropped on has made the older generation of Romanians cautious to the point of paranoia. Lord knows, the state has given them good reason."

"Not difficult to understand their reactions."

Rouleau turned on the radio and they listened to the end of a song followed by the weather report. "Good that Petran's arriving mid-afternoon. I don't expect the meeting will take more than an hour and we might make it home before the storm hits in full force," he said. "I don't relish driving home in a blizzard."

"I brought an overnight bag in case we have to stay but I'd rather come home if we're able." She glanced over at his profile. "You seem in a good mood this morning. Any reason?"

"Nothing special. Happy for a day out of the office."

She smiled at him. "It's been a while since we were on the road together."

The drive was uneventful and they reached the outskirts of Montreal half an hour before Petran's arrival time. Rouleau left Autoroute 20 and merged onto Chemin Herron. At the roundabout, he took the Autoroute 520 east exit and less than a kilometre farther on, the Romeo-Vachon north exit to the Pierre Elliott Trudeau Airport. Rouleau pulled into the dropoff/pickup zone and pulled out his cellphone. "Petran's plane landed fifteen minutes ago and he's on his way out the main door. I'm guessing he only brought carry-on so we should see him any minute. I'll send him a text to let him know we're here."

"What does he look like?" Kala asked.

Rouleau looked up from his phone. "Last time I saw him, he had thick black hair but that was ten years ago. He has pale-blue eyes and usually wears a beard. Medium height and build."

"I'll keep an eye out."

"And I'll finish this text."

Petran was as Rouleau had described him, although his thick black hair and beard were now grey and his blue eyes were both kind and tired. Rouleau and Petran hugged and slapped one another on the back and hugged again. Kala shook his hand and climbed into the back seat so that he and Rouleau could catch up.

"Where to?" Rouleau asked.

"I'm booked at the Sheraton, which is close by. I'll get some sleep and catch the morning flight back. I've made this trip many times before."

Kala let her mind wander as the two men exchanged their news on the short drive to the hotel. She was pleased to see the snow holding off and hoped they'd be able to make the trip home after the meeting. The exhaustion of the last few days was beginning to catch up with her and the car stopping in the hotel parking lot jolted her awake from a state of half sleep. Rouleau decided Petran should check in and drop off his bag while they waited for him in the restaurant.

"Seems like a nice man," she commented after the waitress handed them menus.

"First rate."

"Does he have a family?"

"He's married with two grown sons who are also cops. His wife is a judge so they're immersed in crime and punishment, you could say."

They ordered coffee and club sandwiches once Petran arrived. He waited until after they'd eaten and gotten refills of coffee before he handed Rouleau a file folder. They were seated next to the fireplace away from two other tables of customers and Petran appeared satisfied that he could talk freely without being overheard.

"When I got your call, Jacques, I had a team search through the files kept on its citizens during the Ceauşescu regime. It took some digging because they aren't digitalized, but we found the files on both Boris and his sister."

"Sister?"

"Antonia Vasilescu is her married name. From what you told me, she reverted to her maiden name when she and her brother moved to Canada."

"Necessary, since she and Boris were passing themselves off as a married couple to the neighbours."

"Boris had a past he was eager to bury back in Romania. He was a member of the Secretariat. The secret police. He was a skilled and cold-blooded interrogator, feared by Ceauşescu's enemies, who often disappeared into the prisons never to emerge." Petran's eyes glinted with renewed energy. "As you can imagine, we are very interested in having Boris Orlov extradited to Romania to be tried for war crimes, including the torture and murder of hundreds of men and women. We have witnesses who will testify but they're getting older and time is of the essence. I brought this file to you personally so that you know what we are dealing with and to let you know that we're preparing to apply for his extradition once we confirm his identity."

Kala met Rouleau's eyes and took a moment to absorb the horror of what he'd told them. She asked, "Was Antonia also part of the Secretariat?"

Petran turned his gaze on her. "No. The opposite, in fact. Her husband, Cezar Vasilescu, was a dissident who worked to oust Ceauşescu. While typewriters were confiscated by the state, Cezar kept one hidden away and used it to type up newsletters to expose the atrocities going on under Ceauşescu."

"What happened to him?"

"Cezar Vasilescu was arrested and sent to Râmnicu Sărat prison, where he was tortured and died two years later."

"Don't tell me that Boris tortured his own brother-in-law," said Rouleau, giving voice to Kala's own terrible thought.

"Not that we're aware of. Cezar and Antonia had two children and we don't have the details on what happened to them, although we know they went into an orphanage a year after their father went to prison. This wasn't uncommon. Destitute parents would put their children in the orphanage for a period of time and take them out when they were able to look after them financially."

"Boris and Antonia didn't arrive in Canada with children," said Kala. "I wonder what happened to them."

"The notes in her file don't keep track of the children, but we know that she cleaned houses in Bucharest after moving into a housing complex when her own home was bulldozed soon after Cezar was arrested. A little over two years later, Antonia was admitted to a mental institution after she received the news that Cezar had died." Petran removed his reading glasses and sighed. "Our mental institutions were considered worse than the prisons in some respects, and sadly, many haven't advanced as they should. They were dumping grounds for the mentally ill but also housed the elderly or spouses who were left bereft. This could have been the case for Antonia."

"Perhaps the children went into the orphanage when Antonia went into the mental institution," said Rouleau.

Petran checked his notes. "They were in the orphanage six months before she was admitted. More likely poverty was the reason she put them into the orphanage and she intended to bring them home when she could. Somehow, they were adopted out from under her while she was ill. Boris rescued her from the asylum after Ceaușescu and his wife were executed on Christmas Day 1989, and got her out of the country." He put a black-and-white photograph on the table between Rouleau and Kala. "This is Boris Orlov when he was living in Romania some thirty years ago. Can you tell if it is the same man who lives in Kingston?"

Kala picked up the picture and studied the man's features, comparing them to the man she'd interviewed in his kitchen only days before. "They have the same bone structure and eyes. I would say they are the same man."

Petran smiled. "A good start. I will send word to my colleague in Bucharest to organize the survivors from that time. I'll need you to send current photos and video if possible."

"I can arrange this," said Rouleau. "Will you be coming with us to Kingston to see him for yourself?"

"Next trip. I'm due back in Romania tomorrow for another pressing court case but I'll be in Canada next week with a witness if he's able to travel." He checked his watch. "I have a meeting about another matter in an hour so this trip is killing two birds, so to speak."

Kala considered what Antonia's tragic history and Boris's brutal past had to do with the murders of Zoe Delgado and Vivian McKenna. Rouleau must have been on the same wavelength. He said, "We don't have any evidence that Boris Orlov murdered two women in Kingston, but we now know he was capable. The coincidence of him living next door to the location of Zoe's murder and being home when

Vivian left for her walk … at the very least, we need to bring him in for questioning. We should have enough to get a search warrant."

"You might want to hold off on a search. This could alert him to something more going on. He's nobody's fool," said Petran.

"I understand."

Petran nodded. "Boris had no conscience when he worked in the prisons. He could have killed those two women without losing a wink of sleep. We need a few weeks to lay the groundwork for his extradition at our end. We have much paperwork to complete and our governments must get involved in the process."

Rouleau said, "Of course. We'll keep our inquiries strictly to the murder investigations when we approach him and Antonia. I'll have the photos and video of him taken without them knowing."

"Perfect." Petran's phone rang and he excused himself to return to his room. After he'd gone, Kala looked out the window. "We could start back to Kingston," she said. "The storm is holding off and hopefully we'll be home before the worst of it."

Rouleau checked the weather app on his phone. "The snow starts in Kingston around seven tonight according to this and is sweeping up from the southeast. You're eager to get back?"

"Yes. I have an uneasy feeling and I'm not sure if it's about the case or Dawn. Maybe both."

"Then let me pay the bill and I'll tell Petran that we're leaving."

CHAPTER THIRTY-FOUR

Lauren's phone beeped to let her know she'd received a text. She stepped back from the window and clicked on the message from Matt.

Need to see you before you leave Kingston.

She hesitated as she thought about replying before tossing the phone onto the end table. What would be the use of seeing him again? She didn't think her heart could bear another round of longing and rejection, especially if Matt was only coming around because he wanted her to pin Zoe's murder on Tristan. She had no illusions about his sudden interest, even factoring in his passionate kiss. She'd used and been used enough to know.

She looked out the window again and Boris Orlov's car had rounded the corner and disappeared from sight. Even if he was only gone to the store, she should have time to whip in and out of his house. She could say that her mother had sent her over if he came home before she left. Perhaps she was being crazy, but she couldn't get Antonia's sad, drugged eyes out of her head. She had to know what was going on — whether Antonia was being held captive by Boris, for that was how it seemed, and even more far-fetched, perhaps, was whether he'd killed Zoe and Vivian. She shook her head at the thought, because once articulated, the ideas were preposterous. Boris had gone fishing with her father and they'd built furniture in the back workshop together, drank beer in the sunshine in lawn chairs, and laughed at each other's jokes. Her dad knew Boris better than anybody and would have seen signs.

He'd have known.

Even so, she put on her mother's winter coat and boots and crossed the lawn to stand at the Orlovs' side door one more time. She knocked and rang the bell and waited, finally peering in through the lace curtain on the window and trying the door knob without success. She stood thinking for a frustrated moment and decided to try the front door, which Boris and Antonia rarely used. She was careful not to create new boot prints as she made her way around the house and up the front steps. At the top step, she looked up and down the street feeling exposed and jumpy. No sign of Boris returning home so she reached for the door and tried the handle. Surprise made her cry out in triumph as the knob turned and the door swung open.

The lights were off in the hallway leading to the staircase and she didn't dare turn any on. She took off her boots and left them tucked in next to the umbrella stand, out of sight if Boris came home, although if she was still in the house, he'd find out soon enough even without seeing her boots. She first looked in the kitchen for Antonia. The teapot and mug remained on the table but Antonia wasn't sitting in her chair.

Lauren retraced her steps and climbed the stairs in the murky grey light, pausing on the landing before walking directly to Antonia's bedroom at the end of the corridor. The door was pulled closed and she pushed it open while calling Antonia's name. It took a few seconds for her eyes to adjust to the darkness in the room as she crossed the carpet to the bed.

Antonia was lying flat on her back but her eyes were open and staring up at her. "You came back," she said and offered a toothless grin. Her dentures were resting in a glass of water on the bedside table.

"I came to make sure you're feeling better." Now that Lauren was standing a second time in this old woman's bedroom, she began to feel foolish. *What am I doing here snooping like a neurotic neighbour?*

"I pretend to swallow pills." Antonia's eyes glinted, looking sly and secretive in the light from the gap in the curtains. "Boris can't know."

Lauren stepped closer. Without her teeth, Antonia's words were slurred and wet with saliva. "Of course not. What kind of pills is he giving you?"

"To sleep. Punish me ... but he's wrong ... nobody."

"Wrong?"

"I watch her walk from your house. She wear blue coat and boots with heels. No hat. Red scarf."

Lauren's heartbeat quickened. "You watched Vivian leave on her walk that day? The day she was killed?"

"Went to put on my coat and boots. I run to catch sight of her again. Can't tell who she is with. They at Portsmouth Street, walking fast."

"Did she leave the house with the other person or meet them along the way."

"Not see."

"Was it a man or a woman?"

Antonia shook her head and her mouth settled into a stubborn line. She closed her eyes.

"What way did they turn on Portsmouth?"

"Left."

They could have been going toward Sherwood Drive and the Rideau Trail. Lauren wanted to shake her and scream at her to keep talking. How could she have kept silent all this time about Vivian's last moments alive? What else was Antonia hiding?

"Antonia, why is Boris giving you sleeping pills during the day?"

Silence.

"Is he your brother?"

"Boris."

His name spoken without expression. Lauren was aware of the clock ticking and the cold in the room that made her shiver even through the down of her mother's winter jacket. She looked desperately around the room and her gaze landed on the photo of the couple with the two children. She strode the short distance to the dresser and picked it up.

"Are these your children, Antonia? What happened to them?" She held the picture at chest level and moved closer to the bed.

Antonia reached out one shaky hand for the photo. Tears seeped out of the sides of her eyes and trickled down her cheeks onto the pillow. "Sorry, sorry, sorry," she chanted. "Sorry, sorry, sorry."

"Why are you sorry? What happened to your family?"

"Cezar. I tell Boris you are in resistance and he … tell them. My fault. My fault."

"Boris killed Cezar?"

Antonia snatched the photo from her hand and cradled it against her breasts. "My children. All gone. My fault." She began rocking from side to side and moaning like a wounded animal. She lapsed into Romanian between guttural screeches that made the hair on Lauren's arms and neck stand on end.

Lauren wanted to run out of the bedroom and out of the house but she couldn't make her feet move. Antonia's distress was rising in volume and she felt terribly responsible. She squatted down next to the bed and rubbed Antonia's arm through her thin nightgown. "Everything's okay," she said. "Hush now. I'm leaving. I'm sorry to have brought back this pain. Hush. It's going to be okay."

Antonia turned her face to Lauren and gripped on to her wrist with claw-like fingers that dug into her flesh. "Didn't know what I was doing. I thought was in Romania and she was taking my children. I took knife from back shed to stop her …" Antonia stopped and looked toward the door. Her eyes grew large and frightened. She half rose from her lying position. "Boris home. Quick! Hide! Can't find you here."

"Where?"

"In closet. Go!"

"But this is craz—" Lauren took another look at the terror on Antonia's face and cut herself off. She skittered across the bedroom and into the closet, pushing aside shoes and bags to squeeze in under the clothes swinging on hangers. She listened for noises downstairs. *Maybe she's making it up*, she thought. *"I took the knife to stop her"*? Zoe had been killed with a knife. Antonia followed Vivian and someone else the afternoon she went missing.

The dark claustrophobic closet and the smell of mothballs were making her lightheaded. Panic coursed through her and she felt as if she were suffocating. Frantic, she pushed the door open. She scanned the room before straightening from her crouched position and lurching out of her hiding place. Antonia was watching her from the bed, wide-eyed and silent. Lauren started toward the door but stopped when she heard footsteps crossing the floor in the downstairs hallway and then starting heavily up the stairs. Antonia hissed at her to hide.

Lauren dove back into the closet and pulled the door closed behind her.

Boris reached the doorway to his sister's room and looked in. She was still sleeping, flat on her back, hands folded on top of the covers. The pills should keep her that way until suppertime and he'd make a tray to bring upstairs. She'd be groggy and it would be easier to feed her in her room than to negotiate the stairs supporting her with his one good arm.

He took a step into the room and watched her lying so peacefully and wondered how long he could carry this off before the police were back to talk to her. She was slipping into the past more and more now but maybe when he stopped feeding her sleeping pills and anti-anxiety medicine, she'd come back to herself. She'd insisted she hadn't followed Vivian McKenna up the Rideau Trail, but her grasp on reality was not good at the best of times. He doubted if she'd remember killing this second one. She'd only admitted to Zoe Delgado because he'd found her washing the blood out of her clothes in their kitchen sink and even at that, she hadn't fully understood what she'd done for several weeks. A psychotic break. She'd had one in Romania and he knew the signs. He hadn't dared risk sending her back to the hospital in Kingston. Who knew what she would tell them? He couldn't take the risk.

In a moment of weakness, several months after the murder, he'd told David that Antonia had killed the Delgado girl and regretted it ever after. It had been after David had confessed to him about moving her body. They'd both had secrets to conceal and agreed to keep silent unless the wrong person was charged because Antonia would have died trapped in another asylum. He'd convinced David of this and played on his goodness and compassion. David had helped to keep an eye on her all these years but she'd fooled them again when he'd gone into the hospital this last time. Boris had thought she was cured of the monsters in her head and that was his mistake.

He'd been wrong and now he had to find a way to keep her safe.

Her breathing looked strong and steady and he turned to leave, pausing when he heard a noise.

He looked back into the semi-dark room. Antonia was rolling onto her side and the sheets rustled as she moved. He'd thought the noise had come from inside the wall but perhaps he'd heard a mouse. He'd have to check the traps later.

He kept walking down the hall, stopping for a piss in the bathroom before continuing on downstairs. He was in the kitchen filling the kettle for a cup of instant coffee when the phone rang. Caller ID gave the number as private and he let it go to voicemail. A few seconds later and the phone rang again with the same private ID. A telemarketer would not call back so soon. He picked up and listened. The caller greeted him in Romanian and with sick trepidation Boris said his name and returned the good afternoon. Then he listened without interrupting, thanking the voice on the other end before hanging up. He swore and staggered back a step, grabbing on to the counter to keep himself upright. He closed his eyes and inhaled deep breaths to steady his heart. *Everyone pays the piper eventually. You are no different.* A fatalistic calmness stole over him. His old contacts had come through even after all these years. *Finishing the circle. Paying the last debt.*

He stood motionless looking at the paint cans where he'd left them on the floor while he let the caller's words sink in. A surge of anger made him straighten his shoulders and slap his hand against the wall. War crimes, his contact had called them. What did this pampered generation know about surviving a brutal regime when a person was forced to do whatever it took to stay alive, including selling out their own sister's husband?

I've paid my debt to you, Cezar. I saved Antonia from the mental institution and gave her a life. She forgave my betrayal of you.

He knew that he was lying to himself. If she'd known that he had sold her children while she was inside, she would never have come with him to Canada. She would have damned him to hell.

If there is a God, I am doomed.

He'd turn eighty on Saturday so he supposed this was as good a time as any for the truth to come crawling out of its hiding place. Yet he would not become one of the broken old men he'd seen on trial with stoic, resigned faces in front of television cameras and reporters, being condemned by people in middle-class houses with jobs and two cars in the garage and soft bellies. People who'd never had to choose between selling their soul to stay alive and eternal darkness. People who lived in freedom that they thought would last forever.

He supposed there was nothing for it but to end this quickly as he'd planned when the day came.

It is time for the screaming faces to stop haunting my dreams.

He climbed the basement stairs and entered his workshop, patting the roof of one of his birdhouses as he walked past. They'd have to do without red trim, but so be it. He pulled a chair over to the centre of the room and climbed up. The black PSM pistol was wrapped in the cloth tucked up in the rafters. When he was a trusted interrogator, he'd been given the Russian handgun for protection and smuggled it into Canada before all the airport security that would have made its transport impossible. He reached up and took down a package containing a round of spitzer-pointed high-velocity bullets. They were capable of penetrating forty-five layers of Kevlar soft body armour at close distances and he trusted they were up to this final task. He loaded the bullets into the eight-round magazine and walked wearily upstairs to the kitchen.

He thought about making a final meal for Antonia: baked salmon in white wine and herbs, small roast potatoes and turnip mixed with carrots as she liked to cook on special occasions, but what would be the point of prolonging the last moment? Besides, she had an uncanny intuitiveness and would know that he was up to something. He didn't want to deal with her hysteria, or worse, whimpering. No, far easier to make a swift end now while he had the wherewithal to carry out what needed to be done. If he was lucky, she'd still be asleep.

When he reached Antonia's bedroom, she was sitting up holding the photo of Cezar, Gabriela, and Iuliu in her hands resting on the blanket in front of her.

She knows what I am about to do, he thought.

"Remember how happy we were?" she asked. Her eyes were bright and a red flush in her cheeks made her look younger, like the woman she'd once been back in Romania before she'd lost Cezar and her children.

"Yes," he lied because he couldn't remember ever being truly happy. He kept the gun hidden behind his back and her eyes went to his arm and back to his face.

"I told the girl to go into the closet," she said, switching to Romanian. She held up a hand and pointed. "It's time for her to go home."

Boris looked toward the closet. The door wasn't completely closed and he knew it had been. He strode across the room and pulled the door open with his hand while still holding the pistol. The McKenna daughter was crouched in amongst the shoes looking up at him like a scared rabbit.

"Come out," he ordered.

She looked at the gun in his hand and cowered back into the closet.

He softened his voice. "I won't hurt you. You need to go home now." It didn't matter how she'd come to be in Antonia's closet or why.

His words seemed to reassure her and she scrambled out to stand in front of him. "What are you going to do?" she asked. She looked like a child waif, her short white hair standing every which way, her eyes wide and scared.

"My dear, you do not need to concern yourself." He kept the gun pointed at the floor.

"Let me take Antonia with me to visit my mother." She begged him with her eyes.

"Antonia will be staying with me."

The girl was hesitating and he respected her concern for his sister even when she had to know the risk of standing her ground. He loosened his grip on the gun and remembered that David had loved her the best. David had blamed himself for not standing up to Evelyn, as cold a mother as Boris had ever seen, and he had known some hardened women in his day.

"Antonia and I are old and not afraid of what is to come. You can tell your brother Tristan that she is sorry for letting the police think he killed his girlfriend and wife. She's responsible and regrets not coming forward, but you must understand that she's been ill. She has episodes. Psychotic breaks, the doctors call them. I've tried to protect her. Now, you must leave. Your father would not forgive me if I let any harm come to you."

The girl took one last look toward the bed and back at him. "Is there nothing I can do to change your mind?" she whispered.

"Don't concern yourself. This ending was set in motion many years ago and understand that this is for the best. Antonia and I are tired of suffering. We are both ready."

He watched her leave the room, only glancing back once, and heard her footsteps running down the stairs. He could follow her and lock the door, but he had enough time to do what he had to do without locking anybody out.

He crossed to the bed and kissed Antonia on the forehead. She looked up at him, trusting and silent. He hoped that she forgave him. "I love you, my little sister," he said. He lifted the gun from his side and shot her in the head so quickly that her mouth was still forming the words *I love you* back. Then he bent and kissed her bloody cheek before he lay down next to her with his head leaning against the headboard and his body resting against hers. He placed the pistol under his chin and welcomed the final darkness.

CHAPTER THIRTY-FIVE

Rouleau found a parking spot behind a police cruiser, rested his hands on the steering wheel, and turned his head to look at Stonechild. "Well, we got here in record time. Petran will have wasted a trip if this turns out to be true. Are you set?"

"As set as I'll ever be."

The street was choked with first-response vehicles; two ambulances, a firetruck with red lights flashing, police cars, and reporters and cameramen setting up across the road from the Orlovs'. Darkness had fallen and snowflakes tumbled to earth in the yellow glow of the streetlights. They met Bennett outside the house.

"What have we got?" asked Rouleau.

"Murder suicide. Boris Orlov shot his wife and then himself."

"Antonia was his sister," said Stonechild, "not his wife."

"Who found them?" asked Rouleau.

"Lauren McKenna called it in. We haven't taken her statement yet but she's at her home next door waiting for one of us to go over. She said that Boris talked to her before he did this and she's quite shaken up. Woodhouse and Gundersund are inside the Orlov house."

"Did he leave a note?"

"Nothing."

"I could speak with Lauren," Stonechild offered. "I interviewed her before and we seemed to develop a rapport."

Rouleau liked the idea but thought he should clear it with Woodhouse, since he was still the lead investigator. "Let's have a look inside first."

The house was constructed in the 1950s with furnishings from the '70s: an old brown couch covered in a crocheted afghan, a fake leather recliner, round coiled rug in blue and white in the living room, yellow Formica table with chrome legs and four chairs covered in red dahlia print, and ancient white appliances in the kitchen. Dust had gathered in the corners of the rooms and on the stairs, which he climbed with Stonechild right behind him. They met Woodhouse and Gundersund on the landing.

"It's grisly," said Woodhouse. "Looks like he shot her in the head first, lay down next to her and blew his own head off. The coroner and Forensics are in there now."

"A hunting rifle?" asked Rouleau.

"Pistol. Russian make. Bloody powerful, so he wasn't leaving anything to chance. We'll wait here if you want to have a look."

Rouleau and Stonechild continued to the bedroom but stayed near the doorway to let Forensics do their work unhindered. The smell of blood and death was strong and nauseating. They stood silently for a moment, taking in the scene.

"I'm going to stay and talk to the coroner. Why don't you go see if Woodhouse wants you to interview Lauren? Tell him that I'd like him to handle the media." Rouleau smiled at her. "That ought to make his delegation duties easier."

The direction of her gaze left the bed and swept the room before meeting his. She agreed, but without enthusiasm. Rouleau was well aware that she didn't like the idea of answering to Woodhouse, but knew that it was better for her to volunteer than for him to suggest, which Woodhouse would take as interfering.

After she'd gone, he surveyed the room again, taking in the details, getting a sense of Antonia in the simplicity of the furnishings and the unadorned walls, save for the religious art over her bed. The bedspread was an old quilt darned in places and faded so that the patchwork pattern looked washed out, except for the bright-red blood staining the top half. His eyes lifted to the heavy blood splatter on the headboard and wall before lowering to the bed and the position of their bodies and the tragedy of these old people with nobody left to grieve them. Brother and sister. Was Boris's final act one of love or self-preservation? Rouleau thought about the timing.

Somebody got to him.

Rouleau waited for the coroner to look up. He walked closer when Clarence nodded in his direction. "Are you certain this was a murder suicide?"

Clarence said, "I'll run some tests, but I'd say so. He was holding the gun and there's no sign of a struggle. The woman looks almost peaceful. The man is harder to tell. His face is gone." He held out a baggie. "She was holding this framed photograph when she was shot."

Rouleau took the bag and looked at the photo through the plastic. The man wasn't Boris but the woman resembled Antonia. This must be her husband who died in prison and the two children who disappeared. Petran had believed Boris to be a brutal monster capable of selling out his own family, torturing and killing prisoners, murdering Zoe Delgado and Vivian McKenna. They should not be feeling any sadness for his death.

If they'd died by Boris's hand as it certainly appeared, he must have received word that authorities were beginning proceedings to have him tried for war crimes. Petran's visit and what lay before him could not be a coincidence. Rouleau only wished that Boris had left a note confessing to the murders. He'd feel more confident closing their files with that final admission of guilt.

Kala filled in Gundersund on the information that she and Rouleau had received from Petran earlier that afternoon as they walked down the Orlov driveway and up the road to the McKenna house. She stopped talking when they reached the reporters lining up on the side of the road with cameras angled to film the Orlov house in the background even with visibility marred by the falling snow. Marci Stokes broke away from the cameraman she was talking with and caught up to them halfway between the two houses.

"Woodhouse is giving a statement in a few minutes," said Gundersund. "We have nothing to say."

"Is it true Boris Orlov murdered Zoe Delgado and Vivian McKenna?" asked Marci, shaking snow from her hair and wiping the melting flakes from her eyelashes with a gloved hand. "The rumour is that's the reason he killed himself."

"No comment."

"No comment because you don't know or no comment because you do?"

Kala and Gundersund kept walking and Marci fell back. "That woman's everywhere," mumbled Gundersund. "Like a bad penny."

"She's doing her job."

"The question is, where's she getting her information? She's at the crime scenes practically before we are."

A police officer was guarding the McKenna house. "They're all inside," he said and knocked on the door, stepping aside to let them by.

Adam McKenna ushered them into the hallway. "This is crazy," he said. "Boris must have killed Zoe and Vivian. We're reeling."

"We're here to speak with Lauren," Kala said.

"She's upstairs." He turned and saw his wife in the doorway. "Mona, can you go get her?"

He brought them into the living room where Tristan and Evelyn were sitting. Tristan stood and Evelyn remained seated. Her eyes were red from crying.

"I can't believe Boris would do such a thing. Poor Antonia. Why would he kill her?"

Tristan moved across the room to stand next to Adam. "Lauren won't tell us what happened. She's in shock."

Evelyn said, "Why she was over there in the first place, I'll never know."

"Let it go, Mom," said Tristan. "The only reason we're all still here is because of the storm. Toronto is already snowed in and we'll be next. Lauren wanted to check on Antonia because she was worried."

"I told her not to bother them. Antonia has sick spells and comes around when she feels up to it. Why didn't your sister listen to me for once?"

"I'm quite sure that Lauren's visit had nothing to do with Boris killing himself."

"How can you know that, Tristan? Maybe she said something or got him angry."

"Mom, stop it." Adam's voice cut across the room like ice. "You can't say things that have no basis in fact. We can't turn on each other."

Kala touched Gundersund's arm. "Why don't I go upstairs and see if Lauren feels up to speaking with us?"

He nodded, his blue eyes seeking hers and signalling that they couldn't end the sniping too soon for his liking. "I think that would be helpful." He lowered his voice so that only she could hear. "I'll stay here and keep a lid on things."

"Her room's at the end of the hall," Tristan offered.

Kala took the stairs two at a time, happy to be away from the negative energy in the living room while also filing away the insight that the exchange had given them into Evelyn's relationship with Lauren. Mona was walking down the hallway toward her. Her eyes were puffy from crying as well and her voice was dangerously close to wailing. "She won't let me in. I don't know what to do."

"Join the others downstairs. I'll speak with Lauren and make sure she's okay. I imagine it's the shock."

"I can't take this in."

"I know. It's hard to understand sometimes why people act as they do." She put an arm around Mona's shoulders. "Are *you* okay?"

"No, but I have to be for the family."

"Don't hesitate to seek out someone to talk to when you get back home. A counsellor will help you to deal with the trauma."

"I'll remember. Please go carefully with Lauren."

Kala approached the closed door at the end of the hall as she heard Mona descending the stairs. She rapped sharply with her knuckles and said Lauren's name, asking to be let in. She listened to the silence on the other side of the door for ten seconds and was deciding whether to break in or wait a bit longer when the sound of feet hitting the floor made the choice for her. Lauren pulled open the door and flung herself back onto the bed where she stretched out on her back and covered her eyes with one arm. Kala followed her to the bed.

"Do you mind if I sit with you?"

When no answer came, Kala slowly lowered herself to the edge of the single bed so that she was even with Lauren's legs. "You've suffered a terrible shock," she said. "Would you like to see a doctor?"

"I'm fine. I wouldn't mind if Jack Daniels put in an appearance, though." She'd dropped her arm and was attempting a smile but tears were brimming in her eyes.

"That can be arranged. In fact, a shot of something will help with the shock. I'll be right back."

Kala called to Gundersund from the bottom of the stairs and he soon met her with a bottle of Scotch and a glass. "How's it going?"

"This should help her to relax. She's not in great shape. How are the rest of them doing?"

"Let's say I could do with some of that myself." He touched the bottle and then her hand. "Call if you need backup."

"I will."

"We'll debrief after this and then destress somewhere." His eyes were concerned.

"I can handle it."

"I know you can."

She returned to the bedroom. Lauren was sitting up, her back against the headboard. Her white hair was standing in patches and her pale skin was bruised purple under her eyes. She accepted the tumbler of Scotch, closed her eyes, and took a couple of quick gulps. She held the glass against her chest. She said, "I now know what it's like to think you're about to die."

"You were there when Boris shot Antonia and turned the gun on himself?"

"I went in to check on Antonia because I'd been in her room last week and she said things … that Boris was her brother, and her husband and children were gone. She seemed so drugged out and we hadn't seen her like we normally do for a few weeks. She usually spent afternoons at our house." Lauren took another drink from the glass. "Both times I went over when Boris was out."

"Why?"

"I thought she'd be more willing to talk with him gone and I doubted he'd let me in anyway."

"Did she tell you anything about her life or what was going on with Boris?"

"Yes. She said … she said that she killed Zoe with a knife and when Boris found me in the bedroom, he said much the same. He said she'd had a psychotic break and killed Zoe and Vivian."

"So Boris came home and you were still in the house?"

"Yes, it was so strange. Antonia heard him first and panicked. She made me hide in the closet." Lauren's face flashed a look of embarrassment. "I felt like a kid hiding from the bogeyman. Boris came upstairs and looked in on her but left right away. She must have been pretending to be asleep. He went downstairs and a few minutes later the phone rang. I heard him speaking in what sounded like Russian because I'd left the closet and was at the door thinking about making a break for it. Antonia got agitated and I went over to the bed to calm her down and then Boris started back upstairs. I'm humiliated to say that I hid in the closet again, but Antonia was frantic."

"Then what happened?"

"He came into the room and they said something to each other and then he pulled open the door. I saw the gun in his hand and just about passed out. He told me to get out of the closet, and after I did, he said that he wasn't going to hurt me. I knew he was planning to kill Antonia and himself. He said they were old and had suffered enough."

"And he told you that Antonia had killed Zoe."

"Yes. He said that she'd killed Vivian too. He was trying to protect her and I think that was why he killed her. He didn't want her locked up." Tears were rolling down her face now and Lauren took another gulp of Scotch. Her hand was shaking. "I asked if I could take her to see my mother but he wouldn't let me. I knew that he would kill her if I left, but I was scared he'd kill me too. I was at the front door putting on my boots when I heard the shots. Two shots. I ran home and called 911. I hadn't brought my phone with me to the Orlovs' and I didn't even think about using their phone. I couldn't get out of there fast enough." Her voice rose like a wounded child's. "I left her there with him. I left her to die."

"You had no choice, Lauren. He had a gun and he'd made up his mind. He probably had this planned for a long time. You mustn't blame yourself."

Kala thought about Evelyn and the vicious way she talked about her only daughter and knew Lauren would get no comfort there. Lauren reminded her of Rose, tough on the outside and seeking love in all the wrong places, now doing time for accompanying her boyfriend on an armed robbery spree. She reached out a hand and took hold of Lauren's. "You did all that you could and I'm amazed by your compassion. You've suffered a terrible shock and it will take you time to recover, but what you're feeling now will recede and you'll regain your equilibrium. We have good people to help you through this and I'll give you a phone number that you can call whenever you feel overwhelmed. Will you promise to reach out and take this help if you need it?"

Lauren used the back of her hand holding the glass of Scotch to swipe at her eyes. The false bravado returned to her voice. "Sure, why not?"

Kala squeezed her hand and wouldn't let her look away. "You don't have to be alone in this. I'm going to check up on you every day until I know you're okay."

"I'll be in Toronto."

"That's why God invented telephones."

Lauren finally smiled as she said, "You aren't like other cops, you know that?"

Kala withdrew her hand and laughed. "So I've been told."

Lauren took a long shuddering breath and set the empty glass on the bedside table. She slapped her thighs with both hands. "What next?"

"If you're up to it, I'd like to get you to HQ to make a formal statement."

"I figured. Yeah, I can do that. May as well get it over with now so I can be home for supper."

"Good. I'd say that after all this, you've earned a good meal and time to decompress. I find a long walk helps to clear the head after a shock like you've been through."

"I might take you up on that idea. Might be better than mine."

"Which is?"

"Buy myself a big bottle of vodka and get shitfaced."

CHAPTER THIRTY-SIX

The team met up at the Merchant after Lauren gave her statement to Woodhouse at HQ. The snow was making driving tough with several centimetres on the ground and no let up predicted overnight, but they needed to wash away the sight of the Orlovs' bloody bodies and to digest the news that Antonia Orlov had killed Zoe Delgado and Vivian McKenna.

Kala finally reached Dawn on her cellphone as she waded through the snow to the pub's main entrance. She stood with a hand over one ear, protecting the phone from the wind and falling snow, squinting to keep the moisture out of her eyes as she stared at the lights shining in the windows of the limestone buildings across the street. "I won't be long," she said, raising her voice to be heard above the wind. "Everything okay with you?"

"Yes."

"Take whatever you want out of the freezer and heat it up if you haven't already eaten. I'll have some when I get there or I'll make a sandwich."

"I'm not home yet."

Kala pulled the door open with some effort and stepped inside the Merchant's front foyer. "Where are you?"

"Waiting at the bus stop, but the bus is late. I could start walking."

"I'll come get you. Tell me where you are." Kala strained to listen as static and background noise filled her ear, followed by the sound of breathing and Dawn's voice.

"I see the bus. I'll meet you at home."

"I could ..." but Dawn had hung up and left Kala with an uneasy feeling. She checked her watch and wondered what Dawn was doing in town so late. She'd been skipping school and hanging out with friends when she was staying in the foster home. Could she be returning to the street again?

She turned to get back in her truck and collided with Gundersund on his way inside. He reached out and steadied her. "Hold on there, lady! Warmth and drinks are thatta way," he said pointing toward the bar.

"Gundersund, I should get home. Dawn is on the bus and I'm not sure where she's been. Besides, the weather is getting terrible."

"She's on the bus?"

"Yes."

"Then nothing to worry about. Come in and decompress and we can follow each other home."

Kala hesitated and the shock of the day began to steal over her, making her legs tired and her shoulders ache. She knew that an hour talking out the images and making sense of the deaths with colleagues who understood the trauma of facing violent death would help her to cope. Dawn would be a while getting home anyhow. "All right," she said, giving in to the need to relax for a few moments. She let herself be swept into the room where Rouleau, Bennett, and Woodhouse sat waiting with jugs of beer and a plate of nachos already on the table.

Dawn hadn't been entirely truthful with her aunt about seeing the bus coming down the road but knew that one would be along soon after checking the schedule on her phone. She wasn't sure why she was keeping her after-school life a secret from Kala, but thought it had something to do with not trusting Emily or the reason she wanted to hang out. By not talking about Emily, she felt that Kala wouldn't pity her when Emily stopped needing her help with math and stopped talking to her. Keep Kala from hoping that she was fitting in and she wouldn't be disappointed. Dawn knew this was the best way to get by. No expectations and no pain.

She'd stayed late and helped Emily get caught up on the math she'd missed in the morning class, but Emily had been eager to get home to see her brother and wanted to leave by four. She seemed happier than Dawn had ever seen her before and when they packed up their books, Dawn said, "You're having a good visit with your brother. Is he home long?"

Emily smiled. "A few days. He's my best friend." Her smile disappeared. "He's gay and my parents took a long time to accept it. They sent him away to military college but he refused to go back after the first six months. They finally agreed to let him go to university out West. My parents are all about appearances. I think they've finally come around."

"Is that why …?" Dawn trailed off awkwardly, her gaze flickering away from Emily's face and down to her arm.

Emily nodded slowly. "I cut myself? I know you saw and thanks for not asking. I'm seeing a shrink, but that's another family secret. We're full of them." She laughed. "We're going on a family ski vacation at Christmas, so we're all trying."

"I never would have guessed."

"Nobody would. That's part of the problem. It's exhausting to have to pretend all the time, but letting go of that isn't easy either."

After she'd gone, Dawn lingered to take a book out of the library before leaving with the last stragglers. She hadn't felt like going home yet knowing that Kala would be working late again. Taiku would be waiting but he could last inside a few more hours.

The thick cloud cover made the late afternoon feel like evening and moisture dampened her face as she descended the front steps. She looked across the street where the man had been standing but he wasn't there. She was relieved but also oddly disappointed. He had seemed lonely like her. Out of place.

Instead of going toward the bus stop, she began walking toward the downtown. When she was living in the foster home, she'd walk for hours from one end of the city to the other, usually finding a quiet spot near the lake to sit and watch the water. She'd been approached a couple of times by homeless men who — and she knew people might not believe her — asked if she was okay. A few of them would sit nearby and talk to her and she was surprised by the lives they'd left behind. One guy named Greg had been an engineer in a big mining company, married with three kids until he started drinking. Last time she saw him, he was heading south for the winter.

The snow hadn't started yet but the dampness worked its way through her jacket, making her chilled. She stopped at a corner coffee shop and sat inside reading her library book with a cup of hot chocolate. When the lady behind the counter cleaned the table next to her twice with sideways glances in her direction, she left and kept walking toward the waterfront. She scanned the length of the pathway in front of the Visitors' Centre, searching for the man who'd been watching her school, but he was nowhere to be seen.

She walked partway down the snowy path but people seemed to be avoiding being outdoors. She took the boardwalk around the Delta Hotel toward Ontario Street and looked to her right, seeing the Lone Star Restaurant where she'd had supper with Kala and Gundersund several months before. After they'd finished eating, they'd walked to an art gallery and the owner had invited her back whenever she liked. She thought that she remembered where it was and turned in that direction. Halfway down the block, she reached the entrance and stepped inside. A woman with black dreadlocks and the biggest gold hoop earrings Dawn had ever seen invited her to look around. The next hour was a blur as Dawn studied every painting on the walls of the two rooms. She never wanted to leave.

"Do you paint?" the woman at the desk asked as Dawn started toward the door.

"I used to take lessons at a community centre."

"We have classes in charcoal and watercolour on Saturday mornings if you're interested. Here's a brochure."

Dawn took it and looked at the front page. *Four hundred dollars for an eight-week course.* She couldn't ask Kala for anything so extravagant. "Thanks," she said. "I'll think about it." She tucked the brochure into her jeans pocket.

"My name is Simone and I'm here weekdays if your mom has any questions."

"I'll let her know."

Dawn left the gallery and pulled out her phone to check the arrival time of the next bus. She wondered if Kala would be back from Montreal yet and not long after she reached the stop, the phone rang and Kala was telling her to take something out of the freezer. That was when she told the fib about seeing her bus coming up the street.

The snow had started falling while she was inside the art gallery and she was soaked by the time she trudged up the road after the bus dropped her off at the end of Old Front Road. She took Taiku outside after she changed into dry clothes but they didn't linger. She'd only just put a lasagna into the oven and sat down at the kitchen table to begin her homework when Kala arrived home.

"That storm is getting bad," Kala said as she wiped snow from her hair and hung up her parka. "It's so good to be home." She kicked off her boots and bent to greet Taiku before joining Dawn in the kitchen. Dawn had a pot of tea steeping on the table with two mugs set out and Kala sat across from her and poured a cup. "You're wonderful," she said, taking a sip and leaning back with a sigh. "Good day?"

"Fine." Dawn set her pen down. "I saw your note. How was Montreal?"

"We learned some interesting history about a suspect but when we got back to Kingston found out he'd killed himself and his sister. They were elderly but still, very sad."

"That's why you're so late."

"I had to go to the scene and interview the woman who found them and then we went back to HQ. When I called you, we were debriefing at the Merchant. I hadn't realized quite how late it was." Kala took another sip of tea. "Were you with friends after school?"

"No. I helped Emily with her math in the library and then went for a walk." Dawn opened her iPad and typed in a search on Google. "I've been reading about one of our Yankton ancestors and have a surprise for you." She turned the screen to show Kala.

"Goodness." Kala pulled the screen closer. She was momentarily speechless.

"I know, right?" said Dawn. "She looks so much like you that I almost fell off my chair when I saw her. She even wears her hair the same as you."

Kala read her name aloud. "Kitkla-Sa. She lived from 1876 to 1938."

"Her name means Red Bird. She was a writer, musician, and political activist in the U.S. and she's the spitting image of you."

Kala stared at the black-and-white photo and the dreamy, haunted eyes of her ancestor and for the first time felt an overwhelming connection to her past and her Dakota lineage.

"She's so beautiful," said Dawn. "And she was strong and talented, like you."

"You humble me. I'd like to know more about her and read some of her writings."

"The past is important, Aunt Kala." Dawn met her eyes. "I was thinking that I'd like to visit my mother."

Kala kept her response casual, not wanting Dawn to hear in her voice the surprise and relief that she was feeling. "I should have time to take you now that this case is wrapping up. We'll have to clear it with the prison authorities but I don't think there'll be a problem. Your mother needs to agree as well. May I ask what changed your mind?"

"I miss her and reading up on our history helped me to put what happened with my mom into perspective."

"She's embarrassed for you to see her in prison. We might need to convince her."

"Tell her that I have to see her to get better. She won't be able to say no."

CHAPTER THIRTY-SEVEN

The storm raged overnight and by morning freezing rain mixed in with the snow. The windows were coated in ice while snow had drifted against the panes, accumulating in soft drifts on the ledges. The wind rattled the glass and gusts buffeted the house with less strength than a few hours before but it was still enough to make Lauren want to stay snuggled under the blankets for an extra half hour. Evelyn was in bed when Mona, Adam, Tristan, and Lauren gathered around the island in the kitchen to discuss their 9:00 exit strategy.

"The storm is cutting a swath across the GTA and hit Ottawa and Montreal overnight," said Adam. Flights are cancelled and not expected to resume until nightfall. "Much as I'd like to get out of here, I think we'll need to aim for tomorrow."

"Your mom has suffered another shock," said Mona. "We should stay with her today anyway."

"I'm not convinced she's all that broken up," said Lauren. "Dad was friends with Boris, but Mother appeared to tolerate Antonia, and now that we know she killed Zoe and Vivian, even if she was crazy, Mother's shallow well of mercy will have pretty much dried up."

"Do I detect a note of bitterness?" asked Tristan.

"Perhaps a titch." Lauren sent him a sideways smile.

"Have the police decided Antonia killed Zoe and Vivian?" asked Adam and they all fixed their eyes on him.

"I told them that Antonia and Boris both said she'd killed them," said Lauren and then a stab of confusion momentarily stopped her. The entire exchange with the Orlovs had been shrouded in fear and an unreal quality and details were only beginning to come back. Boris had believed Antonia killed both, but hadn't Antonia said she'd seen Vivian walking far ahead with somebody else? Antonia had only admitted to killing Zoe — or had she?

Mona said, "It's turned out as best as we could hope for then. We can go back to our lives without suspicion hanging over any of us."

"I wonder if the media will be printing an apol ogy for all the years of hell they put me through," said Tristan. "At least I won't have to go through it a second time."

Mona put her hand on his back and rubbed in a circular motion. "We knew you'd never hurt Vivian. Now the world knows it, too."

Lauren was watching Adam when Mona defended Tristan and the curious expression on his face startled her.

He knows something, she thought and followed his gaze, which was focused on Mona and Tristan. *What is going on in his head?*

Tristan saw Adam staring at him. "What is it?" he asked. "You're looking at me as if I got away with something."

"Nothing like that. It's just ..."

"What, Adam?" asked Mona, lowering her arm from Tristan's back.

Adam raised both hands. "I'm just glad this insanity is over. We can get back to our lives."

"I have no life to go back to," said Tristan. "Not that you'll lose any sleep over it."

"That's not fair," said Mona, moving away from Tristan. "We love you, Tristan, and only want what's best for you. Sometimes going through pain now can prevent worse pain later."

"That's okay, Mona," said Adam. "A fighting Tristan is preferable to the one wallowing in self-pity."

"What the hell is wrong with you, Adam?" asked Lauren. "Tristan lost his wife and baby and his girlfriend fourteen years ago to a crazy woman and you act as if he shouldn't grieve. When did you get so sanctimonious and hard-hearted?"

"I know he's lost a lot but that doesn't give him the right to lash out at his family. I should have known you'd fight his battles for him."

"Stop it," said Mona. "Stop it! All of you! We've been under stress for so long. Now is not the time to fall apart."

"Mona's right," said Adam. "I'm sorry, Tristan." He moved sideways and put an arm around Mona's shoulders. "I'm sorry, sweetie. I need to relax."

"I hate it when we fight." She swiped at a tear before it rolled down her cheek. "I just want to get home to Simon and back to how things were."

"Yeah," agreed Tristan but he remained stone-faced, his eyes angry.

"I feel like we're stuck in this bloody house. When will the damn storm let up?" asked Lauren, walking over to the counter and staring up at the sky through the window. She said, more quietly, "I need to get out of here."

Her phone beeped a message and she pulled it out of her pocket.

I'm outside. Need to see you.

A message from the gods. She texted back and rejoined her brothers and Mona. "I'm going for a walk."

"Are you crazy?" asked Adam. "It's a blizzard out there."

"I won't be long. I need some air."

She bundled up in her borrowed parka and found Matt waiting for her two houses over. She climbed into his car and he drove to the end of the street where the road curved around the median of conifer trees. He parked but left the engine running. Snow sifted onto the windshield and hail rattled against the roof and windows.

"The police were by the house and told us that Antonia Orlov killed Zoe. They also believe she killed Vivian. Dad and I are relieved the truth has come out but gobsmacked. Had you any idea?"

"No. In fact, since I've been home, I'd begun to suspect Boris."

"The police said that you were in their house before Boris killed her and himself and that they confessed to you."

"That's right."

Matt was silent, staring at her as if searching for the truth on her face.

"What is it?" she asked, uncomfortable under his scrutiny.

"Dad isn't buying it and told the police that you're an unreliable witness since you'd do anything to get Tristan off."

"Wow, that came out of nowhere."

"He's pressuring the police to keep the investigation into Zoe's death open."

"Why are you telling me this?"

"I want you to know that I believe you. Before this gets any uglier."

"And why should you believe me?"

"Because even after all this time, with all that's gone down in our lives, you're the same person that I remembered. I want to see more of you."

The well of anger and grief threatened to boil over and her eyes filled with tears of rage. "I'm so tired of my family and all this pain." She thumped against the headrest, staring straight ahead and trying not to cry. "I have no idea why you want to see me again after all this time. I'm not the same girl you knew before Zoe died. Before I moved to Toronto and tried to forget. How could I be?" She turned her head sideways to look at him. "Look at me, Matt. Really look at me. I'm a mess and you can't even be certain that I'm not lying. God, I could use a cigarette."

"I see you, Lauren. I'm going to have Sundays and Mondays off and I can come to you in Toronto. We can take it slow if you're willing to give me a chance. No long-term promises or regrets if we don't work out. I'd only have regret if we didn't try."

He looked so earnest that she laughed out loud. "You never could take no for an answer, could you, Delgado?"

"I've waited a long time to see you again."

"And got married to help pass the time."

"I settled for a while."

Lauren could fall back in time when she looked at Matt but that was the path to insanity. She tried not to be seduced by memories. He was still damn attractive with an elusive quality she'd never found in any of the many men she'd been with, but she was scared to start up with him. When he'd dumped her, and with Zoe gone too, she'd been broken. She'd been slowly killing herself in a futile attempt to fill the holes they had left in her heart ever since.

She took her time answering. "If you have even an iota of feeling left for me, Matt, you'll stop this game you're playing and leave me alone because I can't take anymore. Not from you too." She opened the car door and stepped outside into the storm without waiting for his response. She ran through the wind and hail to her mother's front door without once turning around.

Kala left Dawn and Taiku sleeping and picked up Gundersund on her way to work. His Mustang wouldn't do well on the unplowed streets, while her truck was reliable no matter the weather. They stopped for coffee and bagel sandwiches near HQ. Most people were staying home and barely anybody was on the roads, making a difficult drive somewhat easier.

"I'm thinking we'll be able to call it an early day," said Gundersund when he left her at her desk to enter Rouleau's office. "Should be quiet now that we know the identity of Vivian McKenna's killer except for a press conference at nine at which I'll be backup singer for Woodhouse and Rouleau."

"I'll update the file. Did you ever receive the report on her from Forensics?"

"I'll get Vera to check on it."

"Thanks."

Kala ate the bagel while she opened emails. Woodhouse and Bennett came into the office at the same time but neither spoke to the other. Bennett detoured for coffee before coming over to say good morning. Woodhouse dropped his jacket on his chair and kept walking toward Gundersund's office.

Tanya Morrison stopped by Kala's desk as she was taking the last bite of sandwich. "Hard to believe the neighbour killed both women. Were you as surprised as I was?"

"She wasn't my first choice."

"Coffee later?"

"Sure."

Kala pulled her cellphone from her parka, which she'd slung over the back of her chair. She scrolled through the contacts until she came to Rose's support worker's number at the Joliette prison. She had to clear Dawn's visit and needed to go about this carefully. Rose had been adamant that she didn't want Dawn to see her in Joliette but Kala was prepared to do whatever it took to make the reunion happen. They needed each other.

She left a message for Linda to call her back while simultaneously clicking on a new email from Julie Gaudette, the cop who'd escorted her around Edmonton. Kala had asked her to follow up on some avenues she'd been pursuing, but that was before the murder cases were solved. She'd been vague with Gaudette about the thinking behind her queries, preferring to wait until all the pieces came together, including a call to Adam's supervisor. She reminded herself to reply with an update to let Gaudette know to close the file. She clicked on her message.

I've gone through Tristan's electronic calendar and copied the dates that he was away on tour, cross-checking them against the black dots in Vivian's Day-Timer. The dots are all on the days he was away and in a couple of cases, she notes a time and location: Murphy's Pub on 50th Avenue in Leduc. I've included the times and dates in the attached file. Good luck with your hunch.

Kala opened the file and printed a copy out of curiosity more than a need to know now that Vivian's murder was solved. She skipped over the unopened email from Air Canada but scrolled back to find it and printed that attachment as well. While she waited, she brought up a map of Edmonton and located Murphy's Pub on the map. Her heartbeat began to quicken. She looked up to find Woodhouse standing next to her desk.

"What're you working on?" he asked.

"Putting the murder file to bed," she said, even though she was doing the exact opposite.

"Gundersund said to tell you that Vivian McKenna's autopsy report is in the system."

"Great. Thanks."

He raised his voice. "I'm leaving now for the media briefing and will be back after lunch if anyone's looking for me."

She met Bennett's eyes smiling at her from across the room and quickly looked away. Woodhouse wanted everyone to know that he was important enough to be included in the briefing. Like a rooster strutting around the henhouse. "Sounds good," she said, because he seemed to need validation and it didn't hurt her to give it.

After he and Gundersund were gone, she spread out the printed attachments and started highlighting dates. The pattern could not be a coincidence. She pondered the significance before opening Vivian's autopsy. She'd been strangled with her own scarf and died where she was found. Kala knew the forensics team hadn't been able to confirm where Zoe had died and were being extra careful with Vivian. She thought the location combined with the use of Vivian's own scarf showed a crime of opportunity. Likely one of passion or anger, which could realistically fit with Antonia Orlov's state of mind. Vivian had died close to

2:00 p.m. Her unborn baby was also analyzed and found to be male and twenty-three weeks or five and three-quarter months along.

That can't be right.

Kala opened Vivian's police file and began sifting through the interviews until she reached Tristan's statement, the one he'd given to her the first time when Vivian was missing but hadn't yet been found dead. She hadn't misremembered and realized the lie that Vivian had fed Tristan. Counting back, she must have become pregnant in August, in the summer when they'd been having trouble in their marriage. Tristan had been on a three-week book tour in the southern U.S. through most of August and they'd patched up their marriage in September. Vivian had told him she was pregnant in October.

Her colleague had said she was having an affair. The neighbour saw a man leaving Vivian in a red negligee early one morning when Tristan was on tour.

Had Tristan suspected?

The phone rang on Kala's desk and she glanced at the number, which caller ID did not identify. She picked up anyway and was surprised to hear Lauren McKenna's voice at the other end.

CHAPTER THIRTY-EIGHT

They met at the Tim Hortons coffee shop on Bath Road, a five-minute drive from the McKenna house. Lauren arrived first and was sitting with a full coffee at a table in the front section of the restaurant when Kala entered, shaking snow out of her hair. She bought a tea at the counter and joined Lauren, who was staring at the ice-crystal designs on the window. Kala slid into the seat across from her and shrugged out of her parka.

"How are things going?" she asked, taking the lid off her cup.

Lauren turned her face to look at Kala. The expression in her eyes was conflicted: worried and hesitant at the same time. "I've been better." She looked back out the window. "I think I misled you, maybe because I can't stomach the alternative."

"Tell me."

"I really believed that Boris and Antonia both said she killed Vivian as well as Zoe, but the longer I think about that afternoon, the more I remember. Boris thought she'd killed both women and that's why he was keeping her drugged and away from everyone: to protect her from herself, but Antonia told me that she'd only killed Zoe." Lauren looked at Kala with tortured eyes. "And I have to ask myself, could there have been two killers? Could someone else have wanted Vivian dead?"

"You think someone in your family could have done it."

"Maybe. I don't know." Her voice dropped away.

"Do you have anyone in mind?"

"This is very hard." She took a shuddering breath. "Vivian wasn't my favorite person but she was pregnant and that baby was innocent. Whoever killed her would have known they were taking two lives. What kind of a person would do that? How could we protect them and live with ourselves?"

Kala took a sip of coffee while she thought over how to approach this. The fact Lauren was putting forth the possibility of another killer instead of letting them believe Antonia had killed both women clinched for Kala that Lauren was innocent — raising the idea would be ludicrous if she were the killer. As it stood now, a dead woman who couldn't defend herself was marked for both deaths. Kala sent out a feeler. "Do you believe that Vivian was faithful to Tristan?"

Lauren appeared to seriously consider the idea. "She and Tristan weren't doing well last summer. I almost expected them to call it quits. She might have been seeing someone else. Tristan and I spoke by phone a couple of times and he said that he was doing so much publicity to get money to keep her happy. She'd told him that he had misrepresented himself to her as a bestselling author when he was a one-hit wonder. I never saw her as anything but opportunistic."

"So you wouldn't be shocked if I told you that I have two separate confirmations that she was having an affair while Tristan was on tour?"

"No, that wouldn't shock me at all."

"Did Tristan know?"

"I don't ..."

"Think back. Did he say anything to indicate he didn't trust her?"

"God, I don't ... wait a minute. I met him in Phoenix in late July. I was at a business conference and he was doing some readings and we got together for supper and drinks. He called Vivian when I went to the washroom and when I came back I overheard him telling her that she had to make up her mind before he came home or that was the end. I thought he sounded frustrated and resigned at the same time, if that makes any sense. I always wondered because next thing I knew, she was pregnant and all was rosy between them. I put what I overheard out of my mind since he hadn't wanted me to know." She paused. "Do you know who she was sleeping with?"

Now was the time to fish or cut bait. Kala studied her reactions. "Nobody has said, but based on timelines and schedules, I believe she was having an affair with Adam. Vivian made notations in her datebook indicating rendezvous locations and times that coincided with Tristan being out of town. Adam was flying the western route at the same time and was staying overnight in Edmonton the same dates. The bar where they met was near the airport. The neighbour saw a man leave their apartment one morning when Tristan was away and he wore a blue coat, which is the colour of Air Canada's pilot overcoats."

Kala expected that Lauren would get angry or dismiss the idea out of hand or defend her brother Adam, but she didn't foresee the silence that followed her revelation. After she waited a while for Lauren to say something, she added her final bit of evidence. "There's one more discrepancy from the autopsy. Vivian was five months and three weeks pregnant, not four and a half as she was telling everyone. The timing of her pregnancy appears to have occurred in the window when Tristan was on tour and when Adam was spending overnighters in Edmonton. Could you see an affair with Adam as a possibility or am I way off base?"

Lauren shrugged. "I saw the attraction between the two of them the first time we were all together. I always thought Vivian was more suited to Adam than Tristan. They're both used to being the centre of attention and suck up all the energy in a room."

"So, the two of them hooking up would not surprise you?"

"No. My brothers were spoiled by my mother, particularly Adam. He's used to getting whatever he wants. He always treated Tristan like he was second-best." Her eyes were worried. "This doesn't mean one of my brothers killed Vivian, though."

Kala said gently, "It gives each of them a motive, but you're right. This doesn't prove that either of them killed Vivian, or which one, if it comes to that."

"Which brings us back to whether or not I believe someone in my family could have killed her." Lauren ran a shaky hand through her hair. "What should we do now?"

The million-dollar question. Kala hesitated. Sharing scenarios with Lauren went against all police protocol. She said, "There is another option we have to consider."

"Oh yeah?"

"The Delgados believed your brother Tristan killed Zoe. One or both of them could have sought revenge by murdering his wife."

Lauren flinched and a grimace crossed her face, but she didn't give her opinion on this possibility.

Kala studied her and wondered if she was as tough as she pretended or if she should let this drop and try another avenue to get at the truth. "If this is too painful, you don't have to get involved any further," she said. "I can keep probing with my team."

"No, I want to help. I need to find out."

"You know your family better than anybody. How can we get them to talk?"

Lauren smiled. "They have one Achilles heel in common that always gets them to lower their guards, unite in anger, and sling mud."

"And what would that be?"

"Me."

Gundersund called Kala before they left the coffee shop, almost as if he knew she was up to something. She could have carried on and kept him in the dark, but caution seemed the better course of action and she filled him in while Lauren went to the washroom.

"The media scrum is wrapping up so I'll meet you at HQ in fifteen," he said.

"I've already called Morrison to get the electronic equipment ready."

"Perfect. I'll fill in Rouleau if I get him alone."

"Gundersund, thanks for not questioning the sanity of this. I know it might come to nothing in the end and it's putting a lot of people out."

"I was never completely convinced the two murders were done by the same person. I'm as keen to check this out as you are."

Lauren followed her to police headquarters on Division and Kala was pleased to see that the major roads had recently been plowed so the trip was easier than earlier in the day. The temperature was dropping and now well below zero so the freezing rain had turned into lightly drifting snow. Gundersund and Morrison met them inside the station and went over their strategy before a technician fitted a wire on Lauren, who fortunately was wearing a bulky sweater that would easily hide the mic.

"What about Woodhouse and Bennett?" Gundersund asked Rouleau. "Should we bring them in?"

"I think we're good with who we've got here. If this doesn't end with a confession, we'll be wise not to have involved them on an evening off."

"Fair enough."

Kala and Rouleau sat with Lauren while Gundersund organized the rest of the outing. Rouleau asked Lauren if she had any questions.

"If nothing comes of this ..."

"We'll destroy whatever is not pertinent. You have my word."

"Good, because I don't want my family maligned in the press or set up to be embarrassed."

"I'll make sure that doesn't happen."

Kala touched Lauren's arm. "Are you having second thoughts?"

"Yes, but I know we have to do this. I couldn't live with myself believing that someone in my family killed Vivian and her baby. I'm not lying when I say that I fervently hope this comes to nothing."

"As do we." Kala added, "What you're doing takes courage, Lauren."

"I'm not sure about that. I lived the last fourteen years with Zoe's murder hanging over us and I can't deal with watching over my shoulder again, never sure who killed her or if new acquaintances are going to discover my dirty laundry."

Vera walked into the office waving a piece of paper. "The judge signed off so you're okay to proceed. She questioned the speed of this but I explained that the family would be leaving Kingston tomorrow morning."

"Thanks, Vera." Rouleau said as he got up from his desk. "I'll go make certain we're ready to roll."

Kala watched the smile on Vera's face disappear as Rouleau walked past her without looking in her direction. He was oblivious to her interest, which Kala had long seen and wondered at. Vera was much younger than Rouleau and seemed an unlikely match, but she appeared steadfast in her attraction to him. She left them without her usual wide smile.

Lauren was watching Vera and turned to give Kala a wry look. "He's clueless, isn't he?"

"About what?"

"About her. He has no idea. She's gorgeous, by the way. Most men would have her in the sack if she ever gave them the time of day."

Kala didn't respond, not wanting to engage, although she was impressed by Lauren's powers of observation and thought for the first time that the plan to get her family talking might have a chance.

Gundersund came into the room and said to Lauren, "Will your family be wondering where you are? It's past five o'clock."

"They won't be wondering. They'll be more surprised when I show up on time for supper."

"Well, we can get going. The camera is clipped on the front pocket of your purse. Try to angle it toward wherever you're gathered, but don't worry if you can't. We'll get the audio."

"We'll be outside if you need us," said Kala. "Leave the front door unlocked if you can."

"Mother doesn't lock up until nighttime if she's got company."

Kala smiled in an attempt to take the worry from Lauren's eyes. "Then I think we're ready to give this a whirl."

"Do you believe she's up to it?" asked Gundersund on the drive over to the McKenna house. He took his eyes off the road and glanced over at Stonechild. She was sitting rigidly in the passenger seat staring out the side window. The wind was whipping the snow against his car in short bursts of energy and she appeared to shiver each time a blast pummelled her window. The windshield wipers were having trouble keeping the glass free of ice and snow.

Kala squared around in her seat. "I feel responsible. She's only doing this because she trusts me, but I can tell she's got a lot to lose."

"Perhaps she's doing this for her own peace of mind."

"I hope we can give her that."

He was still finding this case twisted and seeming to slither away every time he thought he'd figured out what was going on. "Who do you think killed Vivian? he asked. "If you had to guess?"

"I don't know. Tristan maybe. He could have found out the baby was his brother's, but then why would he incriminate himself by killing his wife in the same location where his high school girlfriend was murdered?"

"You've talked yourself out of Tristan."

"No, just thinking out loud. Jealousy can cloud reason and I understand he has the green-eyed temperament." She paused, her face thoughtful. "Adam might have wanted to keep Vivian quiet too. Not to mention the Delgado men believed Tristan killed Zoe and could want to seek revenge. This exercise won't flush them out."

"I hope we find the killer and this doesn't drag out another fourteen years."

"Don't we all."

She turned to look out the window again and was silent the rest of the way to Grenville Crescent.

Gundersund matched her silence with his own, wondering what kind of a person could kill a pregnant woman and slide back into their own life as if nothing had happened.

When he pulled in behind the van with their mobile unit, she turned to him. "In answer to your question, I think Lauren is up to this," she said. "I see a toughness in her eyes mixed in with the pain. She has a strength of character that you can't fake."

CHAPTER THIRTY-NINE

She heard the murmur of their voices in the dining room and took a deep cleansing breath. *Here we go*, she thought and didn't know if she'd actually said the words aloud. Clemmie met her at the bottom of the stairs, obviously woken up from a nap. He stretched his front legs and licked her hand, his tail wagging back and forth at a half-hearted speed as if the angry energy in the house had drained him too.

"Here we go," she said out loud, this time knowing she was speaking to Clemmie and those listening in the van outside. They'd told her they'd be parked a few doors down but close enough to record every word being said. Officer Stonechild would be in the van too, listening and watching the TV monitor with her intelligent black eyes, ready to rush in if necessary. The thought of her nearby gave Lauren strength.

She stood in the doorway to the dining room for a moment. Her brothers were seated across from each other while her mother and Mona brought in the food from the kitchen. She smelled roast beef and gravy and watched Mona put a large bowl of mashed potatoes on the table next to Adam.

"There you are," she said, beaming in Lauren's direction. "I set you a place just in case."

"Thanks," said Lauren. She remembered at the last second to set her purse with the camera on the end of the hutch and angled it to catch as much of the table as possible.

Mona went back into the kitchen and returned with a bowl of green beans and another of salad. Evelyn followed her with the platter of beef already sliced. Her mother's eyes flicked over Lauren and her mouth formed a tight line of disapproval.

"I suppose you've been in the bar again. I trust you aren't here to make a drunken scene."

"I've made so many."

"Leave Lauren alone," said Tristan without any force behind his words.

Lauren looked closer at his pale face and red eyes. He must have spent the afternoon smoking dope in his room again, steeped in his grief. She told herself that he didn't deserve the impatience she was feeling for how long he was taking to get himself together. His lack of backbone was making her weary. She had to ignore the guilt she was already feeling for what she was about to do that would add to his pain.

She took a seat next to Tristan while Mona sat down next to Adam, directly across from her, with Evelyn taking her usual spot at the head of the table, nearest the kitchen. They began passing the food and filling their plates. Lauren took enough to make it look as if she planned to eat even though she doubted she'd be able to swallow a bite.

"The storm's letting up. Did you make your plane reservations for tomorrow?" asked Evelyn, looking from Adam to Tristan and back again.

"You trying to get rid of us, Ma?" asked Adam, grinning at her, his boyish charm on full display.

Her stern face thawed into a quick smile. "You need to get on with your lives."

"We leave on the afternoon flight for Vancouver." He took a bite of roast. "Delicious as always, Mom."

"I thought you and Mona were coming with Tristan and me to Edmonton for Vivian's cremation," said Lauren.

Eyes on her, Adam chewed and swallowed. "Mona wants to get home to Simon and I need a day before I start back on the flight rotation."

"I was hoping you'd be there with us," added Tristan. "It would have meant a lot to Viv."

Lauren made her voice sound antagonistic, playing the role of the loyal sister defending her weak younger brother. "Adam, would it kill you to take one extra day before you go home? What if the police had kept us here another day? You could have managed. I can't believe you aren't going to support Tristan through this."

Mona had kept her head down until now. She looked at Tristan. "I really need to get home to Simon. I'm sorry, Tristan. Perhaps you could come visit us afterward."

"You're asking a lot of Adam and Mona," said Evelyn, who could never keep quiet when Adam's golden boy status was being questioned. As if pronouncing the final verdict on the matter, she added, "Vivian won't know one way or the other anyhow."

Lauren knew this was the opening she needed but she was reluctant to split the wounds open. She looked at Tristan, her wreck of a brother, and Adam, sitting across from him, so self-assured. It was as if Adam grew stronger the more Tristan struggled. He'd slept with his own brother's wife, for god's sake. She picked up her fork and scooped into the potatoes.

She lobbed as casually as she could. "Vivian told me that she considered herself very close to you, Adam."

Adam's eyes widened but he held her stare. "We were good friends as well as relatives. That doesn't change the face that Mona and I have a son with special needs waiting for us. He doesn't understand why we've been away so long and he's been upset that he's out of his routine." He patted Mona's fore-arm and they exchanged quick, sad smiles.

Lauren poked her fork into the mound of pota-toes and made a hole in the middle. "Vivian told me that you stayed at their apartment, Adam, when you had stopovers in Edmonton, so you must have had a more solid connection than any of us realized."

Tristan raised his head. "When was that?"

Lauren half-turned to look at him. "Last sum-mer, I think when you were on tour, Tristan. August for sure. Vivian must have told you."

"No, no, she didn't." His jaw tightened and he looked across at Mona and Adam. "How often did you stay over while I was away last summer, brother?"

Adam wouldn't stop staring at Lauren and she knew he was threatening her with his eyes. Mona sat as still as a closed door next to him.

"Once, maybe? It was no big deal."

"Then why didn't either of you tell me?" Tristan appeared to be calculating dates in his head and suspicion crept into his eyes. "It was more than once, wasn't it, Adam? Were you sleeping with my wife?" His voice rose. "While I was out trying to make enough money to keep her happy, were you screwing *my* wife in *my* bed?"

Evelyn let out an angry shriek and dropped her knife with a clatter onto her plate. Adam raised both hands in the air, pushed back his chair, and slapped his hands on the table. "I slept over one time, one time and no, I didn't sleep in *your* bed with *your* wife." He glared across the table. "What the hell are you playing at, Lauren?"

Lauren tried to still the beating of her heart by focusing on Mona, who hadn't even flinched when the voices rose around her. "I'm not playing at anything," she said calmly. "I know Vivian would want you at her cremation." She put a small forkful of potatoes into her mouth. "She told me that you stayed over many times last summer, Adam. I thought you knew, Tristan."

Adam and Tristan both jumped up and Tristan's chair hit the wall as he kicked it back. "She wouldn't tell me who she was sleeping with but I knew she was seeing someone. I could tell that somebody had been in the condo while I was away. She wanted to separate last summer. She said she was in love with someone else and I told her she had to choose. I couldn't understand why she came back, but you turned her down, didn't you, Adam? You took the overseas route so you wouldn't have any more stopovers in Edmonton and she got the message. She knew you wouldn't leave Mona for her."

Adam shook his head. "That's not how it was. You're crazy to think I'd sleep with Vivian. Lauren is making this all up. It's her you should be angry with, not me."

Evelyn's voice cut like ice. "Sit down, the both of you. This has gone far enough. Lauren, I think you should pack up your things and go stay at a motel for the night and go back to Toronto where you belong. You've obviously been drinking and I won't have you in my house any longer in this condition."

Lauren picked up her knife and began cutting into a slice of beef. "Actually, I haven't been drinking."

"Why, you smart-alecky girl! Who do you think you are?" Evelyn jumped up and lunged across the table, her hand raised to slap Lauren on the face. Tristan blocked her path and Evelyn began screaming for him to get out of her way. Adam rounded the table behind their mother and grabbed her by the shoulders, yelling at her to calm down.

Mona's scream stopped everyone in their tracks.

"Enough! Enough!" She covered her ears with her hands. "I can't take this anymore. All this ugliness. Your lies, Adam. How many times can you lie to me with a straight face and blame Lauren for finally … *finally* … telling the truth. You had an affair with Vivian that went on all last spring and summer and you played me and Tristan for fools."

"Mona, no." Adam let go of his mother and turned to step toward her. She held up a hand to stop him.

"Vivian told me. *She told me.* That day, I passed her on the stairs with my mug of tea and she asked me to go for a walk with her. I was so happy thinking she might really like me and want to become closer with the baby coming. I actually *believed* that we could become like sisters. What kind of pathetic fool does that make me?"

"Did you walk with her?" Lauren asked, willing Mona to keep talking.

Mona looked at her and nodded. "We were having such a nice chat and she suggested we walk up the Rideau Trail a bit to enjoy the quiet of the woods. She waited until we were standing looking up at the sky through the spruce trees to tell me that she'd been having an affair with Adam and he wanted to leave me because she was having his baby. She said she was having his *normal* baby and he could stop booking all the overseas flights that he'd been doing to escape me and my damaged son. She lied to you, Tristan. I'm so sorry. When she turned away from me, I ... I grabbed her scarf and I don't remember. I don't remember." She dropped her head into her hands.

Adam moved closer to her and faced the others now standing motionless with dawning horror on their faces. "Nobody tells anybody what went on in this room," he said. "Mona, don't say anything else. We'll work through this."

Lauren waited a moment longer before slipping out of the dining room. Clemmie was standing with tail down near the staircase and he followed her the length of the hallway. She opened the front door and let in Officer Stonechild and the cop who looked like a Viking warrior before she climbed the stairs to pack her bags to leave. If she was lucky, she'd be home in Toronto before midnight. She'd invite Tristan to join her and they could catch the flight to Edmonton in the morning as planned. They would bury Vivian and the baby and put all of this pain behind them.

She would not cry for Mona.
She
would not
cry
for Mona.
Not yet.

CHAPTER FORTY

"More chicken balls, Dawn?" asked Gundersund. She nodded and he scooped a few onto her plate. He saw Stonechild smile across the table where she sat between Rouleau and his father, Henri. They were seated in Kai's Delight Chinese restaurant on King Street West in Portsmouth Village on Saturday evening, a few days after Mona McKenna confessed to killing her sister-in-law.

Henri had requested they join him for dinner, which was to be his treat. Rouleau knew that his father had organized the gathering so that he could speak with Dawn about helping him with his research over the March break.

"You'll come work in my office at the university and I'll pay you minimum wage. If you enjoy the work, I can apply for a grant to have you work for me over the summer at an increased salary."

"Am I old enough?" she asked.

"I had my first summer job when I was twelve, so I believe you are."

"Then that would be great. Thanks so much, Mr. Rouleau."

"If we're to be working together, I insist that you call me Henri."

"Henri."

"Do you have plans for the money?" asked Gundersund, picking up a shrimp with his chopsticks.

"Yes. I'm going to take an art course."

Kala broke off her conversation with Rouleau and looked at Dawn. "I was going to surprise you, Dawn, but I've already enrolled you. I found the brochure in your pocket when I went to wash your jeans and called. You can start whichever session you'd like."

"You mean it?"

"I do. You'll have to find another use for your money once you earn it."

"Thank you so much, Aunt Kala."

Rouleau watched Dawn's eyes light up and exchanged a smile with Kala. The two of them had come a long way toward being a family as far as he could see and the relationship was helping them both to heal. He noticed Gundersund looking at Kala, too, with an intensity that he hid most of the time. Gundersund's wife, Fiona, would be home in the spring and Rouleau knew she'd been calling Gundersund at work, refusing to let him forget he was still married. He'd be better off making a clean break with her, but Rouleau knew all about conflicted relationships and would not offer advice. Gundersund would have to decide on his own what he needed to do to be happy.

Kala checked her watch and then set down her fork. "Dawn, it's time to go." She turned to Henri and kissed him on the cheek. "Thank you again for supper and your company, but we have to dash because

Dawn's meeting friends for a Shawn Mendes concert at the K-Rock Centre. I'm her chauffeur tonight."

"We'll do this again soon, my dear." Henri winked at Dawn. "Enjoy yourself, young lady."

"I will."

Kala and Dawn found a parking spot near the Merchant pub and walked the rest of the way to the K-Rock. The night was clear and crisp but not so cold that they minded being outside.

"I'm glad you decided to take in the concert." Kala looked sideways at Dawn as they walked. "Even if I had to convince you."

"I thought Emily was only trying to be nice so that I'd help her with her math. She's not really in my circle."

"What changed your mind?"

Dawn shrugged and scuffed at the snow before stepping off the curb to cross the road. "She has everything you'd think she needs for a happy life but she hurts inside. I guess it took me a while to see who she really is."

"The best friendships can start out slowly."

As they got close to the stadium, the groups of teenagers, mainly girls, became thicker and more boisterous. Dawn seemed to withdraw inside herself, her eyes scanning the crowd.

"Where did you say you'd meet up?" asked Kala.

"By the main doors. Maybe they're not coming. I don't have to wait —"

Dawn's words were cut off by a girl calling her name. Kala turned and saw three tall blond girls cutting through the groups of teenagers. The one in the lead was beaming and lovely. The other two girls hung back as she approached.

"You made it, Dawn."

"Aunt Kala, this is Emily, the girl I've been helping with math after school."

"Great to meet you." Emily extended her hand and Kala reached out to shake it.

"Nice to meet you, too, Emily." Kala waved at the other two girls and turned to Dawn. "I'll be back and waiting here for you after the concert. Have fun."

Kala watched them thread their way through the crowd and disappear inside the building. Dawn turned at the last moment and waved.

Kala walked back toward her truck, enjoying the brisk air and the night sky visible above the buildings and city lights. The sidewalks had been cleared of snow for the most part with snow piled high wherever space allowed. She was happy that Dawn was out for an evening with kids her own age. A first step. Rose hadn't given the green light for them to visit her in Joliette yet, although she and Dawn had exchanged letters and a phone call was scheduled for Sunday. More steps in the right direction.

She started across the street when she looked up and saw Gundersund waiting for her on the other side. Her heart felt lighter at the sight of him and she quickened her steps. He took her arm when she reached him and said, "I needed to stretch my legs. Dawn met up with her friends okay?"

"She did and now I have a few hours before I go back to get her again."

He held the door to the pub open and they gladly stepped inside the warm foyer. Henri had gone home and they found Rouleau deep in conversation at a table with reporter Marci Stokes, who was dressed in an emerald-green turtleneck that complemented her auburn hair and creamy complexion. Kala had never seen her looking so relaxed and glowing. She looked from Marci to Rouleau and saw that something good was going on between them. She wondered if Gundersund noticed too.

Once she and Gundersund settled in at the table and their drinks arrived, Marci said, "I never in a million years would have suspected two different killers for the Delgado and McKenna murders. Both utterly tragic for everyone involved. My in-depth piece comes out in the *Whig* tomorrow so say whatever you like. I've already put the subject to bed."

"Mona McKenna is co-operating fully and her remorse is evident," said Rouleau. "She's been charged with second-degree murder and we'll have to see if she receives some degree of leniency in sentencing."

When Marci left to go to the washroom, Kala asked Rouleau, "How did Petran react when you told him that Boris Orlov was dead?"

"He was disappointed and is undecided about pursuing the file further. He's sensitive to opening old wounds, but needs to balance this with closure for those who suffered under Orlov. He confirmed that his visit to see us tipped off somebody from the old regime who called Boris that afternoon when he killed himself and his sister."

"So many years living on that quiet street without detection," said Gundersund.

"Did Petran find out what happened to Antonia's children?" Kala asked.

"They were adopted outside the country. He's still trying to track them down." Rouleau's eyes met hers. "I hope loving families adopted them both and that something good came out of all the misery."

"That is always the hope," Kala said, but she had seen too many children harmed by the system to be completely optimistic. She couldn't forget the other foster children crying for their parents, trying to find a place to belong. They survived but many were irreparably scarred. Since Dawn had come to live with her, she'd begun to understand the importance of learning about their own ancestry as a step toward healing the past and the present — toward being at home in their own skins and embracing their strength together.

Dawn would beat the odds. Kala would make sure of it because now their life stories were forever joined.

The best we can do is to fight against injustice and what has gone before, she thought. *To keep going through the darkness until a path leads us home.*

"I bought the house," she blurted out to Gundersund after Marci rejoined them. "Dawn and I are now your official neighbours on Old Front Road."

Delight filled his face. He grinned and raised his beer. "To putting down roots," he said, and they clinked glasses.

"Welcome home," said Rouleau, raising his glass to hers. "And to being where you belong with your newfound family."

Marci leaned over and hugged her. "I'm so pleased for you," she said.

CHAPTER FORTY-ONE

Lauren sat at her desk staring out the window. Night was falling and her reflection shone back at her in the dusky window. She heard someone at the door to her office and turned. Salim was leaning against the door frame with a grin on his handsome face. There was a time this would have been enough.

"Want to grab some drinks and supper?" he asked. "A new Italian bistro opened up near my apartment building."

"Not tonight. I'm tired and want to turn in early."

"That was part of my plan, too." His grin widened.

"We aren't doing this anymore, Salim. I thought I made myself clear enough."

"I was hoping you'd weakened at the sight of my new suit jacket."

She laughed. "Not going to happen. Find yourself a nice girl and slot me back into just being your boss."

"Not my first choice but I'll adjust over time and several martinis. See you tomorrow?"

"Tomorrow." She pretended not to see the look of longing on his face and shut down her own weakening resolve.

Ten minutes after she'd heard him shut the main door and clomp down the stairs to the street, she packed up her desk and put on her coat and boots. Tomorrow would be the start of a new month: March. *March madness*. Would the change in the calendar move her forward or would she be stuck in the depression she'd fallen into after her trip to Edmonton with Tristan?

Somehow, she'd functioned. Work had been a solace and she'd put in long hours, taking on more clients than she should have, but needing to keep her mind busy. She'd stopped her nightly drinking and kept away from men in bars and Salim, whom she should never have started up with. She'd even managed to keep away from cigarettes. She was breaking old patterns. Trying to find herself. Maybe finding some happiness that she hadn't known in a long time.

She walked up to Kensington Market to buy something fresh for supper. Making her own meals was another resolution. She took her time, strolling through the quirky neighbourhood, enjoying the shoppers hustling down the narrow sidewalks cleared at long last of snow with brightly covered awnings offering a haphazard cover. Victorian houses were converted into clothing and food shops, the brick facades of some painted bright blue, yellow, and orange. When she began to feel chilled, she entered a corner food shop and picked out lettuce and vegetables to make a salad and fresh chicken breasts, which she planned to bake with tomatoes, feta, and olives. She returned through the thickening darkness to the parking lot near her office to retrieve her car and drove east through the downtown to her apartment in the Beaches.

She parked in the outdoor lot a block away, where she had a reserved spot. The temperature was dropping and a wind cut through her wool coat. She hoped the wind would strengthen once she was tucked inside her apartment because she loved the sound of it howling outside her window when she lay in bed at night. She quickened her steps, hurrying toward the lights of the three-storey brownstone that she'd moved into six months earlier. She used her key to enter the front door and climbed the stairs to the second floor, where her two-bedroom apartment took up the southwest corner. She knew her neighbours enough to say hello but she'd kept to herself, for this place to be a haven where nobody asked anything of her.

She pushed open the door on the landing and stepped into the corridor. She had her head down and was almost at her apartment door when she saw a man leaning against the wall. Her initial response was fear and an instinct to run back outside, but he turned and she felt the adrenaline turn to relief, leaving her weak at the knees.

"Sorry to drop by on you without warning," Matt said. "We finally got the second new hire sorted out and I'm starting my two days off tomorrow. If this isn't a good time, I can go, but I'm hoping you'll let me take you to dinner."

She looked down. He was holding on to his cap with sinewy hands; embedded into his skin were traces of oil and grease that he could never scrub away. They were strong hands but she remembered how they used to touch her. She raised her eyes to look into his face.

"It's been almost two months and I didn't hear from you."

"I'm sorry. Dad had a heart attack the day after your sister-in-law was arrested. I guess holding in all that hate and grief finally got to him. Anyhow, I've been working double shifts and looking after him. I was trying to get myself into a position to come see you, but it took longer than I thought it would."

She asked, "How's your dad now?"

"The doc unblocked his artery and he was back at work as of Monday."

"I'm glad." She took her apartment key out of her pocket and opened the door. "I've got food for supper if you don't mind eating in."

She heard the relief in his voice. "I'll help cook."

She left him in the kitchen chopping tomatoes and went into her bedroom to change into jeans and a T-shirt. *What does he want?* She asked her face in the bathroom mirror. She was wary of the hope she saw in her eyes.

He'd poured her a glass of red wine from the bottle she'd left on the counter and they talked about life in Toronto while they worked side by side. She was surprised by how quickly the years slipped away, and they were back to the easy friendship of high school. They sat across from each other at the island that divided her galley kitchen from the living room and ate their meal with the rest of the bottle of wine.

"How are your brothers doing?" Matt asked.

"My mother is selling her home in Kingston and moving to Vancouver to look after Simon while Adam resumes his overseas flights. I imagine Simon will miss having Mona around more than Adam will. Adam always finds a way to land on his feet. Tristan has a bidding war going on for his latest book, which is expected to be a bestseller. If Vivian had bided her time, she'd have hit the jackpot." Lauren laughed but the sound came out bitter rather than joyous.

Matt put down his glass, reached across the counter, and covered her hand with his own. He didn't need to say anything. He knew all her family secrets.

"I'm sorry for your mother," he said after a while.

"And why would that be?"

"She's never given you the credit you deserve and she's missed out. I feel sorry for her because she's a fool."

Lauren wanted to weep at the compassion she saw in his eyes. She pulled away her hand and picked up her wine glass. "Where is this going, Matt?" she asked, angry at the trembling in her hand. She set down her glass.

"I wanted to make an entrance like Richard Gere in that movie when he picks up the girl in the factory and carries her away to cheers and clapping."

"*An Officer and a Gentleman?*"

"I guess, but we both know that kind of drama's not in me. As an alternative plan, I thought we could take things slowly, at whatever pace you want, and get to know each other again."

"Like date?"

"Yeah."

This was the moment. The crossroads. Would she look back on her life and think *I should have but I was too scared*? Would she live in regret from this day forward? He would be disappointed for a day, maybe a month, and then he'd find someone better. A sudden memory of her father came out of nowhere. She was in the kitchen, looking out the window, swallowing the sobs that threatened to push up out of her throat. Zoe had been dead three months and she'd refused to cry. She'd kept herself together by freezing out the pain, but she couldn't keep out the darkness. The idea of killing herself was a fire in the pit of her belly, pulling her into its heat. The thought was seductive, like Matt's eyes when he used to meet her in the park before they'd find a warm, dark place to lie under the trees. Death would be warm like that. It would hold her and comfort her and take away the panic that wouldn't let her sleep. That morning in January, she'd decided not to fight the darkness anymore, to take a straight razor into the bathtub and slit her wrists after her mother went downstairs to do the laundry, but her dad had come up behind her and clasped his hand on her shoulder. "I see you and I know you're hurting," he'd said. "Let me help you." He'd spun her around and held on to her, his arms a vise around her as she struggled to push him away. But he'd held on until her arms had gone limp and she'd collapsed against him, his arms all that were keeping her from falling in a heap on the floor. He'd held her until the sobs erupted from deep inside her and she'd soaked his shirt with her tears. And she hadn't killed herself that day. She'd chosen to keep going. And now, this moment, she could turn away from Matt. She could close him down and continue living in the darkness she'd learned to contain, but had never really shaken. She looked into his eyes. Dark, trusting eyes that stared into hers without wavering. And she knew then that they saw her: the girl who loved him and Zoe fourteen years ago and still did. The core of her being had not changed. A sense of peace filled her like it had that morning when her father told her that he'd never let her go. She took a deep breath.

"I'm willing to give it a shot —" she held up a hand before he finished his move toward her "— on one condition."

"Name it."

"We'll always be honest with each other. About our feelings. About our warts. No matter what."

"I can manage that."

"And you'll let me know if it's not working."

"I'm not planning for that to happen."

"But if it does —"

"We'll talk. I won't disappear on you, Lauren."

"Promise?"

"I promise." He stood and collected their dishes, then returned to stand next to her. "If you're done with your wine, I'd like to take you for a ride in my car so we can find a quiet place to watch the water, listen to the wind, and you can reclaim your title as best kisser this side of the Atlantic." He grabbed her hand and pulled her up from the chair and wrapped his arms around her in a hug. "I think that somewhere up there, Zoe's smiling down on us."

And my dad.

Lauren let herself relax against his chest. "And if I know Zoe, she's probably wondering what in the hell took us so long."

ACKNOWLEDGEMENTS

Thank you first of all to the Ottawa Public Library for the loan of two books that helped me to anchor the storylines: *The Dakota of the Canadian Northwest: Lessons for Survival* by Peter Douglas Elias, and *Kiss the Hand You Cannot Bite: The Rise and Fall of the Ceauşescus* by Edward Behr. That said, the characters and storylines in *Bleeding Darkness* are complete works of fiction, originating somewhere in the crevices of my brain.

I have a terrific team at Dundurn who helped bring *Bleeding Darkness* to readers. Thank you to freelance editor Shannon Whibbs and assistant project editor Jenny McWha, who polished the manuscript until it shone. Thank you also to designer Laura Boyle for this dark, slightly menacing cover design, which perfectly depicts the mood of the book. My thanks to Michelle Melski and Margaret Bryant, publicist and director of marketing respectively, for all of your work bringing my books to readers and for all of your support. And of course, my gratitude to Dundurn president and publisher Kirk Howard and VP Beth Bruder for believing in Canadian authors and the stories we continue to create and share.

I've been blessed to have so many friends quietly and loudly supporting me and my books. A special thank you this time around to Nancy Reid; Barbara, Gary, and Darren McEwen; Joey Taylor; Derek Nighbor; Mary Jane Maffini; Denise Hoekstra; Della Faulkner; Beth Wood; Oleg Zadorozny; Maureen and Earl Morris; Art and Fran Olson; Art and Jeannie Miskew; Marlita Perrault; Sandra Brown; Janice and Doug Kreviazuk; Sue Schmidt; Joyce Garinther; Alex Brett; Jill Austin; Kendall Loughheed; Edith Harvey; Frank Kinahan; Brenda Phillips; Barbara Fradkin; Linda Wiken; Judith Kalil; Jolynn Sommervill; Graham Law; Eileen and Geoff Wilson; Marilyn Zerr; Robert Cook; and Holly and Craig Homan.

Finally, thank you to my entire family, including but not limited to Janet Chapman; Laura Chapman; Donna, Blake and Laura Russell; Steve and Lorraine Chapman; and Ian and Cynthia Black. Thanks and love to Lisa Weagle, Robin Guy, and Julia Weagle. With special thanks to my husband and field-trip companion Ted Weagle, who was more than happy to accompany me to all the Kingston pubs and bars named in the series, although he was starting to have second thoughts about visiting the murder sites. Happily, I can report that the drinking establishments are not works of fiction. ☺

dundurn.com   dundurnpress
@dundurnpress   dundurnpress
dundurnpress   info@dundurn.com

FIND US ON NetGALLEY & GOODREADS TOO!

DUNDURN

31901063451597